QUO VADIS?

HENRYK SIENKIEWICZ

THOMAS NELSON AND SONS LTD

LONDON EDINBURGH PARIS MELBOURNE JOHANNESBURG
TORONTO AND NEW YORK

Henryk Sienkiewicz was born at Wola Okrzejska, Poland, in 1846, educated at Warsaw University, and died in Switzerland on 15 November 1916.

'Quo Vadis?' the most popular of his numerous novels, was published in 1896.

QUO VADIS?

PART I

CHAPTER 1

PETRONIUS awoke about mid-day, very tired as
usual, for he had been at a banquet in the palace
the night before. For some time his health had not
been so good, and wakening had become a matter of
greater difficulty; but the morning bath and skilful
massage always stirred the sluggish circulation of
his blood and restored his strength so completely,
that he left the *oleotechium* (the last bath chamber)
a new man, with shining eyes, and handsome enough
to put Otho himself in the shade. Well indeed might
men call him the Arbiter of Elegance.

And so on the day after the feast, at which he had
been discussing with Nero, Lucan, and Seneca the
question whether woman possessed a soul, he lay
stretched upon a massage table covered with snowy
Egyptian linen, while two stout bathmen rubbed
his muscles with their well-oiled hands.

He waited with closed eyes until the warmth of
the *laconicum* and of the friction should penetrate
him, and drive away his weariness. At last he
opened his eyes, and inquired about the weather
and about some precious stones that Idomeneus the
jeweller had promised to let him see. He was told
that the day was fine, with a light breeze off the

Alban Mountains, and that the jeweller had not yet put in an appearance. Petronius shut his eyes again, and was about to be taken into the *tepidarium,* when the nomenclator lifted the curtain and announced that Marcus Vinicius had called.

Petronius bade him show the visitor into the bath-room, and at once had himself carried there. This Vinicius was the son of his eldest sister, who had married Marcus Vinicius, a consul in the time of Tiberius. The young man had been fighting the Parthians under Corbulo, and now that the war was over had returned to Rome. Petronius was fond of him in a way, for Marcus was a young man of fine presence and athletic build, who knew how to preserve, even in his debaucheries, that moderation which Petronius valued above all things.

' Hail, Petronius! ' he said. ' May all the gods rain blessings upon you, especially Asclepias and Cypris.'

' Welcome to Rome and a pleasant rest to you after your warlike toils,' replied Petronius, freeing his hand from the folds of the fine linen garment which he wore. ' What news from Armenia ? Did you get as far as Bithynia during your stay in Asia ? '

Petronius, now famed for his effeminate tastes and his love of pleasure, had once been governor of Bithynia, and moreover an energetic and just governor. He was fond of recalling the time when he had proved what he could have done and what he could have risen to, had he been so disposed.

Vinicius replied that he had gone to Heraclea for reinforcements for Corbulo, and began to speak about the war. But Petronius closing his eyes, the young man changed the subject and inquired about his uncle's health. His health ?—Poorly. Vinicius had just committed him to the care of Æsculapius

4

and Cypris. Now he, Petronius, had no faith in Æsculapius: did they know exactly whose son he was, this Æsculapius? Was he Arsinoë's, or Coronis' maybe? And when there are doubts as to the mother, what about the father? Who nowadays could swear to his own father? Here Petronius smiled and went on:

'As for Cypris, to whom you have also commended me, perhaps it's her favour I have to thank for the twinges that I've had in my right leg. Still she's a kindly goddess, and I believe that you too, sooner or later, will offer white doves on her altar.'

'True,' replied Vinicius. 'The Parthian arrows have not touched me, but I was smitten in the most unexpected fashion by Love's arrows no great way from the city gates.'

'By the white-kneed Graces,' exclaimed Petronius. 'You must tell me the whole story. Let us go into the anointing room.'

Once there, however, Vinicius' attention was occupied by the wonderful women slaves, two of whom, negresses, began to rub Petronius' body with Eastern perfumes, while others, Phrygians skilled in hairdressing, stood by with steel mirrors and combs in their supple fingers. Two more, Greek girls from Cos, stood ready to drape their master's toga in the flowing lines of a statue.

'By Zeus the cloud compeller,' said Marcus Vinicius, 'what a choice collection! Brazenbeard himself has not more lovely figures in his palace.'

Petronius indulgently replied: 'You are my kinsman, and I am neither so selfish as Barsus nor so strict as Aulus Plautius.'

'What put Aulus Plautius into your head?' asked Vinicius, raising his head quickly. 'Do you know that when I sprained my wrist at the city gates I stayed in his house a fortnight, where one of his slaves, a doctor called Merion, cured me. That's just what I wanted to speak to you about.'

'Really! You're not in love with Pomponia by any chance? If so I'm sorry for you. She's not young, and she's virtuous. A bad business.'

'No, it's not Pomponia, unfortunately.'

'Who is it, then?'

'I wish I knew. But I don't even know her name properly; whether it's Lygia or Callina. They call her Lygia among themselves because she comes from the Lygian country, but her own name is Callina. What a queer house Plautius has! it's full of people, yet quiet as the groves of Subiacum. For ten whole days I had no idea that a goddess dwelt there. But one morning I caught sight of her bathing in the basin of a fountain under the trees. And the rays of the dawn were playing right through her body—I swear it by the foam that gave Venus birth. I thought the rising sun would make her disappear before my eyes like the dim light of morning. I have seen her again twice, and since then I have known no peace—I have not known what it means to desire aught else. I don't care now for all the town can offer—women are nothing to me, gold, Corinthian bronzes, amber, mother of pearl, wines, feasts—all I want is Lygia. My heart goes out to her, Petronius, as the dream does to Paisitheia on the mosaic in your tepidarium. I long for her day and night.'

'If she is a slave, buy her.'

'She isn't a slave.'

'What is she then? One of Plautius' freed-women?'

6

'She's never been a slave, so she can't be a freed-woman.'

'Well, then?'

'I don't know. A king's daughter——'

'That's very interesting, Vinicius.'

'It's not a long story. Perhaps you knew Vannius, the king of the Suevi. When he was driven from his own country he dwelt for a long time in Rome, where he distinguished himself by his luck at dice and his skill in chariot racing. Then Drusus gave him his throne again, and at first he ruled quite well and had some success in war, but later on he went over the score and took to fleecing his subjects as well as his neighbours. So his nephews, Vangio and Sido, the sons of Vibilius, king of the Hermanduri, made up their minds that he should go back to Rome—and try his luck with the dice again.'

'I remember: it was in Claudius' time, not so very long ago.'

'Yes. Well, war broke out. Vannius called the Yazygians to his assistance, while his good nephews supported the Lygians. Claudius had no wish to be mixed up in the Barbarians' quarrels, but he wrote to Atelius Hister, who was in command of the Danube Legion, bidding him follow closely the various stages of the war and see that the peace of the empire was not disturbed. Hister exacted from the Lygians a promise not to cross the frontier; and in addition to their promise they gave him hostages, among whom were the wife and the daughter of their chief. As you know, the Barbarians take their wives and children with them on their campaigns. Well, my Lygia is this chief's daughter.'

'How did you discover that?'

'Aulus Plautius himself told me so. The Lygians did not indeed cross the frontier. But the Barbarians arise like a storm and pass away like one. So did the Lygians vanish, with their bulls' horns on their heads. They defeated Vannius' Suevians and the Yazygians; but their king was slain, so they retired with their booty, leaving the hostages in Hister's hands. The mother died soon after. In order to get rid of the child, Hister sent her to Pomponius, the governor of Germany. After the war with the Chatti he returned to Rome, and Claudius, as you know, allowed him the honours of a triumph. The girl walked behind the victor's chariot that day; but after the ceremony, as a hostage cannot be treated like a captive, Pomponius uncertain in his turn what to do with her, entrusted her to his sister, Pomponia Græcina, the wife of Plautius. In his house, where all is virtuous, from the master and mistress to the very fowls in the henhouse, she grew up, I am sorry to say, as virtuous as Græcina herself, and so lovely that beside her Poppæa would be like an autumn fig beside an apple of the Hesperides.'

'Well, what then?'

'As I said, I've been in love with her since I saw the light playing through her body.'

'I know Aulus Plautius, and although he doesn't approve of my way of life he has a liking for me. He knows I've never been an informer like Domitius Afer, for instance, and Tigellinus, and the whole gang of Nero's friends. So if you think I can do anything for you with Aulus, I am at your service.'

'Well, suppose you spoke to Aulus? You have some influence with him, and besides, you're never at a loss for a plan.'

'You're overrating my influence and my resource,

but all the same I'll speak to Plautius as soon as he returns.'

'He returned two days ago.'

'Well, then, let's go into the dining-room: breakfast is waiting; and after we have refreshed ourselves, we'll betake ourselves to Plautius.'

'I was always very fond of you, but now I will put your statue among my household gods; as fine a statue as this,' said Vinicius, pointing to a figure of Petronius as Mercury with his staff, 'and offer sacrifices to it. By the light of heaven, if Paris was like you, 'tis easy to understand Helen's conduct.'

And this exclamation contained as much sincerity as flattery, for Petronius, though older and less athletic, was even handsomer than Vinicius. The women of Rome admired the Arbiter of Elegance, not only for the quickness of his mind, but also for the grace of his body; and this admiration was evident even in the faces of the two maidens from Cos, who were then arranging the folds of his toga, and one of whom, Eunice, was looking into his face with humble adoration. Petronius, however, paid no attention to her emotion, but with a smile replied to Vinicius in Seneca's phrase about women, '*Animal impudens*——' Then laying his hand on Vinicius' shoulder, he led him into the dining-room.

In the anointing room the two young Greeks, the Phrygians, and the two negresses were putting the utensils and the perfumes in order, when the heads of the bathmen appeared round the curtain, which had been raised from the side of the cold room, and a slight hissing noise was heard, at which the Phrygians and Ethiopians and one of the Greek girls vanished. This was the time when games and revelry took place in the baths, to which the overseer, himself a lover of such things, made no objection. Petronius was not sure about them, but being a broad-minded man he shut his eyes.

Eunice alone remained in the anointing room. With bended head she listened for a moment to the voices and laughter as they died away in the direction of the laconicum; then she went and took the amber and ivory chair on which Petronius had been sitting and placed it in front of her master's statue.

Standing on the chair, she threw her arms round the neck of the statue, her hair falling in a golden stream over her back. Her body clung to the marble, and her mouth was pressed closely against the cold lips.

CHAPTER 2

THE two friends took their seats in the litter, and told the men to take them to Aulus' house, in the Vicus Patricius. The gigantic negroes lifted their burden and set off, while other slaves went on ahead. Petronius was inhaling the scent of verbena from his hands, and appeared to be thinking.

'I'm just thinking about it,' he said. 'Did you speak to this woodland nymph of yours? Did you tell her you loved her?'

'As I told you, I saw her bathing, and have seen her twice since. While I was with Aulus I occupied a part of the house reserved for guests, and as I had a sprained wrist, I could not sit at table. It was only on the evening before I left, at supper, that I met Lygia, and I couldn't get a word with her. I had to listen to Aulus telling about his victories in

Britain, and lamenting the decline of small holdings in Italy. Then another time I met Lygia in the garden near the cistern as she was watering some clumps of iris. Look at my knees. I swear by Hercules' shield, they never trembled when the Parthian hordes burst yelling on our troops. But tremble they did beside that cistern. For a long time I was as nervous as a child who still wears the amulet, and I could not utter a word. My eyes alone appealed to her.'

Petronius looked at him with a sort of envy.

'And you did not speak to her?'

'Yes I did. Recovering myself, I told her that, just when I had to leave that hospitable roof, I learned that to suffer there was pleasanter than pleasures anywhere else, that sickness there was sweeter than health in any other place. She too was uneasy, and listened to me with bended head, while she traced some lines on the yellow sand with a reed. Then she raised her eyes, looked down again at the figure she had traced, lifted them once more to me as though she would ask me a question, and suddenly ran away like a nymph from a stupid faun.'

'What did she trace on the sand?'

'A fish.'

'A what?'

'A fish, I tell you. Did that mean that the blood in her veins was cold? I've no idea. But please interpret it for me.'

'My dear fellow, you'll have to ask Pliny; he's the man who knows about fish.'

There the conversation rested, for now the litter was passing through crowded streets, and soon, by way of the Via Apollinis, they reached the Forum.

Crowds of people were walking about beneath the

11

arches of the Basilica of Julius Cæsar, and crowds were sitting on the steps of the Temple of Castor and Pollux, or walking round the little Temple of Vesta, showing up against this marble background like many-coloured swarms of butterflies and beetles. From above, over the enormous steps of the temple dedicated to Jupiter—*Jovi Optimo Maximo*—flowed down fresh multitudes.

Near the Rostra people were listening to some popular orators.

Hawkers were offering in a loud voice their fruit and wine and water mixed with fig juice; quack doctors were singing the praises of their remedies; soothsayers, treasure finders, and interpreters of dreams puffing up their skill. The timbrel, the Egyptian sambuca, and the Greek flute helped to swell the din. Here were the rich and the pious bearing their offerings to the gods. Among the feet of the passers-by the pigeons stole the grain of the sacrifices from the pavement, rose for an instant amid a whirl of wings, then settled again on the places left empty by the eddying throng. Groups of people separated to make way for litters in which might be seen some lovely woman's face, or maybe the careworn visor of a knight or senator. From time to time a cordon of soldiers or watchmen broke up some too rowdy assemblage, marching through it with firm step. On every side could be heard the Greek tongue—as frequently as Latin.

Vinicius, who had not seen the city for many a day, was looking curiously upon this Roman Forum, that dominated all this vast sea of races, and was yet submerged beneath them. 'The nest of the ancient Romans—without the Romans,' said Petronius, guessing his friend's thoughts. And indeed the Roman element was almost lost among this mob.

Here were negroes from Ethiopia; there were fair-haired giants from the dim regions of the North, Britons, Gauls, Germans, and Serians with slanting eyes, men from the banks of the Euphrates and men from the banks of the Indus with brick-red beards, Syrians from the Orontes with soft, dark eyes, shrivelled desert Arabs, hollow-chested Jews, Egyptians with fixed smile, Numidians and Africans; Greeks from the mainland, joint rulers of the city with the Romans, supreme in science, and art, and cunning, Greeks from the isles and Asia Minor, from Egypt, from Italy, and from Gallia Narbonensis. There were priests of Serapis, with palm branches, and priests of Isis, the goddess whose altars were more lavishly covered than those of Jupiter Capitolinus; priests, too, of Cybele, carrying maize stalks, and priests of some nomad deities. There were Oriental dancers in their mitres, vendors of amulets, snake charmers, and lastly, the people with no occupation, who every week came to the stores on each side of the Tiber to obtain food, who scrambled for lottery tickets in the Circus, passed their nights in the broken-down houses beyond the Tiber, and their days in some portico or other, in the notorious slums of the Suburra, on the Milvian bridge, or in front of some rich man's house, where from time to time they had thrown to them scraps from the slaves' table.

The litter stopped before Aviranus the bookseller's, and Petronius went in and bought a beautiful manuscript, which he handed to Vinicius.

' That is a present for you,' he said.

' Thank you,' replied Vinicius, looking at the title. ' " The Sattyricon " ? Is it new ? Who wrote it ? '

' I did: but nobody knows anything about it, so tell nobody.'

'But I see a lot of verse here mixed with the prose.'

'When you read it, pay heed to the banquet of Trimalchio. As for the verses, I'm sick of them since Nero has written his poem. When Vitellius wants an emetic, he uses an ivory spoon, which he passes down his throat: others use a flamingo's feather steeped in oil or in a decoction of thyme: what I do is to read over Nero's poetry, and the effect is instantaneous. Then I can praise them, if not with a clear conscience, at least with a clean stomach.'

With that he stopped the litter opposite Idomeneus the goldsmith's shop, and after arranging about the jewels, he told his men to take them to Aulus' house.

The door leading to the porch was opened by a powerful young doorkeeper, a captive magpie according them a hearty ' Salve.'

As they passed into the atrium, Vinicius said: 'Did you notice that the doorkeeper wears no chains ? '

'It is a queer house,' replied Petronius in a low voice. 'You've heard, no doubt, that Pomponia Græcina is suspected of being a votary of the Oriental superstitions founded on the worship of one called Christus ? '

'I'll tell you another time about what I've heard and seen here.'

They were now in the atrium. The slave in attendance there sent the nomenclator to announce the visitors, while other slaves brought them chairs and footstools.

Petronius, who had thought this grave mansion given over to eternal *ennui,* and so never visited it, looked around him with a certain disappointed surprise, for there was nothing gloomy about the bright hall. From above, through a large opening in the roof, descended a column of radiant light, which broke into a thousand beams when it met the water thrown up from a square basin, the *impluvium*, surrounded by anemones and iris. It was evident that lilies were the favourite flowers here, and there were whole clumps of them, white and red. There were also sapphire-coloured irises, with delicate petals, silvered over by a liquid dust of spray. There was an air of quiet comfort everywhere, quite different from luxury, but dignified and reposeful.

Presently a slave drew aside the curtain between the hall and the tablinum, and Aulus Plautius appeared.

He was a man already in the evening of his days, still powerful, with a strong face, which, albeit too short, had something aquiline about it. At the moment his face expressed astonishment, and even uneasiness, at the unwonted company of the companion, friend, and confidant of Nero.

Petronius, too much the man of the world, and too acute not to notice this, after the first greetings went on in his most lively and engaging fashion to account for his presence. He had come to thank Plautius for the attention shown his nephew in this house, and gratitude was the sole reason for his visit, which moreover he was emboldened to make because of their long-standing friendship.

'You are welcome,' said Plautius; 'and as for gratitude, it is I who am your debtor, though probably you do not suspect the cause.'

No; Petronius raised his hazel eyes, and ransacked his memory in vain—he could not guess.

'You saved the life of Vespasian, whom I appreciate and like so well,' said Aulus, 'that day when he was unlucky enough to fall asleep while listening to Cæsar's poetry.'

'Say rather "lucky enough,"' replied Petronius, 'since he did not hear it: but I admit his good fortune might have had a bad ending. Nero was set on sending the friendly advice by a centurion that he should open his veins.'

'And did you, Petronius, laugh at Cæsar?'

'Not at all. I pointed out that if Orpheus could put the wild beasts to sleep by his singing, it was no less a triumph to succeed in sending Vespasian to sleep.'

'Ah, well, these are sad times,' Aulus went on. 'I have lost two front teeth—they were broken by a stone slung at me by a Briton—and now I make a hissing noise whenever I speak. Still I consider the time I spent in Britain the happiest of my life.'

'Because it was then you won your victories,' Vinicius broke in. But Petronius, fearing that the old soldier would start talking about his campaigns, changed the subject and began to flatter Plautius about his house and the good taste which prevailed in it.

'It is an old house,' replied Plautius, 'and I've made no changes since I inherited it.'

The curtain separating the atrium from the tablinum being drawn, the house was open from one end to the other, and across the tablinum and through the peristyle and the adjoining hall could be seen the garden, like a bright picture set in a dark frame. The happy laughter of a child floated up from below to the atrium.

'Ah, general,' exclaimed Petronius, 'let us hear that frank laugh nearer at hand; 'tis a kind that is rare nowadays.'

'Certainly,' replied Plautius, as he rose; 'it is

16

my little Aulus playing at ball with Lygia. But surely, Petronius, that's how you spend your time, laughing ? '

' Life is laughable, so I laugh,' said Petronius ; ' but this laughter has a different ring.'

' True,' added Vinicius. ' Petronius does not laugh all day : say all night, rather.'

Talking thus they traversed the length of the house, and arrived at the garden.

Petronius threw a hasty glance at Lygia. Little Aulus ran up to greet Vinicius, who, as he came forward, bowed to the lovely girl, standing motionless with the ball in her hand, her dark hair slightly disarranged : she was a little out of breath with the exercise, and her cheeks were tinged with colour.

But Pomponia Græcina was seated in the garden triclinium, overshadowed by ivy, vine, and honeysuckle, and they went forward to greet her. Petronius knew her, having seen her at the house of Antistia, the daughter of Rubellius Plautus, and also at the houses of Seneca and Pollio. He could not refrain from a certain respectful surprise at the serene melancholy of her face, and her noble presence, bearing, and words.

And even as he spoke and thanked her for her care of Vinicius, he used the word ' *domina*,' which he did not think of using in conversation with Calvia Crispinilla, for example, Scribonia, Valeria, Solina, and other great ladies.

Little Aulus, who was a friend of Vinicius since his stay in the house, invited him to a game at ball. Lygia had entered the triclinium after the child, and beneath the curtain of ivy, with the half lights playing on her face, she seemed to Petronius more beautiful than at first sight—a creature truly half divine. And

17

as he had not said a word to her yet, he rose and
bowed, and repeated the words of Ulysses' greeting
to Nausicaa:

> ' Goddess or mortal, I am at your feet ;
> If thou art mortal dwelling on the earth,
> Thrice happy are thy father and thy mother dear,
> Thrice happy are thy brothers. . . .'

Even Pomponia appreciated the clever courtesy of
this man of fashion. As for Lygia, she listened to
him, confused and blushing, her eyes bent on the
ground. But presently an arch smile flickered round
the corner of her lips, her lovely features wavered
undecided, and she replied in the words of Nausicaa,
which she repeated all at a breath, somewhat like a
lesson learnt by heart:

' Stranger, thou seem'st no man of lowly birth or little wit.'

Then she ran away like a frightened bird.

It was now Petronius' turn to be surprised. He
had not expected to hear a verse of Homer from the
mouth of a girl of barbarian origin, as Vinicius had
told him she was. He looked questioningly therefore at Pomponia, who smiled when she saw the pride
that was expressed on her husband's face.

Despite the prejudices of an old Roman, which
obliged him to denounce the Greek tongue and the
spread of it, Aulus was glad that this scholar and man
of culture should have found in his house somebody
able to reply to him in the language and in the very
words of Homer.

' We have a teacher here, a Greek,' said he,
turning to Petronius, ' who gives our son lessons,
and the girl is always there.'

Petronius was now looking through the lattice of

ivy and honeysuckle at the garden and the two who were playing there. Vinicius, clad in his tunic alone, was throwing a ball to Lygia, who, with lithe, easy movements endeavoured to catch it. At first Petronius had thought her somewhat frail, but seen now in the full light of the garden, she looked like the living image of the dawn, with her clear rose-flushed cheeks, her lips made for kisses, eyes of deepest blue, her marble-white forehead, and dark hair with gleams of bronze and amber. And what grace of form in that slender body, young with the youth of an early May, like a bud new opened! She was a springtime idyll, this dainty little maiden. Like a lamp with the light playing through it, her lovely form revealed the pure soul which lent it radiance.

Now, however, they had ceased to play, and after a short walk had sat down on a seat beside the fish-pond. Presently little Aulus rose to go and tease the fish, and Vinicius went on with the conversation which he had begun as they walked.

'Yes,' he said in a low trembling voice, 'I was scarce more than a child when I joined the army in Asia. I never had time to know the city, or life, or love. As a child I went to Musonius' school, and he used to teach us that happiness consisted in wishing for what the gods wish, and hence depended on ourselves. But I think there is another happiness, far greater and more precious, that does not depend on ourselves—it is love alone that can give it. It is a joy the gods themselves seek, and I, Lygia, who till now never knew what it was, wish to follow in their steps, and I too am seeking her who will make me happy.'

She listened, as though it had been the sound of a Greek flute or a cithara, to this strange music that poured into her ears, that stirred her blood, and filled her heart with weakness and dread and yet with a joy divine. His words told of something that already existed in her, but which she could not have expressed.

A rosy light fell on the motionless cypress trees, and the whole air was charged with it. Lygia lifted her eyes to Vinicius as though awakened from a dream, and of a sudden, as he bent towards her, his eyes trembling in entreaty, he seemed to her more beautiful than all other men, nay, than all the gods whose statues she saw on the temple pediments. He took her gently above the wrist and said:

'Do you not guess, Lygia, why I speak so to you?'

'No,' she whispered, so low that Vinicius scarce heard her. But he did not believe her, and pressing her arm more lightly, he would have drawn her to his heart, had not old Aulus just then appeared on the myrtle-edged path, and said as he came up:

'The sun is sinking. Beware of the evening chill, and do not trifle with Libitina.'

'I have taken off my toga,' replied Vinicius, 'but I am not cold.'

'Still, the sun is more than half sunk behind the Janiculum,' replied the old soldier. 'This is not like Sicily, where the people meet at evening in the squares to sing their evening hymn to the setting sun.'

And he went on to talk at length of Sicily, where he had a large interest in farms.

He vaunted his orchards and his flocks, his house hidden among the trees, and his hills covered with garden thyme and wild thyme, over which hummed his swarms of bees.

Petronius, on a seat beside Pomponia, was enjoying the view of the setting sun, the garden, and the people who were standing near the fishpond. Their clothes stood out in the golden rays of the sun against the dark background of myrtles. Away on the western horizon purple and violet turned to opal; the vault of heaven took on a lilac hue; the dark outlines of the cypresses made them seem more dense, and the calm of evening pervaded men and trees and all the garden.

Petronius was surprised at this peacefulness. Upon the face of Pomponia, of Aulus, of their son, and of Lygia there was something that he was not used to see upon the faces which he saw of an evening. He saw them surrounded by a radiant gentle calm that resulted from their daily life, and he felt that there might exist a beauty and a charm which he, ever on the search for the beautiful and charming, had never known. Unable to refrain from expressing this idea, he turned to Pomponia and said:

' How different is your world from that which our Nero governs.'

Raising her refined face towards the evening light, she replied simply:

' It is not Nero who governs the world; it is God.'

Both were silent. On the walk were heard the footsteps of the old general and Vinicius with Lygia and little Aulus, but before they drew near Petronius spoke again:

' So you believe in the gods, Pomponia ? '

' I believe in God, who is one, who is just and all-powerful,' she replied.

CHAPTER 3

'I MUST congratulate you on your choice,' said
Petronius when he was in the litter alone with Vinicius. 'She's a real "rosy-fingered Aurora." Do
you know what she reminded me of also? Of spring.
Not our Italian spring, with an apple tree here and
there in blossom and the olive trees always dusty
gray, but such a spring as I've seen in Helvetia,
youthful, fresh, bright green.'

Vinicius, his head bent, made no answer for a
moment, then:

'I longed for her,' he said, 'and now I long the
more for her. When I pressed her hand, a breath of
fire kindled my blood! She must be mine. I came
to you for advice, but if you have none, I must find
it myself. Aulus looks on her as his daughter, so
why should I look on her as a slave? Since there is
no other way to get her, so be it! She shall smear
the wolf fat on my house door, fasten the wreath
upon it, and come to my fireside as my wife.'

'Calm yourself, O frenzied scion of consuls! We
do not drag the Barbarians behind our chariots with
ropes round their necks, and then marry their
daughters. Do not go to extremes: calm yourself.
Remember that if she wants to leave these people
and come to you, they cannot keep her. I promise
you I'll give the matter thought, and Petronius is no
longer himself if he cannot hit on some plan.'

'I thank you, Petronius; the gods shower blessings
on you. Where are you going to?'

'Where! to Chrysothemis, of course.'

'Lucky man, to have the woman you love.'

'I lucky? Do you know the only thing about
her that amuses me now? The fact that she is

unfaithful to me with my own freedman, Theocles the lute player, and thinks I don't know it.'

So they were taken to Chrysothemis' house. But in the porch Petronius laid his hand on Vinicius' shoulder and said :

' Stop, I think I have it now.'

' May all the gods reward you!'

' Yes. It cannot fail. Listen to me, Marcus Vinicius.'

' I'm listening, O Pallas Athene.'

' Well, in a few days the divine Lygia will eat the grain of Demeter in your house.'

' Cæsar himself is not so great as you,' exclaimed Vinicius.

CHAPTER 4

AFTER his visit to Chrysothemis, Petronius slept the whole day ; but in the evening he was taken to the Palatine, where he had a special audience of Nero, and on the following day there appeared before Plautius' house a centurion with fifteen of the Prætorian Guards.

In those days of terror and uncertainty such messengers were often the heralds of death. When the centurion made the knocker resound on Aulus' front door and the hall porter announced the soldiers, terror spread through the house. The whole family crowded round the old general, convinced that he was the one threatened. Pomponia, throwing her arms about his neck, strained herself to him, muttering incoherent words with her blanched lips ; Lygia, pale as a sheet, kissed his hands ; and little Aulus clung to his toga. Slaves of both sexes swarmed from all parts of the house, uttering cries of grief. The women sobbed, and some of them were already tearing their faces and covering their heads with their garments.

Aulus went into the hall, where the centurion awaited him. It was old Caius Hasta, who had once been under his command in Britain.

'Hail, General,' said the messenger. 'I bring you a command from Cæsar with his greeting: here are the tablets and the seal to prove my authority.'

'I am grateful to Cæsar for his greeting, and will obey his orders. Welcome, Hasta; deliver your message.'

'Aulus Plautius, Cæsar has learnt that the daughter of the Lygian king dwells in your house, she who was given to Rome by that king as a hostage. His Majesty thanks you, General, for the hospitality you have shown this maiden; but wishing no longer to burden you with her, and considering moreover that as a hostage this Lygian girl should be under the care of himself and the Senate, he commands you to give her over to his keeping.'

Aulus was too old a soldier and too strong a man to utter vain words of regret or recrimination on receiving an order. He examined the tablets and seal, and then raising his eyes to the old centurion he said calmly:

'Wait in the hall, Hasta; you shall have the hostage.'

So saying, he returned to the interior of the house, to the room where Pomponia, Lygia, and little Aulus had taken refuge.

'Neither death nor exile in a distant island threatens anyone,' he said, 'yet Cæsar's messenger brings ill tidings which concern you, Lygia.'

'Lygia? exclaimed Pomponia.

'Yes.'

Then turning to the girl he said:

'Lygia, you have been brought up in our house, and we love you, Pomponia and I, like our own daughter. But Cæsar has the right to your guardianship, and he now claims you.'

'Aulus,' cried Pomponia, 'it were better she should die.'

As Lygia, clinging to her, cried aloud, 'Mother, my mother!' Aulus' face once again showed his grief and rage.

'If I were alone in the world,' he said in a sad voice, 'I would not hand her over alive, and my friends might this very day bring their offerings to Jove the Liberator. I will go to the emperor and beg him to reconsider his decision. I know not if he will hear me. Meanwhile, Lygia, farewell. Remember we always blessed the day that brought you to our hearth. You are our joy and the light of our eyes—farewell!'

He returned hastily to the hall, that he might not be overcome by emotion unworthy of a Roman and a soldier.

But Pomponia, taking Lygia to her bedchamber, spoke to her in words that sounded strangely in that house where Aulus Plautius, ever zealous at their shrine, offered sacrifices to his household gods.

'The hour of trial is come,' said Pomponia. 'Once upon a time Virginius smote his own daughter to the heart to deliver her from Appius, and Lucrece bought back her honour with her life. The house of Cæsar means dishonour. If the more holy law that we two live under forbids us to take our own life, it allows and commands us to defend ourselves from disgrace even at the price of life itself.'

The girl fell upon her knees, and hiding her face in the gown of Pomponia, remained a long time silent. When she rose her face was calmer.

'It is a great grief to leave you, mother, and my father and brother, but I know that resistance would be useless and would destroy you all. At least I will never forget your words when I am in Cæsar's house.'

Then she bade farewell to young Plautius, to the old Greek who taught them both, to the servant who had been her nurse, and to all the slaves.

One of them, a great broad-shouldered Lygian who was called Ursus in the house, and who had come to the Roman camp along with Lygia and her mother, fell at Pomponia's feet and said:

'Allow me, lady, to go with my mistress and serve her and protect her in Cæsar's house.'

'You are not our slave, you are Lygia's,' replied Pomponia; 'but will they allow you to pass the emperor's door? And how will you succeed in protecting her?'

'I know not. I only know that I can break an iron bar like wood.'

Aulus Plautius, far from objecting to Ursus' proposal, declared that all Lygia's suite must, along with her, pass under the protection of the emperor.

Pomponia wrote afterwards to Acte, Nero's freedwoman, commending Lygia to her protection. She was not one whom Pomponia met at the meetings of the initiate, but she heard it said at these meetings that Acte never refused her assistance to the Christians, and that she was an eager reader of the epistles of Paul of Tarsus.

Hasta himself undertook to deliver the letter to Acte, and the soldiers then led Lygia off to the palace amid the cries of little Aulus, who wanted to protect his sister, threatening the centurion with his tiny fists.

The general ordered a litter, and while awaiting it, retired with Pomponia into the picture room.

'Now listen, Pomponia,' said he. 'I intend to go

to Cæsar, although I believe such a proceeding is in vain; and though Seneca has lost his influence with Nero, I will visit him too. It is Sophonius, Tigellinus, Petronius, and Vatinius who have the influence now. As for Cæsar, probably he never heard of the Lygians in his life; and if he has demanded that Lygia be handed over, it is because somebody has suggested it to him. It is not hard to guess who that is.'

' Petronius ? '

' Exactly. And Petronius has not taken her from us for Cæsar's benefit,' continued the old general in his hissing voice, ' for he'd be afraid to estrange Poppæa, so it's either for himself or for Vinicius. I will find out this very day.'

A moment later, the litter was bearing him towards the Palatine.

CHAPTER 5

AULUS was right in expecting to be denied admission to Nero, for on his arrival he was informed that Cæsar was engaged in singing with Terpnos the lute player. Besides, he only received persons who were summoned by himself.

Seneca, however, though suffering from a fever, did receive the old general.

' I can only do you one service, most noble Plautius,' he said with a bitter smile—' never to let the emperor see that I sympathise with your grief.'

He would not advise him to seek out Tigellinus, nor Vatinius, nor Vitellius. Possibly money might do something; possibly they would be glad to injure Petronius, whose influence they were undermining;

but more probably they would tell Cæsar how dear Lygia was to Plautius, and Cæsar would then keep her all the more jealously for himself.

'You have been silent, Plautius, silent for years, and Cæsar does not love those who are silent. How dared you fail to be enraptured by his beauty, his goodness, his singing, his eloquence, his poetry, and his skill in the chariot races? Why did you not applaud the death of Britannicus, and panegyrise his mother's murder? Why did you not congratulate him on having Octavia smothered?'

The general interrupted these bitter reflections.

'My noble Annæus,' he said, 'it is Petronius who has had our child taken away. Tell me what means to employ, and what influences he will be amenable to, and you yourself make use of all the eloquence that your old friendship for me will lend you to persuade him.'

'Petronius and I,' said Seneca, 'are in two warring camps. It may be that he is a better man than the other rascals in Nero's entourage, but as for pointing out to him that he has done an evil action, it's a waste of time; good and evil are all one to him now. But show him that his proceedings were inartistic, and he'll be ashamed. When I see him I'll say to him: 'Your conduct is worthy of a freedman.'' If that does not succeed, nothing will.'

'I thank you, in any case,' replied the general.

Then he proceeded to Vinicius' house, and he found him fencing with his *maître d'armes*. When they were alone, Aulus' anger broke forth in a torrent of reproach and invective; but Vinicius turned so deadly white at the news of the outrage that all suspicion left Aulus' mind. Beads of perspiration stood on the young man's forehead; his eyes flashed; his lips uttered incoherent questions. Jealousy and anger overcame him by turns. He felt that Lygia, once over the threshold of the palace, was lost to him for good. But when Aulus mentioned Petronius' name a suspicion flashed like lightning across the young man's mind. Petronius had fooled him. He wanted to gain fresh favour with Cæsar by offering Lygia to him, or else he was going to claim her as his own.

Violence was hereditary in the family of Vinicius.

'General,' he said in a broken voice, 'I assure you that Petronius shall account to me for this outrage to Lygia, though he were my own father. Return home and wait for me. Neither Petronius nor Cæsar shall have her. I will kill her sooner, and myself with her.'

With that he set out to find Petronius.

Aulus returned home a little more hopeful, and comforted Pomponia; then they waited for news from Vinicius. Several hours went past, and it was not till evening that they heard the knocker resound on the door.

A slave entered with a letter for Aulus, which read thus:

'Marcus Vinicius to Aulus Plautius, greeting. What has happened is by the emperor's command, to which you must bow, as do Petronius and I.'

CHAPTER 6

PETRONIUS was at home, and the doorkeeper did not dare to stop Vinicius as he dashed into the hall and then into the library, where Petronius was writing. Vinicius snatched the pen from his hand

and broke it. Then gripping his uncle's arm tightly, he said in a hoarse voice: 'What have you done with her? Where is she?'

Petronius, however, the effeminate Petronius, grasped the young athlete's hand that encircled his arm, caught the other also, and holding both in his one hand as in a vice, said:

'You see it's only in the morning I'm weak; in the evening I get back my strength.'

With that he released his hands, and Vinicius stood before him, ashamed and enraged.

'You have a hand of iron, but by all the gods in Hades I swear that if you have played me false, I will plunge a knife in your throat, though it were in Cæsar's own presence.'

'Let us talk quietly,' replied Petronius. 'Your coarseness is very painful to me; and if human ingratitude could still surprise me, I should be surprised at yours.'

'Where is Lygia?'

'In the brothel; otherwise, Cæsar's palace.'

'Petronius!'

'Sit down and be calm. I made two requests of Cæsar, and he has promised to grant them. First of all to take Lygia away from Aulus' house, and then to hand her over to you.'

There was a pause. Vinicius looked at Petronius as though stupefied and then said:

'Forgive me. I am in love with her, and my affection makes me uneasy.'

'Didn't I manage cleverly, Marcus? This is what I said to Cæsar the day before yesterday: "My nephew Vinicius is fallen so deeply in love with a poor chit of a girl whom Aulus' people have brought up, that his sighs are turning his house into a vapour bath. You, Cæsar, you and I, who only love genuine beauty, wouldn't give a thousand sesterces for her, but this fellow had always as much sense as a three-legged stool." '

' Petronius! '

' Well, if you don't understand I talked like that in order to secure Lygia's safety, I'll begin to think I was telling the truth. I convinced Nero that a man of taste like himself could not look on her as a beauty ; so as he doesn't dare see save with my eyes, he'll not want her. It was absolutely necessary to get on the safe side of the buffoon and keep him in hand. " Take Lygia," I went on casually, " and hand her over to Vinicius. You have the right, for she is a hostage, and at the same time you'll be playing Aulus a nice trick." So he gave his consent. You will be the official guardian of the hostage. This Lygian treasure will be entrusted to your keeping, and so far from squandering it, you will see that it multiplies! Fortunate mortal! '

' Is it quite true, then, that she's in no danger in Cæsar's palace ? '

' If she had to live there, Poppæa would mention her to Locusta ; but for a few days there's no fear. To-morrow there's a banquet at the palace, and I have got them to keep a place for you beside Lygia.'

' Why did you not have Lygia sent direct to me ? '

' Because Cæsar wants to keep up appearances. The affair will cause some sensation in Rome, and people will talk. Since Lygia is being taken away as a hostage, she shall remain in the palace so long as the stories go about. Then you shall have her sent you quietly.'

' So I shall see her to-morrow, and afterwards have her in my house for ever, until my dying day.'

'Yes, you will have Lygia, and Aulus will consign me to all the gods in Hades.'

'Oh, Aulus came to see me, and I promised to let him hear about Lygia.'

'Write and say that our "divine" emperor's will is the supreme law, and that you'll call your first son "Aulus." Suppose I asked Nero to invite him to the banquet to-morrow? He would see you at table beside Lygia.'

'No, don't do that,' said Vinicius. 'I am sorry for both of them, especially Pomponia.'

He then sat down and wrote the letter that was to take away the old general's last hope.

CHAPTER 7

ONCE upon a time the haughtiest head had bowed before Acte, the mistress of Nero.

She had earned the gratitude of many, and had made herself no enemies. Even Octavia did not go the length of hating her. Now she was considered too unimportant to cause any jealousy. She continued to love Nero in a hopeless fashion, sustained only by the memory of the hours that were gone for ever, and Poppæa did not even demand her dismissal from the palace.

From time to time she was invited to the emperor's table, where her beauty adorned the imperial banquets.

But Cæsar had long ceased to be fastidious in his choice of guests. There were senators at his table, chiefly such as were content to play the part of mountebanks; there were patricians old and young, wasted with lives of pleasure, luxury, and debauchery; ladies who bore great names, and who yet when darkness fell, disguising themselves with yellow wigs, walked the dim lit streets in search of adventure; and there were priests who mocked their own gods with their cups held on high. At another time there would be a gathering of singers, actors, musicians, and men and women dancers; poets who, while they spoke their verses, were thinking all the time of the money they would get for praising up Cæsar's own poetry; starving philosophers who followed each plate with greedy eyes; famous chariot drivers, jugglers, magicians, story-tellers, mountebanks, and a swarm of wretches to whom fashion or folly had lent a momentary fame, and not a few of whom hid beneath their long hair the pierced ears that were the badge of slavery

The most notorious of them took their places at the table, while the smaller fry furnished amusement during dinner, watching for the moment when the servants would give them the remnants of meat and drink to feast upon. This last class was recruited by Tigellinus, Vatinius, and Vitellius, who had more than once been forced to furnish these super-numeraries with garments in some measure suited to the splendour of the palace. Cæsar, however, liked such company, and the luxuriousness of the court made all resplendent.

Today Lygia was to be present at the banquet. She was torn with anxiety. She was afraid of Cæsar, afraid of the men, afraid of this palace in an uproar, and afraid, too, of these feasts, whose disgraceful nature was known to her from hearing the conversation of Aulus and Pomponia and their friends. Though still quite young she was no innocent. In these troubled times ideas of evil reached even the ears of children. So she knew that they would plan her ruin in this palace. But her soul burned with the enthusiasm of a lofty teaching, and she swore not to yield.

Since neither Aulus nor Pomponia could any longer be held responsible for her actions, she began to wonder if it would not be better to disobey Cæsar and not appear at the banquet. A desire sprang up of proving her courage by exposing herself to torture and death. Had not her Divine Master set an example? And had not Pomponia told her that the more earnest among the brethren longed and prayed for this test?

But Acte, when she spoke of her doubts to her, stared at her in amazement.

Would she disobey Cæsar, and so from the very first day call down his wrath? Such conduct was the conduct of a child that did not understand the purport of its actions. From Lygia's story it appeared that she was not, properly speaking, a hostage, but a girl forgotten by her countrymen, and so not protected by the law of nations. Cæsar had been pleased to take her, and henceforth she was at his disposal: she was the plaything of his will, which owned no superior in all the world.

' Yes,' she went on, ' I, too, have read the letters of Paul of Tarsus, and I know that beyond the world are God and the Son of God that rose from the dead. But upon earth there is nought save Cæsar. Besides, your fears are vain; for I know the palace well, and from Cæsar, I am sure, you need fear no harm. If it had been for himself that he had you taken away, they would not have brought you to the Palatine. Poppæa is supreme here, and Nero, since her son was born, is more than ever dominated by her. Petronius has asked me to look after you, and since Pomponia has also written me, they are probably acting together. Perhaps, too, you may find somebody besides Petronius who will intercede for you. Did you never meet any of Cæsar's intimate friends at Aulus' house ? '

' I've seen Vespasian and Titus there.'

' Cæsar does not like them.'

' And Seneca.'

' When Seneca advises one thing, Nero does the opposite.'

There was a blush on Lygia's fair cheek as she said :

' I have met Vinicius too.'

' I do not know him.'

' He is a relative of Petronius, and came back recently from Armenia.'

' Does he stand well with Nero ? '

' Vinicius ? Everybody is fond of Vinicius.'

' And would he plead your cause ? '

' Yes.'

Acte smiled tenderly.

' Well, you'll probably see him at the banquet. You must be there. First of all, if you want to return to Aulus, you must use this as an opportunity to ask Petronius and Vinicius to intervene for that purpose. Come, Lygia, do you hear the sound of voices in the palace ? The sun is low on the horizon already, and the guests will soon be arriving.'

' You are right, Acte,' replied Lygia. ' I will follow your advice.'

She could not herself have said precisely whether her desire to see Petronius and Vinicius was greater than her natural woman's curiosity to witness for once in her life such a feast ; to behold Cæsar there, his court, the famous Poppæa, the other beauties, and all the magnificence of which she had heard such accounts.

Acte took her to her own private anointing room to rub her with scents and dress her for the feast ; and although Cæsar's palace had no lack of women slaves, she determined, out of sympathy for the charming young girl, to attire her with her own hands. It soon appeared that the young woman, despite her seriousness and her assiduous perusal of the epistles of Paul of Tarsus, had retained much of the old spirit of Hellas, to which nothing makes stronger appeal than a perfect body. When she had undressed Lygia, she could not restrain a cry of admiration at the sight of this graceful yet well-formed figure, which seemed compact of roses and mother of pearl. It was a peerless vision of spring that stood before her.

'Lygia,' she cried at length, 'you are a hundred times more beautiful than Poppæa.'

The young girl, brought up in the strict Pomponia's house, where propriety was observed even among the women themselves, stood there in her perfect beauty, all blushing with shame, her knees together, her hands to her throat, her eyes hidden beneath her queenly lashes.

On a sudden she raised her arms, and drew out the pins that fastened her hair ; then with a movement of her head she shook her hair free, and so covered herself from head to foot in a flowing mantle.

Acte touched the dark masses of hair.

'I will not powder it with gold—its waves already gleam with it ; perhaps here and there just a suspicion of powder, to touch it with sunlight. It must be a wonderful place, this Lygia of yours, to boast of daughters such as you.'

36

'I do not remember it now,' replied Lygia. 'Ursus has told me that at home it is all forests, forests, forests.'

'And flowers in the forests,' said Acte, dipping her hands in a vase filled with verbena which she rubbed on Lygia's hair. Then she lightly rubbed her body with scented oils and clad her in a gold-embroidered tunic, easy fitting and sleeveless, over which was to go the snow-white *peplum*.

When the first litters arrived at the main door, both women took up their position in a peristyle which commanded a view of the entrance, the galleries, and the principal court.

It was just sunset; the last rays of the sun rested on the yellow marble of the columns, and warmed them with play of rosy light.

Between the columns, beside the white statues of the Danaids and beside the statues of gods and heroes, flowed a ceaseless stream of men and women, stately figures draped in the toga, in the *peplum,* and in gowns that fell to the ground in graceful folds.

Acte pointed out to Lygia the broad-edged toga of the senators, their coloured tunics, and their sandals adorned with crescents; she showed her the knights, the famous artists, the ladies in Roman or Greek dress or in the fantastic finery of the East, their hair arranged in serpents' coils, in pyramids, or lying low upon their foreheads and decked with flowers, like the statues of the goddesses

It was a new world to Lygia; its beauty dazzled her eyes, but her mind could not reconcile the contrasts which it presented to her. The half lights of the evening, the rows of pillars that lost themselves in distance, these men that looked like statues,

produced an impression of infinite calm: here, amid
the simple grace of the marble pillars, might demi-
gods have dwelt in joy and peace. Alas! Acte in
a low voice revealed to her little by little all the
tortuous secrets of the palace and the people who
thronged it. Over there was a portico with pillars
and tiled floor still red with the blood that bespattered their whiteness when Caligula fell to
Cassius' dagger; there was the spot where his wife's
throat was cut, his son dashed to death on the
pavement. Below yonder wing of the palace was
a dungeon where the younger Drusus, tortured by
starvation, was forced to eat the flesh of his hands,
and where his elder brother was poisoned; there
Gemellus roared aloud for terror; there Claudius
writhed in convulsions; and there were heard the
groans of Germanicus.

Acte fell silent, and Lygia continued to look at the
crowd as though in search of somebody. Suddenly a
blush spread over her cheek. Petronius and Vinicius
had just emerged from the row of columns, and were
walking majestically towards the banqueting-hall.

Lygia felt lighter of heart: she was not quite
alone now. Her mournful longing for Pomponia
and for her home no longer pained her. The desire
to see and talk with Vinicius stilled all other desires
in her. In vain did she remind herself of Acte's
words and the warnings of Pomponia. She felt all
of a sudden not only that she must be present at the
banquet, but that she was eager for it.

Acte took her hand and led her towards the
banqueting-hall. Lygia went forward with clouded
eyes and a humming in her ears. As though in a
dream, she saw on tables and walls myriads of
dazzling lamps; she heard the cry with which men
greeted Cæsar. As it were through a mist, she saw

the emperor himself. She scarcely noticed that Acte, after placing her at table, lay down upon her right.

On her left she heard a quiet, well-known voice say:

'Greeting to the most lovely maiden in the world, the fairest star of heaven; greeting to the divine Callina!'

Vinicius was without his toga, according to custom, and wore only a scarlet tunic, that left bare his arms with their golden bracelets, arms that were perhaps too muscular, and made rather for soldiers' work with sword and shield. He wore a wreath of roses. With the single sweep of his eyebrows that met in one, with his splendid eyes and tanned face, he was the personification of youth and strength. To Lygia he seemed such a glorious figure that she scarce could stammer out in reply:

'Greeting to you, Marcus.'

'Happy are my eyes to gaze upon you,' he said, 'and my ears to hear your voice, that is sweeter than flute or lyre. It is you, my divine Lygia, that I should choose, were Venus herself your rival. I knew I should see you again here, and yet at your coming my whole soul thrilled with a new joy.'

His eyes shone with boundless happiness, and he gazed on her as though he would have bathed himself in the radiance of her beauty. Lygia felt that in this crowd and in this palace he was the sole being who was near to her, and she began to question him about all the things which she did not understand and which were full of terror for her. How did he learn that he would find her in Cæsar's house? Why was she there? Why had Cæsar taken her

away from Pomponia ? She was afraid of everything in the palace. She wanted to be with her
mother again. She would have died of grief and
anxiety had it not been for the hope that Petronius
and Vinicius would plead her cause with Cæsar.

Vinicius told her how he had heard from Aulus
himself that she had been carried off.

As for the reason, he was ignorant of it. Cæsar
was not in the habit of giving any one reasons for
his decisions. However, she must not fear ; Vinicius
was near her, and would remain near her. She was
life itself to him, and he would watch over her as
over his own soul. Since she was afraid in Cæsar's
house, he swore she should not remain there.

And though he spoke evasively and made up his
story as he went along, his voice preserved a note
of sincerity, since his feelings were sincere.

A genuine pity had seized him, and Lygia's words
went to his heart. So when she began to thank
him, promising that Pomponia would love him for
his goodness, and that she herself would be grateful
to him till her dying day, he could no longer
control his emotions. His heart was bursting with
happiness.

Lygia's beauty intoxicated him, and he felt a
passionate desire for her, but at the same time he
knew that he loved her beyond all telling, and that
he could worship her as though she were a goddess.
And in the waxing din of the feast he bent towards
her and began to murmur sweet simple words to
her, words that came from his heart, harmonious as
music and maddening as wine.

And Lygia was intoxicated with his words. In
the midst of the strangers who surrounded her he
was ever nearer and more dear ; so worthy of trust
and so devotedly her slave. Before, at Aulus' house,

he had only spoken generally to her of love and its joys ; but now! Her cheeks caught fire, her heart leapt, and her lips parted in wonder.

Fear seized her as she listened to these things, and yet she would not for the world have lost a word. Now and then she would lower her eyes, and then raise them again to Vinicius with a radiant look, at once timid and beseeching, as though she would have said, ' Speak on.' The noise, the music, the scent of flowers and incense, began again to overcome her. Vinicius was lying beside her, full of youth, and strength, and love, and burning with desire. And Lygia, infected by the ardour that breathed from him, experienced a feeling of shame that was yet full of pleasure.

But the proximity of Lygia had its effect also on Vinicius. A flame devoured his breast, that he tried in vain to quench with wine.

The wine maddened him, but far more than the wine, that lovely face, those bare arms, the virgin breasts that swelled the golden tunic, and the body outlined beneath the folds of her robe : these made him every minute grow more and more frantic. Suddenly he caught her wrist, as he had done in Aulus' garden, and whispered with trembling lips :

' I love you, Callina. Darling, I love you.'

' Let me go, Marcus,' said Lygia.

But there was a mist before his eyes :

' My darling, love me, love me!'

Then Acte spoke :

' Cæsar is watching you,' she said.

Vinicius was seized with a sudden fit of anger against Cæsar and Acte. The words had broken the spell. Even the voice of some one beloved would have seemed to him out of place at such a time. He thought that Acte had meant to interrupt his talk.

Raising his head and looking at the young freed-woman over Lygia's shoulders, he said angrily:

'The days are gone, Acte, when you lay by Cæsar's side at the banquets, and they say you are turning blind; how did you read the emperor's face so clearly?'

With a touch of sadness in her voice, she replied:

'And yet I did read it. He, too, is near-sighted, and he is looking at you through his emerald.'

Lygia, who at the beginning of the feast had only seen Cæsar through a mist, and then as she hung on Vinicius' words had forgotten to look at him, now turned her anxious and frightened eyes upon him.

Acte was right, for Cæsar, leaning on the table, with one eye half closed, and his emerald monocle to the other, was looking at them.

His eye caught Lygia's, and the girl's heart turned to ice. When she was a child, at Aulus' estate in Sicily, an old Egyptian slave woman used to tell her about dragons that dwelt in caves; and now she seemed to see the blue eye of one of those monsters fixed upon her. Like a frightened child she caught Vinicius' hand, while a whirl of ideas followed each other rapidly in her mind. So this was Nero—Nero the terrible, the all powerful? She had never seen him before, and she had pictured him different. She had pictured a face on which madness had set its irremovable stamp. But here she saw an enormous head set on an enormous neck, a head that was fearsome indeed yet grotesque, resembling in the distance the head of an infant. His amethyst tunic, forbidden to mere mortals, imparted to his short, broad face a bluish tinge. His dark hair was dressed, after the fashion set by Otho, in four rows of curls one above the other.

He had no beard, having but lately offered it at

Jupiter's shrine, for which all Rome made thanks-giving to him, though it was whispered that he had made the sacrifice because, like the rest of his family, he had a red beard. And yet, in the broad forehead that rose above his eyebrows, there was something godlike, and his drawn brows showed he was aware of his omnipotence. But beneath this half-divine brow grinned the face of an ape; a face still young yet swallowed up in fat; full of fickle desires; the face of a drunkard and a mountebank.

Turning towards Petronius, he asked:

'Is that the hostage Vinicius in in love with?'

'Yes,' replied the other.

'What are her people called?'

'Lygians.'

'Does Vinicius think her beautiful?'

'Yes. But I can read the verdict already on your face, oh infallible judge; she is too narrow in the hips.'

'Too narrow in the hips,' repeated Nero, his eyes half closed.

The feast grew more lively. Bowls of wine were drawn each instant from large ivy-hung vases filled with snow. Roses rained from the ceiling.

Petronius begged Nero, before the guests became completely drunk, to add glory to the feast by singing, and the company to a man echoed his request. At first he refused. But Lucan implored him in the name of art and of humanity. Everybody knew that the divine poet, the fearless singer, had composed a new hymn to Venus, beside which Lucretius' was but the howling of a wolf cub. Let him make of this feast a feast indeed. Their generous emperor should not torture them by his silence.

'Be not implacable, O Cæsar!'

'Be not implacable!' repeated the crowd.

Nero stretched out his hand as a sign that he yielded, seeing that they compelled him. Every face assumed an expression of gratitude, and all eyes were turned towards him. He commanded Poppæa to be told that he was about to sing. The empress had been unable through illness to come to the banquet, and nothing would do her so much good as Cæsar's singing.

Poppæa at once appeared. True, she still held undivided sway over Nero's heart, but it would have been dangerous to irritate him where his vanity as singer, charioteer, or poet was concerned. She entered in her fair beauty, clad, she too, in an amethyst tunic, her neck adorned with enormous pearls, part of the spoils of Massinissa. This woman, although a wife, and already twice divorced, had the aspect and the face of a maiden. She was hailed with acclamation and oft-repeated cries of 'Divine Augusta!' Never in her life had Lygia seen such beauty. She could not believe her eyes. Was this the notorious Poppæa who had urged Cæsar to murder his mother and his wife; she whose statues were overturned at night in the city, who was lampooned on city walls? Lygia had never thought of heavenly spirits as clothed in beauty more exquisite.

Uproarious applause marked the end of the hymn; on all sides were heard cries of 'Heavenly voice!' Some of the women had raised their arms in ecstasy, and remained in this position although the song was over; others wiped tears from their eyes. Throughout the hall there was a ceaseless hum of voices. Poppæa, bending her gilded head, pressed Nero's hand to her lips, and held it awhile in silence. Pythagoras, a young Greek of marvellous beauty, whom afterwards the half-mad Cæsar was to wed with all ceremony in presence of the priests, knelt at his feet.

But Nero was looking closely at Petronius, whose praise he valued above all. Petronius spoke:

'My opinion about the music of this hymn is that Orpheus must be as green with jealousy as our friend Lucan there; as for the verses, I could have wished them not so good in order that I might have found praise not unworthy of them.'

Nero was overjoyed. He pointed out the verses which he himself considered finest, and then he rose to accompany Poppæa, who was really ill and who wished to retire. A moment later he returned, eager to witness the display which he had arranged with Petronius and Tigellinus.

First of all there were dialogues, whose extravagance could not redeem their senselessness. Then Paris, the famous actor, gave a representation of the adventures of Io the daughter of Inachus. It was not a dance, but a picture which unveiled the inmost mysteries of love. Then entered Corybants along with Syrian dancing girls, and performed with savage cries a Bacchic dance to the sound of cithara, flute, cymbal, and tambourine, till Lygia thought the ceiling would crack and fall on the heads of the guests.

And still the golden net stretched above showered roses, and ever more roses, upon them. Vinicius, lying half drunk beside Lygia, said:

'I saw you at Aulus' house, beside the fountain, and loved you from that moment. It was at daybreak; you thought nobody saw you, and I saw you—I! As I saw you then, I see you always, in spite of your gown that hides you. Let it fall, like Crispinilla's. Look, both gods and men are athirst for love! There is nothing, nothing in all the world but love! Lay your head on my breast and close your eyes.'

Her blood beat strongly in her temples and her wrists; she felt as though she were giddy and falling. Vinicius, instead of helping her, was drawing her towards the abyss; he, too, was her foe. She felt a fresh dread of this feast; dread of him; dread of herself.

And the end of the orgy was not yet in sight.

The slaves continued to serve fresh dishes, and to fill up the cups adorned with green. In front of the table, arranged in a half circle, appeared two wrestlers. Straightway they closed. Their bodies, gleaming with oil, seemed welded into one piece, while their bones cracked as they strained their arms of iron, and their teeth could be heard to grate. The saffron-strewn tiles resounded with the thud of their bare feet. For a moment they would pause, motionless, like a marble group. The Romans followed with delight each movement of backs bent double, of thigh and of sinewy arm. But the fight could not last for ever. Croton, the master gladiator and chief of the school, was held with reason to be the strongest man in the empire. And soon his opponent's breath came fast, he began to choke, his face turned blue, and he sank to the ground coughing blood.

The end of the struggle was hailed with applause. Croton, with one foot on the spine of his foe and his mighty arms crossed on his breast, gazed upon the company with the rolling eye of a conqueror.

The music was now only a confused din of cithara, flute, Armenian cymbals, Egyptian sistra, trumpets, and horns. The air, impregnated with the scent of oils applied incessantly to the guests' feet by beautiful youths, heavy with saffron and the scent of flowers and of men's bodies, was no longer fit to breathe. The lamps burned with a dull pale flame; wreaths fell awry on brows damp with sweat.

Vitellius fell below the table. Nigidia, naked to the waist, and dead drunk, laid her baby face on Lucan's breast, who began in a drunken fashion to blow off the golden dust from the girl's hair.

Petronius was not intoxicated, but Nero, who at first, out of regard for his heavenly voice, had refrained from drinking, had swallowed cup after cup, and was now drunk. He even wanted to sing some more of his verses, Greek ones this time, but he could not remember them, and by mistake struck up an ode of Anacreon's. Pythagoras, Diodorus, and Terpnos accompanied him, but as neither one nor other of them had any voice left, they soon stopped.

Vinicius was no less drunk than the rest, and besides his passion, a mad desire to quarrel was aroused in him. His dark face had grown pale, and in a loud voice he cried out to Lygia:

'Give me your lips! To-day or to-morrow, it is all one. I have waited long enough. Cæsar took you away from Aulus' house to give you to me, you understand? To-morrow at nightfall I will send for you, you understand? Cæsar has promised you to me! You must be mine. Your lips, I say; give me your lips! I will not wait for to-morrow. Come, give me your lips!'

He embraced her, though she struggled desperately, feeling that she was about to yield. Her strength failed her. In vain she leaned back and turned her head away to avoid his kisses. He raised himself up and, catching her arms, drew her head down upon his breast, and then panting with eagerness, began to overwhelm her bloodless lips with kisses.

But at that moment a hand of iron loosed his arms like a child's and threw him back as though he had been a straw or a dry leaf. What had happened? Vinicius rubbed his eyes stupidly, and saw, towering above him, the enormous form of the Lygian, Ursus.

Ursus stood calm and motionless, but the eyes that flashed on Vinicius had so singular an expression that the young man felt the blood run cold in his veins. Then the giant lifted his queen in his arms, and with a firm step left the hall.

Vinicius paused for a second as though petrified. Then he sprang to his feet and made for the door.

' Lygia, Lygia!' he cried.

But desire and amazement, rage and drunkenness, took his legs from under him. He reeled and stumbled, and clinging to the naked shoulders of a Syrian bacchant, he asked her, with blinking eyes:

'What has happened?'

The woman, with a smile in her clouded eyes, held out a cup of wine, and said:

' Drink!'

Vinicius drank, and collapsed upon the floor. Most of the guests were scattered below the table; some were staggering about the hall, knocking against the walls; others were asleep round the table, snoring or coughing up in their sleep the wine which they had swallowed to excess.

And upon these drunken consuls and senators, on drunken philosophers, knights, and poets, upon dancing girls and noble ladies, upon this society, which still ruled but which had lost its soul and was rolling towards the abyss in one supreme and splendid debauch, the golden net stretched across the ceiling sent down its ceaseless shower of roses. Out of doors the day was breaking.

CHAPTER 8

NOBODY stopped Ursus; nobody questioned him. Such of the guests as were not yet below the table had left their places; the attendants, seeing a lady in the arms of the giant, imagined that it was a slave taking home his drunken mistress. Moreover Acte was with them, and her presence would have dispelled any suspicion.

From the banqueting-hall they passed into a neighbouring apartment, and thence to the gallery which led to Acte's rooms.

This part of the palace was deserted; the music and the noise of the feast sounded but faintly here. Ursus laid Lygia upon a marble seat, and Acte began to exhort the girl to be calm and try to sleep, assuring her that she was in no danger, since the guests would sleep till evening. But for a long time Lygia could not calm herself. She held her head in her hand and repeated like a child, ' Take me home! Take me home to Aulus!' Ursus was ready. At the doors, to be sure, were the Prætorian Guards, but the soldiers did not stop departing guests. In front of the triumphal arch there was still a swarm of litters, and soon the people would be leaving in batches. Then they would join the crowd and go straight home.

Lygia kept saying: ' Yes, Ursus, let us get away.'

Acte was compelled to call them to reason. Go away! Yes, they might go without let or hindrance. But to run away from Cæsar's house was treason. They could go, and in the evening a centurion with a posse of troops would announce the death sentence to Aulus and Pomponia, and fetch back Lygia to

49

the palace. Then she would be lost indeed. If Aulus took them in, his death was certain. She must choose between destroying Plautius and his family and destroying herself. Before the feast she had hoped that Petronius and Vinicius would intercede for her and take her back to Pomponia. Now she knew it was they who had suggested to Cæsar the idea of taking her away. Lygia had the choice of becoming the mistress of the young and handsome Vinicius, or ensuring the ruin of Aulus' family and herself. Acte was sure that she could not hesitate.

'In Cæsar's house,' she said, 'you would be no safer than with Vinicius.'

She did not reflect that, although true, her words meant: 'Resign yourself to your fate and become Vinicius' mistress.' But Lygia, whose lips still burned with the kisses of his brutal passion, blushed deep with shame.

'Never! I shall remain neither here nor with Vinicius—never!'

Acte was surprised at her defiant attitude.

'Do you loathe him so much?' she asked.

'No,' replied Lygia. 'I am forbidden to do so; I am a Christian.'

'I know, Lygia; and I know, too, from Paul's Epistles, that you are forbidden to submit to dishonour, and bidden to fear sin more than death. But tell me, does your faith allow you to cause another's death?'

'No.'

'Then how could you venture to draw down Cæsar's vengeance on the house of Aulus?'

There was silence for a moment. Once more an abyss yawned before Lygia.

The young freedwoman went on:

'I ask you that because I am sorry for you, and for dear Pomponia and Aulus and their son. I have lived a long time in this house, and I know what Cæsar's anger means. No, you cannot run away. You can do but one thing: entreat Vinicius to take you back to Pomponia.'

But Lygia fell on her knees to make entreaty of Another. Presently Ursus knelt also, and in Cæsar's own house they both offered up prayer to God.

Acte could not take her eyes off the profile of Lygia, who raised her head and hands towards heaven as though she expected her deliverance thence. The dawn lit up her dark hair and white robe, and was mirrored in her bright eyes. In this pure light she looked like purity itself. Her pale face, her parted lips, and her beseeching eyes all told of a supernatural exaltation. Acte understood then why Lygia could be no man's mistress.

At last she rose, her face peaceful again. Ursus rose too and crouched beside the seat, looking at his mistress and waiting for her to speak.

Lygia's eyes grew dim, and two great tears rolled slowly down her cheeks.

'May God bless Pomponia and Aulus,' she said. 'I have no right to cause their ruin, and I will never see them more.'

Then, turning to Ursus, she said that he alone remained to her, and that henceforth he must be her protector and her father. If they could not take refuge with Aulus, no more could they remain with Cæsar or Vinicius. So Ursus must take her, get her away from the city, and hide her somewhere, where neither Vinicius nor his people could find her.

The Lygian was ready. In token of obedience he kissed her feet. But Acte, who had expected a miracle, showed her disappointment in her face. So that was all the effect of the prayer ? To flee from the palace was to commit the crime of treason, for which they would be punished ; and even if Lygia succeeded in hiding, Cæsar would revenge himself on Aulus' family. If she must run away, let her run away from Vinicius' house. And then Cæsar, who did not care to trouble himself about other people's affairs, would perhaps refuse to help Vinicius to find her.

That was almost Lygia's own idea. Aulus' people would not know where she was—even Pomponia would not. She would escape on the way, and not from Vinicius' house. In his drunken carelessness he had told her that he would send slaves to fetch her that evening. Ursus should go at once to the bishop, Linus, and ask his help and advice. He would instruct the Christians to go to the rescue, and they would deliver her by main force.

Her face grew rosy and radiant. She threw herself on Acte's neck, and with her lovely mouth on Acte's cheek she whispered :

' You will not betray us, Acte, will you ? '

' By the shade of my mother, I will not. Pray to your God that Ursus may succeed in saving you.'

CHAPTER 9

As it was already broad daylight, with the sun pouring in on the banqueting-hall, Acte urged Lygia to take the rest that was needful after a sleepless night. Lygia made no objection, and both retired to the bedroom whose luxurious fittings recalled the days of Acte's liaison with Cæsar. They lay down side by side, but Acte, despite her fatigue, could not sleep.

The thought of the dangers that threatened Lygia filled her with an immense pity. A sort of maternal feeling established itself in her, and she covered the girl's dark hair with kisses. Lygia was sleeping as peacefully as though she had been at home under the protection of Pomponia. Not till midday did she open her eyes and look round the bedchamber in utter perplexity. She was not in Aulus' house, then ?

' Is that you, Acte ? ' she said at last, noticing the young woman's face in the shadow.

'Yes, Lygia, it is I.'

' Is it evening yet ? '

' No, my child, afternoon.'

' Has Ursus come back ? '

' Ursus did not promise to come back ; he said that he would lie in wait for the litter to-night.'

' Yes, I remember.'

They left their room and went to the bath. After the bath and after breakfast, Acte took Lygia into the palace gardens, where they need fear to meet nobody, as Cæsar and his friends were still asleep. It was the first time that Lygia had seen these splendid gardens. Amid the cypresses, the pines, the oaks, and the olive and myrtle trees, gleamed a crowd of statues ; the glistening spray of the fountains watered clumps of roses, and swans swam majestically on the clear water of the ponds.

Having walked awhile, they sat down among a group of cypresses and began to talk about Lygia's escape.

The sound of footsteps interrupted them, and ere Acte could see who was coming, Poppæa appeared in front of the seat accompanied by a few slaves. Two women were waving screens of ostrich feathers gently above her head. An Ethiopian woman, her breasts swollen with milk, was carrying in her arms an infant wrapped in purple.

Poppæa stopped.

'Acte, the little bells which you sewed on to the doll were badly sewn, and the child tore one off and put it in her mouth, but fortunately Lilith noticed it in time.'

'I ask your Majesty's pardon,' said Acte, crossing her hands on her breast and bowing her head.

Poppæa looked at Lygia and said:

'What slave is this?'

'This is no slave, most divine Majesty; she is an adopted child of Pomponia Græcina's, and the daughter of the King of Lygia, who gave her to Rome as a hostage.'

'Has she come to visit you?'

'No, madam. She has come to live in the palace; she came yesterday.'

'Was she at the feast?'

'She was.'

'By whose order?'

'By Cæsar's.'

Poppæa looked more attentively at the girl, and a wrinkle appeared between her eyebrows. Jealous for her supremacy, she lived in perpetual dread of seeing some lucky rival supplant her, as she had supplanted Octavia. And at a glance she had seen how marvellously beautiful Lygia was.

'A perfect creature indeed,' she said to herself; 'Venus must have given her birth. Immortal gods, she is as fair as I am, and younger.'

Her eyes had a hard look beneath their golden lashes. She turned to Lygia and said calmly:

'Have you spoken to Cæsar?'

'No, madam.'

'Why do you prefer this to Aulus' house?'

' I do not prefer it. Petronius urged Cæsar to take me away from Pomponia. I am here against my will.'

' So you desire to return to Pomponia ? '

This question was put in a more friendly tone. Lygia's heart leapt with hope.

' Madam,' she said, stretching out her hands, ' Cæsar intends to hand me over to Vinicius as his slave. But you will intercede for me and send me back to Pomponia ? '

' So Petronius got Cæsar to take you away from Aulus to give you to Vinicius ? '

' Yes. Vinicius said he would send for me this very day. But you will be kind and take pity on me ? '

She stooped, and taking hold of the edge of Poppæa's robe she waited with throbbing heart. Poppæa looked at her with a wicked smile and said:

' Well, I promise you shall be Vinicius' slave this very day.'

She moved away, a bewitching, malevolent vision. The cries of the child, who had begun to weep, reached the ears of Lygia and Acte. Lygia's eyes were full of tears. She caught Acte's hand.

' Let us go in,' she said. ' We must hope for help only where help may lie.'

They then returned to the atrium, from which they did not stir again. They listened anxiously for the sound of footsteps. The conversation was constantly broken, and in the dull silence which ensued, their ears played them many a trick.

After nightfall the curtain of the antechamber moved, and a man with a dark, pock-marked face appeared. Lygia recognised Atacinus, a freedman of Vinicius, whom she had seen in Pomponia's house. Acte shrieked.

Atacinus bowed low and said:

'Greetings to the divine Lygia from Marcus Vinicius, who awaits her. The feast is spread; and the house is decked with green.'

'I am ready,' she said, with pale lips.

And throwing her arms round Acte's neck, she bade her farewell.

CHAPTER 10

GAILY decked indeed with green was Vinicius' house. The walls and the doors were adorned with festoons of ivy and myrtle; garlands of vine leaves encircled the pillars.

The bright light of the lamps was toned down by globes of Alexandrian glass, or broken into rays of pink and yellow, blue and purple, by hangings of Indian gauze. The table in the dining-room was laid for four guests, since Petronius and Chrysothemis were to be present at the banquet.

Vinicius had followed Petronius' advice on every point, and Petronius had advised him not to go and bring Lygia home himself, but to send Atacinus for that purpose, provided with the emperor's warrant.

'You were drunk last night,' he said; 'I saw you. You behaved like a quarryman from the Alban Mountains. Don't be too much in a hurry, and recollect that good wine requires time for its discussion. Remember, too, that though it is sweet to desire, it is sweeter still to be desired.'

The slaves brought in tripods and threw sprigs of myrrh and spikenard upon the coals.

'They must be at the corner of the Carinæ by now,' said Vinicius, as though speaking to himself.

'He cannot keep away,' exclaimed Chrysothemis;
'he will go and meet them—and probably miss
them.'

Vinicius smiled foolishly.

'Not at all,' he said.

Petronius shrugged his shoulders.

'Not an ounce of philosophy in him,' he said.
'I'll never make a man of this son of Mars.'

Vinicius did not even hear him.

'They must be at the Carinæ now.'

And in fact they were at that moment turning
towards the Carinæ. The litter was preceded by
lamp-bearers and surrounded by foot-servants, with
Atacinus directing the procession. Progress was
slow, as the lanterns in the unlit streets gave but a
poor light. The streets, moreover, which near the
palace had been deserted, with only here and there
a man moving quietly along with a light, were becoming unwontedly busy. From every little lane
three or four people in sombre garments would come
out, carrying no torches. Some went along with the
procession, mingling among the slaves, while other
more compact bodies advanced towards them from
the opposite direction. Some were staggering about
as though drunk, and at times the difficulty in forcing
a passage was so great that the slaves who carried
the lamps were forced to cry out:

'Make way for the noble tribune, Marcus
Vinicius!'

Through the half-drawn curtains Lygia noticed
these dark groups, and her heart was filled alternately
with hope and with terror.

'It is he—it is Ursus with the Christians. The
time is come,' she murmured with trembling lips.
'Christ help us! Christ preserve us!'

Atacinus, who at first had paid no attention to this

unusual commotion, became uneasy. The lamp-bearers had to cry out even more frequently: 'Make way for the litter of the noble tribune!' These unknown figures thronged about it so closely that at last he gave the command to his men to drive them off with sticks. Suddenly a tumult sprang up in front, and every light was extinguished forthwith. Now Atacinus understood; it was an attack! He was terror-stricken. All Rome knew that Cæsar often entertained himself along with the Augustans in making night raids in the Suburra and other districts, and that sometimes he even came by knocks and bruises in the course of these nocturnal expeditions. But he who defended himself was a dead man, though he should be a senator. Around the litter raged an inextricable mass of men, struggling and kicking and falling. An idea flashed on Atacinus' mind; above all, he must recover Lygia and escape with her, leaving the rest to their fate. He snatched her from the litter, and taking her in his arms he attempted to get away in the darkness.

But Lygia cried out:

'Ursus! Ursus!'

In her white robe she was easy to distinguish, and Atacinus was covering her with his own cloak, when his neck was seized from behind in a grip of iron and his skull resounded with a blow as from a club. He collapsed like a poled ox.

The slaves were mostly lying on the ground, or knocking themselves against the angles of the walls in their haste to escape. The litter was lying smashed in the struggle. Ursus carried Lygia off into the Suburra, and his comrades dispersed.

The slaves met again in front of Vinicius' house, and laid their heads together. They did not dare to enter. After a moment of deliberation they returned to the scene of the attack, where they found some who had been killed, and also Atacinus, who was still gasping, but who after one last convulsion stiffened and lay motionless.

Taking up his body they once more went and stood in front of the door. It was necessary, however, to inform their master of what had happened.

'Gulo shall tell him,' some voices whispered; 'he has blood on his face like us, and our master is fond of him. He is in less danger than the rest.'

Gulo, an old German slave who had nursed Vinicius, and whom the latter had inherited from his mother, said:

'Yes, I will tell him; but we must all go, so that his anger may not fall on me alone.'

But now Vinicius was losing patience. Petronius and Chrysothemis laughed at him as he walked up and down the atrium repeating:

'They ought to be here! They ought to be here by now!'

And he would have gone out if they had not restrained him.

Suddenly in the outer hall steps were heard, and a crowd of slaves entered the hall. They stood beside the wall and began to groan with uplifted hands:

'Ah—aaaaah!'

Vinicius flew towards them.

'Where is Lygia?' he cried in a terrible voice.

'Aaaaah!'

Gulo came forward and suddenly broke out in a mournful voice:

'Look at the blood, master! We defended her! Look, master, look at the blood!'

Before he had finished, Vinicius shattered the

slave's skull with a brass candlestick. Then seizing
his head in his hands and running his fingers through
his hair, he cried hoarsely:

' Woe is me!'

His face became livid, his eyes started, and he
foamed at the mouth.

' Lashes!' he cried at last in an inhuman tone.

'Master! Aaaah! Have mercy,' groaned the
slaves.

Petronius rose with an expression of disgust.

' Come, Chrysothemis,' he said. ' If you have a
mind for raw flesh, I'll have them carry off a
butcher's booth from the Carinæ.'

And they walked out of the atrium.

So the house, clad as it was with green and decked
out for the feast, resounded until morning with the
groaning of slaves and the whistling of the lashes.

CHAPTER 11

VINICIUS did not lie down all that night. The
groans of the slaves under the lash satisfied neither
his sufferings nor his wrath, and late in the night he
led out another band of slaves, and embarked on a
search for Lygia. He explored the Esquiline, the
Suburra, the Via Scelerata and all the adjoining
streets. Then, rounding the Capitol, he passed over
the Fabrician bridge, hastily scoured the island, and
finally made a search through the district across the
Tiber.

He did not return till daybreak, when the carts
and mules of the kitchen-gardeners began to appear,
and the bakers were opening their shops. Throwing
himself down on a couch in the atrium, he began to

reflect in a confused fashion about ways and means of finding Lygia again.

To give her up and lose her for good seemed to him an impossible thing, and the very thought filled his heart with rage. He would not and could not resign himself to his fate, for never had he desired anything so passionately as he desired Lygia. At times he felt against her a rage that bordered on madness. He wanted her, were it only to beat her, to drag her by the hair to his bedchamber and torture her.

And then a terrible longing for her voice, for those eyes of hers and the outline of that sweet face, took hold of him, and he would fain have grovelled at her feet. He called to her, he bit his nails, he clapped his hands to his head. At last the idea flashed across his mind that it could be none but Aulus who had carried her off ; at least he would know where she was hiding.

He started to his feet to go to Aulus' house. If they did not give her up, and if they paid no heed to his threats, he would go to the emperor, accuse the old general of disobedience, and so obtain his death warrant.

Suddenly his heart sank as a dreadful suspicion occurred to him :

' Suppose it was Cæsar himself who had carried off Lygia ! '

Everybody knew that Cæsar frequently made these nocturnal raids in order to banish *ennui,* and Petronius himself had taken part in the fun.

The idea was chiefly to catch some pretty girls and make them bounce up and down from a soldier's cloak till they were exhausted. Nero used to refer to these expeditions as pearl fishing, for sometimes they fished up a real pearl of youthful beauty. Then they would either send the pearl to the Palatine or to one of Cæsar's innumerable villas, or else Cæsar would hand her over to one of his companions. Such an adventure might have happened to Lygia. Cæsar had looked at her during the banquet, and Vinicius made no doubt that he had been fascinated by her. Of course, he might have kept her at the palace, but then, as Petronius said, Cæsar had not the courage of his failings. And, besides, he had to handle Poppæa carefully.

If this was the case, Lygia was lost for ever. She could be snatched from the hands of all save Cæsar. Now he saw how dear she was to him. Like a drowning man, who in an instant remembers his whole past, Vinicius remembered Lygia. He saw her, he heard every word she had said. He saw her beside the fountain, in Aulus' house, and at the banquet. He felt her near him, he felt the heat of her body, he remembered the perfume of her hair, and the ecstasy of the kisses with which he had crushed those innocent lips at the banquet. And just before he had thought that he could not live if he did not recover Lygia, so now he saw that it would be impossible for him to die without avenging her.

It was this idea of vengeance that alone afforded him any consolation. 'I will be your Cassius Chærea,' he kept on saying. Taking a little earth from the flower-pots which surrounded the fountain, he swore a terrible oath to Hecate, to Erebus, and to his household gods, that he would be revenged on Nero. At least he had now something to live for. He bade his men take him to the palace, where he could first of all see Acte, and perhaps learn something from her. On arriving in front of the arched doorway, he said to himself that if the guards made the least difficulty, or attempted to ascertain whether he was armed—and he had forgotten to arm himself—that would prove that Lygia was in the palace by the command of Cæsar. But the oldest centurion came up to him with a friendly smile, saying:

'Greeting, noble tribune! If it be your desire to pay your duty to the emperor, you are unlucky, for I do not know if you will be able to see him.'

'What is the matter?' asked Vinicius.

'Her Highness the young princess has taken suddenly ill, and the emperor and empress are in her room with the doctors.'

This was an event of importance. At the birth of this child, Cæsar had been mad with joy. Before the birth, the Senate had solemnly commended Poppæa's womb to the protection of the gods. A dedicatory service had been held at Antium on her recovery; there had been splendid games, and a temple had been raised to the two Fortunes. Nero, incapable of moderation in anything, loved the child immoderately, and Poppæa, too, was fond of her, since she had strengthened her position, and made her influence irresistible.

Upon the health and the life of the little princess might depend the fate of the empire. But Vinicius was so utterly absorbed in his love that he paid no heed to the soldier's reply.

'I only want to see Acte,' he said, and passed on.

Acte also was with the child, and he had to wait. She did not come till midday.

'Acte,' exclaimed Vinicius, seizing her hand and drawing her into the middle of the room, 'where is Lygia?'

'That is what I wanted to ask you,' she said reproachfully.

Thereupon Vinicius, though he had resolved to question her calmly, cried out, his face contorted with grief and rage:

' She is not with me. She has been carried off on the way.'

Then, controlling himself, with his face close to Acte, he said through his clenched teeth:

' Acte, if you value your life, if you would not be the cause of disasters whose consequences you cannot even imagine, tell me the truth: is it Cæsar who has carried her off ? '

' Cæsar did not leave the palace yesterday.'

' Swear by your mother's spirit, swear by all the gods, that she is not in the palace.'

' I do swear, Marcus ; she is not here, and it is not Cæsar that has taken her. The little princess has been ill since yesterday, and Nero has not left her cradle.'

Vinicius breathed again.

' Then,' he said, as he sat down and clenched his fists, ' it must be Aulus' people, and woe betide them.'

' Aulus Plautius was here this morning. He could not see me, as I was with the child, but he questioned Epaphroditus and the rest of Cæsar's suite, and told them he would come back to see me.'

'He was wanting to prevent suspicion falling on him. If he had not known what had become of her, he would have come to me to ask about her.'

' He left a message for me on a tablet. He knew that Lygia had been taken from him at Petronius' desire and yours, and expecting that she had been sent to you, he went to your house this morning, where your people told him what had happened.'

She went into the bedroom, and returned with the tablet which Aulus had left.

Vinicius read its contents and remained silent. Acte seemed to be reading his crestfallen countenance, and presently she said:

'No, Marcus, what has happened, has happened at Lygia's own desire.'

'Then you knew she wanted to escape?' exclaimed Vinicius.

'I knew she would not consent to be your mistress.'

His clouded eyes assumed a look that was almost severe:

'And you—what have you been all your life?'

'Yes, but I was a slave.'

Still Vinicius did not cease to vent his wrath. Cæsar had given Lygia to him, and he would find her though she were hidden beneath the earth, and then do as he liked with her. Yes, she should be his mistress. When he was tired of her, he would give her to the lowest of his slaves, or harness her to a hand mill on one of his African estates.'

Becoming impatient, Acte said:

'Beware of losing her for ever when Cæsar finds her again.'

'What do you mean?'

'Listen, Marcus. Yesterday, in the gardens, Lygia and I met Poppæa, and Lilith, the negress, with the little princess in her arms. In the evening the child fell ill, and Lilith makes out that the strange woman must have bewitched her. If the child recovers, they will forget; if not, Poppæa will at once accuse Lygia of witchcraft, and then when she is found all hope of saving her will be gone.'

After a moment's silence Vinicius said:

'Perhaps indeed she *has* cast a spell on the child— and on me, too.'

'Lilith recollects that the child began to cry as

soon as she had passed us. That is true ; she did begin to cry, and no doubt she was ill before. By all means look for her, Marcus, but until the child is well again, do not speak of her. Her eyes have shed tears enough through you.'

' Do you love her, Acte ? ' asked Vinicius in a sad voice.

' Yes, I have learned to love her.'

' You love her. And she has not returned your love with hatred like mine? '

' You blind, headstrong man ; she did love you.'

Vinicius started.

It was not true, he said. She hated him. Where did Acte learn the contrary ? Did Lygia confide in her after a day's friendship ? What sort of love was this that preferred a life of wandering and poverty, uncertainty about the morrow, and even perhaps a miserable death—that preferred all that to a life of luxury and happiness ? What kind of love was this that was afraid of pleasure and thirsted for suffering ?

It was now the turn of Acte, usually so mild, to grow angry. How had he tried to win her ? Instead of going humbly to Pomponia and Aulus, and asking them for her, he had carried her off by surprise from her friends. He had wanted to make her, not his wife, but his mistress—her, the daughter of a king. He had offended her innocent eyes by the sight of that shameful debauch. Did he forget what Aulus' house was like ? And what Pomponia was—her adopted mother ? He had not understood that this pure girl would prefer death to dishonour. No, Lygia had not confided in her, but she had told her how she expected him, Vinicius, to save her. She blushed when she spoke of him.

Her heart beat for him, but he had terrified her, insulted her, outraged her.

'It is too late,' he groaned.

An abyss yawned before him. He knew not what to do, what to attempt, whither to turn. Like an echo Acte repeated, 'Too late,' and these words in the mouth of another sounded to him like a death-knell.

He was about to depart without even taking leave of Acte, when suddenly the curtain of the atrium was raised. Vinicius saw before him the grief-stricken face of Pomponia Græcina. She, too, had heard of Lygia's disappearance, and thinking it would be easier for her to gain admission to Acte than for Aulus, she had come to ask her for news. When she saw Vinicius, she turned her pale, delicate face to him and said:

'Marcus, may God forgive you for the wrong you have done to us—to us and to Lygia.'

Vinicius stood with bowed head, conscious of his misfortune and of his own responsibility for it, but unable to understand what god it was that was to pardon him, or could do so, and why Pomponia should speak of pardon when she should have spoken of vengeance.

At last he went out, destitute of hope and weighed down by his thoughts.

In the principal courtyard and beneath the gallery anxious groups crowded together. They were senators and knights, come to inquire for the little princess, or at least to show their loyalty, if only before the emperor's slaves. Some newcomers, seeing Vinicius leaving, accosted him in their search for information, but he passed on without replying. Suddenly, Petronius stopped him.

Vinicius would have given free rein to his rage

against this man, whose scheme had had such disastrous results for him, but on leaving Acte he was so dejected that his natural quickness of temper was in abeyance. However, he pushed Petronius aside, and would have passed on had Petronius not caught his arm.

'How is Her Highness?'

Vinicius, compelled to stop, grew angry once more.

'May Hades swallow her and the whole house with her,' he replied through his clenched teeth.

'Be quiet, you fool!' said Petronius.

Then, casting a furtive look around, he added:

'If you want to hear something about Lygia, come with me. No, it is no use. I'm going to say nothing here. Come along with me and I will tell you my ideas about it.'

He put his arm round Vinicius and drew him away. That was his chief aim, for news he had none. But as he felt himself responsible for the events that distracted Vinicius, he had indeed already taken some steps, and once in the litter he said:

'I have all the city gates watched by my slaves, and I have given them an exact description of the girl and of that giant who carried her out of the banqueting-hall the other day; beyond doubt, it was he who carried her off again yesterday. If my people do not see her at the gates, that will prove that she is still in the city, and we'll begin our search again this very day.'

CHAPTER 12

WHEN they left the litter on their arrival at Petronius' house the porter told them that none of the slaves sent to watch the city gates had returned.

'You see,' said Petronius, 'they are still certainly within the walls, and we shall find them.'

They went into the inner peristyle, and sat down on a marble seat to talk.

'The thing has happened in a mysterious fashion,' said Petronius. 'It is neither Cæsar's nor Aulus' doing. Yet the Lygian could not have managed it alone, so they must have had help.'

'Who could help them?'

'The people of her own faith.'

'What faith? Who are her gods? And yet I should know that better than you!'

'There's scarcely a woman in Rome who has not gods of her own. Apparently Pomponia has brought her up to worship the divinity she herself worships. What worship is that? I know nothing about it; but one thing is certain: nobody has ever seen its votaries offer sacrifices in any temple to any of our gods.'

'Well, I met Pomponia in Acte's room, and she said to me: "May God forgive you for the wrong that you have done to us—to us and to Lygia."'

'It would seem that their god is a very good-natured sort of guardian. Ah, well, I hope he'll pardon you, and to prove it, give you back the girl.'

'I would offer up a hecatomb to him tomorrow if he restored Lygia to me. I cannot eat, nor bathe, nor sleep. I'm going to put on a dark cloak and prowl about the city. Perhaps I shall find her in that disguise. I am ill.'

Petronius looked at him pityingly, for his eyes were sunken and burned feverishly; his strong chin was covered with a two days' beard; his hair was in disorder, and he appeared to be really unwell. Iras and Eunice also cast pitying glances at him, but, like Petronius, Vinicius paid less heed to them than he would to little dogs playing about his feet.

'You're in a fever,' said Petronius.

'Yes.'

'Well, listen. I don't know what a doctor might do for you, but I know what I should do in your place. Until the one is found again, I should go to another for what is lacking at the moment. I have seen some beauties in your house. You can't deny it— Yes, yes, I know what love is, and that if you desire one woman, no other can take her place. But one can find passing amusement in a pretty slave.'

'I have no desire,' replied Vinicius.

'Possibly your own women have lost the charm of freshness for you,' said Petronius, after a moment of friendly reflection. But '—and he examined Eunice and Iras in turn, finally laying his hand on the hip of the fair Achæan—'but just look at this rival of the Graces. A few days ago, young Fonteius Capito offered me in exchange three lovely youths from Clazomenæ, for never did Scopas himself fashion more perfect beauty. I don't understand how I have been insensible of her charms till now; it was certainly not the idea of Chrysothemis that restrained me. Well, I will give her to you, take her.'

Eunice grew suddenly pale, and awaited Vinicius' reply with her eyes fixed upon him in terror.

He pressed his hands to his head, and began to

speak very quickly, like a sick man who is being annoyed.

'No, no ; I don't want her ; I don't want anybody. I thank you, but I don't want her. I'm going to look for the other in the city. Get them to bring me a Gallic cloak with a hood. I'll go across the river. If only I could see Ursus !'

He went hastily out, and Petronius did not try to stop him. But ascribing Vinicius' refusal to a temporary loathing of all women save Lygia, and unwilling that his kindness should be in vain, he turned to the slave and said :

'Eunice, go and bathe, and then, after perfuming yourself, go to Vinicius' house.'

But Eunice fell on her knees, and with clasped hands implored him not to send her away. She would not go to Vinicius ; she would rather remain and carry wood for the furnaces than be the chief woman in his house. She would not! She could not! She besought him to have mercy. Let him have her whipped every day, but not send her away.

Petronius listened in amazement to this slave who was bold enough to question a command, and who said 'I cannot; I will not.' Such a thing was so unheard of in Rome that at first he thought he did not hear aright. At last he frowned. He was too refined for cruelty. His slaves had more liberty than those of others, but it was on condition that they did their duties in an exemplary fashion, and respected their master's will as highly as that of the gods. Should they fail in those duties, Petronius also could punish them as custom demanded. Besides, he put up with no opposition. So he looked for a moment at the weeping girl who knelt before him, and said to her :

'Go and find Teiresias.'

Presently she returned with Teiresias, a Cretan, who had charge of the atrium.

'Take Eunice,' said Petronius, 'and give her twenty-five lashes, but do not injure her skin.'

So saying, he passed into the library, and sitting down at a table of pink marble he set to work on the 'Banquet of Trimalchio.'

But Lygia's escape and the illness of the princess were too much on his mind to allow of his writing long. The latter especially was an important event. If Cæsar let himself be persuaded that Lygia had cast a spell on the child, Petronius might find himself in a fix, since the girl had been summoned to the palace by his request. But he would take the first opportunity to explain to Cæsar the full absurdity of such an accusation. He counted, too, on Poppæa having taken a fancy to him, which she did not conceal so well as to blind him to it. Shrugging his shoulders at his fears, he determined to dine at home and go afterwards to the palace, from there to the Campus Martius, and lastly to Chrysothemis.

As he went into the dining-room he noticed among the other slaves at the entrance to the service passage the slender figure of Eunice, and forgetting that he had commanded Teiresias only to whip her, he looked frowningly around for him.

Not seeing him, he said to Eunice:

'Did you receive the lashes?'

She threw herself again at his feet and kissed the hem of his toga.

'Yes, master, I received them. Yes, master!'

Her voice seemed to tremble with joy and gratitude. Evidently she thought that the fact of her having been whipped meant that she was to remain in the house. Petronius, understanding this, was astonished at such a desperate resistance; but he knew human nature too well not to be aware that only love could account for such obstinacy.

'So there is somebody here you love ? ' he said.

She lifted her eyes to him, full of tears, and replied in a voice scarcely intelligible:

'Yes, master.'

Her eyes, her disordered golden hair, and her pathetic face were so beautiful that Petronius felt a sort of sympathy for her.

'Which is your lover ? ' he asked, pointing to the slaves.

There was no reply. Eunice bent her face to her master's feet and remained motionless.

Petronius cast a glance on the men, some of whom were very handsome. Not one of their faces told him anything, though they all smiled meaningly. He looked for a moment at Eunice, lying stretched at his feet, and passed on to the dining-room without a word.

After the meal he was taken to the palace, and then to Chrysothemis' house, where he remained very late. On his return to the house he asked Teiresias:

'Did Eunice receive the lashes ? '

'Yes, master. But you said I wasn't to mark her skin.'

'I gave no other order about her ? '

'No, master,' replied the doorkeeper uneasily.

'Very well. Which of the slaves is her lover ? '

'None of them, master.'

'What can you tell me about her ? '

Teiresias replied in an uncertain voice:

'Eunice never leaves the bedroom at night where she sleeps with old Acrisone and Ifis. After you bathe, master, she never remains in the bathroom.

The other women laugh at her: they call her Diana.'

'That will do,' said Petronius. 'My relative Vinicius, to whom I presented her this morning, has not accepted her, and she will remain here. You may go.'

'May I say something further about her, master?'

'I have told you to tell me what you know.'

'All the slaves, master, are talking about the flight of the girl who was to live with the noble Vinicius. After you left, Eunice came to me and told me she knew a man who could find her.'

'Ah, who is he?'

'I do not know him, master.'

'Well, tomorrow this man shall come and meet the tribune. Go now and beg Vinicius in my name to come here in the morning.'

CHAPTER 13

WHEN Teiresias told him about a man who was confident of being able to find Lygia, Vinicius hastened, ere it was too late, to Petronius' house, and began at once to question him.

'There's talk of somebody,' said Petronius, 'whom we can make use of in our search. Eunice, who knows this person, is coming in a moment to arrange my toga, and she will give us further information.'

'Eunice, the girl you wanted to give me yesterday?'

'The girl you refused; and, by the way, I am obliged to you for that, because she is the best at arranging the toga in all Rome.'

With that the girl entered, and having opened out a toga she began her task of arranging it on Petronius' shoulders. When it was in position, Eunice wound it, and as she stooped the better to dispose the folds, he could see the delicate carnation pink of her arms and the pearl-white beauty of her throat.

'Eunice,' he said, 'is the man there whom you told Teiresias about yesterday?'

'Yes, master.'

'His name?'

'Chilon Chilonides, master.'

'What is his profession?'

'He is a doctor, a sage, and a fortune-teller, who can see into men's destinies and foretell the future.'

'And has he told your future?'

Eunice's face and neck turned pink.

'Yes, master.'

'And what did he foretell for you?'

'That I should suffer and that I should be happy.'

'You suffered yesterday at Teiresias' hands, the happiness is still to come, I suppose?'

'It has come already, master.'

'How?'

She murmured:

'I have remained here.'

Petronius put his hand upon her fair head.

'You have arranged the folds well, and I am pleased with you.'

At the touch of Petronius' hand Eunice's eyes became misty and her throat swelled.

Petronius and Vinicius passed into the atrium where Chilon was waiting. He made them a low bow as they entered.

The man who stood before them was a blend of the pitiful and the ridiculous. He was not old, though here and there his curly locks and dirty beard showed a stray white hair. His stomach was sunken, and his shoulders so rounded that at first sight he seemed to be a hunchback. On top of all was a huge head, and his keen face had something of both the fox and the ape in it. His skin was covered with yellow pimples, which clustered also upon a nose empurpled with wine. His plain dress and his tunic and cloak of goatskin revealed a state of wretched poverty, genuine or feigned. At the sight of him Petronius thought of Homer's Thersites, and replying to his greeting by a gesture, he said:

'Hail, Thersites. How are the bumps that the divine Ulysses gave you under the walls of Troy ? And what is become of him in the Elysian Fields ? '

'Noble sir,' replied Chilon Chilonides, 'the wisest of the departed, Ulysses, sends greetings through me to Petronius, the wisest of the living, and begs he will cover my bumps with a new cloak.'

'By Hecate,' exclaimed Petronius, 'the answer merits one.'

But here the conversation was interrupted by Vinicius, who put the question directly:

'Do you know exactly what it is you undertake ? '

'Night before last,' replied Chilon, 'a maiden called "Lygia," or rather "Callina," an adopted child of Aulus Plautius, was carried off. Your slaves, sir, were taking her from Cæsar's palace to your house. I undertake to discover her in the city, or else, if she has left it, which is unlikely, to show you, noble tribune, where she is in hiding.'

'Very good,' said Vinicius, pleased by the clearness of the reply. 'And what means will you employ ? '

Chilon smiled maliciously.

' These are in your power, sir ; I have only the brains.'

Petronius smiled also—he was quite satisfied with his guest.

' How do you come to know Eunice ? ' he asked.

' She came to consult me, for my fame had spread so far.'

' What did she consult you about ? '

' About a love affair, sir. She wanted to be cured of a love that was not returned.'

' And did you cure her ? '

' I did better, sir. I gave her an amulet which secures a return of affection. At Paphos, in Cyprus, there is a temple where Venus' girdle is kept. I gave her two threads from it inside an almond shell.'

' For which you made her pay sweetly ? '

' A love that is returned is above all price. As for me, I lack two fingers of my right hand, and I want to save up for a clerk to write down my teaching, and so pass it on to the generations to come.'

' To what school do you belong, divine sage ? '

' I am a Cynic, sir, as you see by my ragged cloak ; I am a Stoic, for I endure my wretchedness in patience ; and a Peripatetician because, having no litter, I go on foot from tavern to tavern, and by the way bestow the benefits of my teaching on such as will pay for a stoup of wine.'

' With that in front of you, you become an orator ? '

' Heraclitus has said, " All things are fluid." Now it is undeniable, sir, that wine, too, is fluid.'

' Heraclitus also said that fire was divinity, and

hence it is to honour this divinity that your nose lights its altars ? '

' But the divine Diogenes of Apollonia has taught that air is the very essence of things, and that the warmer the air the more perfect are the beings it produces, and that the warmest air engenders the souls of sages. But since autumn brings cold weather, the true sage must warm his soul with wine. For you cannot deny, sir, that a jar, even of sour Capuan or Telesian—you cannot deny, I say, that this jar is a heat conductor for the whole framework of our mortal covering.'

' Chilon Chilonides, where were you born ? '

' On the shores of the Euxine. I am from Mesembria.'

' You are a great man, Chilon.'

' And unappreciated,' added the other dolefully. ' Virtue and honour are so little esteemed to-day that even philosophy is forced to seek other means of living.'

' What are yours ? '

' To know all that goes on and offer information to such as need it. When a valuable slave escapes, who is it that finds him again? Who but my father's son ? When some inscription, too flattering to the divine Poppæa, appears on the walls, who is it who points out the culprits ? Who hunts out satires on the emperor in the bookshops ? Who reports all that is said in the houses of knights and senators ? Who carries letters that are not to be trusted to a slave? Who listens to the talk in barbers' shops ? Who is in the confidence of pot-house keepers and bakers ? Who is the slaves' confidant ? Who can tell all that happens in a house from the porch to the garden ? Who knows every street, every blind alley, and every hiding-place ? Who knows all that is said in the baths, at the circus, in the markets, in the gladiators' schools, in the slave-dealers' barracks, and even in the sandpits ? '

'Heavens above! Peace, illustrious sage,' exclaimed Petronius, 'or we shall be submerged beneath the waves of your merit, your goodness, and your wisdom. Enough! We wanted to know who you were—now we know.'

Vinicius was satisfied, for he considered that such a man, like a hound, once put on the trail, would not stop till he found his quarry's hiding-place.

'Good,' said he ; 'do you require any information ? '

'I require arms.'

'Arms ? ' said the astonished Vinicius.

The Greek opened one hand and pretended to count money into it with the other.

''Tis the nature of the times, sir,' he said with a sigh.

'So you are the ass which carries the stronghold by means of a sack of gold ? '

'I am but a poor philosopher,' replied the other humbly ; 'it is you who carry the gold.'

Vinicius threw him a purse, which he caught in mid-air with the three fingers of his right hand.

Then, raising his head, he said :

'Sir, I know more about this than you think. I did not come here with empty hands. I know that the maiden has not been carried off by Aulus' people, for I have already spoken with their slaves. I know that she is not at the palace, where everybody is busy with the little princess ; and I fancy I even know the reasons why you prefer my services to those of the watch and the soldiers. I know that her escape was planned by a slave from the same country as herself. He had no assistance from the slaves, for they stand by one another, and would have given him no help against your slaves. He can only have obtained assistance from those of the same faith.'

'You hear that, Vinicius!' Petronius broke in. 'Did I not say so ? '

'I feel much honoured, sir,' said Chilon. Then, turning to Vinicius, he continued: 'The maiden is certainly a worshipper of the same deity as Pomponia, most virtuous of Roman women. I have also heard that Pomponia was tried for her worship of strange deities, but I could not learn from her people what sort of deity it was, or the name of those who worshipped it. If I could find that out, I'd go to them and become the most pious of disciples, and so win their confidence. But you, sir, who, as I know too, spent a fortnight in the noble Aulus' house, can you not throw some light on the matter ? '

'No,' said Vinicius.

'Well, you have questioned me about all sorts of things, noble sirs, and I have answered your questions. Allow me now in my turn to put a few to you. Illustrious tribune, did you never notice any ceremony or anything connected with their worship—a statuette perhaps, or a sacrifice, or an amulet ? Did you never observe them drawing any symbols that only Pomponia and the young foreign girl could understand ? '

'Symbols ? Wait now! Yes! One day I saw Lygia trace a fish on the sand.'

'A fish ? Oh! Indeed! Only once, or more than once ? '

'Once.'

'And are you sure, sir, that she traced a—a fish ? Oh!'

'Yes,' said Vinicius, becoming curious. 'Do you know what it means ?'

'Know what it means!' exclaimed Chilon.

Then with a bow he added:

'May Fortune ever load you with her favours, most illustrious masters.'

'Get them to give you a cloak!' said Petronius.

'Ulysses thanks you on behalf of Thersites,' replied the Greek.

He bowed once more and departed.

'What think you of yonder honourable sage ?' asked Petronius.

'I think he'll find Lygia,' said Vinicius joyfully; 'but I think also that if there were a kingdom of scoundrels in this world, he'd be the king.'

'Indisputably. I must make the better acquaintance of this Stoic, but meantime I'm going to have the atrium disinfected.'

Chilon Chilonides rattled in his hand beneath his new cloak the purse that Vinicius had given him, and remarked with delight its weight and its pleasing sound. He walked along slowly, turning round to see that nobody was watching him from Petronius' house. Then he walked on past the Porticus Livia, and when he came to the corner of the Clivus Vibrius, he turned in the direction of the Suburra.

'I must go to Sporus,' he said to himself, 'and pour out a drop or two in honour of Fortune. Oh, she traced a fish on the sand, did she ? If I know what that means, may I choke on my next mouthful of goat cheese! But I'll get to know! One more purse like this and I'll be able to throw away my beggar's wallet and treat myself to a slave.

But then, what say you, Chilon, if I advised you to buy not a man but a woman slave ? I know you! You won't turn up your nose at that! And if she were as pretty as Eunice, for instance, you would grow visibly younger beside her, and you would even find in her a means of honest and certain gain. I sold poor Eunice two threads of my old coat. She is very stupid, but I'd take her if Petronius gave her to me. Yes, yes, Chilon, son of Chilon, you have lost father and mother ; you are a poor hopeless orphan ; allow yourself at least the consolation of such a slave. True, she must have somewhere to live, so Vinicius shall take a house for her, and you can live in it too. Then she must have clothes, so Vinicius shall pay for them too. She must eat—Vinicius shall provide her food. Ah, how bitter a thing is life ! Where are the days when for a farthing a man could have as much pork fat and beans as his two hands could hold, or else a fine red slice of goat sausage, a slice as long as a twelve-year-old boy's arm ? Here I am at Sporus'—the old robber! This tavern is the best place for news.'

He entered the tavern and ordered a flask of ' dark ' wine. At the host's incredulous look he rummaged in his purse and drew out a gold piece, which he laid on the table.

' Sporus,' he said, ' I worked to-day with Seneca from daybreak till noon, and this is what my friend gave me when I left him.'

Sporus' round eyes grew rounder still, and the wine was placed forthwith before Chilon, who dipped his finger in it and drew a fish on the table.

' Do you know what that means ? ' he asked.

' A fish ? What a question. A fish—it's a fish!'

'And you—you're an ass, although you do add enough water to your wine to keep a fish alive in it. Let me tell you then that in the language of philosophy this is a symbol meaning the "smile of Fortune." Had you guessed it, perhaps you'd have made a fortune. Respect philosophy, I tell you, or I'll go elsewhere, as my old friend Petronius has long been urging me to do anyhow.'

CHAPTER 14

For the next few days Chilon was nowhere to be seen. Vinicius, who, since he learned of Lygia's feelings, longed more passionately than ever to find her, began to search for her in person, for he would not and could not ask for help from Cæsar, distracted as he was by the illness of the princess.

Neither sacrifices, nor prayers, nor vows, nor doctors' skill, nor all the craft of sorcery that was employed in the last extremity, could avert the disaster. The child died after a week of illness.

The court and the city were plunged in mourning. Cæsar, who had gone mad with joy at the child's birth, was now mad with despair. For two whole days he took no food, and although the palace was besieged with crowds of senators and Augustans come to offer their sympathy, he would see nobody. The Senate held an extraordinary meeting, at which the dead child was deified: a temple was dedicated to her, and a special priest was appointed for her worship. In the other temples, too, sacrifices were offered in her honour, statues of her were cast in precious metals, and her funeral was an immensely solemn occasion. The people marvelled at the uncontrollable grief of the emperor, and they wept with him, holding out their hands the while for largesse, their chief emotion delight in the rare spectacle offered to them.

Petronius was exceedingly uneasy. The whole town knew now that Poppæa attributed the child's death to witchcraft. The doctors, anxious to explain away the failure of their skill, repeated the story; so did the priests, whose sacrifices had proved of no avail, and the magicians, now trembling for their lives; so did the populace. Petronius was glad that Lygia had disappeared, but as he wished no harm to Aulus' family, and was anxious for his own and Vinicius' safety, he hastened, as soon as the cypress placed in token of mourning before the palace had been removed, to the reception which was to be held for senators and friends of Cæsar. In order to act with his eyes open, he must know what hold this witchcraft theory had obtained over Nero.

His eyes staring fixedly into space, Nero listened with a face impassive as stone to the words of consolation lavished upon him by knights and senators. It was plain that, even though he was suffering, he was thinking above all of the effect which his grief was making on those present. He started on seeing Petronius, and said in a tragic voice:

'Alas! You, too, helped to cause her death! It was through you that the evil spirit entered these walls which with one look drained the life from her heart. Woe is me! I would my eyes had never looked upon the light of the sun! Woe is me! Alas! alas!'

He raised his voice and uttered heartrending cries.

But Petronius resolved suddenly to hazard all on one throw. Stretching out his hand, he snatched off the scarf which Nero wore round his neck and put it to his mouth.

'Sire,' he said regretfully, 'set fire to Rome and all the universe in your grief, but spare us your voice!'

Those round about were struck dumb. Even Nero was at a loss. Petronius alone remained unmoved. He knew quite well what he was doing, for Terpnos and Diodorus had been formally commanded to close Cæsar's mouth as soon as he raised his voice unduly and exposed his throat to danger.

'Cæsar,' he went on, with the same sad dignity, 'we have suffered a stupendous loss. May this treasure at least be left to console us.'

Nero's face quivered, and in a moment the tears fell fast from his eyes. He leant with both hands on Petronius' arm, laid his head on his breast, and sobbed as he said:

'You are the only one—the only one who thought of that. Only you, Petronius, only you!'

Tigellinus was green with jealousy. But Petronius went on:

'Go to Antium! It was there she saw the light of day; there you knew what joy was, and there you will find comfort. The sea air will restore your divine voice, and your lungs will breathe in its briny moisture. We, your faithful friends, will follow you anywhere, and while we strive to soothe your grief by our friendship you will console us by your singing.'

'Yes,' said Nero in a sad voice. 'I will write a hymn in her honour, and I will set it to music.'

'And then you will take the sun at Baiæ.'

'And then seek forgetfulness in Greece.'

'In the cradle of poetry and song.'

A conversation sprang up, still sad, but full of plans for the future—travelling, art, and the receptions to be given on the approaching visit of Tiridates, King of Armenia. Tigellinus made another attempt to introduce the subject of witchcraft, but Petronius, confident of victory, joined issue with him directly.

'Tigellinus,' he said, 'do you think witchcraft can affect the gods?'

'Cæsar himself spoke of it,' replied the courtier.

'It was his grief which spoke—not Cæsar. But what is your own opinion?'

'The gods are too powerful to be affected by witchcraft.'

'Then you do not admit the divinity of Cæsar and his family?'

'*Peractum est!*' murmured Eprius Marcellus, who stood beside Petronius, using the phrase employed by the people to denote that a gladiator had been wounded in such wise as not to require a finishing stroke.

On his way from the palace Petronius called on Vinicius and recounted the incident to him.

'Not only have I warded off danger from Plautius and Pomponia, but also from ourselves, and even from Lygia, whom they will not look for. I suggested, in fact, to that yellow-bearded monkey that he should go to Antium, and then to Naples and Baiæ. During that time we can search for Lygia as we like, and have her put in some safe place. Whatever you find out, let me know, for I must go to Antium.'

'Very well.'

They were taking leave of one another when a

slave announced that Chilon Chilonides was waiting in the anteroom and had asked to be shown in to the master.

Vinicius bade him be shown in at once.

' My greetings and respects to the noble tribune, and to you, sir,' said Chilon as he entered. ' May your good fortune equal your glory, and may that glory spread through all the world, from the pillars of Hercules to the frontiers of the Arsacidæ!'

' Hail, framer of the laws of wisdom and goodness,' replied Petronius.

Feigning calmness, Vinicius asked:

' What news do you bring ? '

' The first time, sir, I brought you hope ; now I bring you the assurance that the girl will be found.'

' And that means you haven't found her yet ? '

' It does, sir. But I have found out the meaning of the symbol which she traced before you ; I know who the people are who have taken her away, and I know what god it is they worship.'

Vinicius would have started from his seat, but Petronius laid his hand on his shoulder and said:

' Go on.'

' Are you perfectly sure, sir, that the maiden traced a fish on the sand ? '

' Yes.'

' Then she is a Christian, and it is the Christians who have her.'

There was silence for a moment.

' Hark 'ee, my friend,' said Petronius at last, ' My nephew has promised you a large sum of money if you find the girl, but an equally large number of lashes if you try to take him in. In the former case you will be able to buy yourself not one but three clerks ; in the latter, all the philosophy of the seven sages, with your own thrown in, will be of little use as an ointment to heal your wounds.'

'The girl *is* a Christian, sir,' exclaimed the Greek.

'Now just think, Chilon; you are not a fool. Do you want us to believe that Pomponia and Lygia both belong to the sect of these enemies of mankind, these poisoners of fountains and wells, these worshippers of an ass's head, who sacrifice their children and practise the most shameful debauchery ? Think, Chilon, whether this theory which you maintain before us may not recoil upon your own head.'

Chilon made a sign with his hands that it was not his fault. Then he added:

'Repeat this phrase in Greek, sir: Jesus Christ, Son of God, Saviour.'

'Well, there you are. What now ? '

'Now take the first letter of each of these words and join the letters so as to make a new word.'

'Fish!' exclaimed Petronius in astonishment.

'That's why the fish is the emblem of Christianity,' Chilon replied proudly.

They were silent, for there was something unanswerable in the Greek's argument. The two friends could not hide their surprise.

'Vinicius,' said Petronius, 'are you not mistaken ? Did Lygia really trace out a fish ? '

'By all the gods in Hades, this is enough to drive a man mad!' exclaimed the young man furiously. 'If she had traced a bird, I would have said it was a bird.'

'Then she is a Christian!' repeated Chilon.

'And that means,' said Petronius, 'that Pomponia and Lygia poison wells, slay children whom they find in the streets, and go in for debauchery! The

thing is absurd! You, Vinicius, made a longer stay
in their home than I did: I was only there a moment,
but I know Aulus and Pomponia, and Lygia too,
well enough to say it is a piece of stupid calumny.
If the fish is the emblem of Christianity, which
seems undeniable, and if they are Christians, then,
by Proserpine, the Christians are not what we
imagine.'

'You talk like Socrates, sir,' replied Chilon. 'Has
anybody questioned a Christian ? Does anybody
know their beliefs ? Three years ago, on my way
to Rome from Naples (why did I not remain there),
I had as a travelling companion a certain doctor
called Glaucus, who, they said, was a Christian,
and yet I found him a good and virtuous man none
the less.'

'Is it from this virtuous man that you've just
learnt what the fish stands for ? '

'Alas, no, sir! During our journey the worthy
old man was stabbed in an inn, and his wife and
children were taken away as slaves by some dealers.
As for me, I lost these two fingers in trying to save
him. But seeing that the Christians are aided, as
I'm told, by miracles, I'm in hopes that my fingers
will grow again.'

'What ? You haven't turned Christian, have
you ? '

'Since yesterday, sir, since yesterday. It's this
fish that has done it. Listen to me, good sirs. This
discovery that I have made is important. I haven't
found the girl yet, but I know the lines to go upon
now. Be patient with me for a moment. I walked
yesterday till I had sores on my legs. I visited
taverns and bakehouses and butchers' shops, and
I went to the fish sellers and olive sellers, all to get
people to talk ; I was through every street and alley

and in every runaway slave's hiding-place; I lost nearly a hundred *asses* playing at *mora*; I was in laundries, dry-rooms, and cookshops; I saw muleteers and stonecarvers, men who cure bladder troubles and men who pull teeth; I talked to fig merchants and visited the cemeteries. And why did I do all this? In order to draw this fish in front of them all; then look them full in the face and see what response was forthcoming. For a long time I observed none, till at last I saw a slave drawing water at a fountain and weeping. I went up and asked him why he was weeping. We sat on the steps, and he told me that he had been slowly saving up all his life in order to buy back his son whom he was fond of, and now his master, one Pansa, had taken his money from him but still kept his son as a slave. "And so I cry," said the old man, "because it's no good my saying, 'God's will be done!' Poor sinner that I am, I can't keep back my tears." Then I had an idea, and wetting my finger in his pail I traced out a fish, at which the honest fellow said: "My trust is also in the Christ." I said: "You recognised me by this sign?" He replied: "Yes, peace be with you." Then I began to draw him out, and the old fellow told me everything. His master, Pansa, is himself a freedman of the great Pansa's, and his business consists in bringing stones up the Tiber to Rome, which are unloaded from rafts by slaves and workmen and taken by night to houses in course of erection. Among these men are many Christians, and his son is one. As the work was too much for the young man's strength, his father wanted to buy him back, but Pansa preferred to keep both money and slave. As he spoke, he began to cry again, and I mingled my tears with his; which I found easy, from the kindness of my heart and the pains which I had after all that walking. I expressed my regret that, having arrived from Naples only a few days ago, I knew none of the brethren, and did not know where they met for prayer. He was surprised that the Christians in Naples had not given me letters to their brethren in Rome, but I told him they had been stolen on the way. Then he told me to come down to the river at night, and he would introduce me to the brethren, who would take me to the meeting-houses, and to the houses of the elders who rule the Christian community. At these words I was so overjoyed that I gave him there and then the sum necessary to buy back his son, hoping that the generous Vinicius would repay me twice the amount.'

' Chilon,' broke in Petronius, ' in this story of yours there are lies floating about among the truth, as oil floats on water. I am convinced that our search has taken a decided step forward, but it is useless for you to spread your news over with a thick layer of rascalities. What is the name of the old man who told you that Christians know each other by this sign ? '

' Euricius, sir. Poor, unhappy old man !'

' I believe you really have made his acquaintance and will be able to turn it to account. But you gave him no money ; not one penny, you understand. You gave him nothing.'

' No, but I helped him to carry his pails, and I spoke of his son with the greatest sympathy. It is true, sir, nothing can escape the far-seeing mind of Petronius. I did not give him money, or rather I did give him it in imagination, in my inner consciousness, and that should have been good enough for him, if he was a genuine philosopher.

Petronius turned to Vinicius and said :

'Well, tell them to pay our friend five thousand
sesterces—in imagination and in your inner consciousness.'

Vinicius said:

'I'll give you a servant with the money ; you will
tell Euricius that he is your slave, and you will hand
the old man the money in the slave's presence.
Still, as you have brought news of importance, you
shall have a like sum yourself. Call this evening for
the man and the money.'

'There spoke a very Cæsar!' said Chilon.
'Euricius told me that all the rafts were empty and
there would be more coming from Ostia in a few
days' time. Peace be with you—that's the Christian
form of leavetaking. I'll buy myself a woman—I
mean a man slave. We catch fish with a line, and
Christians with a fish.'

CHAPTER 15

M.-C. VINICIUS to Petronius:

'Still no news of Lygia. I wanted to see whether
Chilon was not fooling me, and the night when he
came for that money for Euricius, I wrapped myself
up in a military cloak and followed him and the
young slave without his knowing it. When they
came to the place mentioned, I hid behind a pillar on
the wharf some distance off, and watched them, and
I am sure now that Euricius is no myth. On the
lower ground, near the river, some fifty men were
busy unloading stones from a great raft by the light
of torches and piling them on the bank. I saw
Chilon approach them and enter into conversation

with an old man, who presently threw himself on his knees, while the others crowded round with cries of astonishment. Before my eyes, my young slave handed the bag of money to Euricius, who fell to praying, his hands stretched to heaven. Beside him knelt a young man, evidently his son. Chilon pronounced some further words which I could not catch, and blessed the two men who knelt before him as well as others present, making a sign in the air in the form of a cross, at which all bent the knee. I felt inclined to go down to them and promise three bags of the same value to the man who would hand over Lygia to me, but I feared to spoil Chilon's plans, and after hesitating for a moment I went away.

' That was at least twelve days after you left. He has been to see me several times since. He tells me he has gained great influence among the Christians, and he makes out that the reason why he has not found Lygia yet is that even in Rome their numbers are large, and so they don't all know each other and are not aware of everything that goes on in the community. Besides, they are reserved and prudent for the most part ; but he asserts that once he gets access to their elders, or priests, he will manage to extract their secrets from them.

' He has also discovered that they have meeting-places for their common worship, often outside the city gates, or in empty houses, or even in the sand-pits. There they adore the Christ, they sing their hymns and hold their feasts. The meeting-places are numerous, and Chilon is of opinion that Lygia purposely goes to others than those favoured by Pomponia, so that the latter, should she be tried and questioned about it, may be able to swear that she does not know the girl's hiding-place. Possibly their priests advised them to this prudent course. As soon as Chilon knows one of these places, I'll accompany him there, and if the gods grant that I see Lygia, I swear by Jupiter she shan't slip through my hands this time.

' You say one must know how to love. Even I know how to speak of love to Lygia. But now I am wasted with sorrow, I look for Chilon every moment, and the house is hateful to me. Farewell.'

CHAPTER 16

CHILON was so long in putting in an appearance that Vinicius did not know what to think.

In the strain, with its torturing suspense and sorrow, he was losing both his strength and his beauty. He had become a cruel and merciless master. His slaves and even his freedmen trembled whenever they approached him, and as unjust and terrible punishments rained on them without cause they began secretly to hate him. He felt that too, as he felt his loneliness, and he avenged himself the more cruelly upon them. Only in his dealings with Chilon did he restrain himself, for he feared that the Greek might give up his search ; and Chilon, noticing this, set himself to overreach him, and became more and more grasping.

One day he arrived with so doleful a countenance that poor Vinicius grew pale at the sight of him, and bounded towards him with scarce strength enough left to say:

' She is not with the Christians ? '

' Yes, sir,' replied Chilon. ' But I have discovered Glaucus among them—Glaucus the doctor.'

' What's that you say ? Who is he ? '

' Have you forgotten, sir, about the old man with whom I travelled from Naples to Rome, and the two fingers I lost in defending him ? The robbers who carried off his wife and children stabbed him with a knife. I left him dying in an inn near Minturnæ, and many a tear I shed for him! Alas! I have found out that he is still alive and is a member of the Christian community in Rome.'

' But since you defended him, he will surely be grateful to you and help you.'

' Ah, noble tribune, even the gods are not always grateful, while as for men——! Yes, he should be grateful. Unhappily he is an old man with a brain weakened and clouded by age and misfortunes, with the result that, so far from being grateful to me, he charges me, as I have learned from his fellow-Christians, of having acted in concert with the robbers and of being the cause of his misfortunes. That's how he repays me for the loss of my two fingers.'

' I'm quite sure that in point of fact his story is the true one,' said Vinicius.

' Then you know more of the matter than he does,' replied Chilon in a dignified way, ' for he only supposes that is what happened. But that won't prevent him appealing to the Christians to help him to a cruel revenge. Doubtless that's what he will do, and they will help him. Fortunately he doesn't know my name, and he didn't notice me in the house of prayer where we met. My impulse was to throw myself on his neck, but I was restrained by my prudence and by the habit I have of thinking about every act before I do it. I inquired about him, and those who know him told me he was a man who had been betrayed by a fellow-traveller on the way from Naples. Otherwise I should not suspect the stories he was telling about me.'

' What's all this to me ? Tell me what you saw in the meeting-house.'

' Indeed, sir, it's not much to you, but seeing it concerns my skin, and as I am anxious that my teaching should survive me, I had rather give up the reward you promised me than risk my life for the things of this world, without which I, as a true philosopher, can live to continue my search after the divine truth.'

But Vinicius came up to him threateningly and said in a husky voice:

' Who told you you should die at Glaucus' hand and not at mine ? How do you know, you dog, that you won't be buried in my garden in a minute ? '

Chilon, who was a coward, looked at Vinicius, and saw at once that an imprudent word might cost him his life.

' I will look for her, sir,' he exclaimed hastily, ' and I will find her.'

A silence ensued, broken only by the rapid breathing of Vinicius, and farther off, the singing of the slaves at work in the garden.

The Greek, seeing that the young patrician was growing somewhat calmer, said:

' No, sir, I did not say I had given up looking for the girl ; I only wanted to let you see that these proceedings are very dangerous for me now. Glaucus is alive, and if once *he* sees me, *you* will never see me again. And then who will find the girl ? '

' Well, what am I to do ? What's the remedy ? What do you propose ? ' asked Vinicius.

' Aristotle teaches us that we must sacrifice little things to great, and as King Priam used often to say, old age is a heavy burden. Now Glaucus has long been crushed beneath the burden of his age and misfortunes, so much so that death would be a blessing for him. What is death, says Seneca, but a deliverance ? '

' You can play the buffoon with Petronius—not with me. Tell me what you propose.'

' If virtue is buffoonery, God grant I stay a buffoon all my life! I propose, sir, to get rid of Glaucus.'

' Well, hire men to club him to death ; I'll pay them. How much do you need ? '

' A thousand sesterces. Remember, sir, I must find honest ruffians who won't pocket your money and disappear without doing anything. A good job done is worth a good price. I ought to have something for myself, to help dry the tears I shall shed over Glaucus. I'll find the men this very day, and tell them that for every day Glaucus lives after to-morrow night I shall deduct a hundred sesterces. Besides, I have a plan that cannot fail.'

Once more Vinicius promised Chilon what he wanted, and then asked him what news he brought, where he had been, and what he had discovered during all this time. But Chilon had no news of importance to give him.

He had been, he said, in two meeting-houses, and had paid careful heed to all who were there, especially the women, but had seen nobody who resembled Lygia. But now the high priest of the sect, who had been a disciple of Christ and who had been entrusted by Him with the guidance of the faithful throughout the world, was expected daily at Rome. All the Christians would certainly want to see him and hear his teaching. There would be great gatherings, at which he, Chilon, would also be present, and what was more, as it is easy to escape

observation in a crowd, he would get Vinicius in too.
And then they could not fail to find Lygia. Once
Glaucus was out of the way, they would run no
serious risk at all.

CHAPTER 17

IT really was a matter of moment for Chilon to get
rid of Glaucus, who, although an old man, was no
mere decrepit dotard. The story which Chilon had
told Vinicius contained much that was true. He
had indeed known Glaucus, whom he had betrayed
to robbers, torn away from his family, despoiled,
and planned to murder. These events, however, sat
lightly upon his memory, for the wretch had left
Glaucus in his death agony, not in an inn, but in a
field near Minturnæ. He had foreseen everything
save that Glaucus would recover from his wounds
and get the length of Rome. Now the question was,
how to get rid of him.

With this in view he sought out Euricius that
same evening. He knew that the old man was devoted to him body and soul, and would do anything
to save him. Prudent by nature, Chilon had no
intention of disclosing his real purpose to him,
which, moreover, would have come as a rude shock
to the confidence reposed by Euricius in the goodness and piety of his benefactor.

The old man, having bought back his son, had
taken one of the little booths that swarmed in the
neighbourhood of the Circus Maximus, where he
sold olives, beans, unleavened bread, and honey
water to the spectators at the games. Chilon found
him in his shop arranging his wares. He greeted

him in the name of Christ and began to explain the matter that brought him there. He had done them a good turn, and he counted on their gratitude. He needed two or three strong, brave men in order to parry a danger that threatened himself and the whole Christian community. He was poor, indeed, but he could pay for this service, on condition that the men would trust him and carry out his orders faithfully.

Euricius and his son Quartus declared themselves ready to do whatever he should bid them do, convinced that such a devout man could not call upon them to do anything inconsistent with the teaching of Christ.

Chilon assured them that they were right, and raising his eyes to heaven he appeared to pray. He was really engaged in reflecting whether he would not do well to accept their proposal, which might save him a thousand sesterces. But after a moment's reflection he refused it. Euricius was an old man, not so much stricken with age as worn out by grief and illness. Quartus was only sixteen years old, and Chilon had need of active and, above all, robust men. As for the money, he thought that he could save a good part of it by means of the plan which he had hit upon.

Then Quartus said:

'I know Demas the baker, sir, who has a number of slaves and hired servants working at his mill. One of these servants is as strong as any four men, let alone two. I've seen him myself lifting stones that four men together couldn't move.'

'If he is one of the faithful, fearing God, and able to sacrifice himself for his brethren, let me know him,' said Chilon.

'He is a Christian, sir,' replied Quartus, 'like

most of Demas' men. Demas has day and night workers, and this man is a night worker. If we went now, we should get there during their evening meal, and you could talk with him at your pleasure. Demas lives near the harbour.' Chilon willingly agreed to this. The harbour, or Emporium, was at the foot of the Aventine, and so not far from the Circus Maximus. It could be reached without going round the hills by way of the river and the Porticus Æmilia, which shortened the road still further.

'I am old,' said Chilon, when they were under the colonnade, 'and sometimes my memory fails me. Our Christ was of course betrayed by one of His disciples, but at this moment I cannot remember the traitor's name.'

'It was Judas, sir ; he hanged himself,' replied Quartus, somewhat astonished that anybody could forget that name.

'Oh yes, Judas ! Thank you,' said Chilon.

They walked on awhile in silence, and when they came to the Emporium, which was already shut, they passed by it round the grain stores, where the distributions were made, and took to the left in the direction of the houses which lined the Ostian road as far as Mount Testacius and the Forum Pistorium. There they came to a stop in front of a wooden building, from which came the sound of the crushing of grain between the millstones. Quartus went in, but the prudent Chilon remained outside.

'I am curious to see this Hercules of the mill,' said he to himself, looking up at the moon, which was shining brightly. 'If he is a ruffian with some sense, it will cost me a little more ; but if he is a virtuous Christian and a fool, he will do all I ask for nothing.'

These reflections were interrupted by the return of Quartus, who came out of the building with another man wearing only the workman's coat, which left the right arm and side bare. Chilon heaved a sigh of satisfaction at the sight of the newcomer. Never in his life had he seen such an arm nor such a chest.

'Here, sir,' said Quartus, 'is the brother whom you wished to see.'

'May the peace of Christ be upon you,' said Chilon. 'And now, Quartus, tell this brother if I am worthy of confidence and then return home, for the love of God, for you must not leave your old father alone.'

'This is a holy man,' said Quartus, 'he has given up all his fortune to redeem me from slavery, though I was a stranger to him. May our Lord and Saviour give him his reward in heaven.'

At these words the gigantic workman bowed and kissed Chilon's hand.

'What is your name, brother?' asked the Greek.

'My father, I received the name of Urban in holy baptism.'

'Urban, my brother, have you time to talk with me awhile?'

'Our work does not begin till midnight, and just now our evening meal is being prepared.'

'Then we have ample time. Let us go to the riverside, where you shall hear what I have to say.'

They went and sat down upon a stone on the river bank, where the silence was only broken by the distant sound of the mills and the murmuring of the river.

Chilon examined the workman's face, which seemed to him, despite the somewhat sad, hard look

101

common among the barbarians living in Rome, expressive of goodness and sincerity.

'Yes,' thought he, 'this is a good, stupid soul, who will kill Glaucus for nothing.'

'Urban,' he said, 'do you love Christ?'

'I love Him from the bottom of my heart.'

'And your brothers and sisters, and all who have taught you the truth and faith in Christ?'

'I love them also, good father.'

'Then peace be with you.'

'And with you too, father.'

Chilon, with eyes upturned to the moon, began in a hushed voice to speak of the death of Christ. He spoke not as though he were addressing Urban, but as though he were confiding the secret to the sleeping city. There was something touching and solemn about it all. The workman shed tears, and when Chilon began to groan and lament that at the moment of the Saviour's death there was none to protect Him from the insults of the soldiers and the Jews, the barbarian's huge fists clenched in sorrow and suppressed anger.

Chilon suddenly asked him:

'Urban, do you know who Judas was?'

'I know, I know; but he hanged himself.'

And in his voice was a trace of regret that the traitor should have done justice on himself.

Chilon went on:

'But suppose he hadn't hanged himself; suppose some Christian met him, on land or sea; should he not avenge the Saviour's torture and blood and death?'

'Who would not?'

'Peace be with you, faithful servant of the Lamb! Yes, we may forgive a wrong done to ourselves, but wrongs done to God who may pardon? Just as serpent begets serpent and wickedness wickedness, and treachery begets treachery, so from the poison of Judas is sprung another traitor. Just as the one sold the Saviour to the Jews and the Roman soldiers, so the other, who dwells among us, would betray the Lord's flock to the wolves. And if nobody prevents this treachery—if nobody crushes the serpent's head in time—then we are all lost, and with us will disappear the glory of the Lamb.'

The workman looked at him in extreme uneasiness, as though he did not understand the words which he heard.

The Greek, covering his head with the flap of his cloak, repeated in sepulchral tones :

'Woe unto you, servants of the true God! Woe unto you, sons and daughters of Christ!'

Again there was a silence, broken only by the grinding of the mills, the low singing of the workmen, and the murmuring of the river.

'Father,' said the workman at last, 'who is this traitor ? '

Chilon lowered his head.

Who was this traitor ? A son of Judas, begotten of his treachery, who passed himself off as a Christian and haunted the houses of prayer with the one aim of bringing accusations against the brethren before Cæsar, saying that they did not admit his divinity, that they poisoned wells, offered their children in sacrifice, and that they sought to destroy the city and not leave one stone upon another. In a few days the guards would be ordered to put the old men, the women, and the children in irons and lead them to their death. This was the work of a second Judas. But when nobody punished the first one ; when nobody undertook to defend Christ in the hour of His trial, who would punish this one ; who would crush this serpent's head and cause him to vanish ere he could speak to Cæsar ?

Urban, who till then had remained seated on the coping of the wall, suddenly stood up and said:

' I will, father.'

' Then go to the Christians, to the meeting-houses, and inquire of the brethren where Glaucus the doctor is, and when they show him to you, kill him, in the name of Christ.'

' Glaucus ? ' repeated the workman, as though seeking to engrave the name on his memory.

' Do you happen to know him ? '

' No, I don't know him. There are thousands of Christians in Rome, and they do not all know one another. But tomorrow night every man and woman of them will meet at the Ostrianum, for the great apostle of Christ has arrived and is to preach there ; and there our brethren will point Glaucus out to me.'

' At the Ostrianum ? ' said Chilon. ' But that's outside the gates. All the brothers and sisters ? By night, outside the city, at the Ostrianum ? '

'Yes, father, that is our cemetery out there, between the Via Salaria and the Via Nomentana. Did you not know that the great apostle was to preach there ? '

' I have not been home for two days, that's why I did not receive his letter ; and I do not know where the Ostrianum is, because I have not long since arrived from Corinth, where I am in charge of the Christian community. But at any rate all is well, and since Christ has sent you this inspiration, go, my son, to the Ostrianum, find out Glaucus in the midst of the brethren, and kill him on the way back to the city. As a reward, all your sins shall be forgiven you. And now, peace be with you!'

' Father——'

'I am listening, child of the Lamb.'

A look of great uneasiness was on the workman's face. Not long ago, he said, he had killed a man, perhaps two, and the Christian doctrine forbids killing. True, he had not killed them in his own defence, for that too was forbidden. Nor for his own advantage, Christ forbid! The bishop had even allowed him certain of the brethren to assist him, but had not given him permission to kill, and yet he *had* killed, without meaning it, for God had punished him by giving him too great strength, and now he was suffering cruelly in expiation. The others might sing at their work, but he, poor wretch, could only think of his own sin and his outrage against the Lamb.

And now once again he had promised to kill a traitor. Ah well, he would kill him, since it was only wrongs done to oneself that must be forgiven. He would kill him under the eyes of all the brothers and sisters assembled to-morrow at the Ostrianum. But in the first place Glaucus must be condemned by the chief men among the brethren, by the bishop or by the apostle.

'There is not time for a trial, my son,' replied Chilon ; 'for the traitor will go straight from the Ostrianum to Cæsar, at Antium, or else take refuge in the house of a nobleman whom he serves.'

'Father,' said the man once more, in a tone almost of supplication, 'will you charge your conscience with this deed ? Have you heard with your own ears Glaucus speaking treason against his brethren ? '

Chilon felt that he must give some proof of his words and mention some names.

'Listen, Urban. I live in Corinth, but I come originally from Cos, and I am teaching the doctrine

of Christ to a young countrywoman of mine called
Eunice, who is a slave here in Rome. She acts as
the personal attendant of one Petronius, a friend of
Cæsar's. Well, in this house I heard Glaucus undertake to betray all the Christians, and promise,
moreover, to another of Cæsar's intimates, Vinicius,
to find a certain young maiden among the Christians,
and restore her to him.'

He stopped and looked with amazement at his
companion, whose eyes had suddenly lit up, like
those of a wild beast.

' What's the matter ? ' he asked, almost afraid.

' Nothing, father. I'll kill Glaucus to-morrow.'

CHAPTER 18

PETRONIUS to Vinicius:

' It is evident that Venus has disturbed your mind,
and caused you to lose reason and memory and the
ability to think about anything at all save love. If
some day you read over your answer to my letter,
you will see how indifferent your mind has become
to everything except Lygia: you will see how it is
busied with nothing else ; how it reverts continually
to her, and how it hovers above her, like a hawk
above its prey.

' By Pollux, if the fire that is consuming you does
not reduce you to ashes, you will become like the
Egyptian Sphinx that fell in love, as they say, with
the pale Isis, and became deaf and indifferent to all,
awaiting only the night, when it might see its beloved
with its eyes of stone.

' At night you should disguise yourself and scour

the city ; even visit the Christian houses of worship
with your philosopher. Everything that begets
hope and kills time is of value. But in friendship
for me do this one thing : hire Croton, and do not go
out save with him and the Greek, for Lygia's slave,
Ursus, is a man of extraordinary strength. That
will be a more sensible plan, and will lessen the
danger. Given that Pomponia Græcina and Lygia
are of their number, then the Christians are certainly no desperadoes. All the same, their rescue of
Lygia proves that they are no triflers when some ewe
lamb from their flock is in danger. When you see
your beloved, I know that you will want to carry her
off there and then. How would you manage that if
you had only the son of Chilon to help you ? But
Croton would see the thing through, were she
defended by ten Lygians like this Ursus.

' They have stopped talking here already about the
little princess and saying that her death was caused
by magic. Poppæa sometimes alludes to it, but
Cæsar's mind is taken up with other things. At any
rate, if it is true that Her Divine Majesty is again
in an interesting condition, the memory of the first
child will not be long in fading away.

' Take good care of yourself, and take Croton into
your service, or else they'll wrest Lygia away from
you a second time. When you have no further use
for Chilon send him to me, wherever I am. Perhaps
I can make another Vatinius of him, and have
consuls and senators trembling before him, as they
do before the knight of the bradawl. It would be
worth living on to see that. Tell me when you get
Lygia back, and I will offer up to Venus in her little
round temple at Baiæ a pair of swans and a pair of
doves. I dreamt I saw Lygia on your knee, asking
to be kissed. See that you take steps to make my

dream come true. May there be no clouds in your skies, or, if there be, may they have the colour and scent of roses.'

CHAPTER 19

VINICIUS had scarcely finished reading when Chilon entered the library without being announced, the servants having received orders to let him enter at any hour of the day or night.

'May the holy mother of Æneas, your great-souled ancestor, be as kind to you as Maia's son to me!'

'Which means ? ?'

'Eureka!'

'You have seen her ? '

'I have seen Ursus, sir, and have spoken to him.'

'And you know where they are hidden ? '

'No, sir. It is enough for me to know that Ursus works near the Emporium, with a miller who is called Demas, like your freedman. And that is enough, because in the morning any one of your confidential slaves can follow him and find out their hiding-place. I bring you only the certainty that as Ursus is here, the divine Lygia is also in Rome, and I bring too the news that in all probability she will be at the Ostrianum to-night.'

'The Ostrianum ? Where away is that ? '

'It is an old burial-place between the Via Salaria and the Via Nomentana. The great Christian priest I told you about, sir, whom they did not expect till much later, has arrived, and to-night he is to preach and baptize in this cemetery.'

'You shall not be disappointed in relying on

my generosity, but you must come with me to the Ostrianum.'

'To the Ostrianum?' said Chilon, who had not the slightest desire to go there. 'Noble tribune, I promised to show you where Lygia was, but I did not promise to carry her off. Reflect, sir, upon my fate if that Lygian bear should discover his mistake after tearing Glaucus to pieces.'

Vinicius took a purse from a box and threw it to Chilon.

'There are *scrupula*,' he said. 'When Lygia reaches my house, you shall have another like it, only filled with *aurei*.' ★

'A very Jupiter indeed!' exclaimed Chilon.

'They'll give you something to eat here, and then you may rest. You will not leave the house before evening, and when night comes you will go with me to the Ostrianum.'

For a moment fear and hesitation were portrayed on the Greek's features, but finally he calmed himself and said:

'Who could resist you, sir? For my part, these "scruples" of yours'—here he jingled the purse—'have outweighed mine, not to speak of your company, which is an honour and a pleasure to me.'

Vinicius interrupted him impatiently, and questioned him a long time about his conversation with Ursus. It appeared, indeed, as though that night they would discover the girl's hiding-place, or even carry her off on the road as she returned from the Ostrianum.

Vinicius, remembering Petronius' advice, told his slaves to bid Croton come to him. Chilon, who knew everybody in Rome, was mightily reassured

---

★ The scripulum, or scrupulum, a small gold piece, was equivalent to the third of a golden denarius, or aureus.

when he heard the famous athlete's name, and so it was in a contented frame of mind that he took his place at table when invited by the slave in charge of the atrium.

The meal over, he lay down on the seat, put his cloak beneath his head, and fell asleep. He only awoke, or rather was only awakened, when Croton arrived. Then he went into the atrium. Croton had already made his terms with Vinicius, and was saying :

' I undertake, noble sir, to seize with this hand any one you point out, with this other hand to defend myself against seven Lygians like Ursus, and to finish up by bringing the girl home here, though all the Christians in Rome were after me like Calabrian wolves. If I do not, then let me be scourged in this very hall.'

' Don't let him do that, sir,' exclaimed Chilon. ' They will throw stones at us, and what good will strength do then ? Would it not be better to capture her when she gets home again, and so risk neither her life nor ours ? '

' That's what I mean, Croton,' said Vinicius.

' It is you who pay, so you must give the orders.'

Chilon went on :

' Here is an idea, sir, that has occurred to me. The Christians have, no doubt, certain tokens of recognition, certain *tesseræ*, without which nobody is admitted into the Ostrianum. I know it is so in the meeting-houses, and I once got a thing of this kind from Euricius ; so allow me to go and find him, ask him about all the details, and provide myself with these tokens if they are necessary.'

' An excellent idea, noble philosopher,' Vinicius replied gaily. ' You speak like a prudent man and deserve to be congratulated. Go, therefore, to

Euricius, or wherever else seems good to you, but for greater safety leave the purse I gave you on this table.'

Chilon, who never willingly parted with money, made a face at this. However, he obeyed, and went away. It was no great distance from the Carinæ to the Circus, where Euricius' little shop was, and he was back long before nightfall.

'Here are the tokens, sir,' he said.

When it began to grow dark, they wrapped themselves up in Gallic cloaks with hoods, and provided themselves with lanterns and daggers. Chilon also put on a wig which he had obtained on his way back from Euricius. Then they left the house, walking quickly in order to arrive at the Porta Nomentana before it closed.

CHAPTER 20

In this way they passed through the Vicus Patricius, and along the Viminal, as far as the old Viminal Gate, which adjoins the plain where Diocletian afterwards built his magnificent baths. They passed the ruined wall of Servius Tullius, and arrived at the Via Nomentana through some quiet streets. Then turning to the left towards the Via Salaria, they found themselves in the midst of hills honeycombed with sand-pits, with here and there a graveyard. Night had now fallen, and as the moon was not yet up they would have had difficulty in finding their way, had not the Christians themselves, as Chilon had anticipated, shown it to them. For to right and left, and in front of them, they made out dark figures cautiously proceeding in the direction of the sandy gullies. The few passers-by and country people returning from the city doubtless mistook these pilgrims for workmen going to the sand-pits, or for members of some funeral society on their way to a nocturnal celebration. But as the young nobleman and his companions proceeded, the lanterns and figures around them grew more numerous. Some of those who passed were singing in a hushed voice hymns which struck Vinicius as full of sadness. Now and then he heard a broken sentence in which Christ's name occurred. The road was beginning to seem long, when at last a light shone out in the distance, like the glare of torches or a camp fire. Vinicius bent towards Chilon, and asked if this was the Ostrianum.

Chilon, who was unpleasantly impressed by the night, by the distance from the city, and by the ghostly forms around, replied in a trembling voice :

' I do not know, sir. I have never been at the Ostrianum. But I wish to goodness they would worship Christ a little nearer the city.'

They walked on in silence for a moment, and then Chilon, whose terror grew with every step that took them farther from the gates, said :

' What with this wig and the two beans I've put up my nose, they'll never recognise me, and even if they do, they won't kill me. They are not bad people. Indeed, they're very worthy people, and I love and honour them !'

' Don't try to flatter them too soon,' replied Vinicius.

They were now in a narrow gully above which ran an aqueduct. The moon had just emerged from the clouds, and they saw at the end of the gully a wall thickly covered with ivy. They had arrived at the Ostrianum.

At the gate two quarrymen were collecting the tokens. The next moment Vinicius and his companions found themselves in a large open space surrounded by walls. In the centre was a crypt, and before the door of it a fountain was playing. Here and there was a gravestone, and throughout the enclosure people were swarming in the uncertain light of the moon and the lanterns. Whether because of the cold or from fear of traitors, almost all kept on their hoods, and the young nobleman reflected with dismay that if they persisted in this it would be impossible for him to recognise Lygia.

Close by the crypt which occupied the centre of the enclosure some torches were lit and arranged in a little pile. Presently the crowd began to sing a strange hymn, at first in a low tone, then gradually louder and louder. It was a sort of appeal in the night, a timid appeal for help uttered by people wandering in darkness. Their faces, upturned to the sky, appeared to see somebody there, high above them, and their outstretched arms seemed to implore him to descend. More torches were thrown upon the fire, which shed a red glow over all the cemetery and made the lanterns seem pale. At that moment there came from the crypt an old man wearing a hooded cloak, but with his head bare, who mounted upon a rock that lay near the burning pile.

A movement ran through the crowd, and Vinicius heard voices beside him murmur, ' Peter, Peter !' Some knelt, while others stretched out their hands towards him. Then fell a silence so profound that the crackling of the torches could be heard, the rumbling of the carts on the Via Nomentana, and the whispering of the wind in the pine trees near the cemetery.

Chilon leaned towards Vinicius, and said softly:

'That is he: the first disciple of Christos; that's the fisherman.'

The old man raised his hand, and making the sign of the cross blessed those present, who this time fell upon their knees. Vinicius himself and his companions, afraid to betray themselves, followed their example. The young tribune felt that the face which he saw before him was at once ordinary and yet extraordinary, and that it was extraordinary by reason of its very simplicity. The old man had no mitre, nor any wreath of oak leaves upon his head, no palm branch in his hands, no gilded breastplate on his breast, no white or star-spangled vestments —none of the emblems which were worn by the priests of the East, of Egypt, and of Greece, and by the *flamines* at Rome.

At first Peter spoke like a father giving advice to his children, and teaching them how to guide their lives. He exhorted them to renounce excesses and pleasure-seeking; to love poverty and purity and truth; patiently to endure injustice and persecution; to obey their rulers and those above them; to shun the crime of treason; to shun hypocrisy and calumny; and, lastly, to show a good example, even to the heathen. Vinicius, who was impatient of everything that did not help him to recover Lygia, was annoyed by some of this advice. Was the old man, by his exaltation of chastity and resistance to the passions, not condemning Vinicius' love? Was he not arousing Lygia against him? And besides being angry he felt that he had been deceived. He had expected the revelation of some astounding mysteries—he had reckoned at least on a display of eloquence; but he had heard instead a few words of the utmost simplicity, and he marvelled at the reception they met with from the crowd. The old man went on to say that they must love virtue and truth for their own sake, for God was the essence of all good and the everlasting truth, and whosoever loved these things loved God and became His child.

Vinicius did not understand it all, but he already knew, by what Pomponia Græcina had said to Petronius, that according to the Christian belief this God was one and all powerful. But the crowning surprise of all to the young man was to hear the old man say that God was also Infinite Love, and consequently that he who loved mankind fulfilled the most sublime of the Commandments. Nor was it enough to love the men of one's own race, for the God-Man had shed His blood for all. Nor was it enough to love those who used us well, for Christ pardoned even the Jews who gave Him over to death, and the Roman soldiers who crucified Him. We must not only forgive such as have injured us, we must love them and return them good for evil; it was not enough to love good men—we must also love the wicked, for it was only love that could destroy their wickedness in them.

More torches were thrown upon the fire: the noise of the wind in the trees was hushed; the flames rose straight towards the twinkling stars; and the old man, recalling the death upon Golgotha, spoke now only of Christ.

This man had seen these things himself. He told how, after he left the cross, he had spent two days and two nights with John, neither eating nor drinking, overwhelmed with grief and fear and doubt, repeating to himself that He was dead! The third day dawned, and they were mourning still when Mary Magdalene hastened breathless to them, with her hair flowing, and cried: 'They have taken away our Master!' At these words they had rushed to the place where He was buried. John, who was younger, arrived first: the tomb was empty and he dared not go in. When all three were together, he, Peter, who now spoke to them, entered the tomb, and saw the shroud and the graveclothes, but found no body. Thinking that the priests had taken His body away, John and Peter returned to the house in still greater affliction. Then other disciples arrived and made lamentation; now all at once, so that the God of the heavenly hosts might hear them more easily, and now by turns. They had hoped that their Master would redeem Israel, and now they were losing hope, for it was already the third day since His death.

The old man closed his eyes, as though the better to see in his mind the distant past, then he continued:

'While they were lamenting thus, Mary Magdalene came running to them again, crying out that she had seen the Lord. In the dazzling light she could not distinguish Him, and she thought it was the keeper of the garden till He said "Mary," and then she cried aloud "Rabboni," and fell at His feet. He bade her go find the disciples, and then He disappeared. But the disciples did not believe her, and as she wept for joy, some reproached her, and others thought that sorrow had turned her head, for she said too that she had seen angels in front of the tomb, while they, on returning to the tomb, found it empty. Later on, in the evening, came Cleophas, who had gone with another to Emmaus, whence they returned in haste with the news that the Lord was truly risen. Then, when they had shut the door from fear of the Jews, they began to dispute about the matter. Suddenly He rose up in their midst, though none had heard the sound of the door, and He said to them, "Peace be with you."

'And I saw Him, like the rest, and our hearts were filled with light, for we believed that He was risen, that the seas would be dried up, that the mountains would crumble in dust, and that His glory would last for ever.

'A week later Thomas Didymus put his finger on the Master's wounds, touched His side, and fell at His feet, exclaiming, "My Master, and my God!" And He replied: "Because thou hast seen, Thomas, thou hast believed; blessed are those who have not seen and who have believed." And we heard those words, and our eyes beheld Him, for He was in our midst.'

Vinicius listened; he would not allow himself to believe the old man's words, yet here was a man who said 'I have seen.' At times Vinicius thought he was dreaming; but around him he saw the silent crowd; the smoke of the lanterns assailed his nostrils; a little farther off the torches were blazing; and quite near him, standing upon a stone, was an old man with trembling head, not far from his end, who bore witness, and said 'I have seen.'

From the distant houses that lay scattered along the Via Nomentana came the first cockcrows, announcing midnight. At that moment Chilon pulled Vinicius' cloak and whispered:

'Over there, master, not far from the old man, I see Ursus with a young girl beside him.'

Vinicius started like a sleeper suddenly awakened, and turning in the direction pointed out by Chilon, he saw Lygia.

CHAPTER 21

HE saw Lygia, and from that moment he saw nothing else. At last, after all these efforts, after all these days of anxiety and strain and grief, he had found her again! Joy may assail a man like a wild beast, and force the breath from his body. He, who had always thought it Fortune's duty to fulfil all his desires, distrusted his own eyes, and could not believe in his good luck. But for this distrust, his headlong temper might have driven him to do some rash deed : he wanted first of all to be sure that he was not dreaming, and that this was not one of the miracles of which his head was full. No ; it was Lygia that he saw there about a dozen paces away from him. She was standing in the full light of the fire. Her hood had slid down and disarranged her hair, her mouth was slightly open, her eyes turned towards the apostle, and her face all attention and ecstasy. She wore a dark woollen cloak like a daughter of the people, yet Vinicius had never seen her look more beautiful, and despite his agitation, he could not help contrasting the almost servile dress with the high-born dignity of her head. As though on fire, his whole body quivered with a love at once sorrowful and ardent, respectful and passionate. He refreshed his whole being in the sight of her as a man quenches a torturing thirst at some life-giving spring. Beside the enormous Lygian, she seemed to him to be smaller than she was— almost a child, indeed—and he noticed also that she had grown thinner. Her skin appeared transparent, and she suggested to his mind a flower or a spirit. But he desired all the more to possess her, so different as she was from the other women he had seen and enjoyed in the East or at Rome. He felt that for her sake he would sacrifice them all—that he would sacrifice Rome and the whole world.

He would have continued musing so had not Chilon, who feared he might commit some folly, pulled his cloak. But now the Christians had begun to pray and sing.

Then the great apostle baptized with water from the fountain those whom the priests presented to him as ready for baptism. To Vinicius it seemed as though the night would never pass. He longed to follow Lygia and carry her off.

At last some of the Christians left the cemetery. Chilon whispered:

' Let us go now and wait outside the gate, sir ; we haven't lifted our hoods, and people are looking at us.'

They did so, and took up a position from which they could examine every one who came out. It would not be difficult to recognise Ursus by his height.

' We'll follow them,' said Chilon, ' and see what house they enter, and to-morrow—or, rather, to-day —you can guard all the approaches to the house with your slaves, sir, and lay hold of her.'

' No,' said Vinicius.

' What do you mean to do, sir ? '

' We will follow her into the house and carry her off at once. You know what you have to do, Croton, don't you ? '

' Yes. And you can have me as your slave if I don't break the back of that great ox who guards her.'

Chilon adjured them, in the name of all the gods, not to act in this way. They had only brought

Croton to defend them in case they were recognised, not to carry the girl off. If they tried to capture her unassisted, they risked their lives, and, moreover, she might escape them. Why not make quite sure ? Why run risks and endanger the success of their plan ?

Although he had been obliged to use his utmost efforts to prevent himself from taking Lygia in his arms in the open cemetery, Vinicius felt that the Greek was right, and he would perhaps have listened to his advice but for Croton, who did not want to lose the reward promised to him.

' Master,' he said, ' tell that old ninny to be quiet, or let me give him a rap on the head. I don't say you must seize her at once in the middle of the crowd, for they might stone us, but once she reaches home, I'll carry her off and take her where you like.'

' By Hercules ! that's how we'll do it,' said Vinicius.

' That Lygian,' groaned Chilon, ' looks a terribly strong fellow.'

' Well, it won't be your business to hold his hands,' replied Croton.

They had still a long time to wait, and the cocks had already announced the dawn before Ursus and Lygia came out. They were with several other people, among whom Chilon thought he recognised the great apostle, with another old man of much shorter stature beside him, two old women, and a boy who showed the way with a lantern. Behind this little group came a crowd of some two hundred Christians, which Vinicius and his companions joined.

' Yes, sir,' said Chilon ; ' your maiden has powerful protectors. That is the great apostle who is with her. Look, you see the people in front are kneeling before him.'

The day was breaking. The light of morning tinged the top of the walls with faint colour. The trees by the roadside, the buildings and the grave-stones scattered here and there, emerged from the darkness. The road was no longer deserted. Vege-table sellers, with their asses and mules laden with greenstuffs, hastened along to be in time for the opening of the city gates, and at intervals carts full of game came creaking along the road. A light mist, harbinger of good weather, hung around. Men, seen through the mist from a little distance looked like phantoms. Vinicius never took his eyes from Lygia's slim figure.

But now they were drawing near to the gate, and here a strange sight met their eyes. Two soldiers knelt at the feet of the apostle, who laid his hands on their helmets, and made the sign of the cross. It had never before occurred to the young nobleman that Christians were to be met with among the soldiers, and this set him thinking about the marvellous fashion in which this new faith spread. Had Lygia wanted to make her escape from the city, she would have met with sentries who would have closed their eyes to it.

After passing the waste lands that adjoined the city walls, the little groups of Christians began to disperse. It was now necessary to follow Lygia at a greater distance and with greater caution. They walked on like this till just at sunrise they reached the Trans-Tiber, when Lygia's party broke up. The apostle, with the old woman and the boy, took the road by the river, while Ursus, Lygia, and the little old man turned into a narrow lane, and then, after proceeding for about a hundred yards, entered the porch of a house occupied on the ground floor by an oil merchant and a bird-catcher.

Chilon, who was following about fifty yards behind Vinicius and Croton, stopped dead, flattened himself against the wall, and called on them to come back.

They retreated, as in any case there was need of deliberation.

' Go and see,' said Vinicius, ' whether this house has no door opening on to some street.'

Chilon, who a moment before had been complaining about his aching feet, hurried away as quickly as though he had been shod with the winged sandals of Mercury, and was soon back again.

' No,' he said ; ' this is the only door.'

Then clasping his hands—

' In the name of Jupiter,' he exclaimed, ' of Apollo, of Vesta, of Cybele, of Isis and Osiris, in the name of Mithra, of Baal, and of all the gods of East and West, I implore you, master, give up this plan. Hear me——'

Suddenly he stopped, for Vinicius' eyes were sparkling like a wolf's. To look at him was to see that nothing in the world would stop him. Croton had begun to draw deep breaths and to move his great head about from side to side like a caged bear. But there was no trace of uneasiness on his features.

' I will go first,' he said.

' You will follow me,' replied Vinicius in a voice of command.

With that they disappeared in the dark passage.

Chilon had hurried to the corner of the nearest lane, whence he peered out watchful and uneasy.

CHAPTER 22

ONCE inside the passage, Vinicius realised all the difficulty of the undertaking. The house was a farmed-out house, with a number of floors—one of those hastily-constructed hives, too high and too narrow, full of cells and recesses, in which the poorer classes swarmed.

Following the passage, Vinicius and Croton came to a small court surrounded with buildings forming a sort of common atrium for the whole house, with a fountain in the middle, from which water fell into a roughly fashioned basin. Running up the walls were outside staircases, partly of stone and partly of wood, leading to galleries which in turn gave access to the houses. Down below also there were houses, some with wooden doors, others only separated from the courtyard by woollen curtains, for the most part ragged or patched.

As it was early, there was not a living soul astir in the court. Evidently all were asleep, save those who had just come from the Ostrianum.

' What shall we do, master ? ' asked Croton, as he stopped.

' Let us wait here,' replied Vinicius. ' Perhaps somebody will show himself. We must not be seen in the courtyard.'

At the same time he thought that Chilon's plan would have been the practical one. If he had had some fifty slaves with him he could have had the door, which seemed to be the only entrance, guarded, while he had the houses searched. Whereas now he must light upon Lygia's house at once, or else the Christians, of whom there must be many in the house, would give the alarm. For the same reason it was dangerous to ask questions of strangers. Vinicius was just wondering whether it would not be well to go and get some slaves, when from behind the curtain which shut off one of the most distant houses a man came out with a sieve in his hand, and advanced towards the fountain.

' That is the Lygian,' said Vinicius quietly.

' Shall I break his bones straight away ? '

' No : wait.'

Ursus did not notice them, for they kept inside the dark passage, and he began quietly to wash the vegetables that were in the sieve. His task at an end, he returned, and the curtain closed behind him. Croton and Vinicius followed him, thinking at once to hit upon Lygia's house.

Great was their astonishment when they found that the curtain did not separate the court from the house itself, but from a second dark corridor, at the end of which was a garden with some cypresses, several myrtle bushes, and a little house built against the rear wall. There was no other dwelling-place.

They saw that this was a favourable circumstance for them. In the courtyard there might have been a gathering of the occupants, but here the lonely position of the little house made their undertaking easier.

Ursus was just about to enter when the sound of footsteps attracted his attention. He stopped, and seeing the two men, laid the sieve upon the balustrade and turned towards them.

' What are you after ? ' he asked.

' You ! ' replied Vinicius.

Then turning towards Croton, he said :

' Kill him ! '

Croton sprang forward, and in a moment, without giving the Lygian time to recover or to recognise his enemies, he seized him in his arms of steel. Vinicius was too sure of Croton's supernatural strength to await the end of the struggle, so he passed them, dashed towards the little house, and pushing open the door, found himself in a somewhat dark room lit up by the fire which burned on the hearth. The light of the flames fell full upon Lygia's face. There was another person seated beside the fireplace—the same old man who had accompanied Lygia and Ursus home from the Ostrianum.

Vinicius had already lifted Lygia by the waist, and was hurrying towards the door. Holding the girl close to his breast with one arm, he violently pushed back with his free hand the old man who barred his path. As he did so his hood slipped, and Lygia, at the sight of the well-known face, which looked so terrible at that moment, felt her blood run cold. She would have cried out for help, but she could not. She tried to hold on to the door, but her fingers slipped on the stone, and she would have fainted, had not her nerves been shaken by the dreadful sight which she beheld when Vinicius dashed into the garden with her.

There was Ursus holding in his arms a man bent completely double, with his head hanging loose on his shoulders, and blood coming from his mouth. When Ursus saw them he struck the head one last blow with his fist, and straightway sprang like a wild beast upon Vinicius.

'Death!' thought the young nobleman.

Then, as in a dream, he heard Lygia cry, 'Do not kill him!' and he felt that something like a thunderbolt had unwound his arms from Lygia's body. Everything reeled before him, and daylight was blotted out.

All this time Chilon, hidden in the angle of the wall, was awaiting developments, his curiosity struggling with his terror. But the time seemed long: he was becoming uneasy at this silence, and he did not take his eyes off the passage.

' If they do not find her hiding-place, and if they make a noise, she'll escape,' he thought.

This idea was by no means disagreeable to him in point of fact, for in that case he would once more be necessary to Vinicius, and he would get a great deal more money out of him.

' No matter what they do,' he murmured, ' it's for me they're working, though they don't know it. Gods above, permit me only—— What on earth is this ? Immortal gods!'

And suddenly his scanty hairs stood on end.

Ursus had just appeared in the doorway, carrying on his shoulder the lifeless body of Croton. After looking around him on all sides, he pursued his course towards the river.

Chilon flattened himself against the wall like a trowelful of plaster.

' If he sees me, I'm a dead man,' thought he.

But Ursus passed by him, and disappeared behind the next house. Chilon, without further ado, tore down a side street with an agility that would have been surprising even in a young man.

' If he sees me when he comes back, he'll catch me and kill me,' he said to himself. ' Help me, Zeus! Help, Apollo! Help, Hermes! Help me, God of the Christians! I'll leave Rome! I'll go to Mesembria ; only save me from the clutches of this fiend!'

This Lygian who had killed Croton seemed to

him a supernatural being. As he ran, the idea struck him that he was no doubt some god who had assumed the disguise of a barbarian. For the moment he believed in all the deities in the universe, and so it occurred to him that perhaps Croton had been killed by the God of the Christians.

Only after passing through several lanes, and seeing some workmen coming his way, did he grow a little calmer. He was out of breath, so he sat down upon a doorstep, and wiped his perspiring brow with his cloak.

The city was still asleep. Chilon soon felt himself chilled by the cool air, and, rising, he made his way at a slower pace towards the river.

'Perhaps,' said he, 'I shall see Croton's body somewhere. Great heavens! I wish this Lygian were in Hades! I don't want anything to do with him ; his bones are too hard. What am I to do now ? This is a dreadful affair.'

To know Vinicius' fate was essential, and Chilon did not know it. He had seen the Lygian carry Croton's body in the direction of the river ; that was all. Vinicius might have been killed, or he might only be wounded or captured. Not till then did it strike Chilon that doubtless the Christians would not dare to kill so powerful a personage, at once a friend of Cæsar's and holding high command in the army, since such a deed might provoke a general persecution. It was more probable that they were forcibly detaining him in order to give Lygia time to seek a hiding-place elsewhere.

'If that Lygian dragon has not torn him to pieces at the first rush, he is still alive, and if so, he himself will admit that I did not give him away ; and then, so far from having anything to fear, I have a new field open to me. I can inform one of Vinicius' freedmen where his master is ; whether he'll report the matter to the prefect or not is his lookout. Then I can go to Petronius, too, and get a reward there. I looked for Lygia, now I'll look for Vinicius, and after that I'll look for Lygia again.'

There was one thing that made him decidedly happy, he had got two purses. Vinicius had given him one before they set out, and he had thrown the other to him on the way back from the cemetery. In view of this happy circumstance, and in view of all the mental strain to which he had been subjected, he determined to have a better meal than usual, and better wine to it.

At last, when the time came for the wine-shops to open, he put his plan into execution with so hearty a good-will that he forgot about having a bath.

Above all, he desired sleep, and the want of it had so weakened him that he tottered as he made his way home to the Suburra, where the girl whom he had bought with Vinicius' money was expecting him.

On arriving home he dragged himself to his bedroom, threw himself on his bed, and fell asleep at once.

It was not till evening that he awoke, or, rather, was awakened by his slave, who asked him to rise, as a stranger wanted to see him on urgent business.

The wary Chilon was wide awake on the instant. Hastily throwing a hooded cloak about his shoulders, he ventured on a cautious look round the door, when he perceived Ursus' gigantic figure.

He felt his legs and his head turn cold as ice, his heart stopped beating, and thousands of ants seemed to be running up and down his spine.

'Syra, I'm not in. I don't know this—this good man.'

' But I've told him you were in, and asleep, sir,' replied the girl, ' and he insisted on me wakening you.'

' Heavens above, I'll make you——'

But Ursus, doubtless out of patience at all this delay, came to the bedroom door, and putting in his head, called out:

' Chilon Chilonides!'

' *Pax tecum! Pax! Pax!* ' replied Chilon. ' Yes, best of Christians, I am Chilon ; but there's some mistake—I don't know you!'

' Chilon Chilonides,' Ursus said again, ' your master, Vinicius, wants you, and says you are to go along with me and see him.'

129   5

PART II

CHAPTER 1

VINICIUS was awakened by a stab of pain. Three men were bending over him, two of whom he recognised—Ursus and the old man whom he had knocked over as he carried Lygia off. He was in the hands of the third, who was feeling his left arm. So great was the pain that Vinicius, thinking that they were torturing him in revenge, said between his teeth:

'Kill me.'

They seemed to pay no attention to his words. The terrible Ursus, whose rugged face wore at the moment an expression of grief, was holding a packet of bandages, and the old man was saying to the person who was working with Vinicius' arm:

'Glaucus, are you sure that this wound in the head is not mortal?'

'Yes, good Crispus. The giant'—here he pointed to Ursus—'threw him against the wall, and as he fell he tried to save himself with his arm; the arm is broken and dislocated, but the wound on his head is trifling.'

'You have attended more than one of the brethren,' said Crispus, 'and you have the reputation of being a clever doctor. That is why I sent Ursus to look for you.'

'And he admitted to me on the way that yesterday he was ready to kill me.'

'He told me of his plan, and I, who know you and know your love of Christ, let him see that it was not you who were the traitor, but this stranger, who wanted to drive him on to murder.'

'He is the spirit of evil, and I took him for an angel,' said Ursus, with a sigh.

'You shall tell me about it another time,' said Glaucus. 'Just now we must attend to our invalid.'

When the operation was over, Vinicius, who had again become unconscious, woke up.

Lygia stood near his bed holding in both hands a ewer, in which Glaucus from time to time dipped the sponge for bathing the wounded man's head.

'Lygia!' murmured Vinicius.

The ewer shook in the girl's hands as she bent her sad eyes upon him.

'Peace be with you!' she said in a low voice.

'Lygia, you would not let them kill me?'

She replied softly:

'God give you back your strength.'

A sweet sense of weakness stole over him. He felt as though he were falling into an abyss, but at the same time he had a feeling of well-being and happiness. It was as if some deity were hovering above him.

Meantime Glaucus had finished bathing the wound on his head, and was applying an ointment. Lygia put to his lips a cup of wine and water, which he drank eagerly, and when the dressing of his wound was over he was almost free from pain.

'Give me more to drink,' he begged.

Lygia went into the other room to fill the cup, and Crispus, after a few words with Glaucus, came to the bedside and said:

'Vinicius, God has not allowed you to do an evil deed. He has spared your life that you may look into your own conscience. He in whose sight man is but as dust has delivered you helpless into our hands, but the Christ in whom we believe has charged us to love our enemies. So we have dressed your wounds, and your health will be restored to you, but we can no longer look after you. When you are alone, ask yourself if you should continue to persecute Lygia, who through you has lost her home and her guardians, and us, who have returned you good for evil.'

'Do you mean to leave me ?' asked Vinicius.

'We mean to leave this house, where we may look for persecution at the hands of the city prefect. Your comrade is dead and you are wounded: that is not our fault, but it is we who would suffer from the rigour of the law.'

'You need not fear persecution,' replied Vinicius, 'I can protect you.'

Crispus did not care to tell him that they distrusted him too.

'Sir,' he said, 'your right hand is sound. Here are tablets and a pen ; write to your servants and bid them come this evening with a litter and take you home. You are in the house of a poor widow. She and her son will soon be here, and her son will take your letter. As for us, we must find other quarters.'

Vinicius turned pale. If he lost Lygia again, he might never see her more. He was desperately anxious to make his peace with her, but he must have time.

'Listen to me, Christian people,' he said. 'I was with you yesterday in the Ostrianum, and there I heard your doctrine expounded. And even had I not, your deeds alone would convince me of your goodness and honesty. Tell the widow to remain in this house, remain yourselves, and allow me to do so. You, sir, who are a doctor, or at least know how to dress a wound, can say whether I am fit to be lifted. This broken arm should be kept still for several days at least, and so I tell you I will not stir an inch, unless you throw me out of doors.'

He paused for want of breath, and Crispus said:

' Nobody will use force to you, sir. We alone will leave, to save our lives.'

Vinicius, little accustomed to opposition, frowned, but went on:

' Nobody saw us enter this house, save a Greek who went with us to the Ostrianum. I will tell you where he lives. Bring him here, and I will command him to hold his tongue, for he is in my service. I will write home and say I am leaving for Beneventum. If the Greek has already reported to the prefect, I will say it was I who killed Croton and that he broke my arm. I swear, by the shades of my parents, to do this. And so you can remain here in safety. Make haste and bring the Greek. He is called Chilon Chilonides.'

' Then, sir, Glaucus will remain with you,' said Crispus. ' He and the widow will look after you.'

' Old man,' said Vinicius, ' mark well what I am going to say. I owe you a debt of gratitude, and I have confidence in you. But you do not say all that is in your mind. You are afraid I shall summon my slaves and bid them carry Lygia off.'

' Yes,' said Crispus severely.

' Well now, listen. I will talk to Chilon in your presence, and I will write the letter announcing my departure in your presence. After that, you will be the only messengers I shall have. Think of what I say, and do not annoy me any longer.'

Here he lost all patience, his face was drawn with anger, and he said furiously:

'Did you think I would deny that I wanted to stay here in order to see her? But I no longer want to take her by force. Moreover, if she goes away I will use this good hand to tear the bandages off my arm, I will take neither food nor drink, and then my death be on your head and your brethren's. Why did you leave me my life?'

At this moment Lygia came in, and approaching Crispus with a look of inspiration upon her face, she said, as though she were but the echo of some other voice:

'Crispus, let us keep him with us, and not leave him till Christ restores him to health.'

'As you will,' replied Crispus.

This ready acquiescence on Crispus' part impressed Vinicius deeply.

It seemed to him that among the Christians Lygia was a sort of sibyl or priestess, who was obeyed and respected, and he too resigned himself to these respectful feelings. A moment later, when she gave him some water, he would fain have taken her hand, but he dared not. He dared not—he, Vinicius, who had kissed her on the lips at the palace, and who later on had sworn to drag her to his bedroom by the hair or have her whipped!

CHAPTER 2

VINICIUS told the Lygian exactly where Chilon lived; then, having written a few words on the tablet, he turned to Crispus and said:

' I am giving you the tablets, because this Chilon is a suspicious, cunning fellow. Often, when I sent for him, he would have my people told that he was not at home, and he always did this when he had no good news to give me and was afraid of my anger.'

' If I find him I'll bring him along—by force if he won't come willingly,' replied Ursus.

And, taking up his cloak, he went out quickly.

When he found himself in Chilon's presence, he did not recognise him. He had only seen him once, and then by night. And besides, that tall self-possessed old man, who had urged him to kill Glaucus, was so unlike this Greek, doubled up with terror. So Chilon speedily recovered from his first shock, and he was still further reassured by the tablets. At least he would not be suspected of having inveigled the tribune into a trap.

He donned another cloak, careful also to draw over his head a capacious Gallic hood, lest Ursus should recognise his features when they were both again in daylight.

' Where are you taking me to ? ' he asked as they went along.

' Across the Tiber.'

' I've not been long in Rome, and I have never gone there, but no doubt there are to be found some friends of virtue there also.'

Ursus was a simple man, but he knew that the Greek had accompanied Vinicius to the cemetery at the Ostrianum, and had also, along with Croton, been at the house where Lygia dwelt, so he stopped and said :

' Old man, no lies! This very day you were with Vinicius at the Ostrianum, and at our own door.'

' Oh, your house is in the Trans-Tiber region then? I only came to Rome recently, and I get

135

confused between the names of the different quarters. Yes, my friend, I did go to your door, and there, in the name of virtue, I implored Vinicius not to go in. I was at the Ostrianum too, and do you know why ? I've been trying to convert Vinicius for some time, and I wanted him to hear the oldest of the apostles. May the light penetrate to his soul and yours ! You are a Christian, aren't you, and you desire that truth may triumph over falsehood ? '

' Yes,' Ursus replied humbly.

Chilon's courage was completely restored.

' Vinicius,' said he, ' is a powerful nobleman, and a friend of Cæsar's. He is often alive still to the promptings of the evil one, but if a hair of his head were harmed, Cæsar would be revenged on all the Christians.'

' A far higher power protects us.'

' True, quite true ; but what do you mean to do with Vinicius ? ' asked Chilon, once more uneasy.

' I do not know. Christ commands us to be merciful.'

' Well spoken ! Keep that always in mind if you don't want to roast in hell like a pudding in an oven.'

Ursus heaved a sigh, and Chilon made the reflection that he would always be able to do as he liked with this terrible man.

Anxious to learn how things had gone since the attempt upon Lygia, he continued in a severe and magisterial tone :

' What have you done with Croton ? Speak out and speak the truth.'

Ursus sighed a second time.

' Vinicius will tell you.'

' Which means that you've stabbed him, or killed him with a club ? '

'I was unarmed.'

The Greek could not help wondering at the barbarian's uncanny strength.

'May Pluto—I mean may Christ forgive you!'

They walked on for some time in silence; then Chilon said:

'I won't give you away, for my part; but have a care of the watch.'

'It is Christ I fear, not the watch.'

'And rightly so, for there is no greater sin than murder. I will pray for you; but if my prayers are to be of any effect, you must make a vow never to lay as much as a finger upon anybody again, as long as you live.'

'But I did not kill him intentionally,' said Ursus.

Chilon, anxious to secure himself against any regrettable mishap, continued to point out to Ursus the abominable nature of murder, and tried hard to persuade him to make this vow.

Talking thus they arrived at the house, and Chilon's heart once more began to beat uneasily.

The room was somewhat dark. It was a winter evening, with thick fog, and the light of the lamps did little to dispel the darkness. Chilon distinguished a bed in one corner of the room, with Vinicius lying upon it, and without looking at any one else he went towards the tribune, certain that beside him he would be safer than beside the others.

'Oh, sir,' he exclaimed, clasping his hands, 'why did you not take my advice?'

'Be quiet, and listen to me,' said Vinicius.

With his piercing eyes fixed on Chilon, he began to speak slowly, with emphasis on his words, in order that each might be taken as an order and remain for ever graven on the memory of the Greek.

'Croton attacked me; he wanted to kill me and

rob me. Do you understand ? Therefore I killed him, and these people have dressed the wounds I received in the struggle.'

Chilon guessed at once that if Vinicius spoke thus it was only by reason of an understanding with the Christians, and that consequently he wanted to be believed. The look upon his face indicated the same thing, and so at once, without displaying the least suspicion or astonishment, Chilon exclaimed :

'Ah, the notorious villain! But I warned you, sir, not to trust him. All my warnings went for nothing.'

'But for the dagger I had on me, he would have killed me,' continued Vinicius.

'Blessed be the moment that I advised you to provide yourself with a knife at least.'

Vinicius, scanning him closely, asked :

'What have you been doing to-day ? '

'What's that ? Didn't I tell you, sir, I was offering up prayers for your recovery ? '

'Was that all ? '

'And I was just getting ready to come and see you when this good man came to inform me that you wanted me.'

'Here is a tablet : you will go to my house and give it to my freedman. It is to say I am leaving for Beneventum. You are to tell him that I left this morning, and that I was called away by an urgent letter from Petronius.'

He said once more, emphatically :

'I have gone to Beneventum ; you understand ? '

'You have, sir ; this morning I said good-bye to you at the Porta Capena, and since your departure such sadness has taken hold of me that unless prevented by your generosity I shall die of it, sighing even as the unhappy wife of Zethos sighed after the death of Itylus.'

Ill though he was, Vinicius could not help smiling. But being satisfied, since Chilon had caught his meaning at once, he said:

'Well, I'll add a few lines to help wipe away your tears. Give me the lamp.'

Chilon, now perfectly at ease, rose and took down from the wall one of the lamps that burned there.

But as he did so the hood which covered his head slipped down, and the light fell full upon his face. Glaucus jumped up from his seat and confronted him.

'Do you not recognise me, Cephasus?' he asked.

His voice sounded so terrible that a shudder ran through the company.

Chilon lifted the lamp and let it fall almost at once. Then he bent himself double and began to groan.

'I am not Cephasus—that is not who I am! Mercy!'

'There is the man who sold me,' said Glaucus, 'and ruined me, and my family with me.'

Vinicius then saw that the doctor who had attended him was the same Glaucus whose story he had heard.

To Ursus these last few moments and Glaucus' words had come as a flash of lightning in the darkness—he recognised Chilon. Seizing both his arms he held them behind his back.

'This is the man,' he exclaimed, 'who persuaded me to kill Glaucus!'

'Mercy,' groaned Chilon. Then, turning to Vinicius, he cried: 'Save me, master! I relied on you. Intercede for me! Your letter—I'll take it—master, master!'

139

But Vinicius did not care what took place—first, because all the exploits of the Greek were well known to him; and secondly, because his heart was inaccessible to pity. He said:

'Bury him in the garden. Some one else will take the letter.'

To Chilon these words sounded like his death sentence. His bones began to crack in Ursus' terrible grip; his eyes were full of tears.

'In the name of your own God, have pity,' he cried. 'I am a Christian. Peace be with you. I am a Christian. If you don't believe me, baptize me once again, twice a dozen times! Glaucus, it is a mistake; let me speak! Make me a slave! Don't kill me! Have mercy on me!'

His voice, choked with anguish, was growing more and more feeble, when on the other side of the table the apostle Peter stood up and broke the silence.

'The Saviour has said to us: "If your brother has sinned against you, punish him, but if he repents, forgive him. And if seven times in the day he has sinned against you, and seven times turned towards you saying, 'I repent,' forgive him."'

There fell a still deeper silence, and Glaucus kept his face hidden in his hands for a long time. At length he said:

'Cephasus, may God forgive you the wrongs you have done me, as I forgive you in the name of Christ.'

Then Ursus released his arm and said:

'May the Saviour forgive me, as I forgive you.'

Chilon had sunk to the ground. Leaning on his hands he turned his head round like a beast caught in a net, casting scared glances about him, and wondering from which quarter death would come.

He trusted neither eyes nor ears now, and did not dare to hope that they had spared him.

Gradually he came to himself, though his pale lips still trembled with terror. The apostle said to him:

' Depart in peace.'

Chilon rose, incapable of speech. Instinctively he made for Vinicius' bed, as though to implore him for help. Although he had at last seen that they were letting him go free, he was eager to escape safe and sound out of the hands of these incomprehensible people, whose mildness frightened him almost as much as any cruelty of theirs could have done.

' Give me the letter! Give me the letter, sir!'

He seized the tablet which Vinicius handed him, bowed once more to the Christians, and once to the sick man, then slunk along the wall to the door with bent head, and hastily vanished.

Once in the darkness of the little garden, his hair stood on end again with terror. He was sure that Ursus was going to fall upon him and kill him under cover of night. He would willingly have run, but his legs refused to obey him. They were not long in becoming paralysed altogether, for Ursus was at his side.

Chilon fell with his face to the ground and began to moan:

' Ursus—in the name of Christ.'

But Ursus replied:

' Fear not. The apostle has bidden me to go with you as far as the door, so that you may not lose yourself in the darkness. If your strength fails you, I will take you home.'

Chilon raised his head.

' What do you say ? What ? Aren't you going to kill me ? '

'No, I will not kill you; if I caught you too roughly and hurt your bones, forgive me.'

'Help me to rise,' said the Greek. 'You won't kill me, will you ? Take me as far as the street, and then I'll go on alone.'

Ursus lifted him like a feather, led him through a dark passage to the second court, and then to the porch which opened on to the street. As they went through the corridor, Chilon kept saying to himself: 'It's all up with me,' and he was only reassured when they emerged. Then he said:

'I'll go myself now.'

'Peace be with you.'

'And with you ! And with you ! Let me get breath.'

When Ursus left him he took several deep breaths; he felt his hips and his sides as though to assure himself that he was really alive, and then he made off.

After he had gone some fifty yards, he stopped and said:

'But why on earth didn't they kill me ?'

CHAPTER 3

VINICIUS was also unable to account for all that had happened, and in his heart of hearts he was no less astounded than Chilon. That these people should have treated him so, and that, instead of revenging themselves for his attack they should have carefully attended to his wounds, he attributed in a minor degree to the doctrine they held, but in a greater degree to Lygia and to his own importance. But their treatment of Chilon completely surpassed what he had conceived as the limits of human forgiveness. 'Why,' he asked himself, 'did they not kill the Greek ? '

Why did the apostle teach that if one had sinned seven times he should be forgiven seven times ? And why had Glaucus said to Chilon: 'May God forgive you, as I forgive you' ? For undoubtedly Chilon had done him the most shocking injury. At the mere thought of what he, Vinicius, would do to any one who, for example, should kill Lygia, he felt his blood boil. There was no torture that he would not inflict upon her murderer! And here was one who forgave him!

Besides astonishment, however, there was something of pity and contempt in his opinion of the Christians. In them he saw sheep destined sooner or later to be the prey of the wolves, and the spirit of the Roman in him did not find it right to submit thus tamely to be devoured. However, he was impressed by the fact that, after Chilon's departure, every face was radiant with joy. The apostle came up to Glaucus, laid his hands upon him, and said:

' The Christ has triumphed within you!'

At that moment Ursus returned and told how he had escorted Chilon to the street and had asked his pardon for the pain he had inflicted upon him; whereupon the apostle blessed him also. Then Crispus declared that this was the day of a mighty victory. At the word victory, Vinicius completely lost the chain of his thoughts.

When Lygia gave him another refreshing drink he held her hand for a moment and said:

' So you too have forgiven me ? '

' We are Christians, and we are forbidden to cherish resentment in our hearts.'

' Lygia, whatever this God of yours is, I will

sacrifice a hundred oxen to Him, just because He is your God.'

She replied:

'You will honour Him in your heart when you learn to love Him.'

'Only because He is your God,' Vinicius said again in a stifled voice.

He closed his eyes, once more overcome with weakness.

Lygia went out, but soon returned, and approached him to make sure he was asleep. Feeling that she was near him he opened his eyes and smiled; she gently closed his eyelids with her hand, as though she wished to compel him to sleep. Then he felt a great peace steal over him, while at the same time his weakness increased. Nightfall brought with it a return of his fever.

He seemed to see, in the middle of a deserted cemetery, a temple in the shape of a tower, and Lygia was the priestess in the temple. He never lost sight of her. He saw her at the top of the tower in the full light, with a lute in her hand, like those priestesses whom he had seen in the East, singing hymns by night in honour of the moon. He himself was toiling up the winding stair to carry her off, while behind him crept Chilon, who kept saying, his teeth rattling together with terror: 'Don't do it, sir, for she is a priestess, and He will avenge her.' Vinicius did not know who 'He' was, but he understood that he was about to commit a sacrilege, and he was conscious of great fear. When he came to the balustrade which ran round the top of the tower he suddenly noticed, beside Lygia, the white-bearded apostle, who said: 'Do not lay your hand upon her, for she belongs to me.'

Then he awoke and stared in front of him.

The branches of olive were vanishing slowly in glowing embers, but the pine logs, which apparently had just been thrown in the fire, crackled, and sent out flames that enabled Vinicius to see Lygia sitting not far from his bed.

He was stirred to the depths of his soul. She had spent the previous night at the Ostrianum: the whole day she had been busy attending him, and now, while the others rested, she alone was watching beside him. She was sitting motionless, with her eyes closed. Vinicius did not know whether she was asleep or deep in her own thoughts. He studied her face, her lowered eyelashes, her hands folded in her lap, and in his heathen brain a new idea began to unfold itself. Side by side with the Greek and Roman beauty, proud and confident in its glorious nakedness, there was in the world another, a new beauty, perfectly chaste, in which dwelt a new soul.

He could not make up his mind to call Lygia a Christian, but in thinking of her he no longer separated her from the religion which she professed. It was Lygia alone, Lygia whom he had wronged, that watched over him while the others slept. That was because her religion so commanded her. But this belief, which filled him with admiration for Christ's teaching, was at the same time painful to him. He would have preferred that Lygia should act thus from love of him; from love of his face, his eyes, his perfect form—in a word, for all the reasons that had made so many Greek and Roman women throw their white arms round his neck.

Then suddenly he felt that had she been like other women, she would have seemed to him less perfect.

But now she had opened her eyes, and seeing that Vinicius was looking at her, she came over to him and said:

'I am beside you.'
He replied:
'I saw your soul in my dream.'

CHAPTER 4

On the following day he awoke still very weak, but
without fever. He thought he heard the sound of
conversation, but when he opened his eyes Lygia
was no longer beside him. Ursus, bending over the
fireplace, was raking among the gray ashes, looking
for a burning ember. Then he stirred the cones into
a blaze, and the breath from his lungs came with the
force of a blacksmith's bellows. Vinicius remembered that this was the man who had on the previous
day overwhelmed Croton, and as an *habitué* of the
arena he studied with interest his immense frame
and his colossal thighs.

'He didn't break my neck, for which I thank
Mercury,' thought he; 'but, by Pollux, if the rest
of the Lygians are like him, they will give our
Danube legions something to think about.'

He said aloud:
'Slave!'

Ursus drew his head from the fireplace and said
with an almost friendly smile:

'God give you good day and good health, sir, but
I am a freeman, and not a slave.'

Vinicius, who meant to question him about
Lygia's country, felt a certain satisfaction at these
words, for a conversation with a freeman, even of
low birth, was less trying to his dignity as a Roman
and a patrician than a conversation with a slave,

whom neither law nor custom recognised as a human being.

' So you're not one of Aulus' people ? '

' No, sir, I serve Callina, as I served her mother, but of my own free will.'

He once more put his head inside the fireplace to blow upon the cones, on which he had thrown some wood ; then he drew it back again and said :

' In our country there are no slaves.'

Vinicius asked him :

' Where is Lygia ? '

' She has just gone out, and I am to make your breakfast. She sat up all night with you.'

' Why did you not take her place ? '

' Because it was not her wish ; I have only to obey.'

His face grew gloomy, and he added next moment :

' If I had not obeyed her, you would not be alive now.'

' So you're sorry you didn't kill me ? '

' No, sir, Christ has bidden us not kill.'

' What about Atacinus and Croton ? '

' I could not do otherwise,' Ursus murmured.

And he looked with a comical despair at his hands, which had remained frankly heathen, although his soul had received baptism.

Then he put a pot beside the fire, and squatting in front of the fireplace, he gazed at the flames with thoughtful eyes.

' It is your fault, sir,' he said at last. ' Why did you lay hands on her—on a king's daughter ? '

For a moment Vinicius shuddered to hear a common fellow and a barbarian speak to him in such a familiar style, and even venture to blame him. But his desire to learn some details about Lygia's life was stronger than his annoyance.

He began to question the giant about the Lygians' war with Vannius and the Suevians. Ursus needed no pressing, but he could add but little to what Aulus Plautius had already told Vinicius. The latter, however, listened with pleasure, his boundless pride being satisfied by this testimony of an eyewitness to Lygia's royal origin.

'When Cæsar had Callina carried off,' said Ursus, 'I wanted to go away back to our forests and summon the Lygians to the rescue of their king's daughter. And they would have marched on the Danube, for they are a loyal people, although but heathens. And then I should have brought them the good tidings. That will come some day. When Callina returns to Pomponia, I will beg her to let me go home to them; for Christ was born far away from there, and they have never even heard of Him. He knew better than I where He should be born; but if He had come into the world in our land, in the forests, we should assuredly not have made Him a martyr. We should have brought Him up and taken care to see that He had always abundance of game and mushrooms and beaver skins and amber. All the spoil we took from the Suevians and Marcomanni we should have given Him, to allow Him to live in wealth and comfort.'

He put the pot containing the broth for Vinicius on the fire and fell silent. His thoughts were wandering in the Lygian forests while the pot went on boiling. When the broth, poured at last into a deep bowl, was sufficiently cool, Ursus went on:

'Glaucus says you are to stir as little as possible, and not even move your sound arm; and Callina told me to get you to eat.'

Sitting down beside the bed, Ursus lifted the broth from the bowl in a little cup which he put to the sick man's lips. And so much solicitude was apparent in this act, and there was such a kindly smile in his blue eyes, that Vinicius could not believe that he saw before him the terrible person of a few hours ago.

For the first time in his life the young patrician began to reflect on what might go on in the heart of a yokel, a servant, and a barbarian.

But Ursus proved himself a nurse as clumsy as devoted. The cup was lost from sight between his enormous fingers, so that there was no room for Vinicius' mouth, and after a few unsuccessful attempts the giant in great embarrassment said :

' It would be easier dragging a wild bull from its lair.'

Vinicius had often seen in the circus these terrible *uri* brought from northern forests, which the most redoubtable gladiators only attacked with misgiving, and which in size and strength were inferior to the elephants alone.

' Have you really tried to catch those brutes by the horns ? ' he asked in amazement.

' I saw twenty summers before I dared to do it,' replied Ursus ; ' but then I managed it.'

Once more he offered Vinicius the broth, but this time still more clumsily.

' I must get Myriam or Nazarius to come,' he said.

The curtain was drawn aside, and a pale face appeared.

' I'll come and help you,' said Lygia.

And the next moment she came from the bedroom, where she had obviously been preparing for sleep, as her hair was undone, and she was clad only in a *capitium*. Vinicius, whose heart had begun to beat more rapidly as soon as he saw her, reproached her with not yet having thought of rest ; but she replied gaily :

'I was just going to sleep, but first of all I'll take Ursus' place.'

She took the cup, sat down on the edge of the bed, and began to feed the abashed but happy Vinicius. As she bent towards him, he felt the warmth of her body, the masses of her hair touched his breast, and he turned pale with emotion. But in all the tumult and ardour of his passion he knew that nobody in the world was so dear to him, and that the whole world besides was nothing to him.

Once he had only desired Lygia ; now he loved her with all his heart. Then, in his style of life and in his feelings, he had been blindly, unscrupulously egotistical ; now he thought of her as well as himself.

He soon refused more food, and although it would have been a supreme joy to him to see her and feel her near him, he said :

'That will do ; go now and rest, my angel.'

'Do not call me that,' she replied ; 'it is not right for me to hear you speak so to me.'

But she smiled to him, and told him she was not sleepy, and did not feel tired, and would only go and rest when Glaucus came in. Her words sounded like music to him ; increasing emotion, gratitude, and joy stole over his heart, and he racked his brains to find some way of showing his thankfulness.

'Lygia,' he said, after a short silence, 'I did not know you before, but now I see that I have chosen the wrong way to win you. So now I say : " Go back to Pomponia Græcina, and rest assured that in future nobody shall molest you." '

Lygia's face grew suddenly sad.

'I should be glad,' she replied, 'to see her,

even from a distance, but I can never go back to her.'

'Why?' asked Vinicius, surprised.

'We Christians are kept informed by Acte of what goes on at the palace. Did you not hear that after my flight, and before he left for Naples, Cæsar sent for Aulus and Pomponia, and threatened them with his anger, thinking that they had helped me to escape? Fortunately, Aulus was able to reply: "You know, sire, that no lie ever crossed my lips; I swear that we did not help her to escape, and that we know no more than you do what has become of her." Cæsar took his word for it, and forgot all about it. I, for my part, following the advice of our elders, have never written to my mother, so that she can always swear she knows nothing about me; for we are not allowed to tell lies, even though our life is at stake. Only from some distant rumours does Pomponia know that I am living and in safety.'

At the memory of Pomponia her eyes filled with tears, but she soon calmed herself, and went on:

'I know that Pomponia misses me sorely, but we have consolations unknown to other people.'

'Yes,' replied Vinicius, 'your consolation is Christ. Here you are sitting beside me and thinking of Him. Think of me, too, else I'll come to hate Him. The only deity I have is you. I long to kiss your feet and make my prayers to you, to offer you adoration and sacrifices, and bend the knee to you—to you, thrice sacred one! No, you do not know—you cannot know—how dearly I love you.'

These words sounded to Lygia like so many blasphemies, and yet she could not help feeling pity for him and his sufferings. She felt that he loved and adored her supremely. She knew that this ruthless and dangerous man was her slave, and seeing him so humble, she rejoiced in the power which she had over him. In a second she lived through the past again. She saw again the splendid Vinicius, handsome as a pagan god, who had talked love to her in Aulus' house, and had awakened her almost child-like heart as though from a deep sleep —this man whose kisses she felt again on her lips, and from whose arms Ursus had snatched her at the palace. But to-day, with joy as well as suffering written on his haughty face, with white forehead and imploring eyes, humbled by his love, wounded, all adoration and humility, he was as once she could have wished to see him—when she would have loved him with all her heart—and he was dearer to her than ever.

Then suddenly she saw that there might come a moment when love of this man would gain upon her and carry her off like a whirlwind. Was it for this that she had sought safety in flight—for this that she had remained so long hidden in the most wretched parts of the town ? What, after all, was Vinicius ? An Augustan, a soldier, a courtier of Nero's ! He seemed to be changed certainly, but had he not just told her that if she thought of Christ more than of him he would hate Him? Lygia fancied that the mere thought of any other love than the love of Christ was a sin against Him and His teaching. And so she was seized with terror of her own future, and terror at the thoughts that filled her own heart.

CHAPTER 5

FROM that moment Lygia rarely appeared in the common room, and scarcely ever went near the invalid. But she could not recover her peace of mind. She saw that Vinicius followed her with supplicating looks ; that he looked for a word from her as a favour ; that he was suffering without daring to complain, lest he should scare her away ; and that she alone meant health and joy to him.

One day she noticed traces of tears on his eyelashes, and for the first time it occurred to her that she might dry them with her kisses. Full of contempt for herself, she spent the following night weeping.

Vinicius now displayed much less haughtiness in his conversations with Glaucus. He frequently reminded himself that this poor slave doctor and old Myriam and Crispus were also human beings. In the long run he came to love Ursus.

The more frequent were Vinicius' victories over himself, the more did Lygia love him. But although the young tribune might subject his violence to Christian discipline, to bring his mind into sympathy with the religion itself was a difficulty of another kind. He did not venture to doubt the supernatural birth of Christ, nor His resurrection, nor all the other miracles. But this new religion would destroy all order and all supremacy, and would cause social distinctions to disappear. What would become then of the supremacy of the power of Rome ? Could the Romans renounce their world empire, and recognise as their equals all the horde

153

of vanquished races? No, such a thought could never cross the mind of a patrician.

Lygia guessed what was taking place within him. She saw both his efforts to sympathise and his natural aversion from her religion, and she was profoundly grieved. But the silent respect that he manifested for Christ awakened compassion, pity, and gratitude within her, and drew her to the young man.

One day, sitting beside him, she remarked that outside of the Christian religion there was no such thing as life. Vinicius, who was beginning to recover his strength, raised himself on his sound arm, and suddenly laying his head on the girl's knees, he said,—

'Life? You are life to me!'

At those words her breathing stopped, her reason left her, and she seemed to quiver with pleasure from head to foot. She took his head in her hands, and sought to lift him, but as she bent towards him in the effort, her lips touched his hair. For a moment they blindly struggled against themselves and against a love that was forcing them into each other's arms. Then Lygia rose and fled.

Vinicius did not suspect the price he was to pay for this good fortune. But Lygia saw that she herself had need of help then. The following night she spent in wakefulness, in weeping and praying, feeling herself unworthy to address God, and hopeless of being heard. The next day she left her bedroom betimes, asked Crispus to come out into the garden, and there, in the arbour covered with ivy and withered bindweed, she opened her heart to him, and begged him to let her leave Myriam's house, for she was no longer sure of herself, and could no longer struggle against her love for Vinicius.

Crispus approved of her proposal to leave, but had no word of pardon for this love, which he regarded only as a sin. His heart overflowed with indignation at the very thought that Lygia, the fugitive whom he had protected, whom he loved, whom he had confirmed in the faith, whom till then he had regarded as an immaculate lily sprung from the soil of the Christian religion—that she could find in her soul room for a love other than the love of God. He was filled with amazement and bitterness at his mistake.

' Go and ask pardon of God for your faults,' he said to her in a sad tone ; ' seek safety before the spirit of evil, who has bewitched you, lead you to fall utterly, and before you deny your Saviour. Would God you had died—would God the walls of this house had crumbled about your head before this serpent entered your breast and dropped there the poison of his iniquity! May God forgive you and have mercy on you, for until you cast out this serpent, I who looked on you as one of His elect——'

He broke off suddenly, perceiving that they were not alone.

Through the withered bindweed and the green ivy he saw two men, one of whom was the apostle Peter. At first he did not recognise the second, whose face was partly concealed by a cloak, and he thought for a moment that it was the Greek.

Hearing Crispus talking loudly, they had entered the arbour and sat down on a seat. When the apostle's companion disclosed his ascetic face, his bald head, his red eyelids, and curved nose, Crispus recognised Paul of Tarsus.

Lygia had thrown herself on her knees, and was silently hiding her tearful little face in the folds of the apostle's cloak.

Peter said :

' Peace be with your souls.'

He laid his wrinkled hand on Lygia's head, and then, looking at the old priest, he said :

' Crispus, have you never heard that our Divine Master at the marriage in Cana blessed the love of husband and wife ? Do you think, Crispus, that Christ, who allowed Mary of Magdala to cast herself at His feet and who pardoned her sins, would turn His face away from this child, pure as a lily of the field ? You, Lygia, so long as the eyes of your lover are not open to the light of the truth, must avoid him, lest he lead you into sin ; but pray for him, and be assured that your love is no guilty love.'

He laid both his hands on Lygia's hair, and gave her his blessing. His face shone with a heavenly goodness.

' I have offended against mercy,' said Crispus ; ' but I thought that in admitting to her heart a worldly love she had renounced Christ.'

Peter replied :

' I denied Him thrice, and yet He forgave me and bade me be the shepherd of His flock.'

' And then,' Crispus said finally, ' Vinicius is an Augustan.'

' Christ has softened harder hearts,' replied Peter.

CHAPTER 6

VINICIUS to Petronius :

' I have told you about my stay with the Christians, about their treatment of their enemies, among whom they might justly number myself and Chilon, about their kindness and attention to me, and about Lygia's disappearance. Had Lygia been my sister or my wife she could not have nursed me more tenderly than she did. More than once I thought that only love was capable of inspiring such solicitude. More than once I read this love on her face and in her eyes, and then—will you believe it ?—in the midst of these simple folk, in that miserable room, half kitchen half dining-room, I felt unspeakably happy. No, I was not indifferent to her. And yet this same girl has left the house, unknown to me. Now I spend whole days with my head in my hands, wondering why she did so. Did I tell you that I proposed to send her back to Aulus ? But it was not possible, for they had all gone to Sicily, and in any case it would have been imprudent: slaves' gossip passes from house to house, and finally reaches the palace, and then Cæsar might have taken her back. At least she knew that I would persecute her no more, that I had done with violence, and that as I could not cease to love her, nor live without her, my happiness would lie in having her as my wife. And yet she ran away! Why? She had no longer anything to fear. If she did not love me, she could have repulsed me.

' And what if she, too, loved ? In that case she ran away from love. At the very thought I feel I want to send slaves to cry at the door of every house: " Lygia, come back." I could not have forbidden her to believe in her Christ, and indeed I should have put up an altar to Him in the atrium here. What does one god the more matter, and why should I not believe in Him, I who have scarce any belief in the old gods ?

' But it seems that is not enough for the Christians.

The worship of Christ is not the only thing; His teaching must be put into practice; and here you find yourself, as it were, upon the shore of a sea which they say you must cross on foot. Even if I promised to put His teaching into practice, they would feel this was only empty words.

'I am no philosopher, but neither am I such a fool as you may have thought me more than once. And so I say: I do not know how the Christians manage to live their lives, but, on the other hand, I know full well that, where their religion begins, there is an end of Roman supremacy and of this life of ours; there goes the difference between conqueror and conquered, between rich and poor, master and servant; and there is an end of law and order in the world. I admit that Lygia is of more moment to me than the whole of Rome and its empire, and the world may crumble to ruin if only I have her in my house. But that is not the question. It is not enough for the Christians if one renders their religion mere lip service.

'I told you, I think, that she left without my knowledge. But before she went she left me a cross made by herself out of some little boxwood twigs, and when I woke up this cross was near my bed. I keep it in the *lararium*, and without quite knowing why, I approach it with fear and respect, as though it had something divine about it. I love it because it was her hands which bound the twigs together, and yet I detest it because it is this cross which keeps us apart.'

CHAPTER 7

VINICIUS, completely restored to health, returned home, and retired into seclusion. He saw the doctor, Glaucus, from time to time, and nobody else. These visits were precious to him, for then he could talk of Lygia. Glaucus did not know where she had taken refuge, but he assured Vinicius that the elders were keeping anxious watch over her.

One day, moved by Vinicius' grief, he told him that the apostle Peter had blamed Crispus for reproaching Lygia with her worldly love. The young patrician grew pale with emotion. He had often thought that Lygia might care for him, but he had always been plunged again into doubt and uncertainty. Now for the first time he heard confirmation of his desires and hopes from the mouth of a stranger, and that stranger a Christian. He thought, too, that if Lygia loved him, every obstacle was thereby removed, for he himself was ready to worship Christ. He often felt a desire to see Paul of Tarsus, whose words interested and disturbed him. But Paul had left for Aricia, and as Glaucus' visits became more and more infrequent, Vinicius found himself completely alone. He took to scouring the neighbouring alleys of the Suburra, and the narrow lanes of the district across the Tiber, in the hope of catching sight of Lygia even from a distance ; and when this hope failed, *ennui* and impatience took hold of him, so that at last a day came when his old self gained the upper hand with all the violence of a wave which has receded only to beat afresh upon the shore. He determined to forget Lygia, or at least to resume his old amusements, and pursue them without thinking about her. And so he plunged into the whirl of loose living with his wonted ardour.

Everything seemed to favour him. The city, which had been empty and desolate during the winter, was beginning to revive in the hope of Cæsar's early arrival, and a state reception was being prepared for him. Spring was coming. The snow on the peaks of the Alban Hills had melted before the breath of the African winds, and in the gardens the turf was sown with violets. The open spaces and the Campus Martius swarmed with crowds warming themselves in the more genial sun of spring. The Appian Way, the usual haunt of people when taking the air, was thronged with richly decorated chariots. Already excursions were being made to the Alban Hills. Young women, under pretext of worshipping Juno at Lavinium or Diana at Aricia, stole away from home in search of excitement, society, and social pleasures of all kinds.

One day, among these magnificent chariots, Vinicius saw the splendid four-horse car of Chrysothemis, the mistress of Petronius, preceded by two Molossian hounds, and surrounded by a group composed of young men and of senators detained in the city by their official duties. Chrysothemis herself drove her car, which was drawn by four small Corsican horses, and she was lavishing smiles and light taps from her gilded whip on those around her. When she noticed Vinicius, she drew up her horses, invited him to take his place beside her, and took him home with her to a banquet, which lasted the whole night. Vinicius became so intoxicated that he could not remember at what time he was taken home. But he did remember that Chrysothemis had asked if he had any news of Lygia, that he had been angry at this, and, being already drunk, had poured his cup of Falernian wine over her head. And as he thought about it he felt his anger return again. But on the following day Chrysothemis, forgetting his insulting behaviour, came to see him, and took him out driving again on the Appian Way.

She remained to supper with him, and confessed to him that she had long been tired both of Petronius and his lute player, and that her heart was free. For about a week they appeared together, though their intimacy did not promise to be of long duration. Since the incident of the Falernian wine, Lygia's name had never been mentioned, but Vinicius could not succeed in banishing her from his thoughts. He felt always as though her eyes were fastened on him. His indignation against himself was in vain ; he suffered at the thought of giving Lygia pain. On the first display of jealousy by Chryso-themis—it was about two young Syrian women whom he had bought—he showed her the door without more ado.

But he did not alter his style of life. He rather pushed his excesses further, as though to baffle the tyranny of Lygia's memory. But finally he came to see that the young Christian was the sole cause of all his evil deeds, as of all his good ones, and that he had interest in nothing save her. Even the emperor's return did not arouse him from his indifference, and it was only when Petronius sent his own litter to fetch him that he visited even him.

Despite his joyful welcome, Vinicius made but half-hearted answers at first to his uncle's questions. But in the long run, his feelings and thoughts, long pent up, poured forth in a torrent of words. He gave a more detailed account of the events which had overwhelmed him, and he told of his grief at having fallen into such a state of mental chaos that he had lost both his peace of mind and all ability to see things clearly and in their proper light. He was attracted by nothing; he was interested in nothing; and he knew not what plans to make nor how to act. He was ready at once to worship Christ and persecute Him; he understood the lofty character of His teaching, and yet at the same time he felt an invincible repugnance to it. He seemed to be wandering in darkness and groping for a way out.

Petronius noticed Vinicius' changed features, and saw his hands stretched out as though in the search for a road through the darkness, and he reflected. Suddenly he said:

'Surely you have tried to shake off this sadness and to enjoy the pleasures of the world?'

'I have,' replied Vinicius.

Petronius laughed.

'Ah, deceiver! News travels fast when slaves get it; you have robbed me of Chrysothemis!'

Vinicius with a gesture of disgust admitted the charge.

'At any rate, I am grateful to you,' continued Petronius. 'I will send her a pair of pearl embroidered shoes. In my language of love that means 'Good-bye.' I am doubly grateful to you. In the first place, you did not accept Eunice, and now you have taken Chrysothemis off my hands. Now listen to this: you see before you a man who used to rise betimes, bathed and feasted, possessed the woman he wanted, who wrote satires, and sometimes enlivened his prose with verses, but who was as much bored as Cæsar, and often did not know how to drive away his dismal thoughts. And do you know the reason? Because he was looking abroad for something which lay ready to his own hand. A lovely woman is always worth her weight in gold, but one who, moreover, loves in return is priceless, simply priceless. You cannot buy that with all the treasures of Verres. So this is what I tell myself to-day. I fill my life with happiness as I should fill a cup with good wine, and I drink till my hand loses its power and my lips turn pale. Then come what will—that is my new philosophy.'

'You have always professed that. It contains nothing new.'

'It contains a system, which used to be lacking.'

Then he summoned Eunice. She entered, clad in white, with a smile upon her lips. Petronius opened his arms and said:

'Come!'

She ran to him, and, sitting on his knee, she laid her head on his breast. Vinicius saw her cheeks grow gradually redder and her eyes become misty. Sitting together thus, they made a wonderful picture of happy love. Petronius, stretching out his hand, took a handful of violets from a shallow tray and strewed them on Eunice's hair and breast and on her robe. Then he loosed the garments about her shoulders, and said:

'Happy is he who, like me, has found love enclosed in such a body as this! Look—have Praxiteles, Miron, Scopas, and Lysias ever conceived more perfect lines? Is there at Paros or on the Pentelicon a marble so warm, so radiant, and so voluptuous?'

His lips strayed over the neck and shoulders of Eunice. She quivered, and there was a tremor on her eyelids. Petronius turned to Vinicius.

'And now, think what your dismal Christians are compared with this. If you see no difference, well, you are welcome to go back to them. Eunice, my love, bid them prepare breakfast for us and bring us garlands.'

He rose and walked up and down the room.

' Love,' he went on, ' effects in men a transformation, neither more nor less. I too have been transformed by it. Once upon a time I loved the scent of verbena, but since Eunice prefers violets, I have come to love them more than any other.'

He stopped in front of Vinicius and said :

' You tell me Lygia loves you. Possibly, but is not hers a love which will not surrender itself ? Does not that mean that there exists something stronger than itself ? No, my dear fellow, Lygia is not Eunice!'

' Everything tortures me alike,' replied Vinicius. ' I saw you cover Eunice's shoulders with kisses, and at once I thought that if Lygia had uncovered her shoulders for me like that I could have died happy. But at the very idea a sort of fear seized me, as though I had made an attempt upon a vestal virgin, or had sought to violate a goddess. Lygia is not Eunice, indeed, but we do not view the difference between them from the same point of view. Love has altered your sense of smell, and so now you prefer violets to vervain. It is my soul that it has altered. And in spite of the unhappiness of my passion, I prefer that Lygia should not be like other women.'

Petronius shrugged his shoulders.

' Then you lose nothing by your abstinence. But I do not understand.'

' That is the truth,' replied Vinicius hurriedly. ' We can never understand one another again.'

After a short silence Petronius broke out:

' I wish Hades may swallow up all Christians! They have filled you with uneasiness, and perverted your outlook on life. You are wrong in thinking their religion is good. The only good is that which gives us happiness—that is, beauty, love, and strength—and these things are what they call vanities. You are wrong, too, in imagining that they love justice: if we return good for evil, what are we to give in return for good ? And if both meet with the same reward, why should men be good ? '

' They do not meet with the same reward, but, according to their teaching, the reward comes in the life after death, which is eternal.'

' I can't go into these considerations, since we can only verify them later on—if indeed we can verify anything when we have no longer the use of our eyes. Meantime, these people are mere simpletons, and the heritage of the future is not for such as they are.'

' Life begins for them only after death.'

' As though you should say, day begins at nightfall. Do you mean to carry Lygia off ? '

' No, I cannot return evil for good, and besides, I have sworn.'

' Do you mean to adopt the Christian faith ? '

' I should like to, but my whole nature cries out against it.'

' Lastly, are you able to forget Lygia ? '

' No.'

' Then go abroad and travel.'

Just then the slaves came to announce that breakfast was ready, and Petronius continued the conversation as they went to the dining-room.

' You have seen part of the world, but only as a soldier hurrying to his destination and not stopping by the way. What did you see when you were with Corbulo ? Nothing! Did you see the Greek temples as they should be seen ? Spending two whole years on them like me, and passing from one guide to

another? Did you see where the Colossus stood at
Rhodes? Did you see the clay at Panopeus in
Phocis that Prometheus used to make men from?
Did you see Leda's eggs at Sparta, or the famous
Sarmatian suit of armour made out of horses' hoofs
at Athens? Did you see Agamemnon's ship at
Euboea, and the cup that was moulded upon Helen's
left breast? Did you see Alexandria, Memphis, the
Pyramids, and the hair that Isis tore out when she
mourned for Osiris? Did you hear the melancholy
singing of Memnon's statue? The world is wide,
and all does not end at the Tiber. I mean to go with
Cæsar, and on the way home I will leave him and go
to Cyprus. My goddess with the locks of gold is
anxious that we should both make an offering of
doves to Venus at Paphos, and you must know that
whatever she desires is carried out.'

'I am your slave,' broke in Eunice.

He laid his head on her breast and said with a
smile:

'Then I am the slave of a slave. I adore you, my
love, from your head to your feet.'

'Come,' he said to Vinicius; 'come with us to
Cyprus and leave your Christians alone. I tell you
they are fools, that you feel it yourself, and that
your nature revolts from their teaching for the very
reason that you perceive their idiocy. You are a
man of metal; think no more of it, and speak to
me about it no more. We can live and we can die,
and what more can they do? Does anybody know
that?'

These words made an impression upon Vinicius,
and on his return home he began to reflect that
perhaps this goodness and mercy were indeed
simply a proof of their feeble-mindedness. Strong,
well-tempered men, he thought, could not forgive

like this, and hence no doubt the repugnance of
their faith to his Roman mind. 'For our part, we
can live and we can die,' Petronius had said. What
could they do? They could only forgive, but as
for real love or real hatred, these lay beyond their
comprehension.

CHAPTER 8

THE emperor regretted having returned to Rome,
and after a few days he conceived afresh a strong
desire to set out for Achæa. He actually published
an edict announcing that his absence from the city
would be brief and that public business would not
suffer by it. Then, accompanied by the Augustans,
among whom was Vinicius, he proceeded to the
Capitol to offer sacrifices to the gods and return
thanks for their protection on his last journey. But
next day, on the occasion of his visit to the Temple
of Vesta, an event took place which changed all his
plans. Nero did not believe in the gods, but yet he
was afraid of them, and especially of the mysterious
Vesta. At the sight of the goddess and her sacred
fire his hair stood on end, he clenched his teeth, he
trembled in every limb, and fainted away in the arms
of Vinicius, who chanced to be standing behind him.
He was at once taken from the temple to the palace,
where he remained in bed all day. To the great surprise of all present he announced that he had made
up his mind to postpone his journey, as the goddess
had secretly warned him against undue haste. An
hour afterwards it was publicly proclaimed throughout Rome that Cæsar, noticing the sadness on the
people's faces, and swayed by a father's love for

them, would remain in their midst and share their joys and sorrows. The populace, delighted at this resolve, which heralded for them the approach of games and largesse, assembled in crowds before the Palatine Gate, shouting loud in honour of their most august emperor, who at that moment was playing at dice with his friends.

'Yes,' he said, 'I have had to put off my journey. Egypt and the command of the East cannot slip from my grasp, the seers tell me, nor in consequence can Achæa. I shall have the isthmus of Corinth cut through, and we will raise monuments in Egypt that will make the Pyramids look like toys. I will have a Sphinx built seven times the size of the one that looks out over the desert at Memphis, and it shall have my features.'

'A superb gift to mankind!' said Petronius.

'And then in Egypt I mean to marry the Moon, who is a widow, and so I shall be a god indeed.'

'And you will give us the stars as wives, and we shall form a new constellation, to be called the constellation of Nero. You will marry Vitellius to the Nile, to raise a family of hippopotamuses. Give the desert to Tigellinus, and he will be king of the jackals!'

'And what am I to have?' asked Vatinius.

'The blessings of Apis upon you! You arranged such splendid games for us at Beneventum that I cannot wish you any harm. So you make a pair of boots for the Sphinx, for his paws grow cold at night, when the dew falls. Then you can make shoes for the great statues that line the approaches to the temples. Everybody will find a suitable occupation over there. There's Domitius Afer, for instance, he'll be treasurer, being so well known for his honesty. I am charmed, sire, that you are thinking of Egypt, and am only sorry that you have put off your journey.'

But Nero replied:

'Your mortal eyes have seen nothing, for the goddess is not visible to unhallowed eyes. Know then that in the temple Vesta herself rose beside me and said in my ear, "Delay your journey." It happened so suddenly that I was terrified, although I should have been grateful to the gods for so clearly watching over me.'

He thought for a moment and then said:

'Tell me why men fear Vesta more than other gods? Even I, the high priest, was seized with fear. I only remember that I fainted, and I should have fallen if some one had not caught me. Who was it?'

'It was I,' replied Vinicius.

'Oh, you, stern son of Mars? Why did you not come to Beneventum? They told me you were ill, and indeed you have changed. By-the-bye, they told me Croton tried to kill you? Is that true?'

'Yes, and he broke my arm, but I defended myself.'

'With a broken arm?'

'A certain barbarian, who was stronger than Croton, came to my assistance.'

Nero looked surprised.

'Stronger than Croton? Surely you're joking? Croton was the strongest man in the world. Now it's Styphax the Ethiopian.'

'I am telling you, sire, what I saw with my own eyes.'

'Where is this treasure then? He must surely have been made king of the forest of Nemora?'

'I do not know, sire. I have lost sight of him.'

'Do you not even know his nationality?'

169

'I had a broken arm and did not think of questioning him.'

'Find him for me.'

Tigellinus said:

'I will undertake that.'

But Nero continued to address Vinicius:

'My thanks for holding me up; I might have fallen and broken my head. You used to be good company; since the war—since you served under Corbulo—you have turned shy, and I only see you occasionally.'

After a brief pause, he went on:

'How is that girl—the girl with the narrow hips —that you were in love with and that I took from Aulus for you?'

Vinicius grew confused, but Petronius at once came to the rescue.

'I would wager, sire, that he has forgotten her. You see how abashed he looks. Ask him how many he has had since, and I am not sure that he could tell you. The Vinicii play their part as soldiers, but they would play the part of a barndoor-cock even better, though they'd need a whole yard to themselves. Punish him, sire, and do not invite him to the feast Tigellinus promises us in your honour on the basin of Agrippa.'

But Nero only replied:

'I am wearied to death! The will of the goddess has made me remain in Rome, and I cannot endure it. I'll go to Antium. I'm stifled in this shut-in place, in the midst of ruinous houses and filthy lanes. The poisonous air reaches my very garden. Ah! if an earthquake would only destroy Rome, if some angry god would level it with the earth, then I would show you how to build a city fit to be mistress of the world, and fit to be my capital.'

'Cæsar,' said Tigellinus, 'you said, "If some angry god should destroy the city." That is right, is it not ? '

'Yes ; and what then ? '

'Are you not a god ? '

Nero shrugged his shoulders in a tired fashion, and said:

'We shall see what you can do for us on the basin of Agrippa. Then I'll go to Antium. You are all easily satisfied, and you do not understand the great things that I long for.'

He half closed his eyes, as though to intimate that he desired to rest. His friends took their leave one after the other, and Petronius left along with Vinicius.

'So you're invited to the banquet,' he said. 'Well, surely, having conquered the universe, we have the right to enjoy ourselves.'

'The only thing that surprises me is that you're not tired of all that sort of thing now,' replied Vinicius.

'Who said I was not ? I tired of it long ago, but I am not the same age as you. Besides, I have other tastes which you lack. I love books ; you do not. I love poetry, which bores you. I love vases and precious stones, and a horde of things that you'd not look twice at. I have pains in my back, which you have not. And finally, I have Eunice, and you have nothing like her. I delight in art treasures, but nobody could make you a man of taste. I know that I shall never find anything better in life than what I have found, while you are still hoping and looking for something. If death knocked at your door, you would be surprised, despite your courage and your griefs, at having to quit the world so soon ; while I should resign myself to the inevitable end in the firm conviction that there was no fruit in the world of which I had not tasted. I am in no hurry, but I shall require no second bidding. I shall only try to live happily to the end: sceptics are happy people. The Stoics, in my opinion, are fools, but at least Stoicism makes men of metal, while Christians only bring sadness into the world, which is to life what rain is to Nature. But people whose symbol is a cross could not be otherwise. Now listen to me: Greece was a beautiful land, and the birthplace of wisdom, while Rome was the birthplace of power. To what can this religion give birth, think you? If you know, enlighten me, for, by Pollux, I have not the slightest idea.'

Vinicius shrugged his shoulders.

'One would imagine you feared I meant to turn Christian.'

'I fear you'll make a mess of your life. If you cannot be Greece, then be Rome; rule and be happy. Promise me that if you find a Christian waiting for you when you go home you will put out your tongue at him. If by any chance it were Glaucus the doctor, he would not be surprised. I'll see you again at the basin of Agrippa.'

CHAPTER 9

THE Prætorian Guards were posted round the thickets that encircled the pond of Agrippa, to prevent over-many curious eyes from disturbing the pleasure of Cæsar and his guests. Tigellinus was anxious to reconcile Cæsar to the postponement of his journey and to excel all who had ever organised entertainments in his honour. Even when he was with him at Naples and Beneventum, he had this in view, and had sent to the ends of the earth for rare beasts and fish, for birds and plants, and fine vases and stuffs to lend brilliance to the occasion. The revenues of whole provinces were swallowed up in these preparations, but that was a detail which did not trouble the favourite. His influence was growing daily. Nero did not perhaps like him better than his other friends, but he found him more indispensable every day. Petronius, infinitely superior to him in grace of manner, in intellect, and in wit, could keep Cæsar better amused in company, but unfortunately he outshone him, and so made him jealous. His very nickname, ' Arbiter of Elegance,' jarred on the emperor's self-esteem, for who had a right to that save Cæsar ?

Tigellinus had set up the banqueting-tables on an enormous raft made of gilded beams. The edges were ornamented with magnificent shells from the Red Sea and Indian Ocean, with clumps of palms, lotus, and roses, among which were set statues of the gods, with gold and silver cages containing brightly coloured birds, and with fountains which threw up streams of perfume. In the middle was a canopy of Syrian purple, supported by little silver pillars, and beneath this were the tables prepared for the guests, resplendent with Alexandrian glass, with crystal and with porcelain, all brought as plunder from Italy, Greece, and Asia.

The raft, like an island buried in verdure and flowers, was attached by ropes of gold and purple to boats shaped like fish, swans, gulls, and flamingoes ; and in these boats, with their many-coloured oars, sat the rowers, naked men and women, perfect in face and form, with their hair dressed in Oriental fashion or massed beneath nets of gold. When Nero, in company with Poppæa and his friends, had gone on board the principal raft, the boats glided off, the oars dipped in the water, the ropes grew taut, and the raft, with the banquet and the guests, described a circle on the face of the lake as it left its moorings. Smaller rafts escorted them, filled with women playing the harp and the cithara, whose pink bodies, midway between the blue of heaven and the blue of the water, seemed to absorb colour from them and from the golden glitter of their instruments, and blossom out into magic flowers.

From mysterious buildings hidden in the under-growth on shore came the strains of music and singing. Every coppice rang, and all the country-side resounded with the notes of horn and trumpet. Cæsar, seated between Poppæa and Pythagoras, was lost in wonder, and when at last he saw sirens appear, swimming among the boats, he was not stinting in his praise of Tigellinus.

Then were served such dishes as would have made the ideas of Apicius seem foolish, and so many different wines that Otho, who used to offer his guests a choice of eighty, would have hidden below the table for shame. Vinicius outdid all the guests in beauty. There was a time when his face and figure had been too much those of a professional soldier, but now his features were refined by grief and physical suffering, as though the hand of the sculptor had touched them up. His complexion was no longer sunburnt, while still preserving its rich hue of Numidian marble. His eyes were larger and had a shade of sadness ; his body re-tained its powerful appearance, so well suited to a coat of mail, but the manly shoulders were crowned by a head of superlative beauty and refinement.

The wines, cooled in snow, were not long in warming hearts and heads. From the thickets by the waterside boats shaped like grasshoppers and dragon-flies put out each moment. Above them, and attached to silver cords, flew birds from India and Africa. The sun was already high in heaven, and the weather was exceptionally hot, even scorching, on this May day. The surface of the water undulated under the stroke of the oars. There was not a breath of wind, and the leaves of the trees were motionless. The raft glided slowly on, with its passengers growing every moment more hilarious. Already the guests had lost the order in which they sat at table. Cæsar himself had set the example ; he had taken Vinicius' place beside Rubria, and had begun to whisper in the vestal's ear. Vinicius found himself beside Poppæa, who in a few moments stretched out her arm to him and begged him to fasten her robe, which had come undone. The tribune's hand trembled slightly, while Poppæa cast upon him through the drooping eyelashes a half-confused look, and shook her golden head as though in refusal.

But now the sun, grown large and red, was sinking behind the tree-tops. Most of the guests were drunk. The raft was being steered inshore, where among the flowering shrubs groups of men dressed as fauns or satyrs were playing on the flute, on the pipes of Pan, and on the cymbals. Girls dressed as nymphs, dryads, and hamadryads, were gliding about. Twilight was greeted with cries in honour of the moon, and suddenly thousands of lamps lit up the groves. From the buildings erected along the shore issued a swarm of lights, and on the terraces the wives and daughters of the noblest families in Rome flaunted their triumphant nakedness, and with word and gesture invited the guests to join them. At last the raft came to shore, and Cæsar and his friends plunged into the thickets, and swarmed into houses, tents, and grottoes. The madness became universal. Nobody knew what had become of Cæsar ; nobody knew who was senator, soldier, mountebank, or musician. The satyrs and fauns ran shouting after the nymphs ; lamps were struck with the thyrsus to extinguish them ; and some parts of the thicket were in total darkness. From all sides came piercing cries, laughter, whisperings, and laboured breathings.

Vinicius was not drunk, as he had been at the banquet in Cæsar's palace when Lygia was there, but the events of the day had cast their glamour on him too, and the pleasure fever burned in his veins. He plunged into the wood, and ran off with the others to make his choice among the dryads. Groups of improvised goddesses, with a train of fauns, satyrs, senators, and knights, brushed past him. At last he noticed a procession of virgins with Diana at their head, and he bounded up to them to observe the goddess at closer range. Suddenly his heart stopped beating, for he seemed to recognise Lygia in the goddess of the silver crescent. They danced around him in a ring, and then, to incite him to pursue them, they fled like a herd of roe deer. And although this Diana was not Lygia, Vinicius stood still, choking with emotion.

Suddenly he felt an overwhelming sadness at this separation from Lygia. Never had she seemed more pure—never had he loved her so well as he did now in this scent of madness and wild debauchery. A few seconds ago and he himself had been athirst for the festive cup, now he was repelled and disgusted at the idea. He felt over-come by shame; he wanted to breathe fresh air and see the stars in the heavens. He determined to escape from the darkness of this dreadful wood. But he had scarcely gone a yard when he saw a woman's veiled figure in front of him: two hands were laid on his shoulders, and an eager voice whispered:

'I love you! Come, nobody will see us, but make haste.'

Vinicius roused himself as though from a dream.

'Who are you ? ' he said.

For answer she clung to him, and said again:

'Hasten! See how quiet everything is here, and I love you! Come!'

'Who are you ? '

'Guess.'

She wound her arm round Vinicius' neck, and through her veil she pressed her lips to his.

'This is a night of love—a night of madness,' she said, pouting. 'To-night we may do anything. Take me!'

But her kiss renewed his disgust. His mind and his heart were elsewhere, and there was nothing in all the world but Lygia.

He repulsed the veiled apparition.

'Whoever you are, I love another, and I do not want you.'

She leant towards him, and said:

'Lift my veil.'

At that moment there was a rustling among the myrtle bushes; the phantom fled, and her strange evil laugh was heard in the distance.

Petronius appeared.

'I heard and saw all,' he said.

Vinicius replied :

' Let us go.'

They passed the brightly lighted brothels, the wood, and the cordon of mounted sentries, and found their litters.

' I will stop at your house,' said Petronius.

They rode in the same litter, but they kept silence, and it was only in Vinicius' atrium that Petronius said :

' Do you know who it was ? '

' Rubria ? '

' No.'

' Who then ? '

Petronius lowered his voice :

' The Vestal flame has been profaned ; Rubria was with Cæsar. But she who spoke to you——'

Then he added in a whisper :

' —— was the divine Augusta.'

There was silence for a moment, then Petronius went on :

' Cæsar could not hide from her his violent desire for Rubria, and she may have wanted revenge. I disturbed you because if you had recognised her and repulsed her, you would have been lost beyond all hope—you and Lygia, and perhaps myself as well.'

Vinicius broke out :

' I've had enough of it—Rome, Cæsar, feasts, Augusta, Tigellinus, and the whole lot of you! I'm choking! I can't stand it! Do you understand ? '

' You're losing your head, Vinicius ; you're losing all sense and all moderation.'

' I love her alone in all the world.'

' What then ? '

' So I will have no other love. I'll have no more of

178

this life of yours with its revelry and debauchery and crime.'

'What on earth is wrong ? Have you turned Christian ? '

The young man put his hands to his head, and said in a voice of despair :

'Alas! not yet—not yet.'

CHAPTER 10

AT last Petronius learned from Cæsar himself that he meant to leave for Antium in three days. On the following day he went to give the news to Vinicius.

But the latter showed him the list of those invited to Antium, which had been brought to him that very morning by a freedman of Cæsar's.

'My name is on it,' he said, 'and so is yours. You will find a similar list awaiting you at home.'

'If I were not among the guests,' replied Petronius, 'all I could look for would be my death sentence, and I don't think that is due until the journey to Achæa, for Nero will find me too useful there.'

He read the list, and said :

'We're scarcely home before we must leave the house again, and drag ourselves off to Antium. But it's got to be done ; this invitation is as good as an order.'

'Supposing some one disobeyed ? '

'He would receive an invitation of a different nature : one to prepare for a perceptibly longer journey—the journey, in fact, from which there is no return. What a pity that you did not take my advice, and go away while it was yet time! Here you are now, forced to go to Antium.'

'Forced to go to Antium! See what times these are we live in, and what miserable slaves we are!'

'Is this the first time you've noticed that? But let us talk of more serious matters. I said at the palace that you were ill, but there's your name on the list, which means that somebody didn't believe me, and has used influence to have you put on it. It did not matter to Nero, for he sees in you only a soldier, with whom he can discuss, at most, the races, as you have no ideas about poetry and music. If your name figures on the list, you owe the honour to Poppæa, and that means that her passion is no passing fancy: she means to win you.'

'An audacious woman, the empress!'

'Audacious, indeed, for she may ruin herself for good. May Venus inspire her with another love as soon as possible! But while her love lasts, you must be prudent.'

'In the wood I did not know that it was she. You listened, so you know what reply I made, that I loved somebody else and that I did not want her.'

'I implore you, in the name of the gods below, do not lose the little sense the Christians have left you. What, after all, is the difficulty? What are you going to lose by this? Will it stop you loving Lygia? And remember this, too, that Poppæa saw you at the palace, and won't find it hard to guess who it is that causes you to spurn such marked favours from her. Then she will find her out, though she were hidden below the earth. You will bring about not only your own destruction, but Lygia's as well. Do you see?'

Vinicius listened as though his mind were occupied with something else. Finally he said:

' I must see her.'

' Who ? Lygia ? '

' Lygia.'

' You know where she is ? '

' No.'

' So you're going to start to look for her in all the old cemeteries, and across the Tiber ? '

' I don't know, but I must see her.'

' Very well. Although she is a Christian she will perhaps show herself more reasonable than you; indeed she certainly will, if she does not want to cause your destruction.'

Vinicius shrugged his shoulders.

' She saved me from Ursus' clutches.'

' In that case make haste, for Brazenbeard will soon be leaving. Death warrants can issue from Antium as well as from Rome.'

But Vinicius was not listening. He was thinking how to arrange for a meeting with Lygia.

The next day something happened which promised to remove all difficulties. This was an unexpected visit from Chilon.

He arrived starving and in rags, but as the slaves had formerly received orders to admit him at any time, day or night, they did not venture to stop him. He proceeded at once to the atrium, and standing before Vinicius, he said:

' May the gods give you immortality and divide with you the empire of the world!'

For a moment Vinicius felt inclined to have him thrown out of doors, but he thought that the Greek might know something about Lygia, and his curiosity got the better of his disgust.

' Is that you ? ' he said. ' What are you up to now ? '

' Things are bad, O son of Jupiter,' replied Chilon.

' I spent all you gave me in buying books from Atractus. Then I was robbed and ruined ; the woman who wrote down my lectures ran away with all that remained to me of your generosity. I am a poor wretch, but to whom can I turn save to you, O Serapis, you whom I love and for whom I risked my life ? '

' What do you want and what do you bring me ?'

' I beg you to help me, O Baal, and I bring you my misery, my tears, and my love—and also some news that I gathered out of affection for you. I know where the divine Lygia lives, and I will show you the street, sir, and the house.'

' Where is she ? '

' In the house of Linus, the oldest of the Christian priests. She has Ursus with her ; he still works with the miller with the same name as your steward, Demas—yes, Demas, that's it. Ursus works by night, and so if the house is surrounded during the night, he'll not be there. Linus is an old man, and the only other people are two old women. O master, master, it is for you alone to say whether this very night a noble queen shall reign in your house!'

The blood rose to Vinicius' head. His whole being was shaken once more by temptation. Yes, here was a way and a sure way. Lygia once in his house, who could take her away ? Once she was his mistress, what could she do save remain so for ever ? Away with religion! What would the Christians matter, then, with their longsuffering and their dismal beliefs ? Was it not time to shake himself free of all that ? As for Lygia's future conduct, how she would reconcile her new life to her religion, that was a secondary matter, and of no importance! The thing to notice was that she would be his, that very day! As to whether her religion would continue to hold sway over her soul, when she would be living in a world new to her, in the midst of pleasure and enjoyment——

At any rate, if she felt herself outraged, he would marry her, and so wipe out his offence. Yes, that was his duty, for he owed his life to her.

And then he called to mind the day when he and Croton entered her hiding-place, and he called to mind Ursus aiming that blow at his head, with all that happened afterwards. He saw her bending over his bed, dressed like a slave, as though she were some beneficent goddess. In spite of himself his eyes turned towards the household shrine and the little cross which she had left him. Was he going to repay all that by a fresh attempt on her ? Was he going to drag her to the bedroom by the hair, like a slave ? He felt of a sudden that it was not enough to have her by him, not enough to hold her in his arms ; his own love demanded something more, and that something was her own consent, her love, and her heart. Blessed be his house if she came to it willingly, blessed the moment and the day, and blessed be his whole life thereafter! But to carry her off by force was to slay such happiness for ever, and to spoil, to sully, and to render hateful all that he held dearest and most precious in life.

Now the very idea filled him with horror. He cast a glance at Chilon, who had been watching him, and was now scratching himself uneasily beneath his rags. Vinicius was filled with unspeakable disgust, and a desire to trample his old ally under foot like a poisonous snake. Unable to observe moderation in anything that he did, he followed the impulse of his terrible Roman nature, and turning to Chilon, said:

'I will not take your advice; but lest you go away without the reward you deserve, you shall have three hundred lashes in the slaves' dungeon.'

Chilon had turned pale, for Vinicius' handsome face wore a merciless and angry look.

The Greek fell upon his knees, and bowing himself down began to whine in a broken voice:

'What? O King of Persia! Why? O Pyramid of Grace! Colossus of Mercy! wherefore? I am old and hungry and wretched—I have helped you; is this how you show your gratitude towards me?'

'As you did towards the Christians,' replied Vinicius.

And so saying he called his steward.

Chilon clutched convulsively at Vinicius' knees, and his face became deadly pale:

'Master, master! I am old! Give me fifty, not three hundred! Fifty will do! A hundred, not three hundred! Mercy, mercy!'

Vinicius shook him off and repeated his order. In an instant two stalwart Germans laid hold of Chilon by the little hair which remained to him, threw his own rags over his head, and dragged him off to the slaves' dungeon.

'In the name of Christ!' cried Chilon from the door.

Vinicius remained alone. The order that he had just given had excited and revived him. He was now trying to marshal and arrange his scattered thoughts. He was immensely relieved, and his victory over himself filled him with courage. He seemed to have taken an important step towards Lygia, and he felt that he would be rewarded in some way. Yet he wondered if Lygia would approve of his conduct towards Chilon. Did not her religion teach forgiveness ? The Christians had forgiven this wretch, and they had far graver reasons for revenge. Only then did that cry, 'In the name of Christ,' sound through his brain. He remembered that it was such a cry that Chilon uttered as he escaped from the hands of the Lygian, and he resolved to excuse him the rest of his punishment.

He was about to summon the steward for that purpose, when the steward himself appeared and said :

'Master, the old man has fainted, and he may be dead. Are we to go on beating him ?'

'Have him revived, and bring him here.'

The man disappeared behind the curtain, but it was no easy matter to bring the Greek round, and Vinicius was beginning to grow impatient when the slaves led Chilon in, and then at a sign from their master withdrew.

Chilon was as white as a sheet, and the blood was running down his legs on to the pavement of the atrium. He fell to his knees, exclaiming :

'Thank you, master ; you are great and merciful.'

'Dog,' said Vinicius, 'know that I pardoned you for the sake of Christ to whom I owe my own life.'

'Master, I will serve Him and you also.'

'Be quiet and listen. Stand up ! You shall go with me and show me the house where Lygia lives.'

'Truly, sir, I am hungry. I will go, sir, I will go indeed, but I have no strength just now. Bid them give me the leavings from the dog's platter, and I will go.'

Vinicius had some food brought to him, and

gave him a piece of gold and a cloak. But Chilon, weakened by his thrashing and his hunger, could not walk even after this meal, although he feared that Vinicius would mistake his weakness for unwillingness.

'Let me have but a drop of wine to warm me,' he said, while his teeth rattled together, 'and I will be able to walk at once—though it were to Greece itself.'

When he had recovered his strength they set out. The road was long, for Linus lived, like most of the Christians, across the river, and his house was near Myriam's. At last Chilon pointed out to Vinicius a small solitary house, surrounded by an ivy-clad wall.

'There it is, sir.'

'Good,' said Vinicius. 'Now run away, but first of all listen to me. Forget that you were in my service; forget where Myriam and Peter and Glaucus live; forget this house also and all the Christians. You will come every month and see Demas my freedman, who will give you two pieces of gold. But if you continue spying on the Christians, I'll have you whipped to death or handed over to the city prefect.'

Chilon bowed and said:

'I will forget.'

But when Vinicius had turned the corner of the lane and disappeared, he shook his fist after him and cried:

'By Ate and all the Furies! I will not forget.'

Then once again he fainted away.

CHAPTER 11

VINICIUS went straight to Myriam's house, where he found, besides Myriam and her son Nazarius, Peter, Glaucus, Crispus, and Paul of Tarsus, who had recently arrived from Fregellæ.

At the sight of Vinicius, astonishment was depicted on every face.

'I greet you in the name of the Christ you worship.'

'May His name be glorified in all ages.'

'I have learned your virtues and I have experienced your kindness; that is why I come to you as a friend.'

'And we will receive you as one,' replied Peter. 'Sit down, sir, and share our meal; you are our guest.'

'I will, but first hear me. You, Peter, and you, Paul of Tarsus, shall have a proof of my honesty. I know where Lygia is. Just now I stood in front of Linus' house, quite close by. I have rights over her which the emperor gave me, and I possess in my various houses nearly five hundred slaves. So it would be easy for me to surround her hiding-place and seize her, and yet I have not done so, nor do I mean to.'

'And for that the blessing of the Lord will be extended to you, and your heart will be purified,' said Peter.

'In the old days, before I lived among you, I would assuredly have carried her off and kept her by force. But your virtuous qualities and your religion, although I do not profess them myself, have wrought a change in my soul, and I dare no longer to use violence. So I address myself to you, who take the place of Lygia's parents, and I say to you: "Give me her for my wife, and I swear that I will not only not forbid her to avow Christ, but I will set myself to the study of His teaching." '

He held his head high and spoke in a firm voice, yet he was much moved, and his legs trembled below his cloak girded tight round his waist. His words were received in silence, and he went on as though to avert an unfavourable reply:

'I know the obstacles, but she is the apple of my eye ; and although I am not yet a Christian, I am neither your enemy nor Christ's. Another might perhaps say, "Baptize me." I say, "Enlighten me." The thought that Lygia is pure as the snow on the mountains makes me love her all the more, and when I think that she owes this to your faith, then I love that faith and long to know it. They tell me your religion pays no heed to life, to human joys, to happiness, to the laws and to the power of Rome. Is it really so ? Tell me what it is you have to offer. Is it a sin to love, to be joyful, and to wish for happiness ? Are you enemies to life ? Must I give Lygia up ? What is this truth of yours ? I've heard it said too: Greece produced wisdom and beauty, Rome power, but what have they produced ? So tell me what it is. If behind your doors there is light, then open them to me.'

Peter replied:

'We bring you love.'

And Paul of Tarsus added:

'Even if I spoke all the languages of men and angels, without love I should be no more than sounding brass.'

The old apostle's heart was touched by this tortured soul, yearning like a caged bird towards the light, and he stretched out his hands to Vinicius.

'Knock, and it shall be opened unto you. The grace of the Lord is upon you! So I bless you: I bless your soul and I bless your love, in the Saviour's name.'

Vinicius at these words of benediction sprang towards Peter, and then this descendant of the Quirites, who till lately would not admit a foreigner to be a human being, took the hands of the old Galilean and pressed them to his lips in gratitude.

Peter was glad, for he saw that his fisherman's line had caught another soul, and those present cried with a single voice:

'Glory to the Lord in heaven!'

Vinicius' face shone with joy.

'I see,' he said, 'that happiness may dwell among you, since I am happy, and I think you will convince me equally on the other points. But that may not be at Rome. The emperor goes to Antium, and I must go also, for I have received his command. You know that disobedience means death. But if I have found grace in your eyes, come with me and teach me the truth. There you will be safer than I shall be. In the middle of the throng you can spread the truth in Cæsar's own court. I have a house at Antium, where I can receive you under Cæsar's very nose, in order to listen to your teaching.'

The Christians thought with joy of this victory for their faith and of the noise that would be made in the pagan world by the conversion of an Augustan, a descendant of one of the oldest families in Rome. Peter was the leader of the whole flock and could not go, but Paul of Tarsus, who had lately been at Aricia and Fregellæ, and who was preparing for a long journey in the East, to visit the churches there and inspire them with fresh fervour, agreed to accompany the young tribune to Antium. Thence he would take ship for Greece.

Although Vinicius was disappointed that Peter, to whom he felt so grateful, could not come, he thanked Paul heartily, and then turned to the old apostle to make one last request.

'Since I know where Lygia lives,' he said, 'I might go myself and ask her, as is fitting, to be my wife, when I am turned Christian, but I prefer to ask your permission to see her—or to take me to her yourself. I know not how long I may have to stay at Antium and in Cæsar's company; nobody can answer for the morrow. Let me see her before I go; let me feast my eyes upon her and learn from her whether she will forget the wrong I have done her, and make us happy together.'

Peter smiled kindly:

'Who could refuse you so reasonable a pleasure, my son?'

Vinicius bent again to kiss his hands, for he could not master his emotion, and the apostle put his hands on his head, saying:

'Go, and do not fear Cæsar. Verily, I say unto you, not one hair of your head shall be harmed.'

Then he sent Myriam to find Lygia, bidding her not to say who was with them.

The distance was short, and soon Myriam appeared among the myrtles of the little garden, leading Lygia by the hand.

Vinicius would have run to meet her, but at the sight of her dear face, joy paralysed his limbs and he stood still, with his heart beating furiously, a hundred times more dismayed than when he first heard the arrows of the Parthians whistle about his ears.

Now she was in their midst, her face pale and flushed by turns, and fear in her anxious eyes.

She saw only joyful and kindly looks, and the apostle Peter went up to her and said:

'Lygia, do you love him still ? '

For a moment there was silence. Her lips trembled like those of a child about to cry, when forced to confess some fault.

'Reply,' said the apostle.

Then, falling at Peter's feet, she whispered in a humble and timid voice:

'Yes.'

Already Vinicius was on his knees beside her. Peter laid his hands on their heads, saying:

'Love one another in our Lord and for His glory, for there is nothing sinful in your love.'

CHAPTER 12

IN the little garden Vinicius told the maiden in words that came from his heart what a moment before he had confessed to the apostles. He told her of his distress of mind, the changes he had undergone, and the great sorrow that had overcast his life since he had left Myriam's house. He had loved her when he saw her in Aulus' house and at the palace ; he loved her when he saw her at the Ostrianum listening to Peter's words ; he loved her when she watched by his bedside and when she left him. Chilon had just told him where she lived and advised him to carry her off, but he had chastised the Greek, preferring to seek the truth from the apostles and ask for her hand. A blessed moment it was when this inspiration came to him, for now he was near her, and she would never run away from him again.

'But it was not you I ran away from,' said Lygia.

'Why then did you run away?'

She lifted her light blue eyes to him, and then with head bent she replied:

'You know why.'

Overcome by the excess of his joy Vinicius could not clearly explain his feelings to her. Nor could he indeed understand them himself. But he felt that with her there came a new beauty into the world, which was no mere beauty of form, but a beauty of the soul.

He took her hand in silence; he looked at her in an ecstasy of delight; and he repeated her name as though to assure himself that he had found her again and that he was near her.

'O Lygia, Lygia!' he said.

Then he asked her what her own feelings were, and she confessed that she had been in love with him when she was in Aulus' house, and that if he had taken her back to it from the palace she would have told them of her love and tried to appease their anger.

'When Paul of Tarsus shows me the truth,' said Vinicius, 'I will be baptized and return to Rome; I will regain the friendship of Aulus' family, and there will be no further obstacle. Then I will come for you and take you to my home. My darling! My darling!'

Lygia looked up at him with happy eyes, and replied:

'Then I will say: " *Ubi tu Gaius, ego Gaia.*"'

They paused beneath a cypress, near the entrance to the house. Lygia leant against the trunk, while Vinicius said in a trembling voice:

'Bid Ursus go to Aulus' house and bring your belongings and the toys you used to play with to my house.'

Blushing red as a rose or as the morning sun, she replied:

'It is not the custom to do so.'

'I know; the bridesmaid should bring them after the bride, but do this for me. I will take them to Antium with me, and they will remind me of you.'

Clasping his hands he continued:

'Pomponia will return some day soon. Do this for me angel; do it, darling!'

'Well, let Pomponia do it if she thinks right,' said Lygia, blushing still more at the thought of the bridesmaid.

Once again they fell silent, overcome by their love of each other. Lygia was leaning against the cypress, her pale face standing out in the shadow like a flower. Her eyes were downcast and her throat rose and fell rapidly, while Vinicius' face grew paler and his expression changed. In the stillness of the noonday they heard their hearts beating, and their ecstasy turned the cypress, the myrtle bushes, and the arbour into a garden of love.

But Myriam now came to the door and invited them to come and share their meal. They sat between the apostles, who looked at them with delight, seeing in them the new generation which, after their own generation was gone, would continue to sow the good seed.

Peter broke bread and blessed it. There was peace on every face, and a mighty joy filled the room.

'See now,' Paul said at last, turning to Vinicius, 'whether we are enemies of life and happiness.'

Vinicius replied:

'Never have I been so happy as with you.'

CHAPTER 13

THAT same evening, as he was passing through the Forum on his way home, Vinicius noticed at the opening of the Vicus Tuscus the gilded litter of Petronius borne by eight Bithynian slaves. Signalling to them to stop, he came up to the curtains.

' I wish you pleasant and fortunate dreams,' he cried, laughing, when he saw Petronius asleep inside.

' Oh, it's you,' said Petronius. ' Yes, I was dozing ; I spent the night at the palace, and I was going to look for something to amuse me at Antium. What news ? '

' You are making a round of the bookshops ? ' said Vinicius.

' Yes, I don't want to disarrange my library. I'm told there's something new by Musonius and Seneca. I've been to Aviranus, to Atractus at the Argiletum, and before that I saw the Sosii in the Vicus Sandalarius. By Castor ! how sleepy I am ! '

' You've been at the palace ? Then it is I who should ask you for news ; or, rather, send away your litter and your books and come home with me. We'll talk about Antium and about something else as well.'

' Very good,' replied Petronius as he left his litter. ' We set out for Antium the day after to-morrow. Be prepared. The peas in olive oil and the scarf round his great neck have not protected Nero, for he has grown hoarse. Yesterday he wanted to rival Paris. He gave us in a dance the adventure of Leda, and that made him sweat ; then he caught cold. He was as wet and sticky as an eel just out of the water. He was changing his masks every moment, turning round like a top, and waving his arms about like a drunken sailor. He was a disgusting sight with that great belly of his and his spindle legs. He's going to give this pantomime in public, first at Antium and then at Rome.'

' It was bad enough his singing in public, but to think that a Roman emperor should appear on the stage as an actor! No, Rome will never stand it.'

' My dear boy, Rome will stand anything, and the Senate will vote their thanks to the " Pater Patriæ." Indeed the crowd likes to have an emperor for a buffoon.'

' Is it possible to sink lower than this, I wonder.'

Petronius shrugged his shoulders.

' You live at home deep in your meditations, now upon Lygia, now upon the Christians. It is no wonder that you don't know what has happened these last few days. Nero has publicly married Pythagoras. Nero was the bride. That looks like the crowning madness, doesn't it ? Well, the priests came and solemnly united them, and I was present at the ceremony. I can stand a good deal, but I did say to myself that the gods, if there are any, should have given some sign then. But Cæsar does not believe in the gods, and he is right.'

' So he unites in one person the high priest, the god, and the atheist,' said Vinicius.

' Exactly,' said Petronius, laughing. 'What a trinity! And what a world it is! It matters little. Will you allow me to send your litter to fetch Eunice ? My sleepiness is gone and I want to enjoy myself. Get your harpist to play while we eat, and then we can talk about Antium. We must give the thing some thought, you especially.'

Vinicius bade his slaves go for Eunice, but he

declared he had no wish to give himself a headache talking about Antium.

'The world does not end at the Palatine,' he said; 'especially for those who have other things in their hearts and their souls.'

He said this so carelessly and gaily that Petronius looked at him and said:

'What has happened to you? Here you are today just as though you were fresh from school.'

'I am happy,' replied Vinicius; 'and it was to tell you so that I invited you to come home with me.'

'What has happened to you?'

'Something I would not exchange for the whole Roman Empire.'

He leant back in his chair, put his arm behind his head, and began to talk, his face beaming with joy:

'Do you remember the day we went together to visit Aulus? There you saw for the first time a divine girl, whom you yourself likened to Aurora and the springtime. Do you remember that Psyche, that incomparable creature, fairer than all the maidens in earth or heaven?'

'What language is this you're talking? Of course I remember Lygia.'

'I am going to marry her.'

'What?'

Vinicius sprang from his seat and called his steward.

'Summon all the slaves here: every one of them, and at once.'

'You're going to marry her?' Petronius repeated.

Before he had recovered from his astonishment, the huge apartment swarmed with slaves.

Vinicius turned to Demas his freedman.

'All who have been in my service for twenty years

will appear tomorrow before the prætor and receive
their liberty. The rest will receive three pieces of
gold each and double rations for a week. Give
orders in the country to remit all punishments, to
unshackle all the prisoners and have them properly
fed. This is a joyful day for me, and I want
happiness throughout the house.'

The slaves were silent for a moment, as though
unable to believe their ears ; then all hands were
uplifted and every mouth exclaimed:

' Aah, aah, master ; aah!'

Vinicius signed to them to leave him, and despite
their desire to fall at his feet and thank him, they
all hurried out, filling the house from top to bottom
with rejoicings.

' Tomorrow,' said Vinicius, ' I'll gather them all
in the garden and get them to trace whatever signs
they like in front of them. All who trace a fish shall
be set free by Lygia.'

Petronius, who never wondered at anything for
long, had already recovered his self-possession:

' A fish ? Oh, I remember ; Chilon told us that
was the Christians' symbol.'

He stretched out his hand to Vinicius and added:

' Happiness lies always where each man sees it.
May Flora strew your path with flowers for many a
year. I wish you all you can wish yourself.'

' I thank you. I thought you were going to blame
me, and you would have been wasting your time,
you know.'

' I blame you ? Not at all ; on the contrary, I say
you are doing well.'

' Ah, weathercock!' replied Vinicius, ' so you've
forgotten what you said to me that day when we left
Græcina ? '

' No ; but I've changed my opinion. My dear

197

fellow, everything changes at Rome; husbands change their wives and wives their husbands, so why should I not change my opinion? But let me ask you one thing: are you a Christian already?'

'Not yet, but Paul of Tarsus is coming with me to explain Christ's teaching. Then I shall receive baptism. It is not true to say they are enemies of life and joy, as you said.'

'All the better for you and Lygia,' said Petronius. Then shrugging his shoulders, he went on, as though speaking to himself:

'The skill of these people in making converts is amazing. And how they are spreading!'

'Yes, there are thousands and tens of thousands in Rome, in the Italian cities, in Greece, and in Asia. There are Christians in the legions and among the Prætorians, aye, and in Cæsar's palace. Slaves and citizens, rich and poor, the mob as well as the aristocrats, profess the faith. Who knows? perhaps, in a month or a year hence, you may be converted yourself.'

'I!' said Petronius. 'No, by Latona's son! that I will not, though their religion contained all truth and wisdom, human and divine! It would mean exertion, and I don't care to exert myself; it would mean self-denial, and I don't care to deny myself anything in the world. Your ardent and impetuous nature makes such an event as this no surprise, but I have my precious stones, my cameos, my vases, and I have Eunice. I do not believe in Olympus, but I have one of my own here on earth. I shall strive to flourish until the arrows of the divine archer transfix me, or until Cæsar sends me the command to open my veins. I am too fond of the scent of violets and of a well-furnished dining-room. I have even a liking for the gods—as ornaments of rhetoric.

I like Achæa, too, for which I am about to set out in company with our big-bellied friend of the thin legs, the incomparable and divine Cæsar-Augustus, Periodonices, Hercules, Nero——'

He broke off, for a slave came to announce Eunice.

Supper was immediately served, and after they had listened to the lyre for some time, Vinicius told Petronius about Chilon's visit.

Petronius, again overcome by sleepiness, put his hand to his forehead and said:

' The idea was a good one, had you been sure of such a result. As for Chilon, I would have given him five pieces of gold ; but once you had ordered him to be beaten, you should have seen that he died under the lash, for perhaps some day the senators may bow before him as they do today before Vatinius, our knight of the bradawl. Good-night.'

Petronius and Eunice laid aside their wreaths and took their leave. Vinicius went to the library, and wrote as follows to Lygia :

' I want you, my angel, when you open your lovely eyes, to find a morning greeting in this letter. That is why I write tonight, although I am to see you tomorrow. Cæsar is setting out for Antium in two days, and I, alas, must go with him. As I said, disobedience would endanger my life, and now I should not have courage to die. Still, if you do not want me to go, one word and I remain here. Petronius will have to see then to averting the danger from me. On this joyful day I have given presents to all my slaves, and all who have been with me twenty years will be freed tomorrow by the prætor. You, my darling, should be pleased with me for that, as it seems to be in accordance with the religion you profess. I did it for your sake, and I will tell them they owe their freedom to you, so that they may honour your name. I, on the other hand, desire to become the slave of happiness and a slave to you, and I hope I shall never be freed. A plague on Antium and Cæsar's visits! Thrice happy am I not to have Petronius' learning, for then, perhaps, I might have to go to Achæa also. But the thought of you will sweeten the hours of absence for me. As often as I can get free, I will mount my horse and gallop off to Rome to feast my eyes with the sight of you and my ears with the sound of your sweet voice. When I cannot come I will send a slave with a letter and with instructions to bring me news of you.

'I greet you, my angel, and I throw myself at your feet. Do not be angry if I call you angel. If you forbid it, I will obey, but today I know not what else to call you. I send you greetings from the threshold of the house that will be yours, greetings with all my heart.'

CHAPTER 14

IT was known at Rome that the emperor was to go first to Ostia, and proceed thence by the shore road to Antium. Orders had been issued some days in advance, and so from early morning there began to gather at the Ostian Gate a crowd of onlookers, in which the Roman mob rubbed shoulders with representatives of every nation in the world.

Cæsar was in the habit of taking with him on his travels all the objects that he loved to have around him, and even at his shortest halt he could erect about him a familiar array of statues and mosaics. So, in moving from place to place, he was accompanied by a whole host of servants besides the companies of Prætorian Guards, and besides his friends and their own trains.

At daybreak Campanian shepherds had brought in five hundred she-asses, in order that on her arrival next day at Antium, Poppæa might be able to have her daily bath in their milk. The mob was delighted with the sight of a thousand long ears flapping among the whirl of dust, with the sound of the whips and the wild cries of the herdsmen.

Behind the asses came a crowd of young slaves, who swept the road and strewed it with flowers and pine needles. The crowd grew denser as the morning went on. Some had brought their families with them, and spreading their provisions on the foundation stones of the new temple of Ceres, ate their meal there. Here and there people formed themselves into groups and discussed the emperor's departure, his next journeys, and the subject of travelling in general. Old soldiers and sailors were giving marvellous accounts of the countries which they had heard of in their distant wanderings, and in which no Roman had ever set foot. City dwellers who had never been farther than the Appian Way listened open-mouthed to fabulous tales about India and Arabia; about the island off Brittany, where Briareus chained up the sleeping Saturn; about the regions of the Far North; about the seas of ice, and about the roaring of the waters of ocean when the sun sinks to rest in them.

Now came the mounted Numidians of the Prætorian Guard, their dark faces reflecting the golden sheen of their helmets, the points of their lances gleaming as though on fire. Then the procession began.

First of all came wagons loaded with tents of red, purple, and white, Oriental carpets, furniture, kitchen utensils, cages containing birds whose brains or tongues would be served at the imperial table, jars of wine, and baskets of fruit. Such things as might come to harm in the wagons were carried by foot-servants, some of whom bore statuettes of Corinthian bronze, others Etruscan vases, others Greek vases, others vases of gold and silver, or of Alexandrian glass. Small squadrons of guards, mounted or on foot, separated the groups of porters, and each group was watched by men armed with lead- or iron-loaded whips. This procession of slaves carefully bearing the precious objects resembled some solemn religious procession, and the likeness was enhanced by the appearance of the musical instruments—harps, Grecian, Hebrew, and Egyptian lutes, lyres, citharas, flutes, conchs, and cymbals. Surely some Apollo or Bacchus setting out on his travels! Then came acrobats and dancing women, thyrsus in hand, riding in splendid chariots; and after these came the slaves whose duty it was to minister to their masters' passions, young boys and girls from Greece and Asia Minor, with long curls imprisoned in gold hair nets, and faces thickly smeared with grease to protect their complexions from the winds of the Campagna.

Another company of guards followed; shaggy, fair-haired Sicambrians, blue-eyed, and heavy of foot, preceded by standard-bearers bearing aloft the Roman eagles, the standards of victory, the statues of German and Roman gods, and the emperor's bust.

In the next chariots were cages of lions and tigers

tamed by clever trainers, and used by Nero to draw
his car when he desired to imitate Dionysus. They
were held by Hindoos and Arabs in steel chains
completely hidden by flowers. The beasts looked
around them with their sleepy green eyes, from
time to time lifting their mighty heads to sniff the
rank odour of the crowd.

Then more imperial chariots and litters, a squadron
of Prætorians composed entirely of Italian volun-
teers, a great number of well-groomed slaves and
young boys, and lastly Cæsar himself.

The apostle Peter, desirous of seeing Nero, was
standing in the crowd along with Lygia, who wore
a thick veil, and Ursus, whose strength was a sure
guarantee of the girl's safety. The Lygian took a
large stone meant for the new temple of Ceres, and
brought it to the apostle, who stood upon it, the
better to view the procession.

At first the crowd grumbled when Ursus pushed
his way through them like a ship through the waves ;
but when they saw him lift the block of stone which
four of the strongest men there could not have
moved, they applauded him.

There sat Cæsar, in an open car drawn by six
Idumean stallions, alone, save for two deformed
dwarfs squatting at his feet. He wore a white tunic
and an amethyst toga, which gave a bluish tinge
to his face. He was noticeably fatter since his
departure from Naples. A double chin made his
face fuller, so that his lips, always too close to his
nose, seemed now to open beneath his very nostrils.
He wore round his enormous neck a kerchief which
he was constantly adjusting with a fat hand covered
with red hair that looked like smears of blood. He
refused to have these hairs taken out, as he had
been told that this might cause a trembling of the

fingers, which would have prevented him from playing the lute. Boundless vanity was depicted on his features, together with *ennui* and weariness. The picture which he presented was at once fearsome and grotesque.

He was greeted with shouts of, 'Hail, godlike Cæsar! Hail, conqueror! Hail, peerless one! Son of Apollo,' and he smiled with pleasure. But now and then somebody, all unaware how prophetic was his jesting, would mar the universal welcome with: 'Brazenbeard! Brazenbeard! what have you done with your fiery beard? Were you afraid it might set Rome on fire?'

Cæsar paid little heed to these salutations, for he had shaved off his beard, and offered it to Jupiter Capitolinus. But some others, hidden behind heaps of stones and behind the courses of the temple, shouted out: 'Matricide! Orestes! Alcmæon!' Others called out: 'Where is Octavia? Give up that purple cloak!' Poppæa, who came immediately behind, was greeted with cries of 'Yellow head!'—a name given to prostitutes. Nero's sharp ear heard these insults too, and he put his polished emerald to his eye, as though looking for the offenders, to make a note of them. His eye lighted upon the apostle, standing on the stone.

Their eyes met, and thus for one fleeting moment the two rulers of the world were face to face; he who was about to vanish like some bloody apparition, and that other, the old man in the rough woollen garments, who was to take possession of the city and of the whole world for all time.

Immediately behind Cæsar came eight African slaves, carrying a magnificent litter, in which sat the hated Poppæa, wearing, like Cæsar, an amethyst robe, her painted face thoughtful and impassive.

She was followed by a horde of servants of both sexes, and by a string of wagons bearing her dresses and her toilet appliances.

It was long after midday when Cæsar's friends, a long, winding, many-coloured train, began to file past. The crowd smiled in kindly fashion as Petronius passed in a litter, his favourite slave at his side. Tigellinus was constantly rising in his chariot and craning his neck to see if Cæsar was not beckoning to him to join him. Licinius Piso was greeted with applause by the crowd, Vitellius with laughter, and Vatinius with hisses. The court appeared to be endless. Here were Domitius Afer and the feeble Lucius Saturninus; there were Vespasian and his sons, young Nerva, Lucan, Annius Gallio, Quintianus, and a host of women notorious for their luxury and dissolute characters. The brilliant throng seemed to have taken captive the very rays of the sun, and although there was no lack of poor hungry wretches among the crowd, yet the spectacle did not merely provoke their envy—it gave them also a feeling of pride in the might and the unassailable power of Rome, which were the wonder of the whole world.

Vinicius was among the last. Catching sight of the apostle and Lygia, whom he had not looked to see, he sprang from his car.

'You here? How can I thank you, Lygia! God could not have sent me a happier omen. His blessing be upon you! I am saying farewell indeed, but only for a short time. I mean to leave relays of Parthian horses along the road, and each day I am at liberty I will come and spend with you, until I obtain permission to return. Farewell!'

'Farewell, Marcus,' replied Lygia. 'May Christ

go with you, and may He open your heart to Paul's words.'

' My treasure, I hope it may be as you say. Paul prefers to go along with my men, but he is with me here, and he will be my master and my companion. Raise your veil, Lygia, my only joy, that I may gaze upon you before I go. Why have you hidden yourself like this ? '

Raising her veil, and disclosing her radiant face and glorious eyes, she said:

' You don't like it ? '

She smiled with something of a young girl's archness, and Vinicius looked at her in delight.

' No,' he replied, ' for my eyes long to gaze upon you until I die.'

And to the astonishment of the crowd, the distinguished courtier raised the hands of this humble girl to his lips.

' Goodbye.'

He set off at a smart pace, for the imperial retinue was now some distance ahead. The apostle Peter blessed him with an almost imperceptible sign of the cross.

Demas the miller, with whom Ursus worked at night, now approached them. He kissed the apostle's hand, and begged him to come with his friends and refresh themselves in his house, which, he said, was close to the Emporium.

They ate some food and rested awhile in Demas' house, and then, when evening came, they set off for the other side of Tiber. Desiring to cross the river at the Æmilian bridge, they went along the Clivus Publicus, which traverses the Aventine between the Temple of Diana and the Temple of Mercury. From this eminence the apostle looked out over the neighbouring buildings and those which were all but lost in the distance. He reflected on the size and power of this city, where he was come to teach the word of God. He had seen the Roman legions in the various countries which he had visited, but there they were but the scattered members of this mighty voice that seemed to him to-day for the first time to be symbolised in the features of Cæsar. This city, corrupt to the core, and yet unassailable; this emperor, murderer of his brother, his wife, and his mother, with as many spectres as courtiers in his train; this mountebank and debauchee, who ruled the world with his thirty legions; these courtiers clad in gold and scarlet, uncertain of the morrow, and yet more powerful than kings: all this seemed to him to be a very kingdom of iniquity. And his simple heart was amazed that God should have entrusted the world to this monster to shape at will, or cast down and trample under foot amid torrents of tears and blood. 'Master,' he said in his heart, 'what can I do with this city, whither thou hast sent me? To her belong land and sea, the beasts of the earth and the beasts that dwell in the waters, and all the kingdoms and cities of the world. Thirty legions protect her. And I, Master, am but a fisherman from the lakeside. What am I to do? And how shall I overcome the forces of evil?'

His prayer was interrupted by Lygia saying:

'You would think the whole town was on fire.'

And, truly, it was no ordinary sunset.

From the place where they stood they commanded a wide view. To the right they saw the Circus Maximus; higher up were the palaces on the Palatine Hill, seemingly piled one upon another, and opposite them, behind the Forum Boarium and the Velabrum, could be seen the Temple of Jupiter upon the Capitol. Walls, pillars, and temple roofs were all

bathed in gold and purple light. Such parts of the
river as they could see appeared blood-red. And as
the sun sank lower and lower behind the Janiculum,
the glow in the sky appeared more and more like
the light of a conflagration. It enveloped the seven
hills and spread over the great plains around.

' You would think that the city was on fire,' Lygia
repeated.

And Peter said :

' It is God's anger hovering above it.'

CHAPTER 15

VINICIUS to Lygia :

' This is from Laurentum, where we have stopped
on account of the heat. Otho used to have a splendid
villa here, which he gave to Poppæa as a present ;
and although she has been divorced since then, she
has found it convenient to retain this gift. So
Cæsar is Poppæa's guest, and she had prepared a
magnificent reception for him without his knowledge. There were only a few of the Augustans
among the guests, but Petronius and I were of the
number. After the feast we went out sailing in
gilded boats on a sea that was blue as your eyes,
my love. We rowed ourselves, as the empress
evidently found it gratifying to have consuls and
the sons of consuls to do her bidding. Cæsar in his
purple toga stood beside the helm, and sang in
honour of the sea a hymn which he had composed
the night before, with music by himself and
Diodorus. In our train were boats filled with
Indian slaves, skilled players on the sea-horn, while

around us gambolled the dolphins, drawn by the music from the depths of the sea. Do you know what I was doing? I was thinking of you and sighing for you, and I longed to take sea, sky, music, and give them all to you. Shall we come some day, my queen, and live beside the sea, far from Rome? I have an estate in Sicily with a forest of almond trees, which in spring are covered with pink blossoms, and which come down so close to the edge of the sea that the ends of their branches almost hang in the water. There I will love you, and there I will live according to Paul's teaching, for I know now that it is not the enemy of love and happiness. Will you come? But before I hear the answer from your dear lips, I will go on with my story about our expedition. When we were some distance from the shore we saw a sail ahead of us, and a discussion at once arose whether it was only a fisherman's boat or a ship from Ostium. I was the first to guess correctly, and then the empress said that nothing escaped my eyes, and covering her face with her veil she asked me if I would recognise her like that. Petronius at once replied that behind a cloud even the sun was invisible, but Poppæa, as though in jest, said that only love could render blind an eye so sharp as mine, and naming several ladies of the court she questioned me, trying to find out which of them I was in love with. I answered her calmly; but at last she mentioned your name, at the same time unveiling her face and looking at me with a mischievous, inquisitive look. I have to thank Petronius for causing the boat to list just then, and so drawing off the general attention from me, for if I had heard anything spiteful or ironical said about you, I could scarce have refrained from breaking the

wicked creature's head with my oar. You remember
what I told you in Linus' house the day before I
left, about my adventure at Agrippa's pond?

'Petronius trembles for me, and he begged me
again today not to irritate Poppæa's vanity. But
he understands me no longer, and he does not see
that, unless in my own Lygia, there is no pleasure,
beauty, nor love for me, and that the empress only
inspires me with loathing and contempt. Here
is something else that will comfort you. At the
moment of my departure Peter told me not to
fear Cæsar, for not one hair of my head should be
harmed, and I have faith in him. A voice keeps
telling me that all his words will come true, and
that, since he has blessed our love, not Cæsar, nor
all the powers of Hades, nor Fate itself, can
wrest you from me, my Lygia. But now, my
darling, the stars are growing pale, and the daystar
is shining clearer and clearer. Soon the dawn will
tinge the waves with pink. Around me all lies
asleep; I alone am awake. I think of you, and I
love you. I greet you together with the dawn, my
beloved.'

CHAPTER 16

VINICIUS to Lygia:

'My darling, have you ever been at Antium
with Aulus? If not, it will be my happiness to
show you this city some day. All along the shore
from Laurentum there are houses, and Antium itself
is one unbroken row of palaces and colonnades. I
have a house here with some olive trees and a little

wood of cypress trees stretching behind it, and when I reflect that some day this house will be yours, its marbles seem whiter to me, its gardens fresher, and the sea a deeper blue. O Lygia, what a good thing it is to be alive and to love! Old Menecles, my steward, has planted the lawns beneath the myrtle trees with great clumps of iris, and they make me think of Aulus' house, with the fountain and the garden where I sat beside you. These flowers will remind you of your home, and so, I am sure, you will be fond of Antium and this house.

'Since our arrival, Paul and I have had long talks as we sat at table. First we spoke of you, then he began his lesson, and even if I could write like Petronius, I could not give expression to all my thoughts and to all that I felt in my heart.

'Tell me how it is that the world contains at one and the same time men like Peter, Paul of Tarsus, and Cæsar. I ask this because of the evening I spent with Nero after hearing Paul's teaching. First of all he read us his poem about the burning of Troy, and complained that he had never seen a city on fire. He was envious of Priam. Whereupon Tigellinus said, "If your Majesty says the word, I will take a torch and show you Antium in flames before morning." But Cæsar treated this as a fool's idea. "Where should I go then," he said, "to breathe the sea air and take care of this voice which the gods have vouchsafed me, and which you all ask me in the name of humanity to treat with care. Isn't it Rome that is harmful to me, and the sickening stenches of the Suburra and the Esquiline that make me hoarse ? And would not burning Rome be a more splendid and tragic sight than Antium in flames ? " This harangue moved all present to ecstasies of admiration. His poem, he declared, should excel Homer, and what a wonderful city it was that he meant to raise for future ages to wonder at. His drunken guests shouted, " Do it ! do it !" He replied, " I should need more faithful and devoted friends." I admit that at first this proposal filled me with anxiety, for you are at Rome, my beloved, but now I laugh at my fears. Mad though they are, Cæsar and his friends would not commit an act of madness such as this : but see how a man trembles for those he loves. I should certainly prefer that Linus' house should not be situated in a little narrow street across the river. Had I my own way, I would not count the palaces upon the Palatine worthy of you : I am so anxious that you should lack none of the luxuries and comfort to which you are accustomed. So return to Aulus' house, Lygia. If Cæsar were at Rome, the news of your return would soon be carried to the Palatine by the slaves. But he will make a long stay here at Antium, and when he arrives home people will have ceased to talk about the Lygian princess. Linus and Ursus can stay with you. And besides, I live in hope that before Cæsar's return you will be living in your own house at the Carinæ. Blessed be the day, the hour, and the moment when you cross my threshold ; and if Christ, whom I am learning to know, hears my prayer, blessed be His name also. I will serve Him and give my life and my blood for Him. I cannot express myself properly ; but we will both serve Him until the thread of life is cut.

' I love you, and I greet you with all my heart.'

CHAPTER 17

URSUS was drawing water at the well, and as he drew up the two buckets attached to the rope he quietly sang to himself a Lygian song. He watched with joyful eyes the figures of Lygia and Vinicius among the cypresses of Linus' garden. A gold and orange light was stealing gradually over the sky, and in the quiet of evening they held each other's hands and talked.

' Will you not come to any harm, Marcus, through leaving Antium without Cæsar's permission ? ' said Lygia.

' No, my love,' replied Vinicius ; 'Cæsar announced that he meant to remain in seclusion for two days with Terpnos, to compose some new songs. Besides, what does Cæsar matter when I am with you and can gaze on you, my beloved—my treasure ? '

' I was sure you would come. Ursus went twice to the Carinæ at my request to ask for news of you. Both he and Linus laughed at me.'

And indeed she had plainly been expecting him, for in place of the dark garment that she usually wore she had put on a dress of a fine white material, from which her head and shoulders stood out like primroses standing up out of the snow. Her hair was decked with pink anemones.

Vinicius pressed his darling's hand to his lips, and they sat down upon a stone seat in the midst of the flowering hawthorn.

' What peace, and what a lovely world it is,' Vinicius said in a low voice. ' I feel happier than ever before. Tell me why that should be, Lygia ?

I never dreamt of a love like this. I thought that love was only fire in the veins and furious desire; and now I see that a man can love with every breath and every drop of blood, and yet feel a sweet and mighty calm, as though he were being rocked and soothed in a cradle by sleep or by Death.'

She hid her sweet face on the young man's shoulder:

'Marcus, my love.'

She could say no more. Thankfulness and joy, and the certainty that now she had a right to love him, made her eyes swim in tears. Vinicius clasped her to him.

She said in a low voice:

'Marcus, I love you.'

Then they fell silent again. The garden was beginning to turn to silver beneath the rays of the rising moon, and at last Vinicius said:

'I know. I had scarce arrived and kissed your dear hands when I read this question in your eyes: "Has the sacred teaching that I honour reached your heart, and are you baptized?" No, I am not baptized yet, but this is why, my darling: Paul told me he had convinced me that God came to earth, and was crucified to save mankind, but that it was Peter's part to purify me at the fountain of grace, for he was the first to bless me. Then I want you, my treasure, to be present when I am baptized, and I want Pomponia to be my godmother. That is why I am not yet baptized, though I believe in our Saviour and His gentle teaching. What sort of man should I be if I did not long to see truth prevail over lying, love over hate, goodness over crime, faith over treachery, and long-suffering over revengefulness?'

Lygia fixed upon Marcus' eyes her own eyes of blue, that looked in the moonlight like some mystic flowers, and which were dew-laden like flowers.

'Yes, Marcus, your words are true,' she said, as she nestled more closely against her lover's shoulder.

At that moment they both felt supremely happy, for they saw that they were joined by another power than love, a power at once gentle and unyielding, causing love itself to last for ever.

'You will be the soul of my soul and my most precious possession,' said Vinicius in a choking and uncertain voice. 'Our hearts shall beat as one. To think, dearest, that we shall live together, worship our sweet Lord together, and know that after death our eyes will open again as after a happy dream, to behold a new light! Speak but one word, and we will leave Rome and go and live far away.'

Her head on her lover's shoulder, she replied:

'Yes, Marcus. You spoke to me of Sicily. It is in Sicily that Aulus and his family mean to spend their old age.'

'Yes, darling, we are neighbours there. It is a wonderful coast and the climate is milder and the nights calmer than at Rome. Over there life and happiness are one.'

They both remained silent, thinking of the future. He pressed her ever closer to him. In the houses around, inhabited by a population of poor workmen, all was silent.

'And I shall see Pomponia ?' Lygia went on.

'Yes, my beloved. We will invite them to our house, or we shall go to them. Shall we take the apostle Peter with us ? He is broken-down by age and hardships. Paul will come and see us also. He will make a convert of Aulus Plautius, and we will found a colony, like soldiers—a colony of Christians.'

'I love you,' said Lygia.

He bent his lips to the girl's hands. For a moment they heard nothing save the beating of their hearts. There was not a breath of wind and the cypresses stood motionless and silent.

Suddenly the silence was broken by a deep rumbling that seemed to come from beneath the earth. Lygia shuddered.

'The lions roaring in their dens,' said Vinicius.

They listened. The first roaring was answered by a second and a third, and by many more. Sometimes there were in the city several thousands of lions in the dens of the various arenas, and often at night they came and put their muzzles to the bars and uttered their dismal howls. They were giving tongue to their longing for the desert, and their roars, echoing through the stillness of night, made the whole city resound.

Lygia listened, her heart weighed down by an unreasoning fear.

Vinicius threw his arms around her.

'Fear nothing, my beloved. The time of the games is at hand, and so all the beasts' dens are full.'

They went back into the little house, while the animals roared on ever more fiercely.

CHAPTER 18

AT Antium Petronius was winning almost daily victories over the other friends of Cæsar who were striving to curry favour with him. The influence of Tigellinus was completely gone. At Rome he was the indispensable man when it was necessary to crush those who seemed dangerous and to pillage their property, to handle a political crisis, to organise exhibitions, or to minister in any way to the grotesque caprices of Cæsar. But at Antium Cæsar lived in a Hellenic atmosphere. From morning to night there was reciting of verses and discussion as to their composition: music and the theatre were the general occupations, and everything that the genius of Greece has thought of to beautify existence. Under such conditions Petronius, immeasurably superior to Tigellinus and the other courtiers in refinement ; witty, eloquent, and full of subtle ideas, was bound to take the lead. Cæsar courted his society, showed anxiety for his good opinion, asked his advice, and displayed warm friendship towards him. The whole court considered that his supremacy was established.

Petronius, with his habitual indifference, seemed to attach no importance to his position, and remained witty and sceptical. People often thought that he was laughing at them, at himself, at Cæsar, and at the whole world. Sometimes he ventured to criticise Cæsar to his face, and then, when everybody thought him as good as lost, he would suddenly soften his criticism in such a fashion as to make it redound to his advantage and render his position still more secure.

One day Cæsar was reading to his intimate friends a passage from his Troiad. When he had finished amid enthusiastic applause, Petronius, at a questioning look from him, said :

' They would do well enough to kindle the fire with.'

His hearers were thunderstruck.

Terror gripped the hearts of all, for Nero had never before heard such a verdict from any lips. Tigellinus was overjoyed, while Vinicius turned pale, thinking that Petronius, who was never drunk, had taken too much this time.

In a honeyed voice, that trembled nevertheless with the mortification of a wounded vanity, Nero said:

'And what do you find wrong with them?'

Petronius replied, pointing to his audience:

'Do not believe them, they know nothing about it. You ask me what is wrong with the verses? If you want the truth, here it is: they are good enough for Virgil, for Ovid, and even for Homer, but not for you. You had no right to compose them. This conflagration that you sing of has not flames enough; your fire does not burn fiercely enough. Do not listen to Lucan's flattery. Such verses from him, and I would allow he was a genius; but not from you, for you are greater than all of them. We have a right to ask for more from one who has received all the gifts the gods can bestow. But you are giving way to indolence. You rest after the morning meal when you should be hard at work. And so I say it to your face, since you can produce a work to surpass all others: "Make better verses than these."'

He spoke as though he thought his words of no account, mingling reproach with jest, but in Cæsar's eyes stood tears of joy.

'The gods have given me some talent,' he said, 'but they have given me more than that: they have given me a born critic as the one friend who dares tell me the truth to my face.'

With that, Cæsar stretched his red hairy hand towards a golden candlestick, part of the plunder of Delphi, in order to burn his verses.

But Petronius snatched them from him before the flame touched the papyrus.

'No, no,' said he, 'unworthy of you though they are, these verses still belong to humanity. Give them to me.'

'Well, let me send you them in one of my own little boxes,' replied Cæsar, as he embraced Petronius.

'You are right,' he added. 'My Troy burns with a timid flame. Still, I thought that it would do if I equalled Homer, but you have opened my eyes. Do you know why I am at fault ? A sculptor who wants to fashion the statue of a god looks for and finds a model, but I had no model ; I never saw a city on fire.'

'In that case, it is the work of a great artist to imagine the scene as you have done.'

Nero thought for a moment, and then said:

'Answer me one question, Petronius. Are you sorry Troy was burned ? '

'Sorry ? By the bandy-legged spouse of Venus, I am glad. Troy would not have been burned if Prometheus had not given fire to mortals and the Greeks had not declared war upon Priam. Now, had there been no fire Æschylus would not have written his Prometheus, just as Homer would not have written his Iliad but for the war. And I hold the Prometheus and the Iliad of more account than the existence of a little town, probably squalid and miserable, which nowadays would at best be ruled by some wretched procurator who spent his time in endless bickerings with the local council.'

'That is sensible talk,' said Cæsar. 'We have the right, nay the duty, to sacrifice everything to poetry and art. O lucky Achæans, to furnish Homer with the theme of his Iliad, and lucky Priam to see the ruin of his country! And I—I have never seen a city in flames!'

A silence ensued, broken at length by Tigellinus:

'I said before, O Cæsar, give the command, and I will set fire to Antium. Or, should you grudge these mansions and palaces, I will set fire to the ships at Ostia; or else I will have a wooden city built upon the Alban Mountains and you can set it ablaze yourself. Will you allow me ?'

Nero cast upon him a look of contempt:

'What, would you have *me* gaze upon burning wooden sheds ? Your brain is withering up, Tigellinus. And, moreover, you plainly do not appreciate my talent, nor this Troiad of mine, since you think them unworthy of any greater sacrifice.'

Tigellinus turned pale, while Nero, as though anxious to change the subject, went on:

'It is summer now, what a stench there will be in Rome! And yet we must go back for the summer games.'

'Cæsar,' said Tigellinus abruptly, 'when you dismiss your friends, allow me a moment's private audience.'

An hour later Vinicius left the imperial residence with Petronius.

'You terrified me for a moment,' he said. 'I thought you were drunk and that you were lost for good. Don't forget that you are playing with death.'

'That is my arena,' Petronius replied carelessly, 'and I am pleased to think I make a good gladiator. This very evening my influence has increased. If I were firmly set on it, I could ruin Tigellinus, and supplant him as prefect of the guards. Then I should hold Brazenbeard himself in the hollow of my hand. But it would mean too much worry: I still prefer my present way of life—in spite of Cæsar's poetry.'

CHAPTER 19

NERO was playing and singing a hymn, composed and set to music by himself, in honour of the Queen of Cyprus. He was in good voice ; he felt that his hearers were enchanted, and this added such power to his singing and lulled his imagination so pleasantly, that he seemed like one inspired. In the end he turned pale with real emotion. For what was undoubtedly the first time in his life he did not care to listen to the flattery of his audience. He remained seated for a moment, his hands resting on his lyre, and his head bent: then suddenly he rose and said:

'I am tired, and I want fresh air. Have my lyre tuned just now.'

He wrapped a silk scarf round his neck.

'Come with me,' he said, turning to Petronius and Vinicius, who were seated in a corner of the room. 'You, Vinicius, give me your arm, for I feel weak. Petronius shall talk music to me.'

They found themselves now on the terrace, tiled with alabaster and strewn with crocuses.

'It is easier breathing here,' said Nero. 'My heart is sad and anxious, although I feel that after what I sang to you by way of trial I can appear in public and score such a success as never Roman did before.'

'You could appear here or at Rome or in Achæa. I admired your performance with all my heart and soul, most godlike Cæsar,' replied Petronius.

'I know that. You are too lazy to take the trouble

of flattering me. And, like Tullius Senecio, you are sincere ; but you are a far better judge than he is.'

For a moment there was silence, broken only by the sound of their feet upon the crocuses.

' This is a night for confidences,' said Nero, at last, ' and so I will open my heart to you, my friend. Do you think me blind or crazy ? Do you think I do not know of the insulting writings on the walls at Rome ? that I do not know that men call me my mother's murderer, murderer of my wife, monster and executioner, because Tigellinus has obtained some death sentences against my enemies ? So widespread are the stories of my cruelty that sometimes I wonder whether I am not cruel. But they do not see that a man's actions may sometimes be cruel though the man himself is not. Nobody, perhaps not even you, my dear friend, will believe that at times, when my soul is soothed by music, I feel as innocent as a babe in the cradle.'

' People do not know you as I do,' said Petronius ; ' Rome has never learned to appreciate you.'

Cæsar leant more heavily on Vinicius' arm, as though drooping beneath a load of injustice, and said :

' Tigellinus tells me that it is whispered in the Senate that Diodorus and Terpnos play the lyre better than I do. Tell me your honest opinion, for you always speak the truth ; do they play better, or do they play as well as I do ? '

' Certainly not. You have a more delicate touch, and yet greater power. In you we recognise the artist, while they have merely clever fingers. After hearing their playing we realise how much yours is worth.'

' If so, they may live on. They will never suspect the service you have rendered them. Besides, if I condemned them, I should have to replace them.'

'And then people would say that from love of music you were wiping out music in your empire. Never sacrifice art for the sake of art, most sacred majesty.'

'What a difference from Tigellinus,' Nero replied. 'But, you see, I am essentially an artist, and since music opens up for me an infinitude of boundless prospects, I owe it to the gods to explore them. Now, in order to gain admission to the realms of Olympus must I not perform some great act of propitiation ? I am charged with being mad. I am not mad, but I want——'

He put his mouth to Petronius' ear, and said in a low tone so that Vinicius might not hear:

'On the threshold of the unknown world I desired to offer the greatest sacrifice a man could offer. Hence my mother's death and my wife's. But that was not enough. To open the gates of the empyrean a more awful sacrifice is needed. May the word of the oracles come true.'

'What is your plan ? '

'You shall see ; you shall see sooner than you think. Meantime you must know that there are two Neros: he whom men know, and he whom you alone know ; the artist, who slays like Death, and sometimes riots in frenzy like Bacchus—but only out of contempt and loathing for things which should be exterminated. How mean a thing life will be when I am gone! What a burden for a man to be a genius and be ruler of the world!'

'My whole heart goes out to your sufferings, O Cæsar, and land and sea unite with me in sympathy ; not to mention Vinicius, who worships you with all his soul.'

' I have always loved him too,' said Nero, ' though he is a servant of Mars and not of the Muses.'

' Above all, he is a servant of Aphrodite,' replied Petronius.

Then suddenly he determined to set his nephew's affairs in order.

' He is as much in love as Troilus was with Cressida,' he said. ' Allow him, sire, to return to Rome, else he will waste away here under my very eyes. Do you know that the Lygian hostage you gave me has been found ? I did not tell you about it as you were composing your hymn, which is more important than all else. Vinicius wanted to make her his mistress, but as she proved to be as virtuous as Lucrece, he became enamoured of her virtue and now desires to marry her. She is of royal birth, so he is not demeaning himself. But he is every inch a soldier, and so he sighs, and droops, and groans, and yet awaits his emperor's permission.'

' The emperor does not choose his soldiers' wives, so what need for permission ? '

' I told you, sire, of his dedication to your worship.'

' Well, then, I give permission. She is a pretty girl, though her hips are too narrow. Her Majesty brought an accusation against her of having terrified our child in the gardens on the Palatine.'

' And I pointed out to Tigellinus that the gods are not affected by witchcraft.'

' I remember.'

Then turning to Vinicius he said :

' Are you as much in love as Petronius says ? '

' Yes, I love her, your Majesty.'

' Well, I bid you leave for Rome to-morrow ; marry her, and do not appear again before me without a wedding ring.'

'I thank you, sire; with all my heart and soul I thank you!'

'How pleasant it is to make people happy,' said Cæsar. 'I wish I had no other task.'

'Grant us one other favour, most sacred Majesty,' said Petronius; 'and express your will in the presence of the empress. Vinicius would not dare marry a wife whom she had any grievances against, but one word from you, to say you had ordered it so, will overcome all her scruples.'

'I could refuse nothing to you and Vinicius,' said Cæsar.

With that he returned to the house, while they followed him, rejoicing in their success.

In the atrium young Nerva and Tullius Senecio were amusing the empress with their chatter. Terpnos and Diodorus were tuning their lyres. Cæsar went and sat down upon a seat inlaid with tortoise-shell, and after whispering some words in the ear of a young Greek page, he paused.

The page returned with a little gold box, from which Nero took a necklace of large opals.

'Here are jewels worthy of the occasion,' he said.

'They gleam like heralds of the dawn,' said Poppæa approvingly, certain that the necklace was meant for her.

Cæsar toyed a moment with the iridescent stones.

'Vinicius,' he said, 'present this necklace from me to the Lygian princess whom I have bidden you marry.'

Poppæa shot astonished and angry glances at Cæsar, at Vinicius, and then at Petronius. But Petronius was bending carelessly over a harp, passing his hand round the frame as though studying the lines of it.

Vinicius, having expressed his thanks for the gift, went over to Petronius.

'How can I prove my gratitude for all you have done for me to-day?'

'Offer Euterpe a couple of swans, praise Cæsar's singing to the skies, and laugh at omens. I hope the lions' roaring will not disturb your sleep again, nor your fair Lygian flower's.'

'No,' Vinicius replied. 'I am quite easy now in mind.'

'May fortune favour you then! But stop: Cæsar is taking up his lyre again. Hold your breath, listen, and let your tears flow!'

And indeed Nero had now risen, his lyre in hand and his eyes upturned to heaven. Conversation had ceased in the room, and all present remained motionless as though turned to stone. Only Terpnos and Diodorus, who were to accompany Cæsar, kept turning their heads, now towards each other, and now towards Cæsar, awaiting the first notes of the song.

Suddenly there was uproar and shouting in the vestibule ; the curtain was raised, and the emperor's freedman Phaon appeared, followed by the Consul Lecanius.

Nero frowned.

'I crave your pardon, most sacred majesty,' said Phaon in a panting voice, 'but Rome is on fire. The greater part of the town is in flames!'

Everybody rose in haste, and Nero laid aside his lyre, exclaiming :

'Ye gods! I am to see a city on fire then, and so finish my Troiad!'

Then, turning to the consul, he went on :

'If I leave at once, shall I arrive in time to see the fire?'

'Sire,' replied the consul, pale as a sheet, 'the city is one sea of flame, the people are falling down suffocated, or throwing themselves into the fire in their frenzy. Rome is lost, sire!'

There was a silence, interrupted by Vinicius exclaiming: 'Woe is me!'

And throwing aside his toga, he dashed from the palace.

Nero raised his arms to heaven and cried: 'Woe unto you, sacred city of Priam!'

PART III

CHAPTER 1

SCARCELY pausing to bid a few slaves follow him, Vinicius leapt on his horse, and, galloping in the darkness through the deserted streets of Antium, he made for Laurentum. He rode on with his head close to his horse's neck, clad only in his tunic, never looking ahead of him and heedless of all obstacles.

His Idumæan stallion sped along like an arrow. Here and there the sound of its hoofs on the pavement aroused a dog that barked awhile at the mysterious apparition, and then took to howling at the moon. The slaves who galloped behind Vinicius on less fleet horses were outdistanced. Alone he passed through sleeping Laurentum, and turned towards Ardea, where, as at Aricia, Bovillæ, and Ustrinum, he posted relays of horses.

Beyond Ardea it seemed to him that the sky to the north was glowing red. It might be the light of dawn, for the July night was already waning, but Vinicius was unable to suppress a cry of rage and despair, for he thought this must be the glow of the conflagration. He remembered the words of Lecanius, ' The city is one sea of flame,' and for an instant he thought he would go mad, for he had lost all hope of saving Lygia, and even of arriving at the city gates ere Rome was in ashes. His thoughts flew ahead of him like a flock of dark birds of ill omen. He did not know in what part of the city the fire had broken out, but he imagined that the Trans-Tiber district, with its houses huddled together, its wooden stores, and its rickety slave-dealers' sheds, must have been the first to fall a victim to the flames.

The thought of Ursus and his colossal strength flashed across Vinicius' mind, but what could a man or even a giant do against the devastating power of the flames ? It was said that for years the slaves in their hundreds of thousands, had been dreaming of the times of Spartacus, and were only awaiting a chance to take up arms against their oppressors and against the city. And now such a chance had come. Perhaps the glow of the conflagration would be shed upon scenes of massacre and civil war.

He remembered recent conversations in which Cæsar, with strange persistency, had harped upon cities that had been destroyed by fire. Undoubtedly, he had given orders to set fire to Rome. He alone would have ventured to plan such a crime, as only Tigellinus would have dared to carry it out. And if it was by his command that Rome burned, might not this same command have hurled the Prætorians, sword in hand, upon the crowd ?

At that moment a horseman, riding like the wind, called out as he passed Vinicius : ' Rome is lost! ' The word ' gods ' also reached Vinicius' ears, but the rest was drowned in the noise of the horses' hoofs. This word, however, restored him to his senses. The gods! He raised his head, and, stretching out his hand to the starry sky, began to pray :

'It is not to you whose temples are crumbling in the flames that I pray, but to Thee, O Lord! Thou hast suffered, too, and Thou alone are merciful! Thou alone hast understood human suffering! Thou camest to earth to teach men mercy. Show Thou mercy to me now! If Thou art such an one as Peter and Paul say, save my Lygia. Take her in Thine arms, and bear her out of the flames. Thou canst do it! Give her back to me and I will give Thee my blood. If Thou wilt not do it for me, do it for her sake. She loves Thee, and has faith in Thee. Thou has promised life and happiness after death, but she is sure of happiness after death, and she does not want to die yet. Let her live. Thou canst, if Thou art willing.'

He ceased his prayer, which he felt was becoming threatening and sacrilegious, and lashed on his horse more violently than ever. The white walls of Aricia, situated half-way from Rome, glistened before him in the moonlight.

His horse stumbled, and then, checked by the firm hand of its rider, sank back upon its haunches in front of the inn where Vinicius had a relay waiting. The slaves bustled about while Vinicius, seeing a detachment of ten mounted Prætorians, doubtless bound for Antium with the news, hastened to meet them.

'Which part of the city is on fire ? ' he said.

'Who are you ? ' the decurion replied.

'Vinicius, military tribune and Augustan. Answer, as you value your life!'

'The fire broke out, sir, among the booths beside the Circus Maximus. When we were sent off, the heart of the city was in flames.'

'What about parts beyond the river ? '

'They are unharmed so far, but the fire is

spreading to new parts every minute with irresistible force.'

A new horse was brought for Vinicius, and he leapt into the saddle. Passing on his right Alba Longa and its beautiful lake, he made for Albanum. After Aricia the road lay over a steep slope which entirely shut out all view of the horizon. But Vinicius knew that when he reached the top, behind which nestled Albanum, he would see not only Bovillæ and Ustrinum, where horses awaited him, but also Rome. Beyond Albanum the flat expanse of the Campagna lay stretched out on either side of the Appian Way.

' I shall see the flames from there,' he told himself, and once again he whipped up his horse.

But now night had given way to morning, and all the heights around were tinged with the gold and rosy light of dawn, which might have passed, too, for the glow of the conflagration. Vinicius hastened on towards the top, and then he saw.

The valley was overhung with one vast cloud which swallowed up cities, aqueducts, houses, and trees. Nothing was to be seen save this gray motionless pall, and away in the distance beyond it, the city upon its seven hills, one mass of flames.

But the fire did not rise in a column as from a single burning house. It was rather a long, wide belt of flame. Above it rose a bank of smoke, here dense black, there tinged with pink or blood-red, heaped up in swollen masses, which rolled heavily about each other. And this broad riband of fire and this bank of smoke shut out the horizon as would a belt of forests. The Sabine Hills were no longer to be seen.

At first sight it seemed to Vinicius as though not only the city but the whole world were being devoured by the flames, and that nobody would escape from this ocean of fire and smoke.

After passing through Albanum, where the whole population was perched upon roofs and trees to obtain a view of Rome, he recovered his self-possession. Besides Ursus and Linus, the apostle Peter was looking after Lygia. From the moment when Peter had blessed his love and had promised Lygia to him, she was safe from the flames. Before he arrived at Ustrinum he was forced to slow down because of the congestion on the road. Side by side with the foot passengers carrying bundles of clothes upon their backs were horses and mules loaded with baggage, along with carts and litters. Ustrinum was so full of fugitives that it was no easy matter to force a way through them. The Forum, the colonnades of the temples, and the streets swarmed like an ant-heap. Here and there tents were being put up for the shelter of whole families. Many were encamped in the open, crying out, calling upon the gods or cursing their fate. In the midst of this mob it was difficult to obtain information. Those whom Vinicius spoke to made no reply, or else, turning terror-stricken eyes upon him, declared that the city was about to perish and with it the whole world. Every moment saw the arrival from Rome of fresh crowds of men, women, and children, who increased the confusion and uproar.

Already gladiators and slaves of every nationality had begun to pillage the houses, and to fight with the soldiers told off for the protection of the inhabitants.

Junius the senator, whom Vinicius saw standing near the inn in the middle of a troop of Batavian slaves, was the first to give him exact information about the fire. In point of fact, it had broken out near the Circus Maximus, at a point not far from the Palatine and the Mons Cælius, but it had spread with such amazing rapidity that it had invaded all the heart of the city.

'And the district across the Tiber ? '

Junius looked at him in amazement.

'What does that matter to you ? '

'It matters more than all Rome put together!' exclaimed Vinicius passionately.

'You can hardly get to it except by the Via Portuensis, for in the direction of the Aventine you would be suffocated in the smoke. I don't know ; probably the fire had not got that length when I left, but the gods alone can say if it is burning now.'

Vinicius was already urging his horse along the Appian Way.

In front of him lay the city, throwing out a terrible heat, and above the din made by the crowd he could hear the crackling of the flames.

CHAPTER 2

USTRINUM with all its confusion gave but a faint idea of what was taking place beneath the walls of Rome itself.

There was no longer any heed paid to the majesty of the law, to the dignity of the public services, to family ties, or to distinction of classes. Here were slaves mauling citizens, there were hordes of gladiators drunk with wine stolen from the Emporium, striking terror to the heart of free-born Romans, knocking them down, trampling upon them and robbing them. Numbers of barbarians awaiting sale as slaves had escaped from their sheds. For them the fire meant the end of their slavery and the hour of vengeance, and so, while true-born Romans were stretching forth their hands in despair towards the heavens, these wretches fell upon them, robbing the men and outraging the women. They were joined by numbers of slaves actually in service, miserable creatures whose only garment was a woollen waist-cloth, who never appeared by day in the streets, and whose very existence in Rome it was difficult to credit. This mob of Asiatics, Africans, Greeks, Thracians, Germans, and Britons was now revenging itself for all those years of slavery, and was giving voice to its rage in all the languages of the universe.

Vinicius saw that he would have to return towards Ustrinum, leave the Appian Way, cross the river below the city, and join the Via Portuensis, which leads directly to the Trans-Tiber district. But this itself was no easy task. He would have required to force a passage at the sword point, and he was unarmed.

But near the Fountain of Mercury he noticed a centurion with some dozens of Prætorians defending the approach to the temple enclosure. Vinicius bade the centurion go with him, and he, recognising a tribune and an Augustan, dared not refuse.

After many a scuffle, and by dint of clambering over boxes, barrels, costly furniture, kitchen utensils, bedding, carts, and litters, Vinicius and his Prætorians succeeded in freeing themselves from the mob. He learnt from some fugitives that only a few lanes across the river had caught fire, but that undoubtedly nothing would escape its ravages, since there were people spreading it intentionally, and preventing it from being extinguished, acting, as they said, under orders. The young tribune had no longer the slightest doubt that Cæsar had commanded the city to be burnt. And what more could Mithridates himself have done, or any other of Rome's most relentless foes ? Vinicius was sure that the hour of doom had struck for Nero, and that the city as it fell in ruins would overwhelm the monstrous buffoon with all his iniquities. And then daring ideas and plans of vengeance crossed his mind. Vinicius' family, who had given the city many a consul, was well known to every Roman, and the mob wanted but a name.

It was already whispered at court that a prophet had foretold the purple for Otho. Was he not as good as Otho? Perhaps Christ himself would help him with His divine power ; perhaps it was He who was inspiring him at that very moment. ' Then,' thought he, ' I should take vengeance on Nero for the dangers Lygia is undergoing, and for my fears about her ; I should bring about the reign of truth and justice ; I should spread the teaching of Christ from the Euphrates to the misty shores of Britain, and I should clothe my Lygia in the purple, and make her queen of all the universe.'

But now he had traversed the Via Portuensis, which leads directly to the district of Trans-Tiber.

The streets here were filled with smoke and crowded with people, through whom it was now even harder to force a passage, since they had more time and were carrying off and saving more of their belongings. The Prætorians who had accompanied Vinicius remained behind. His horse, wounded in the head by a blow from a hammer, reared up and would not obey him. Recognising the Augustan by his rich tunic, the mob broke out into cries of, ' Down with Nero and his fire-raisers ! '

and hundreds of arms were stretched threateningly towards Vinicius. But his terrified horse carried him clear, trampling his assailants under foot. Vinicius saw now that he could not get through on horseback, so he dismounted and began to run. He held close into the walls, sometimes pausing to allow the crowd of fugitives to pass. He kept telling himself that his efforts were useless. Lygia was perhaps no longer in the city, she might have fled. It would have been easier to find a pin on the seashore than to find the girl in this chaos. Yet he was anxious, though it cost him his life, to reach Linus' house. From time to time he stopped and rubbed his eyes. He tore off a piece of his tunic, and covering his nose and mouth with it he pushed on. As he approached the river the heat grew more intense.

Vinicius remembered that Linus' house was surrounded by a garden, behind which a field stretched towards the river, of no great extent, but free of buildings. This thought renewed his courage. The open space might arrest the progress of the flames. With this hope in his heart, he began to run again, though each breath of wind now brought with it not only smoke, but also thousands of sparks that might spread the fire to the other end of the street and cut off his retreat.

At last, through a canopy of smoke, he caught sight of the cypress trees in Linus' garden. The houses situated in rear of the vacant ground were already blazing like heaps of wood, but Linus' little house was still intact. Vinicius cast a grateful glance to heaven, and although the very air was beginning to scorch him, he dashed towards the door, which stood ajar. He pushed it open and vanished inside.

Not a living soul in the little garden ; the house seemed completely deserted.

'Lygia! Lygia!' he cried. There was silence, save for the distant murmuring of the conflagration.

'Lygia!'

Vinicius rushed into the house. The little atrium was deserted. As he groped for the door which led to the bedroom, he noticed the flickering light of a lamp, and drawing near to it he saw the family shrine, where, instead of the images, there was a cross with a taper burning beneath it. Like a flash the idea entered the mind of the young convert that the cross sent him this light to help him in his search for Lygia. So he took up the taper, and ran into the bedrooms. He drew aside the curtain in the first which he entered and looked round.

It, too, was deserted. Vinicius was sure that this was Lygia's room, for her clothes were hanging from nails on the wall, and on the bed lay a capitium, the close-fitting garment worn by women next to the body. Vinicius took it up, pressed his lips to it, and throwing it upon his shoulder, went on with his search. It was a small house, and he had soon searched all the rooms, even to the cellars. There was nobody to be seen anywhere. Lygia, Linus, and Ursus, with the other denizens of the district, must have sought safety in flight. 'I shall have to look for them in the crowd outside the city gates,' thought Vinicius.

The time had come when he must look to his own safety, for the billows of flame were rolling nearer from the direction of the island and the lane was almost enveloped in clouds of smoke. A draught extinguished the taper which he had used in the house. He dashed into the street, and began to run at full speed towards the Via Portuensis, in the direction whence he had come. The fire appeared to pursue him, now enveloping him in clouds of smoke, now covering him with sparks that fell upon his hair, his neck, and his clothes. Parts of his tunic began to smoulder, but to this he paid no heed, and held on his course lest he should be suffocated. He had the taste of smoke and soot in his mouth, and his throat and lungs were on fire. The blood rushed to his head, and at times everything, even the smoke itself, seemed red to him. Then he said to himself, ' The fire is chasing me ; better to lie down and die.' He was distressed with his efforts. His head, his neck, and his shoulders were bathed in sweat that scalded like boiling water. But for thinking continually of Lygia, and but for the capitium to cover his mouth, he would have fallen. He could not recognise the street in which he was, and he ran like a drunken man, staggering from one side of it to the other.

A cloud hid the end of the street. ' If that is smoke,' thought he, ' I cannot get through.' He put forth all his remaining strength, and casting off his tunic, which was already on fire, he ran along naked, with only Lygia's capitium over his head and mouth. When he came nearer he saw that what he had taken for smoke was a cloud of dust from which proceeded the sound of voices talking and shouting.

' Here is the mob plundering the houses,' he said.

But he continued to run in the direction whence the voices came. There were men there at any rate who could give him assistance. With this end in view he began to shout with all his might. It was his supreme effort. The red film before his eyes grew brighter still, he gasped for breath and fell.

But he had been heard, or rather seen, and two men ran up with flasks of water. Vinicius seized one and drank half of it.

' Thank you,' he said. ' Help me to my feet again, and I'll go on alone.'

The other man sprinkled some water on his head, and both carried him towards their comrades. They crowded round him, asking whether he was much hurt. This kindly interest surprised Vinicius.

' But who are you ? ' he said.

' We are pulling down the houses to prevent the fire from reaching the Via Portuensis,' replied one of the workmen.

' You have saved me, and I thank you for it.'

' It is our duty to help our neighbours,' some of them replied.

Then Vinicius, who had seen nothing since the morning save ferocious mobs, fighting and robbing, looked closely at the faces around him and said :

' May Christ reward you.'

' Glory to His name ! ' exclaimed a chorus of voices.

' Linus ? '

But he did not hear the answer, for he had fainted away, worn out by the efforts he had made. When he came to himself, he was in a garden in the Codeta, surrounded by men and women, and the first words which he uttered were :

' Where is Linus ? '

At first there was no reply, and then came a voice that Vinicius knew, saying :

' Outside the Porta Nomentana ; he left for the

Ostrianum two days ago. Peace unto thee, O King of the Persians!'

Vinicius raised himself, then sank back, astonished at the sight of Chilon.

'Have you seen them?' he asked.

'Yes, master. Thanks be to Christ and all the gods if I have been able to do you a fresh service in return for all your kindness. But I will repay all, divine Osiris, I swear it by the flames that are destroying the city.'

Evening was now coming on, but in the garden all was clear, for the conflagration had increased. It looked as though not merely isolated districts were now on fire, but as though the whole city was burning throughout its length and breadth. The sky was red as far as eye could see, and even the shadows of night were red.

CHAPTER 3

THE wreath of fire about the city encrimsoned the heavens as far as the uttermost horizon. The full moon rose in all its majesty and soon was glowing like molten copper. In the red vaults of heaven red stars were twinkling, but, as on no ordinary night, the earth was brighter than the skies.

From the hills on which the city rested, the flames spread in waves over the low-lying parts filled with buildings of five or six storeys: over the streets crowded with shops and booths, with wooden scaffolding hastily run up for various shows, and with stores of clothes, wood, oil, grain, nuts, and fir cones.

The wildest rumours were in circulation at all the

gates. Some said that Vulcan had let loose his
subterranean fires at Jupiter's command; others
that Vesta was avenging the outrage of Rubria;
while others said that it was Cæsar who had set fire
to the city to get rid of the unpleasant odours of the
Suburra and to obtain a clear site for a new city, to
be called Neronia.

While some called upon the gods of mercy, others
cursed those very gods as the authors of the fearful
catastrophe. Old men stretched out their hands to
the Temple of Jupiter Liberator exclaiming:

'You call yourself Deliverer! Then deliver your
own altar and your city!' The people's wrath was
directed specially against the ancient gods of Rome
whose more particular task they thought it was to
guard the city and who yet appeared to be powerless.
And so when a company of Egyptian priests made
their appearance in the Via Asinaria, bearing the
statue of Isis which had been miraculously rescued
from the flames, the crowd yoked itself to the car,
and, drawing it as far as the Appian Gate, set up the
statue in the Temple of Mars, after knocking down
the priests of Mars who ventured to resist them. In
other districts the mob were calling upon Serapis,
Baal, and Jehovah to help them.

Here and there psalms were raised by old men
and young, by women and children—curious, solemn
hymns of mysterious import, with the ever-recurring
words: 'Behold the Judge draws near, in the day
of wrath and of disaster.'

CHAPTER 4

MACRINUS the weaver, to whose house Vinicius had
been taken, washed and clothed him, and made him

eat some food. When he had recovered his strength, the young tribune declared his intention of at once renewing his search for Linus. Macrinus, who was a Christian, confirmed Chilon's statement that Linus, in company with Clement the arch-priest, had gone to the Ostrianum, where Peter was to baptize a number of converts. The Christians of the district knew that two days before Linus had handed his house over to the care of one Gaius.

Chilon proposed to go through the Campus Vaticanus to the Flaminian Gate, where they could cross the river and continue outside the walls and behind the gardens of Acilius in the direction of the Porta Salaria. After a moment's hesitation Vinicius agreed to this course.

Macrinus, who was in charge of the house, procured them two mules which could be used later on for Lygia's journey.

Vinicius and Chilon at once set out towards the Via Triumphalis by way of the Janiculum.

Having passed the Porta Septimiana, they held along between the river and the splendid gardens of Domitia, with their tall cypresses lit up by the conflagration as though in the light of the setting sun.

The road was becoming less crowded, and only occasionally had they to force their way through the stream of country folk that came pouring in towards the city. Vinicius urged on his mule, while Chilon followed close behind, soliloquising thus:

'And still it burns: still it burns! Soon all trace of it will have vanished from the face of the earth. And where is the world to send its grain, its oil, and its good sterling money then? Who will wring money and tears from it then? Marble does not burn, but it crumbles in the fire. The Capitol will

242

fall in ruins, and the Palatine as well! O Zeus!
Rome was the shepherd, the other nations were the
sheep. When the shepherd was hungry he used to
kill one of his flock, eat its flesh, and offer its skin
to thee, O Father of the Gods! Who will do the
killing now, O Cloud Compeller? To whose hands
wilt thou entrust the shepherd's staff?'

'Come on!' cried Vinicius. 'What are you doing
there?'

'Weeping over Rome, master,' replied Chilon—
'so heavenly a city!'

'Where were you when the fire broke out?'

'I was going to visit my friend Euricius, sir, who
had a shop near the Circus Maximus, and I was
settling down to meditation upon the teaching of
Christ, when the cry of fire was raised. When the
flames were sweeping across the whole Circus, and
were beginning to spread, it was high time to think
of saving my own skin.'

'Did you see people throwing torches into the
houses?'

'What did I not see, O Scion of Æneas! I saw
men forcing their way through the mob sword in
hand; I saw battles; and I saw human entrails
trodden underfoot on the pavement. If you had
seen it you would have thought the barbarians had
stormed the city and had started to massacre. All
around me were people howling in despair, but I
saw others howling with joy: for there are many
wicked people in the world, master, who cannot
appreciate the benefits of your merciful rule and
of those just laws that enable you to take everything from everybody and keep it for yourselves!
Men do not know how to bow before the will of
Heaven!'

Vinicius was too deep in his own thoughts to

notice the irony of these words. Although he had asked Chilon a dozen times about all that he could know, he turned once more to him and said:

'So you saw them with your own eyes at the Ostrianum ?'

'I saw them, son of Venus. I saw the maiden, the worthy Lygian, the holy Linus, and Peter the apostle.'

'Before the fire ?'

'Yes, before the fire, O Mithra!'

The suspicion arose in Vinicius' mind that perhaps Chilon was lying. He drew up his mule and darted a threatening glance at the old Greek.

'What were you doing there ?'

Chilon grew uneasy. He imagined along with a host of others that the destruction of the city meant the end of Roman supremacy, but at this moment he was alone with Vinicius, and he remembered Vinicius' terrible threats in case he should spy upon the Christians, especially Linus and Lygia.

'Master,' he said, 'why will you not believe I love them ? For that is the truth. I was at the Ostrianum because I am already half a Christian. I am a poor man, and while you were at Antium, O Jupiter! I often found myself ready to die of hunger in the midst of my books. Then I would go and sit beneath the wall of the Ostrianum, for the Christians, although very poor themselves, give away more in alms than all the rest of Rome together.'

Vinicius thought this explanation sufficient, and he said in a less severe tone of voice:

'And you don't know where Linus was living during these days ?'

'You punished me once before for my curiosity, sir,' replied the Greek.

They were now passing the hills of the Vatican,

glowing red in the glare of the conflagration. They turned to the right at the Naumachia, intending to return to the river, cross over and make for the Flaminian Gate. Suddenly Chilon reined in his mule.

' Master, an idea!' he exclaimed.

' What is it ? ' said Vinicius.

' There has been no edict issued against the Christians, but the Jews have brought accusations against them before the city prefect of being child slayers, of worshipping an ass, and of spreading a religion not recognised by the Senate. They have been attacking the Christians, and making such furious assaults upon their houses with stones that the Christians are hiding from them.'

' Come to the point.'

' This is it. There is no secret about the synagogues across the Tiber, but the Christians are forced to worship secretly, and so they meet in broken-down sheds outside the city, or else in the sand-pits. Now those who live in the Trans-Tiber quarter have chosen the quarries that supplied building material for the Circus of Nero and the houses beside the river between the Janiculum and the Vatican. The city is on fire, and the true followers of Christ are no doubt engaged in prayer. We shall find a large number of them underground, so I advise you to look in there, more especially as it is on our way.'

' But you said Linus had gone to the Ostrianum,' exclaimed Vinicius impatiently.

' I want to look for the maiden where there is a chance of finding her. We shall find them in the tunnels, busy at their prayers. At the very least we shall learn of their whereabouts.'

' Well, lead on,' said the tribune.

Without hesitation Chilon turned to the left. Leaving the Circus behind, they entered a narrow passage plunged in total darkness. But in the darkness Vinicius saw large numbers of twinkling lanterns.

'There they are,' said Chilon.

'Yes,' said Vinicius, 'I hear them singing.'

And indeed from a dark winding passage the sound of psalm singing floated up. The lanterns were vanishing one by one, but new figures were continually coming in from side passages, and Vinicius and Chilon were soon surrounded by a large crowd. Chilon slid from his mule and beckoned to a young boy who was walking beside them.

'I am a priest of Christ—in fact, a bishop,' he said. 'Look after our mules, and you shall have my blessing and forgiveness for your sins.'

The next moment they were in the quarry, and by the dim light of the lanterns they made their way along a corridor, till they came to a large excavation in the rock. It was brighter here than in the corridor, for besides the lanterns and the candles, there were torches burning. Vinicius saw a crowd of people kneeling in prayer, but he could see neither Lygia, Linus, nor the apostle Peter. On the faces of the people were depicted expectation, fear, and hope. The light was reflected in the whites of the eyes which they turned to heaven. Upon their foreheads, deadly pale, the sweat stood in drops. Some were singing hymns, others were feverishly repeating the name of Jesus, others were beating their breasts. All were awaiting the immediate occurrence of some miracle.

Suddenly the singing ceased, and high above the crowd, in a recess which had been formed by the removal of a huge stone, appeared Crispus. His face was wan and haggard. All eyes were bent upon him in expectation of a message of consolation and hope. But after making the sign of the cross over the multitude, he began to declaim furiously in a voice that rose almost to a shriek:

'Repent of your sins, for the hour is come at last. Upon the city of luxury and crime, upon the new Babylon, the Lord has let loose the devouring flames. The hour of judgment, the hour of wrath and of destruction, has sounded. The Lord has said that He will come again, and soon you shall see Him. But not as the Lamb who offers His blood for the remission of your sins ; nay, but as a dread judge, who will do justice and cast the sinner and the infidel into the pit. Woe unto the world and unto all sinners! For they shall have mercy no longer—I see Thee, O Christ!—The stars are falling ; the sun is darkened ; chasms yawn in the earth and the dead arise! And Thou comest to the sound of trumpets, amid the legions of Thine angels, and amid tempests and thunder. I see Thee, O Christ! I hear Thee!'

He stopped, and lifting his head appeared to gaze fixedly upon some terrifying object in the distance. Suddenly the cave resounded with a dull report, followed quickly by a second and a third. Throughout the burning city whole streets of houses were giving way. But most of the Christians took these noises as conclusive proof that the dread judgment day was come. The fear of God fell upon them, and scores of voices were heard, crying: 'The day of judgment! It is come in truth!' Some hid their faces in their hands, convinced that the earth would rock upon its foundations and that from the depths of yawning abysses, monstrous wild beasts would spring out upon the sinners. Others cried out:

' Christ, have mercy! Saviour, be merciful!' Some confessed their sins aloud, while others flung themselves into the arms of their neighbours, that at the dreadful moment they might feel the heart of a friend beating against their breasts. But some faces there were which showed no fear, but only a heavenly joy. There were people in an ecstasy calling out incomprehensible words in unknown tongues. From a dark corner of the cave came the words: 'Ye sleepers, awake!' Then once again the voice of Crispus rang out above the rest, crying:

' Renounce your worldly goods, for the earth will fall away from beneath your feet! Renounce worldly love, for the Lord will cause that man to perish who has loved wife and child more than Him! Woe unto him who has put flesh before spirit! Woe unto the rich man! Woe unto the spendthrift and the libertine! Woe unto men, women, and children——'

The catacomb trembled with a still greater shock, and all fell forward on their faces, crossing their arms to ward off the evil spirits.

The silence was broken by breathless cries of ' Jesus! Jesus!' and here and there by a child weeping. Suddenly a calm voice was heard, saying:

' Peace be among you!'

It was the apostle Peter, who had just entered the cave.

Their terror vanished like the terror of a flock at the approach of its shepherd. They rose up, and those nearest to him clasped his knees, as though seeking refuge under his protecting wings. He stretched out his hands above the anxious throng.

' Why are you troubled in your hearts ? Who

among you can tell what may happen to him before the hour is come ? The Lord sent fire upon Babylon, which had made the world drunk with the wine of its debauchery, but upon you who are purified by baptism, upon you for whose sins the Lamb atoned, upon you shall His mercy be showed forth, and you will die with His name upon your lips. Peace be with you!'

After the imprecations of Crispus, these words from Peter fell like balm upon the crowd. In place of the fear of God, love of Him took possession of their hearts.

From every side came the cry: 'We are thy sheep.' Those who were nearest knelt at his feet, saying: 'Do not desert us in the day of disaster.' Vinicius caught the edge of the apostle's cloak and said, with head bowed down:

'Help me, master. I have searched for her in the midst of the flames and among the mob, but I have found her nowhere. Still I believe that you can restore her to me.'

Peter laid his hand upon Vinicius' head and replied:

'Have faith and come with me.'

CHAPTER 5

THE flames were drawing near the Palatine. Tigellinus had mustered all the guards, and messenger after messenger was sent off to Cæsar, to tell him that he would miss none of the splendour of the scene, as the fire had spread still further. But Nero, who had already set out, had determined not to arrive before nightfall, the better to feast his eyes on the spectacle. He halted, therefore, near Aqua Albana, and calling the actor Aliturus into his tent, he began to discuss with him the question, whether at the words: 'O sacred city, that seemed more firmly stablished than Ida,' he should raise both hands to heaven, or should let one hand fall to his side holding his lyre, while he raised the other to the heavens. Then he asked Petronius whether in his poem about the catastrophe he ought to introduce some splendid blasphemies against the gods ? Did not true art point to such blasphemy as falling naturally from the lips of one who saw the ruin of his country before his eyes ?

At last about midnight he came in sight of the walls, he and his immense following of courtiers, senators, knights, freedmen, slaves, women, and children. Sixteen thousand Prætorians, drawn up along the road in order of battle, guarded his entry into the city. The mob hurled curses at the procession, yelling and hissing, but they did not dare to offer any violence.

At some places, indeed, there was even applause, but this proceeded from such as, having nothing to lose, had lost nothing, and were looking forward to a more than usually generous allowance of grain, oil, clothes, and money. But shouts and hisses, as well as applause, were suddenly drowned by a fanfare of horns and trumpets blown by order of Tigellinus. After passing the Ostian Gate, Nero stopped for a moment, and cried out:

'The homeless sovereign of a people reft of shelter, where shall I lay my unhappy head to-night ?'

Then, after passing the Clivus Delphini, he ascended a specially erected stairway on to the Appian Aqueduct, accompanied by his friends and by the choir of singers with their citharas and lutes.

All held their breaths in expectation of some words of august inspiration from Nero. But he stood solemn and silent, a purple cloak upon his shoulders, gazing fixedly upon the raging conflagration. Then Terpnos handed him his lute, and he lifted his eyes to the fiery sky, as though awaiting inspiration.

From afar the mob pointed at their emperor as he stood there bathed in the blood-red light. Beyond them hissed and crackled the serpents of flame. Buildings both secular and sacred were blazing ; the Temple of Hercules, built by Evander, the Temple of Jupiter Stator, the Temple of Luna, built before the days of Servius Tullius, the house of Numa Pompilius and the Temple of Vesta, containing the penates of the Roman people—all were ablaze. From time to time the Capitol might be made out through the eddying flames. It was Rome's past that was burning. And there stood Cæsar, with his lute and his tragedian's mask ! His thoughts were not upon his native land, whose ruin he was witnessing. He was thinking of his own pose, and of the phrases best suited to the immensity of the disaster.

He raised his hand, and, drawing it across the strings, he broke forth in the words of Priam :

' O nest of my Fathers ! O cradle dear to my heart ! '

In the open air, and beside the din of the conflagration and the murmuring of the crowd, his voice seemed strangely thin, and the muted strings of the lutes sounded like the humming of insects. But senators, officials, and courtiers all bent their heads and listened in a silent rapture. He sang for a long time, and gradually his voice became tinged with sadness. When he paused for breath the singers repeated the last verses in chorus. Then, with a gesture taught him by Aliturus, he threw his actor's robe over his shoulders, struck a chord, and began to sing again.

When the hymn was over, he started to improvise, seeking for majestic metaphors in the picture spread out before him. Gradually the expression on his face changed. The destruction of his native place had not touched him, but so intoxicated was he with the pathos of his own words that his eyes filled with tears. He dropped his lute, which fell ringing at his feet, and wrapping his robe about him he stood as though turned to stone, like one of the Niobides that adorned the court at the Palatine.

The silence was broken by a storm of applause, but this was answered from afar by the savage yells of the mob. Nobody there doubted now that Cæsar had set the city on fire to provide himself with a spectacle and to sing hymns about it. At this cry from hundreds of thousands of throats, Nero turned to his friends with the sad, resigned smile of a man who is the victim of injustice and malice.

'See,' he said, 'how the citizens of Rome appreciate me, and how they love the Muses!'

'The rascals!' replied Vatinius. 'Bid the guard charge them, sire.'

Nero turned to Tigellinus:

'Can I rely on the soldiers' loyalty ?'

'Yes, your Majesty,' replied the prefect.

But Petronius, shrugging his shoulders, remarked:

'Yes, but there are not enough of them. Stay where you are, for this is the safest place ; but the crowd must be appeased at any price.'

Seneca was of the same opinion, as was Licinius the consul.

But now the uproar below grew threatening. The crowd was arming itself with stones, tent-pegs,

boards torn from carts and barrows, and scraps of
old metal of all kinds. Several commanders of
cohorts reported that the guards were finding difficulty in keeping their line unbroken owing to the
pressure of the crowd, and as they had no orders to
attack, they did not know what to do.

' Immortal gods!' said Nero, ' what a night! On
one side the fire, and on the other the unbridled
masses of the populace!'

And he continued searching for words stately
enough to express the danger of the moment, but
when all around him he saw pale faces and anxious
looks, he took fright himself.

' My dark cloak and a hood!' he said. ' Is it really
going to end in a battle ? '

' Sire,' replied Tigellinus in no very confident
tone, ' I have done all in my power, but still there is
danger. Speak to them, sire. Speak to your people,
and make them promises.'

' Cæsar speak to the plebs ? Let somebody speak
in my name. Who will undertake it ? '

' I will,' replied Petronius, exceedingly calm.

' Go, my friend. You are the most faithful in all
my troubles. Go, and be not sparing of promises.'

Petronius turned to Nero's suite with a careless
but ironical look:

' The senators present, along with Piso, Senecio,
and Nerva, will follow me,' he said.

He slowly descended the stairs from the Aqueduct.
Those who had been mentioned hesitated, and then,
reassured by his calmness, followed him.

Petronius stopped at the foot of the arches and
ordered a white horse to be brought to him. This
he mounted, and followed by his companions he
made his way through the serried ranks of the
guards towards the dark howling multitude. He

was unarmed, having in his hand only the thin ivory rod which he usually carried.

When he came close to them, he rode his horse into their midst.

The shouting grew louder still and burst into an unearthly roar ; stakes, pitchforks, and swords were brandished about his head. Hands were violently stretched out towards his horse's reins and towards himself. But he continued on his course, quiet and disdainful.

Occasionally he struck the boldest of them with his rod as though he were making his way through an orderly crowd, and this coolness made an impression on the rabble.

At last he was recognised, and from many voices came the cry :

' Petronius ! The Arbiter of Elegance ! Petronius !'

The cry was taken up and repeated on all sides, and thereupon the faces of the crowd grew less ferocious and their yells less brutal.

Petronius took off his white scarlet-edged toga, lifted it and waved it in the air as a sign that he was going to speak.

' Silence ! Silence !' shouted voices among the crowd.

There was silence at once, and Petronius, straightening himself in his saddle, spoke in a sonorous tone.

' Citizens of Rome ! Let those who hear me repeat my words to their neighbours, and let all behave like men, not like wild beasts in the arena.'

' Yes, yes !'

' Then listen. The city shall be rebuilt. The gardens of Lucullus, Mæcenas, Cæsar, and Agrippina shall be thrown open to you. Tomorrow there will be the first distribution of corn, wine, and oil, so that every man of you will be able to fill his belly up to the neck. After that, Cæsar will give you games such as the world has never seen, and during the games you shall have feasts and largesse. You will be better off than before the fire.'

He was answered by a murmur that spread like the circles in a pond when a stone is thrown into the water. Those nearest him repeated his words to others farther off, and soon wrathful or approving cries here or there were drowned in one mighty shout:

' *Panem et circenses.*'

Petronius imposed silence with outstretched hand, and said:

' Yes. I promise you bread and games.'

Speaking thus, he turned his horse about, and lightly tapping on head or face those who barred his path, he carelessly made his way towards the ranks of the Prætorians.

Those upon the Aqueduct had not understood the shout of *Panem et circenses*, which they mistook for a fresh outburst of fury. In fact, they never expected to see Petronius return, and when Nero saw him he ran to meet him at the top of the steps.

' Well ? What's happening down there ? Are they fighting ? '

Petronius drew a deep breath or two.

' By Pollux!' he said, ' how they sweat and stink! Give me some strong scent or I shall faint!'

Then he turned to Cæsar and said:

' I promised them corn, oil, games, and access to the gardens. They are worshipping you again, and shouting in praise of you with their cracked lips. Immortal heavens, what an obnoxious smell the plebs have!'

' The Prætorians were ready,' exclaimed Tigellinus, ' and had you not appeased them, their squalling would have been silenced for all eternity. What a pity, sire, that you would not allow me to use force!'

Petronius looked at him a moment, shrugged his shoulders, and said:

' You have lost nothing. To-morrow, perhaps, you may have occasion for it.'

' No, no,' said Cæsar. ' I will have the gardens opened to them, and corn distributed. I thank you, Petronius. They shall have their games, and I will sing in public the hymn I sang you this evening.'

Speaking thus, he laid his hand on Petronius' shoulder, and after a pause he said:

' Tell me honestly, how did I appear to you ? '

' Worthy of the occasion, as the occasion was worthy of you,' replied Petronius.

Then turning towards the burning city, Nero said:

' Let us gaze once more upon it, and say farewell to the old Rome.'

CHAPTER 6

THE apostle's words had restored confidence to the hearts of the Christians. One by one they left the catacombs and returned to their temporary homes. Some of them even made their way towards the region across Tiber, for it was rumoured that the wind was now setting towards the river and that the fire had ceased to spread.

Peter, in company with Vinicius and Chilon, also left the cave. People crowded to kiss the apostle's hands and the hem of his garment; mothers held up their children to him, while others knelt in the dark passage, and lifting their lamps towards him implored his blessing; others again followed him singing. They came to an open space where they could already see the burning city, and the apostle, having thrice made the sign of the cross over Rome, turned towards Vinicius, and said:

'Fear not! The quarryman's hut is close at hand. We shall find Lygia there with Linus and her faithful servant. Christ, who destined her for you, has saved her for you.'

Vinicius turned so faint that he fell at the apostle's feet, and clasping his knees remained thus, motionless and unable to utter a word.

The apostle, in order to check his expressions of gratitude and devotion, said:

'Not to me, but to Christ!'

'Truly, a noble deity!' said Chilon, who was behind them. 'But I don't know what to do with these mules that are waiting.'

'Take them back to Macrinus,' replied Vinicius.

Then they turned to the right in the direction of the hills. As they went along Vinicius besought Peter:

'Master, wash me with the water of baptism, that I may call myself a true convert to Christ, for I love Him with all my heart. Baptize me soon, for my heart is ready. All He bids me I will do. Tell me what more I can do.'

'Love your fellow-man like a brother,' replied the apostle, 'for only by love can you serve Him.'

The quarryman's hut was a sort of cave hollowed out in a buttress of rock, and enclosed on one side by a wall of earth and brushwood. The door was shut, but through the opening that served for a

window the interior could be seen, lit up by the
fire. An enormous figure rose to meet the newcomers, saying:

'Who are you?'

'Servants of Christ,' replied Peter. 'Peace be
with you, Urban.'

Ursus bowed himself at the apostle's feet, and
then, recognising Vinicius, he grasped his wrist
and carried his hand to his lips.

'And you are come too, master! Blessed be the
name of the Lamb for the joy you bring to Callina!'

He opened the door and they passed in. Linus,
who was ill, was lying upon a bed of straw, his face
wasted, and his brow yellow as ivory. Lygia was
seated beside the hearth, with a string of small fish
for the evening meal in her hand.

Busy with her task of unstringing them, and
thinking that it was Ursus who entered, she did
not stir. But when Vinicius went up to her, and
opening his arms called to her, she rose quickly
with a look of joyful surprise upon her face, and
without a word, like a child who after days of terror
sees father or mother again, she sank into the young
man's arms. He pressed her fervently to his heart.
Then, taking her temples between his hands, he
covered her eyes and forehead with kisses.

After this he told her about his departure from
Antium, his arrival in Rome, and his search for her
at the city walls and in Linus' house, and about
his sufferings before the apostle told him where
she was.

'But now,' he said, 'now that I have found you
again, I will not leave you here. I will save you—I
will save all of you. My darling, will you come to
Antium with me? We can embark there for Sicily.
My lands are your lands, and my houses your

houses. We shall find Aulus' family in Sicily. I will restore you to Pomponia and receive you again from her hands. You will come, dear love ? You are not afraid of me any longer ? I am not yet washed in the waters of baptism, but ask Peter if I have not begged him to baptize me. Rely on me. Rely on me, all of you.'

Lygia listened with a beaming face. The departure for peaceful Sicily would open up a new era of happiness in their lives. Had Vinicius proposed to take her only with him, she would probably have resisted the temptation, as she was unwilling to leave the apostle and Linus. But Vinicius had said: 'Come with me ; my lands are your lands, and my houses your houses!'

Lygia bent to kiss his hand and said:

'Your hearthstone shall be my hearthstone.'

Then in confusion at having uttered the bride's words she blushed deeply, and stood motionless in the firelight. Vinicius turned towards Peter.

'It was at Cæsar's command that Rome was set on fire,' he said. 'Who can tell whether he will not now have its people massacred by his army ? Who can tell whether after the fire there will not be other trials—civil war, famine, proscriptions, and murders ? '

'The measure is full,' said the apostle. 'The tale of catastrophes to come will be fathomless and illimitable as the sea.'

He pointed to Lygia and went on:

'Take this child whom God has given you and save her. Linus, who is ill, and Ursus will go with you.'

But Vinicius, who had come to love the apostle with all the strength of his passionate nature, exclaimed:

'I swear to you, master, that I will not leave you here to perish.'

'And the Lord will bless you for your goodwill,' replied Peter. 'But do you not know that thrice beside the sea of Tiberias Christ said to me, " Feed my sheep " ? Now if you, who were given no charge over me, say you will not leave me here to perish, how can you ask me to desert my flock in the hour of danger ? '

Linus looked up with his wasted face and said:

'Vicar of God, why should not I follow your example ? '

Vinicius passed his hand over his forehead, struggling with his thoughts. Then suddenly he caught Lygia's hand, and in a voice vibrating with all his soldier's energy he said:

'Listen to me, Peter, Linus, and you, Lygia! I only said what human reasoning prompted me to say. Yes, I was wrong. I did not understand, for the scales are not fallen from my eyes and the old man is not quite dead in me. But I love Christ and I want to serve Him ; so, although here it is a question of something dearer to me than life itself, I kneel before you, and I too swear that I will fulfil the commandment of love, and will not desert my brethren in the hour of disaster.'

So saying he fell upon his knees, stretched out his arms, and cried out fervently:

'O Christ, do I know Thee at last ? Am I worthy of Thee ? '

His hands shook, his eyes glistened with tears, his body quivered in the fervency of his love and faith. Peter lifted a stone jar, and drawing near to him said in a solemn voice:

'I baptize you in the name of the Father and of the Son and of the Holy Ghost! Amen!'

Thereupon a religious ecstasy fell upon them all. The hut shone for them with a miraculous light; they heard the sound of heavenly music; the rocky roof of the cave opened above their heads and a host of angels descended from heaven towards them. And up above in mid-air they saw a cross and two pierced hands that blessed them.

Outside resounded frenzied cries and the crash of houses collapsing amid the flames.

CHAPTER 7

THE people were camping out in the splendid gardens of Domitia and Agrippina, in the Campus Martius, and in the gardens of Pompey, Sallust, and Mæcenas. They had found shelter under the colonnades, in the buildings set aside for ball-games, in luxurious summer mansions, and in the wild beasts' sheds. Supplies arrived from Ostia in such quantities that a man could walk upon the rafts and barges as upon a bridge, from one side of Tiber to the other. Enormous stores of wine, oil, and chestnuts had been ordered. Large numbers of sheep and cattle arrived daily from the mountains.

But Cæsar's generosity did not check the current of vituperation. The only people satisfied were the hordes of cutpurses, thieves, and vagabonds who could eat and drink their fill and plunder without fear of restraint. But those who had lost their dearest friends, and those whose whole fortune had been destroyed, were not appeased by the opening of the gardens, by the distributions of corn, nor by the prospects of games and money.

In spite of the assurances of his lickspittle

courtiers, and in spite of Tigellinus' lies, Nero reflected with dismay that in his secret, deadly struggle against the Senate and the nobles, the people's support might in future fail him.

His own friends were no less uneasy. Tigellinus thought of summoning the legions from Asia Minor ; Vatinius, who used to smile even though his face were slapped, had lost his good-humour ; and Vitellius had lost his appetite.

Tigellinus took counsel with Domitius Afer, and even with Seneca, whom he hated. Poppæa, well aware that Nero's downfall meant her death, took counsel of her intimates and of the Jewish priests. It was common talk that for several years she had professed the religion of Jehovah. Nero, for his part, put forward suggestions of his own, often shocking in character but more often absurd.

Deliberations took place in Tiberius' house, which had been spared in the conflagration. Petronius thought they should leave their troubles behind and set out on a voyage to Greece, Egypt, and Asia Minor. The proposal had been made long ago : why delay longer ? Cæsar at once fell in love with it, but Seneca objected :

' It is easy to get away, but less easy to return.'

' By Hercules !' replied Petronius, ' we shall return, if need be, at the head of the legions of Asia.'

' I will do it !' exclaimed Nero.

Once more Petronius was to be the man of the moment. But Tigellinus cried out :

' Hear me, Cæsar ! This is disastrous advice. Before ever you reach Ostia civil war will break out, and maybe some doubtful descendant of the divine Augustus will have himself proclaimed emperor.'

' Very well,' replied Nero ; ' we'll see that there's

a shortage of Augustus' descendants. We can easily get rid of the few who are still alive.'

'Yes, quite easily; but there may be danger from others also. Yesterday my soldiers heard it said among the crowd that a man like Thrasea should be made emperor.'

Nero bit his lip.

'An ungrateful and greedy people! They have abundance of corn and abundance of hot ashes for baking cakes with it: what more do they want ? '

'They want revenge,' said Tigellinus.

All were silent, till suddenly Cæsar rose and with uplifted hand declaimed:

> 'Hearts thirst for vengeance, yea, and vengeance thirsts
>   For victims——'

Then, forgetting everything, he cried out with radiant face:

'Bring me my tablets and a pen to write down these verses! Lucan never composed anything like them. And did you notice that I hit upon them in the twinkling of an eye ? '

'O peerless poet!' came the response.

Nero wrote down the verses, and running his eye round the company said:

'Yes, vengeance has need of victims! What if we gave out that it was Vatinius who set fire to the city, and then he could be sacrificed to the fury of the people ? '

'What am I, O divine Majesty ? ' exclaimed Vatinius.

'True. Somebody more important—Vitellius ? '

Vitellius turned pale, but said with a laugh:

'My fat would make the fire break out afresh.'

But Nero was looking for a victim who really

would appease the people's anger. He had found one.

'Tigellinus,' he said, 'it was you who fired Rome!'

A shudder ran through his hearers. They saw that Cæsar had ceased to jest, and that this was a moment big with fate.

Tigellinus' lips curled like those of a dog about to bite.

'Yes,' he said. 'I fired Rome—by your command.'

They stood and gazed fixedly at each other. The buzzing of the flies in the atrium could be heard.

'Tigellinus,' said Nero, 'do you love me?'

'You know I do, sire.'

'Then sacrifice yourself for me.'

'Most holy Cæsar,' replied Tigellinus, 'why do you offer me this sweet draught, when I may not put it to my lips? The populace is discontented and rebellious; would you have the Prætorians rise as well?'

As Tigellinus was Prætorian prefect, these words imported a threat. Nero knew this, and his face became livid.

At that moment Epaphroditus, a freedman of Cæsar's, came to announce to Tigellinus that the empress desired to see him: she had visitors whom she wanted the prefect to see.

Tigellinus bowed before Cæsar and went out, his confidence restored. They had tried to undo him, but he had shown his teeth; and Cæsar was a coward.

Nero was silent awhile, and then, seeing his suite waiting, he said:

'I have taken a serpent to my bosom!'

Petronius shrugged his shoulders as if to say that

it would not be very difficult to wrench that serpent's head off.

'Come, speak, and give me your advice,' Nero exclaimed. 'In you alone have I any confidence, for you have more sense than all the rest put together, and you love me.'

Petronius replied:

'I advise you to set out for Greece.'

'Ah,' cried Nero, disappointed. 'I hoped for better things from you. If I take your advice, who will assure me that the Senate, which hates me, will not proclaim another emperor? The people were once loyal to me, but to-day they would be against me. By Hades, had Senate and people but one head!'

'Allow me to say, sire, that if you want to preserve Rome you must preserve a few Romans,' said Petronius with a smile.

But Nero groaned:

'Oh, what are Rome and the Romans to me? In Greece they would listen to me. Here there is nothing but treason all around me. Everybody is deserting me, and you yourselves are ready to betray me. I know it, I know it! You do not think of the grievance posterity will have against you: that you should have deserted such an artist as I am!'

At this moment Poppæa came in with Tigellinus. Never did a victorious general ascend the Capitol with such pride depicted on his face as Tigellinus showed, when he took his stand before Cæsar and said slowly in a voice clear, yet rasping as iron:

'Hear me, Cæsar, for I have made a discovery. The people desire a victim for their revenge. One victim, did I say? No, but hundreds and thousands. Did you ever hear, sire, of Christos, him

who was crucified by Pontius Pilate ? Do you know
who the Christians are ? I have spoken to you,
I think, of their crimes and their infamous rites ;
and about their prophecies that the world will be
destroyed by fire ? The people already hate them
and suspect them. Nobody has ever seen them
in the temples, for they say that our gods are evil
spirits. They are never seen in the stadium, for
they despise racing. Never has a Christian hand
applauded you. Not one of them ever admitted
your divine origin. They are enemies of humanity ;
enemies of the city ; and they are your enemies!
The people murmur against you ; but it was not
you, O Cæsar, who bade me set fire to Rome, nor
I who did it. The people are thirsting for vengeance ; they shall have their fill. They want
games and blood ; they shall have them. The
people suspect you ; their suspicion shall turn
elsewhere.'

While Tigellinus was speaking, the expression on
the emperor's face changed continually, hovering
between rage and annoyance, between pity and
disapproval. Then suddenly he rose, threw aside
his toga, and stood silent, with both hands uplifted to heaven. At last he broke forth in tragic
style :

'O Zeus, Apollo, Hera, Athene, Persephone and
all ye immortal gods! Wherefore have ye not rescued us ? What has this hapless city done to these
madmen that they should set it ablaze ? '

'They are the enemies of mankind, and they are
your enemies,' said Poppæa.

'Do justice upon them,' came the general cry.
'Punish the incendiaries! The gods themselves
cry out for vengeance.'

Nero sat down and bowed his head in silence,

as though overwhelmed at the sight of an abomination. Then he waved his hands and cried:

'What punishments and what tortures are adequate for such a crime? Still, the gods will inspire me, and with the powers of Tartarus to help me I will set before my poor people such a spectacle that Romans in all ages will speak of me with gratitude.'

Petronius thought of the danger that such a plan meant to Lygia and Vinicius, whom he loved, as well as to all those others whose religion indeed he rejected, but whom he knew to be innocent.

He began to speak, with the nonchalance usual to him when he was criticising or making merry about some ridiculous idea of Cæsar or his friends:

'Yes, hand the Christians over to the people and torture them,' he said, 'but be courageous enough to admit that it was not they who set fire to Rome. By the divine Cleo! Nero, the master of the world —Nero the god it was, who burned Rome, for he was omnipotent on earth as Zeus is in heaven. Nero the poet loved poetry so much that he sacrificed his native land for it! No matter whether the burning of Rome is a thing good or bad: it is a great thing—a thing unparalleled! Beware, Cæsar, of acts unworthy of you. It is only posterity you need consider, and posterity may say: "Nero burned Rome. But coward both as ruler and as poet, he disavowed his great deed, and, like the poltroon he was, cast the blame of it upon innocent folks." '

Petronius was well aware of the consequences involved in the failure of this desperate stratagem. But he had always loved the play of chance and fortune. 'The die is cast,' thought he, 'and now we shall see whether in the soul of this ape fear for his own skin or his love of glory will prevail.'

In his heart of hearts he did not doubt that after all fear would be the stronger.

There was silence. Nero's lips protruded under his nostrils, a sign of indecision in him.

'Sire,' exclaimed Tigellinus, 'let me leave you! You are being urged to expose yourself to the greatest dangers, and at the same time you are being called cowardly emperor, cowardly poet, incendiary, and hypocrite. My ears refuse to hear any more.'

'I have lost,' thought Petronius.

But he turned to Tigellinus, and measuring him with a look that told plainly of his contempt for the rascal, he said:

'Tigellinus, you were the hypocrite I meant, for you are one even now.'

'Because I won't listen to your insults ? '

'Because you pretend to a boundless love for Cæsar, and yet a moment ago you were threatening him with the Prætorians. We all understood it—and so did he.'

Tigellinus, who did not imagine that Petronius would dare play so bold a card as this, turned pale but made no reply. That, however, was to be the arbiter's last triumph over his rival, for then Poppæa exclaimed:

'Sire, how can you endure that such a thought should occur to anybody, or at least find expression in your presence ? '

'Punish him for the insult!' said Vitellius.

Once again Nero's lips curled, and turning his glassy eyes upon Petronius he said:

'So this is the return you make for the friendship I have always shown you ? '

'If I am wrong, show me my mistake,' replied Petronius ; 'but be assured that I only said what my love for you bade me say.'

'Punish him for the insult!' Vitellius repeated.
And all cried out:
'Yes, punish him!'

They moved away from Petronius. Even Tullius
Senecio, his old courtier friend, and young Nerva,
who up till now had shown the liveliest friendship
towards him, moved off. The Arbiter of Elegance
was left alone on the left side of the atrium. He
smiled as with careless hand he arranged the folds of
his toga, waiting for Cæsar to speak.

'You want me to punish him,' the emperor said,
'but he is my companion and my friend. So
although he has wounded my heart, let him learn
that this heart has nought but forgiveness for
friends.'

'I have lost,' thought Petronius, 'and I *am*
lost.'

But now Cæsar had risen: the conference was at
an end.

CHAPTER 8

PETRONIUS returned home, while Nero and Tigellinus went to Poppæa's apartments, where the
people whom the prefect had already seen were
waiting.

These were two rabbis from the Trans-Tiber, clad
in long ceremonial robes and wearing mitres, a young
clerk who acted as secretary, and Chilon. When
Cæsar entered, the priests turned pale with emotion,
and, raising their hands shoulder high, buried their
faces in them.

'You accuse the Christians of setting fire to
Rome ? ' said Cæsar.

'Your Majesty, we only accuse them of being the enemies of humanity, of Rome, and of the emperor, and of having for many a day threatened the city and the world with fire. The rest this man will tell you, whose lips no lie will ever defile, for in his mother's veins there flowed the blood of the chosen race.'

Nero turned to Chilon.

'Who are you?'

'Your servant, divine Osiris, a poor Stoic.'

'I detest Stoics,' said Nero. 'I detest Thrasea; I detest Musonius and Cornutus. Their talk and their contempt for art disgust me, as well as their self-imposed misery and their uncleanliness.'

'Sire, I am a Stoic of necessity. Cover my stoicism, O Radiant One, with a wreath of roses, and set before it a jar of wine, and it will sing Anacreon, this same Stoicism, in a manner that will put the Epicureans to silence.'

Nero, pleased with the title of 'Radiant One,' smiled and said:

'You are an honest fellow!'

'The man is worth his weight in gold!' exclaimed Tigellinus.

'Will your Majesty add of your generosity to that weight?' replied Chilon; 'else the wind will blow away your bounty.'

'Aye, truly, you're not so heavy as Vitellius,' said Cæsar.

'Nay, divine Apollo, my wits are not of lead.'

'I see that your law does not forbid you to address me as a god.'

'Immortal One! you are the law to me. The Christians blaspheme that law, and therefore I hate them.'

'What do you know about them?'

'Will your Majesty allow me to weep ? '

'No,' said Nero, 'I dislike weeping.'

'And you are thrice wise ; for eyes that have looked on you should for ever be free from tears. Defend me, sire, against my foes.'

'Tell us about the Christians,' broke in Poppæa impatiently.

'It shall be as you command, O Isis,' replied Chilon. 'Well, the first Christian my unlucky star brought me in contact with was a doctor at Naples, called Glaucus. From him I came gradually to learn that they worshipped a certain Chrestos, who had promised to exterminate all men and wipe out all the cities upon earth, but to spare them on condition that they would help him in his work of annihilation. That, sire, is the reason why they hate the children of Deucalion, that is why they poison the wells, and that is why they scribble blasphemies all over Rome and on all the temples where our gods are worshipped. Chrestos was crucified, but he promised that on the day when Rome fell he would return to earth and award them the kingdom of the world.'

'Now the people shall learn why Rome was burned,' said Tigellinus.

'Many people know it already, sir,' replied Chilon ; 'for I have been going about the gardens and the Campus Martius telling them. But if you will hear me to an end, you will know why I seek vengeance against them. Glaucus the doctor did not tell me at first that their faith commanded them to hate men. On the contrary, he kept telling me that Chrestos was a kindly deity, and that his teaching was founded upon love. My tender heart was not proof against such doctrines. I came to love and to trust Glaucus. I used to share with him every crust of bread and every penny piece. And do you know how he repaid me? On the road from Naples to Rome he struck a knife in me, and sold my wife, my lovely young Berenice, to a slave dealer. Had Sophocles but known my story! Fool that I am! He who is listening is a greater than Sophocles!'

'Poor man,' said Poppæa.

'He who has looked upon the face of Aphrodite is not poor, most sacred Majesty, and it is her face I gaze on at this moment. When I reached Rome I tried to have speech of their elders, in order to obtain justice against Glaucus. I thought they would compel him to give me back my wife. So I got to know their high priest, and one Paul who was in prison here, though set free later; I knew the son of Zebedee, Linus, Clitus, and many more. I know where they lived before the fire, and where they now hold their meetings; I can show you an underground cave in the Vatican Hill and a cemetery outside the Porta Nomentana, where they perform their disgraceful rites. It was there I saw the apostle Peter. It was there I saw Glaucus slaying children, that the apostle might sprinkle their blood upon the heads of the faithful; and there that I heard Lygia, the adopted daughter of Pomponia Græcina, excuse herself for not having brought any children's blood, by saying that she had at least bewitched the little princess, your daughter, O divine Osiris, and yours, O Isis!'

'Cæsar, you hear?' said Poppæa.

'Is it possible?' exclaimed Nero.

'I could have forgiven the wrongs they did me,' Chilon went on, 'but when I heard that, I longed to put a dagger in her. Unfortunately, the noble Vinicius, her lover, prevented me.'

' Vinicius ?   But she ran away rather than——'

' She ran away, but he searched for her, as he could not live without her.   For a miserable reward I helped him, and it was I who showed him the house where she lived, among the Christians across the Tiber.   We went there together along with Croton your gladiator, whom Vinicius hired for greater safety.   But Ursus, Lygia's slave, strangled Croton.   He is a man of the most fearful strength, sire, a man who could wring a bull's neck as easily as I could twist a poppy stem.'

' By Hercules,' exclaimed Nero, ' the man who strangled Croton should have his statue in the Forum!   But this is either a mistake or a lie, old man, for Croton was stabbed by Vinicius.'

' See how men lie to the gods!   Sire, Ursus crushed Croton's ribs before my very eyes, and then he felled Vinicius.   He would have killed him if Lygia had not intervened.   Vinicius was ill for a long time, but they looked after him, hoping to make a Christian of him by love.   And in point of fact they managed it.'

' To make Vinicius a Christian ? '

' Yes.'

' And Petronius too ? ' Tigellinus asked eagerly.

Chilon wriggled about, rubbed his hands and said :

' I admire your perspicacity, sir ; yes, maybe—it is quite possible!'

' Now I understand his eagerness to defend the Christians.'

But Nero burst out laughing.

' Petronius a Christian!   Petronius turned an enemy of life and its pleasures!   Don't be absurd, and don't ask me to believe that if you want me to believe anything at all.'

'And yet the noble Vinicius is turned Christian. By the glory that emanates from your Majesty, I swear I am telling the truth, and that nothing is so revolting to me as lying. Pomponia is a Christian, so is young Aulus, and so are Lygia and Vinicius. I was his faithful servant, and in return he had me thrashed at the instigation of Glaucus the doctor, although I was old and sick and hungry. And I swore by Hades I would not forget. Sire, punish them for the wrong they have done me, and I will deliver into your hands Peter, Linus, Clitus, Glaucus, Crispus, Lygia, Ursus, and all their elders. I will point them out in hundreds and thousands ; I will show you their houses of prayer and their cemeteries. Your prisons will not be large enough to hold them. In all my troubles till now, I sought consolation in philosophy alone. Let me find it now in the favours that will rain upon me. I am old, and I never knew what it was to live : let me find rest now!'

'You want to be a Stoic, but with a full platter before you ? ' said Nero.

'He who serves you fills his plate at the same time.'

'You're not far wrong, worthy philosopher.'

But Poppæa was not losing sight of her enemies.

'Your Majesty will avenge our child ? ' she said.

'You must make haste,' said Chilon, ' or else Vinicius will have time to hide himself. I will show you the house they went to after the fire.'

'I will give you ten men. Set off at once,' said Tigellinus.

'You did not see Croton in Ursus' hands, sir. Though you give me fifty, I will only show you the house from a distance. Besides, if you don't put Vinicius in prison at the same time, I am done for.'

Tigellinus glanced at Nero.

' Would it not be well, your Majesty, to make an end of uncle and nephew at the same time ? '

Nero thought for a moment.

' No,' he said, ' not at present. Nobody would believe that Petronius, Vinicius, or Pomponia Græcina set fire to Rome. Their houses were too handsome. Today we must find other victims. Their turn will come.'

' Sire, give me an escort of soldiers,' said Chilon.

' Tigellinus will see to that.'

' You will live in my house, meanwhile,' said the prefect.

Chilon's face shone with joy.

' I'll betray them all to you ! But make haste,' he cried in a husky voice, ' make haste !'

CHAPTER 9

On leaving Cæsar, Petronius was taken directly to his house on the Carinæ, which, thanks to the garden enclosing it on three sides, and to the little Forum Cæcilium in front, had escaped destruction.

In thinking over his own position the clear-sighted Petronius saw that he was in no immediate danger. Nero had not let slip the opportunity of uttering some fine high-flown sentences about friendship and forgiveness, which meant that for the moment his hands were tied. He would have to search for a pretext, and it would take him some time to find one.

Thenceforward he thought only of Vinicius, whom

he determined to save. His slaves were hastening through the ruins and the heaps of ashes that still strewed the Carinæ, but he impatiently bade them break into a run. Vinicius, whose mansion had been burned, was living with his uncle, and by good luck he was in the house.

'Have you seen Lygia to-day?' Petronius began by asking.

'I have just left her.'

'Listen to what I am going to say and make your plans at once. It was resolved today at the Palace to attribute the burning of Rome to the Christians. There will be persecutions and torture, and the hue and cry may be raised at any moment. Take Lygia and be off with her instantly to the far side of the Alps or to Africa. And make haste about it, for the Palatine is nearer the Trans-Tiber than this house is.'

Vinicius was too good a soldier to waste time on unnecessary questions. He had been listening with eyebrows drawn, but without alarm. The primitive desire of his nature was the desire to fight.

'I'll go now,' he said.

'Just one word more. Take a purse well filled with gold, arm yourself, and take some of your Christians with you. If you are compelled to do it, carry her off by main force.'

Vinicius was already at the door.

'Send me a slave with news,' cried Petronius.

Once more alone, he began to walk up and down beside the pillars of the atrium, wondering what would come of it all.

His meditations were interrupted by the entry of Eunice, at sight of whom he forgot Cæsar and his disfavour; he forgot the despicable courtiers and the persecution that threatened the Christians; he forgot Vinicius and Lygia, and saw Eunice alone— saw her with the eyes of an artist enchanted with a marvellous form, and with the eyes of a lover for whom this form is instinct with love. In her robe of thin violet gauze, that scarce concealed the rosy pink of her skin, she was divinely beautiful. Well aware of his admiration, loving him with all her heart, and always eager for his caresses, she blushed like an innocent child.

' What is it, O daughter of the Graces ? ' he asked, stretching out his hand towards her.

She bent her golden head towards him and replied:

' Anthemios and his singers have arrived, and he wants to know if you desire to hear him to-day.'

' Tell him to wait; he shall sing us his hymn to Apollo when we are at table. By the groves of Paphos, when I see you in these filmy garments it is as though Aphrodite stood before me veiled in a strip of the skies.'

' O master!' said Eunice.

' Come, Eunice, embrace me and give me your lips. You love me ? '

' I could not love Zeus better.'

And quivering all over, she kissed him on the lips. But Petronius said:

' And what if we had to part ? '

Eunice threw a look of anguish upon him.

' What do you mean, master ? '

' Don't be afraid, but I might be forced to go on a very long journey.'

' Then take me with you.'

Petronius changed the subject and said:

' Are there any asphodels on the garden lawns ? '

'The cypresses and the lawns are all yellow since the fire, the myrtles have lost their leaves, and the whole garden seems to be dead.'

'The whole city seems to be dead, and it will soon be a cemetery. Do you know there is to be a proclamation against the Christians, and that they will be persecuted and killed in thousands ? '

'Why should they punish them ? They are good, quiet people.'

'That is just the reason.'

'Let us go to the sea. Your dear eyes do not love the sight of blood.'

'Yes, but meantime I will have my bath. Come to the anointing room and rub my shoulders. By the girdle of Venus, I never saw you look so lovely. I'll have a bath made for you in the shape of a shell, and you shall be the precious pearl inside. You will come, my darling of the golden locks ? '

An hour later, wearing wreaths of roses and with eyes slightly dimmed, they took their places at a table covered with gold plate, and waited on by youths dressed as Cupids. And as they drank from their ivy-decked cups, they listened to the hymn in honour of Apollo sung to the harps by Anthemios and his singers.

But ere the hymn was over, the slave in charge of the atrium entered.

'Master,' he said, in a voice tremulous with anxiety, 'there is a centurion at the door with a company of soldiers, and he desires to speak with you, by order of the emperor.'

Harps and singers fell silent, and anxiety took hold of the company, for Cæsar did not employ the Prætorians to carry messages to his friends, and their presence at such a time foreboded no good. Petronius alone displayed not the least emotion,

278

merely remarking, like a man annoyed by too frequent invitations:

'They might at least let me dine in peace. But show him in.'

The slave vanished behind the curtain. Next moment was heard a heavy, measured tread, and into the room came the centurion Aper, whom Petronius knew, fully armed and wearing his iron helmet.

'Noble sir,' he said, 'here is a message from Cæsar.'

Petronius carelessly stretched out his white hand for the tablets, and after glancing at them he passed them quite calmly to Eunice.

'He is going to read us some new stanzas of his Troiad to-night, and he invites me to come.'

'I was only told to give you the message,' said the centurion.

'Yes; there is no reply. But perhaps you will rest awhile with us, centurion, and drink a cup?'

'I thank you, noble sir. I will gladly drink a cup to your good health, but I cannot wait, for I am on duty.'

'Why did they give you the writing instead of sending it by a slave?'

'I do not know, sir. Perhaps because I had been sent to this part on other duty.'

'I know,' said Petronius—'to hunt for Christians.'

'Yes, sir.'

'Have they been hunting for them long?'

'There were some detachments sent across the river before midday.'

The centurion spilled a few drops of wine on the tiles in honour of Mars:

'May the gods give you all you desire, sir!'

'Take the cup with you,' said Petronius.

Then he signed to Anthemios to go on with the hymn.

'Cæsar says, "Come if you like," master. Will you go?'

'I am in an excellent temper, and feel equal even to hearing his poetry,' replied Petronius. 'So I mean to go, more especially as Vinicius cannot.'

After dinner he had his hair dressed and his toga arranged, and an hour later, in all his majesty, he set out for the Palatine.

His erstwhile friends, although surprised to see him among the guests, held aloof from him; but, careless and handsome, he made his way into their midst with as much assurance as though he had favours in his gift. Several of them grew uneasy, fearing that they had been over hasty in shunning him.

But Cæsar pretended not to see him, and continued to talk in lively fashion, without replying to his greeting.

Tigellinus, on the other hand, came up to him and said:

'Good-evening, O Arbiter of Elegance; do you still assert that it was not the Christians who set Rome on fire?'

Petronius tapped him on the shoulder as he would have tapped a freedman:

'You know as much about that matter as I do.'

'I would not pretend to compete with you in wisdom.'

'There you are right. For otherwise, when Cæsar reads his new verses of the Troiad, you would find yourself obliged, instead of screeching like a peacock, to give your own opinion, which could not fail to be a ridiculous one.'

Tigellinus bit his lip. He was far from delighted

that Cæsar should have decided to recite this new part of his Troiad today. For this opened up to Petronius a field where he had no rival. And indeed, all through the reading, Nero from long habit kept turning his eyes involuntarily towards Petronius and trying to read his face.

Petronius listened with eyebrows raised, nodding approval now and then and concentrating his attention as though to make sure that he heard aright. Then he praised and criticised, advising alterations, and further polishing of certain lines. Nero himself felt that the rest, with their extravagant praise, had only their own ends in view, and that Petronius was the only one who was interested in the poetry for its own sake, and the only real judge among them. He gradually fell to discussing it with him and arguing with him, and in the end, when Petronius was questioning the appropriateness of certain words, he said:

'You will see why I used this expression when you hear my last verses.'

'Ah,' thought Petronius, 'so I am to hear those last verses!'

More than one courtier who heard Nero's words said to himself: 'Fool that I am! Petronius has some time left him. Perhaps he will return to favour and oust Tigellinus.' And once again they were all smiles to him. But the evening did not close quite so happily, for as Petronius was taking his leave, Cæsar suddenly asked him with a look of wicked joy:

'And why did Vinicius not come?'

Had Petronius been sure that Vinicius and Lygia were clear of the city, he would have replied:

'He has married, by your Majesty's permission, and has left Rome.'

But he noticed Nero's curious smile, and said:

'Your invitation, most sacred Majesty, did not find him at home.'

'Tell Vinicius I shall be glad to see him,' replied Nero, 'and give him my advice not to miss the games, for all the Christians are to take part.'

Petronius was uneasy at these words, which affected him because of what they meant to Lygia. He got into his litter and bade his men go at their utmost speed. A dense yelling mob surged in front of Tiberius' house. They were still drunk, but, far from singing and dancing, they appeared to be furiously angry. In the distance their cries were incomprehensible to Petronius, but they gradually swelled, till they burst forth in a savage roar:

'To the lions with the Christians!'

Fresh gangs of men came running up the ruined streets. From mouth to mouth spread the news that the hunt had been going on from the morning, and that large numbers of the incendiaries had already been captured. In every street, old and new, in ruined lanes, in the neighbourhood of the Palatine, on the hills, in the gardens and throughout all the city, the clamour raged and swelled, ever fiercer and fiercer.

'To the lions with the Christians!'

'Low scum,' thought Petronius, 'but worthy of their emperor!'

He began to reflect that such a people could not last much longer. Rome was the mistress of the world, but she was also the canker at its heart. She smelt of the grave.

'Has the noble Vinicius returned?' asked Petronius on entering.

'He came back a moment ago,' replied the slave.

'So he has not managed to save her,' thought Petronius.

Throwing aside his toga he ran into the atrium. Vinicius was seated on a stool with his head in his hands and his elbows on his knees. At the sound of footsteps on the tiles he lifted up a face in which only the eyes seemed still alive.

' You arrived too late ? ' Petronius asked.

' Yes ; they took her away before midday.'

There was a pause, and then Petronius said :

' Did you see her ? '

' Yes.'

' Where is she ? '

' In the Mamertine Prison.'

Petronius shuddered and looked questioningly at Vinicius, who understood, and said :

' No, she is not in the Tullianum,* nor even in the prison properly speaking. The warder gave up his room to her for a good round sum, and Ursus is lying outside the door, guarding her.'

' Why did Ursus not protect her ? '

' There were fifty Prætorians sent. Besides, Linus would not allow him.'

' And what of Linus ? '

' He's dying ; they did not take him with the rest.'

' What do you mean to do ? '

' Save her or die with her. I also am a Christian.'

Vinicius spoke calmly enough, but there was such a heartrending note of sadness in his voice that Petronius was deeply moved.

' I understand,' he said ; ' but how do you think you can save her ? '

' I paid the warders large sums to prevent them insulting her and to prevent them hindering her escape.'

* A subterranean part of the prison with only an opening from the top. Jugurtha was starved to death here.— *Author's Note*

283

' And when is that to be ? '

' They told me they could not let her out at once, as they were afraid to be detected. But when the prisons are swarming with people, and when they have lost count of the prisoners, then they will hand her over to me. It is a last resort. But by then you will have saved us both, for you are Cæsar's friend. It was he himself who gave her to me. Go and save me!'

Without replying, Petronius called a slave and bade him bring two dark cloaks and two swords.

A moment later they were in the street.

' Now listen,' said Petronius. ' I am in disfavour, and my life itself is hanging by a thread. So I can do nothing with Cæsar. What is more, I am quite sure he would act against my wishes if he could. Otherwise, should I have advised you to run away with Lygia or rescue her by force ? You know that if you had succeeded in escaping, Cæsar's anger would have turned against me. He would sooner do you a favour to-day than me. But think no more about it —it is useless. Get her out of prison, and be off. If that fails, there will still be time to try other means.'

They had now arrived at the Forum, which was not far from the Carinæ. Already the night was beginning to pale, and the outlines of the stronghold were discernible looming up out of the darkness. Suddenly Petronius stopped and said:

' The Prætorians! Too late!'

The Mamertine Prison was surrounded by a double cordon of troops. Their helmets and the ends of their lances gleamed like silver in the first light of morning.

' Come on,' said Vinicius.

When they came up to the ranks, Petronius, who had an excellent memory and who knew not only the officers but also most of the soldiers of the Prætorian Guard, beckoned to one of the leaders of the cohorts.

'What's the matter, Niger ? You're mounting guard round the prison ? '

'Yes, noble Petronius. The prefect feared an attempt to rescue the incendiaries.'

'Have you orders to let nobody pass ? ' asked Vinicius.

'No, sir. Their friends will come to see them, and then we shall catch more Christians in our trap.'

'Then let me pass,' said Vinicius.

At that moment from behind the stone walls and from the very dungeons came floating up the sound of voices raised in song. Hushed at first, they swelled gradually louder and louder. Men, women and children were singing in unison. In the early morning stillness the whole prison had broken into song. These were no voices of sadness and despair ; they were voices that thrilled with a triumphant joy. The soldiers looked at one another in amazement.

Already the sky was tinged with the gold and rosy light of dawn.

CHAPTER 10

THE shout ' To the lions with the Christians ' rang ceaselessly through every street in the city. Nobody doubted that they were the true authors of the calamity, and nobody wanted to doubt it, since their punishment was to furnish a great spectacle. At the same time the belief spread that the disaster would not have assumed such appalling proportions had not the wrath of the gods overhung the city. So expiatory sacrifices were ordered in all the temples.

The whole of Rome was cleansing itself from its sins, sacrificing to the gods and imploring their forgiveness.

Among the ruins new streets of great width were being laid out. Here and there were the foundations of houses, palaces, and temples. But first and foremost were being hurried on the immense wooden amphitheatres where the Christians were to meet their death. Immediately after the council in Tiberius' house the proconsuls had received orders to send wild beasts to Rome. Tigellinus laid violent hands on the menageries of every town in Italy without exception. Cæsar was determined to drown all remembrance of the fire in torrents of blood ; he wanted to make the city drunk with human gore. And never was more glorious slaughter promised.

The people, rendered eager by these preparations, helped the watchmen and the guards in their manhunt. And it was no difficult task, for whole bands of Christians were still camping in the gardens with the rest of the people, and they made no secret of their faith. When they were surrounded, they fell on their knees and gave in without a struggle, singing hymns the while. The prisons were overflowing, and every day the Prætorians and the mob pushed fresh victims within their doors.

Petronius, who could not forget that but for his unlucky device for carrying off Lygia from Aulus, she would still be at liberty, was sparing neither of his time nor his efforts. Within a few days he saw Seneca, Domitius Afer, Crispinilla, whose influence with Poppæa he hoped to gain, Terpnos, Diodorus, the handsome Pythagoras, and finally Aliturus and Paris, to whom Cæsar never refused anything. Chrysothemis was now the mistress of Vatinius, and through her he sought to enlist the latter's support, prodigal in this case as in all the rest of promises and money. But all his efforts were in vain. Seneca, never sure of the morrow, told him that the Christians, even if they had not set fire to Rome, ought to be wiped out for the sake of the city's safety, and that public policy justified such a massacre. Terpnos and Diodorus took his money and did nothing for it. Vatinius complained to Cæsar that an attempt had been made to corrupt him. Aliturus alone, at first hostile to the Christians, was now sorry for them, and he had the courage to speak to Nero on Lygia's behalf. For all reply the emperor said:

' Do you imagine me less stout-hearted than Brutus, who did not spare his own children when Rome's safety was at stake ? '

Petronius, when these words were reported to him, exclaimed:

' Oh, if he has compared himself to Brutus, we're done for.'

CHAPTER 11

Time went on, and the amphitheatres were ready at last. Tickets for the morning games were being distributed.

But on this occasion, by reason of the unheard-of number of victims, these games were to last for days, weeks, and even months. How to dispose of the Christians was now a problem, as fever was raging in the overcrowded prisons. Apprehensive lest the sickness should spread through the city, the authorities determined to hasten matters.

The news reached Vinicius, and bereft him of his last ray of hope. A stony stupor had settled on his features ; his face had turned dark, and resembled one of the waxen masks from the family shrine. When anybody spoke to him, he put his hand to his head mechanically, and looked at the speaker with dull staring eyes. He spent his nights with Ursus at the door of Lygia's cell, and on returning to Petronius' house he walked up and down the atrium till morning. His slaves often found him on his knees with hands outstretched, or else lying face downwards on the ground. He was imploring the help of Christ, for Christ was his last hope.

His mind was still clear enough to know that Peter's prayers would be more efficacious than his own. Peter had promised Lygia to him; Peter had baptized him; Peter could do miracles: let Peter come to the rescue and save him.

He went to the quarryman's house, and learned from the man that a meeting of Christians was to be held in the vineyards of Cornelius Pudens, outside the Porta Salaria. At nightfall they set out, passed through the gate, and traversing some rush-covered hollows, arrived at the vineyards of Pudens.

When he entered the shed, Vinicius saw kneeling there some ten people, the handful of Christians who had escaped capture. A litany was being said, and each moment the chorus of men's and women's voices repeated: 'Christ have mercy upon us!'

Peter knelt in prayer beneath a cross nailed to the wall. Vinicius recognised in the distance his white hair and outstretched hands. He would have picked his way through the people, and thrown himself at the apostle's feet, calling 'Help me,' but the solemnity of the occasion and also his own failing strength caused him to sink to his knees. And so he remained at the door, groaning aloud: 'Christ have mercy upon me!'

All those who knelt around him cherished in their

hearts the idea that Christ was about to show Himself ; that He was about to end their troubles, hurl Nero into the lowest pit, and rule over the world.

Vinicius hid his face in his hands and sank down.

Silence suddenly fell around him, as if terror had paralysed the cries in every throat.

He felt that a miracle was imminent. When he rose and opened his eyes he was sure that he would see the brightness that blinds the eyes of men, and hear the voice that causes hearts to sink.

But nothing broke the silence, till suddenly a woman sobbed aloud.

Vinicius rose and looked wildly around him.

The shed was lit, not by any miraculous brightness, but by the wretched flickering light of the candles, and by the silvery light of the moon that streamed through a chink in the roof. The low whistling of men on the lookout could be heard.

Peter rose, and facing the people, said :

' My brethren, uplift your hearts to the Saviour, and offer Him your tears.'

He was silent. From among the crowd rose a voice, a voice full of bitter complaining and boundless grief :

' I am a widow. I had a son who was life to me. Give him back to me, Master.'

Once more there was silence. Peter, standing there in front of the kneeling group, seemed now the very image of impotent decrepitude. Then another voice wailed :

' These butchers outraged my daughters, yet Christ allowed that !'

A third voice was heard :

' I am all that is left to my children. If they take me, who will give them bread and water ? '

A fourth :

'They spared Linus at first; but now they have taken him too, and are torturing him.'

And yet another said:

'If we go home the soldiers will seize us. We do not know where to hide. Woe unto us! Who will protect us ?'

But now Peter had begun to speak, at first in a voice so low as to be scarcely audible.

'My children, upon Golgotha I saw God, and they nailed Him to a cross. I heard the sound of the hammers, and I saw them lifting up the cross that the multitudes might behold the death of the Son of Man.

'And I saw them pierce His side, and I saw Him when life was gone.

'And when I left the cross, I too cried aloud in my grief: "Alas! O Lord, Thou art God! Why hast Thou suffered this, and why hast Thou died and brought despair to our hearts—to us who be-believed that Thy kingdom would come ?" But God, our Lord and Master, rose on the third day, and remained with us till the day when, with great glory, He entered into His kingdom. And under-standing our little faith, we were strengthened in our hearts, and from that day we went about sowing the good seed.'

Then turning to her who had uttered the first lament, he went on in a louder voice:

'Why do you all complain ? Behold Him who cometh and saith unto you "Follow me." Behold Him who raiseth you up towards Him! And you cling fast with both hands to the earth and cry out, "Help, Lord." I tell you in the name of Christ, what lies before you is not death, but life; it is not grief, but joy unchanging; it is not slavery, but a kingdom! I, who am God's apostle, tell you, poor widow, that your son will not die, but will be born in glory into eternal life, and you shall see him again.

'And the father whose daughters were outraged by these cruel men shall find them again, whiter than the lilies of Hebron. And to all of you who are to see the death of those you love, to all who are in distress, to all who are unhappy or in terror, and to those about to die—in the name of Christ, I say unto you that you will pass out of sleep to a joyful awakening, and out of night into the dawn of heaven. I pray in Christ's name that the scales may fall from your eyes, and that your hearts may be kindled.'

He raised his hand as though he were giving a command. They felt their bodies thrill, and the blood course more strongly in their veins. For before them stood no longer the decrepit old figure, but a mighty man who was snatching their souls out of the slough of despond to bear them off to a far land.

He went on:

' Sow in tears, that you may reap in joy ; wherefore shrink before the powers of evil ?

' The Lord is advancing to the assault of this proud city of crime and oppression, and you are His army. And as He redeemed the sins of the world by His torments and His blood, so in like manner does He desire that you by your torments and your blood should redeem this nest of wickedness. And by my mouth He declares it.'

The apostle stretched forth his arms, raised his eyes to heaven, and remained motionless. His face was radiant, and he gazed on in ecstasy. Then he said:

' Thou art here, Lord, and Thou showest the way! It is not then at Jerusalem, O Christ, but in this city of Satan that Thou art to make the capital of Thy Kingdom! Here, amid blood and tears, wilt Thou establish Thy Church! And here, where Nero reigns, is Thine Eternal Kingdom to be founded! Yea, O Lord, and Thou dost bid these frightened creatures to lay with their bones the foundation of the Holy Zion! And Thou hast commanded my soul to reign over Thy Church and over the peoples of the world! Behold Thou fillest the hearts of the weak with might, that they may become strong; and behold Thou commandest me to feed Thy sheep here till the tale of the ages be told. Praised be Thy command, O Thou who hast bidden us conquer! Hosanna! Hosanna!'

The summer lightning played through the shed.

Peter awoke from his ecstasy, and turned upon the people a face inspired and radiant.

'As the Saviour has overcome your doubts,' said he, 'so shall you go and conquer in His name.'

He knew already that they would conquer, he knew what should be born of their blood and their tears, and yet his voice trembled with emotion as he began to bless them with the sign of the cross.

'I bless you, my children, in your torture, in your death, and in all eternity.'

They thronged about him, beseeching him:

'We are ready, master; but save your own sacred head, for you are the Vicar of God.'

And they clung to his garments, while he laid his hands upon them, and blessed them one by one, as a father blesses his children before starting upon a distant journey.

The apostle set out for his house under the guidance of Nereus, one of Puden's slaves, who took him through the vineyard by a secret path. In the clear night Vinicius followed them, and when they came to Nereus' hut, he threw himself at the apostle's feet.

Peter recognised him, and said:

'What seek you, my son ? '

But Vinicius, after what he had heard at the
meeting, did not dare ask for anything more. He
kissed the apostle's feet, and bowed his forehead
upon them, his very silence calling out for pity.

'I know. They have taken the maid you love.
Pray for her.'

'Master,' groaned Vinicius, clasping more tightly
the feet of the apostle, 'I am but a poor worm, but
you knew Christ ; so do you pray to Him for her !'

Peter was moved by his grief.

By the lightning that flashed across the sky,
Vinicius could watch Peter's lips, hanging on them
for the word of life or death. There was silence,
save for the calling of the quails in the vineyard, and
the dull grinding of the mills on the Via Salaria.

'Vinicius,' said the apostle, 'have you faith ?'

'Master, should I have come here if I had not ? '

'Then have faith to the end, for faith can move
mountains. And even if you saw this young girl
beneath the sword of the executioner, or in the lion's
mouth, have faith still, for Christ can save her.
Have faith and make prayer to Him, and I will pray
with you.'

Then, turning his face to heaven, he said in a loud
voice :

'O Merciful Christ, look upon this sad heart, and
ease its pain. O Merciful Christ, who prayed Thy
Father to turn aside the cup of bitterness from
Thee, turn it aside from the lips of Thy servant !
Amen !'

Vinicius groaned aloud, his hands outstretched to
the stars :

'Christ, I am Thine ; take me instead of her.'

In the east the sky was beginning to lighten.

CHAPTER 12

AFTER leaving the apostle, Vinicius returned to the Mamertine Prison.

All the Prætorians on duty there knew him by this time, and as a rule they allowed him to pass without any trouble. But on this occasion the ranks did not open to make way for him, and a centurion came up and said:

'You must forgive me, noble tribune, today; we are commanded to let nobody pass.'

'Commanded?' Vinicius repeated, turning pale.

The man looked at him with an air of compassion, and said:

'Yes, sir, by Cæsar. There is a great deal of sickness in the prison, and possibly they fear that visitors may spread the infection through the city.'

'But did you not say the order related to today alone?'

'We are relieved at midday.'

Vinicius made no reply, but uncovered his head, for he felt as though the cap which he wore pressed on his head like a leaden casing. The soldier came nearer still, and said in a low tone:

'Fear nothing, sir. Ursus and the warders are beside her.'

So saying, he stooped down and rapidly traced the outline of a fish on the pavement with his long Gallic sword.

Vinicius threw a questioning glance at him:

'And you are a Prætorian?'

'Yes, until they put me in there,' he said, pointing to the prison.

'I too worship Christ.'

294

'Blessed be His name! Yes, sir, I know. I cannot let you go in, but if you give me a letter, it shall reach its destination through the warders.'

'I thank you, brother.'

On returning home he found Petronius, who, true to his custom of turning night into day, had just come in, but had already bathed and been anointed before lying down.

'I have news for you,' he said to the young man. 'I was at Tullius Senecio's yesterday, and Cæsar was there also. I don't know what caused the empress to take the unlucky step of bringing little Rufius with her—possibly to touch Cæsar's heart by his beauty. The child was drowsy, and unfortunately in the middle of the reading he fell asleep, like Vespasian, you remember. Brazenbeard was furious, and threw a bowl at his head, which made a dangerous wound. Poppæa fainted, and everybody heard Cæsar exclaim: "I have had enough of this monstrosity." That, you know, is as good as a sentence of death.'

'The judgment of God hangs over the empress,' said Vinicius, 'but why tell me this story?'

'I tell you because she will now have her own troubles to think about, and will perhaps forget her grievance against you, and be more easily swayed. I will see her this evening and speak to her.'

'Thank you, Petronius; this is good news.'

'Now go and bathe and rest awhile. Your lips are blue, and you are only the shadow of yourself.'

Vinicius said:

'Was the date of the earliest games mentioned?'

'Ten days hence. But they will draw from the other prisons first of all. I will tell the empress something like this to-day: You save Lygia for Vinicius, and I will save Rufius for you. And I will really try to think of something. A word in season to Brazenbeard can save or ruin a man. In any case, we shall gain time.'

They separated, Vinicius going to the library and writing a letter to Lygia.

He took the letter himself to the converted centurion, who went with it into the prison. When he came out he said to Vinicius:

'Lygia greets you. Her answer I will bring you tomorrow.'

Vinicius would not go home, but sat down upon a stone to wait for her letter. The sun was already high in heaven, and people were streaming into the Forum by the Clivus Argentarius.

Suddenly a great shouting arose near the spot where the tribune was seated. The street was swarming with people. Two runners in yellow tunics were parting the crowd with cries and with blows from their long rods, to make way for a splendid litter borne by four enormous Egyptian slaves.

Inside the litter sat a man clad in white, whose face could not be clearly seen, as he had his eyes fixed upon a papyrus, which he seemed to be studying closely.

'Make way for the noble Augustan.'

But the street was so crowded that the litter was forced to stop for a moment. Its occupant impatiently dropped his papyrus, and thrust out his head.

'Scatter these rascals, and be quicker about it!'

Suddenly he caught sight of Vinicius, and at once raised the papyrus to the level of his eyes.

Vinicius passed his hand across his forehead, thinking he was dreaming still.

For in the litter sat Chilon.

The runners had now cleared the way, and the Egyptians were about to go forward once more,

when the young tribune, understanding in a flash
a score of things that had puzzled him till now,
approached the litter and said:

' Hail, Chilon!'

' Young man,' replied the Greek, with haughty
dignity, as he sought by his aspect to express the
calmness that he certainly did not feel—' young man,
I greet you ; but do not detain me, for I must make
haste to see my friend, the noble Tigellinus.'

Vinicius leaned upon the edge of the litter, bent
towards Chilon, and looking him straight in the face,
said in a low voice:

' You have sold Lygia!'

' Colossus of Memnon!' cried the other in terror.

But Vinicius' eyes were in nowise threatening,
and the fears of the old Greek vanished at once.
Reflecting that he was under the protection of Tigellinus and Cæsar, the two powers before whom all
trembled, and that he was surrounded by muscular
slaves, he compared himself to Vinicius standing
there unarmed, his face drawn and his body bowed
with grief.

The thought restored all his insolence, and staring
at Vinicius with his red, inflamed eyes, he muttered
in answer:

' Yes, and when I was dying of hunger, you had
me thrashed.'

For a moment there was silence ; then Vinicius
said in a low tone:

' I did you an injustice, Chilon.'

The Greek raised his head, and, snapping his
fingers contemptuously, replied in a loud voice, that
all might hear:

' Friend, if you have any favour to ask, come to
my house on the Esquiline in the morning ; for it is
then, after my bath, that I receive my dependants.'

At a sign from him the Egyptians lifted the litter,
while the runners brandished their rods, crying:

'Make way for the litter of the noble Chilon
Chilonides! Make way! Make way!'

CHAPTER 13

Lygia hastily wrote a long letter, bidding farewell
to Vinicius. She knew that nobody was now allowed
to enter the prison, and that she would only see
Vinicius again when she was in the arena. So she
begged him to come to the games, as she wanted to
see him once again before she died.

'Whether Christ release me now,' she wrote, ' or
at my death, matters not. By the mouth of the
apostle He has promised me to you, so I am
yours.'

The whole letter breathed joy and hopefulness.
There was mention of but one earthly matter. She
asked Vinicius to remove her body from the Spoliarium, and bury her as his wife in the tomb where
he himself would lie some day.

The following day, when Vinicius arrived at the
prison, the converted centurion left the ranks and
came towards him.

'Hear me, sir. Christ, who has tried you, has but
now shown you a sign of His favour. Last night
the freedmen of the emperor and Tigellinus came to
choose some Christian maidens for their master's
pleasure. They asked for the maiden you love, but
the Lord has smitten her with the fever that is
carrying off the prisoners in the Tullianum, and so
they did not take her. Yesterday evening, indeed,
she was unconscious. Blessed be His name! This

sickness which has preserved her from dishonour may also save her from death.'

Vinicius leaned heavily with one hand on the centurion's shoulderpiece to save himself from falling. The other continued:

'Give thanks to the Lord for His mercy. They seized Linus and put him to the torture, but seeing that he was dying, they let him go. Perhaps now they may let her go also. And Christ will restore her to health.'

'You are right, centurion. Christ, who saved her from shame, will save her from death,' said Vinicius softly.

He remained till evening beneath the prison walls, and then, returning home, he bade his slaves go search for Linus and take him to one of his country houses.

Petronius too had decided upon a further step. He had already seen the empress; now he went to visit her again. He found her at the bedside of little Rufius. The child's skull had been fractured, and he was delirious. Wholly absorbed in her grief, Poppæa at first would not hear Lygia and Vinicius mentioned. But Petronius terrified her.

'You have offended a new and unknown God. Your Majesty, it seems, worships the Hebrew Jehovah, but the Christians claim that Christ is His Son. Ask yourself if the Father's wrath is not hot against you. Is it not their vengeance that assails you, and does not the boy's life depend on your future conduct ? '

'What do you want me to do ? '

'Appease the anger of the gods.'

'And how ? '

'Lygia is ill. Use your influence to persuade Cæsar and Tigellinus to restore her to Vinicius.'

' Surely you do not imagine that I could ? ' she said despairingly.

' Well, there is another way. If Lygia recovers, she will be put to death. Go to the Temple of Vesta and bid the chief vestal be, as though by chance, at the entrance to the Tullianum when the prisoners are being led out to death. Then let her tell them to liberate this girl.'

' But suppose Lygia dies of the fever ? '

' The Christians say that Christ exacts vengeance, but that He is just. Perhaps you may appease Him by your good intentions alone.'

' Let Him give me a sign that He will save Rufius.'

Petronius shrugged his shoulders.

' Your Majesty, I do not come here as Christ's envoy. I come simply to say this to you : Be on good terms with the gods, whether Roman or not.'

Poppæa, who would gladly have offered hecatombs to all the gods of the universe to save Rufius, went that very evening to the Temple of Vesta in the Forum, leaving the child under the care of the faithful Sylvia, her own old nurse.

But on the Palatine the child's fate had already been sealed. Scarcely had the litter of the empress passed through the great entrance, when two of Cæsar's freedmen entered the room where little Rufius was lying. One of them threw himself on old Sylvia and gagged her, while the other, with a blow from a little bronze sphinx, stunned her instantly.

The child did not understand what was going on, and smiled to them, partly closing his eyes in an attempt to recognise them. They took off the nurse's girdle, and putting it round his neck, drew it tight. The boy cried out once, ' Mamma !' and died in a moment.

Then they wrapped a cloth round him, galloped off to Ostia, and flung the body into the sea.

Poppæa, unable to find the *Vestalis Maxima*, who had gone to Vatinius' house with the other vestals, returned to the palace. At the sight of the empty cradle and of Sylvia's cold body she fainted. When she recovered, she began to scream, and her wild cries rang out all through the night and all the next day.

On the third day, however, Cæsar bade her attend a banquet. Donning the amethyst tunic, she went and silently took her place, in all her fair beauty, with a stony look upon her face. A wonderful vision she was indeed, yet sinister as an angel of death.

CHAPTER 14

FROM early morning on the first day of the games crowds of idlers awaited the opening of the doors, listening with profound satisfaction to the roaring of the lions, the hoarse growls of the panthers, and the howling of the dogs. The beasts had not tasted food for two days, and large pieces of raw flesh were passed in front of their cages in order to render them furious with hunger and rage. At times their cries broke out in a storm so appalling that the people waiting in front of the circus could not hear each other speaking.

From daybreak onwards arose within the circus itself the sound of peaceful solemn hymns, which caused the listeners to exclaim in amazement: 'The Christians! The Christians!' During the previous night large numbers of them had been brought to the amphitheatre. In the morning bands of gladiators, led by their masters, the *lanistæ*, began to stream in also. To keep themselves fresh until the appointed time, they marched unarmed, many of them indeed quite naked, bearing wreaths of flowers, and carrying green branches in their hands—young and handsome in the morning light, and full of vigorous life. Their bodies, glistening with oil, looked like granite statues in their formidable strength, and delighted the crowd, always enthusiastic for beauty of form. Their names were well known, and they were greeted with shouts of ' Hail, Furnius!' ' Hail, Leo!' ' Hail, Maximus!' ' Hail, Diomedes!' The young women cast amorous glances at them, while they in turn picked out the prettiest of the girls and bantered them, and threw them kisses, saying, ' Come and take me before death gets me!' Then they disappeared through the doors, which closed on more than one of them for the last time.

Every moment the attention of the crowd was drawn to fresh sights. Behind the gladiators came the *mastigophori*, whose business it was to stimulate the combatants with their whips. Then came mules, drawing in the direction of the *spoliarium* long lines of wagons piled up with coffins. The people were delighted at this, foreseeing the magnificence of the show from the number of the coffins. Following these came the men who killed off the wounded, dressed to represent Charon or Mercury ; then those who kept order inside the enclosure and showed the people to their seats ; slaves to bring round food and refreshments ; and lastly, the Prætorians, whom the emperors always had at their command in the amphitheatre. The doors were opened and the crowd surged in. But so great were the numbers that for hours it continued to flow in a ceaseless stream. The roaring of the beasts, who now smelt the human flesh, had grown louder since the doors were opened, and the people, as they took their places inside the circus, made a murmuring noise like waves fretting upon the shore.

At last came the city prefect, with his guards, and then the litters of the senators, consuls, prætors, ediles, officers of the household, chiefs of the Prætorians, patricians, and women of fashion.

The great folks were greeted with shouts of welcome by the people in the circus. Small detachments of Prætorians arrived from time to time. The priests from the various temples came a little later, and behind them were borne the vestal virgins, preceded by lictors. The show was ready to begin as soon as the emperor should arrive. And Nero, anxious not to abuse the patience of the people, and desirous of propitiating them by his punctuality, soon made his appearance in company with Poppæa and the Augustans, among whom came Petronius and Vinicius in the same litter.

All the warders and attendants in the amphitheatre had been bribed by Vinicius, the arrangement being that the keepers should conceal Lygia in a dark corner of the dungeons until night, then hand her over to a steward of the tribune's, who should set off at once with her to the Alban Mountains. Petronius, who was in the secret, advised Vinicius to go openly with him to the amphitheatre and escape afterwards in the crowd. Then he could hurry down to the cells and, to prevent any mistake, could himself point out Lygia to the warders.

The warders admitted him by a little service door, and one of them, named Syrus, took him at once to the Christians. As they went along he said:

'I don't know, sir, if you'll find the person you seek. We made inquiry for a young girl called Lygia,

303

but nobody replied. It is just possible they don't trust us.'

As he spoke, Syrus opened a door and they entered a vast room, low, and very dark, being lit only by the gratings that shut it off from the arena. At first Vinicius could see nothing: he heard only the confused murmuring of voices in the room itself, and outside the shouts of the crowd in the amphitheatre. But soon his eyes grew accustomed to the darkness, and he saw groups of queer figures resembling wolves or bears. These were the Christians sewn up in the skins of animals. Some were standing, while others knelt in prayer. Here and there long tresses flowing over the shaggy skin showed that the victim was a woman. Mothers clad in wolves' skins were carrying in their arms children in hairy garments.

But from out the skins appeared bright faces and eyes that shone in the dim light with feverish joy. When questioned about Lygia by Vinicius, some made no answer, and looked at him like men suddenly awakened out of sleep. Others smiled to him, a finger on their lips, or else pointed to the bars through which streams of light were pouring. Some of the children alone were weeping, frightened by the roaring of the wild beasts, and the fearsome aspect of their parents.

Vinicius walked along beside Syrus, scanning the faces, searching and asking questions. Now and then he stumbled upon the bodies of men or women overcome by the stifling atmosphere. Suddenly he paused, for he seemed to hear the sound of a familiar voice. He turned, and, making his way through the crowd, he came near to the man who was speaking. A flood of light fell on the man's head, and by its help Vinicius recognised beneath the wolf's skin the severe, emaciated face of Crispus.

'Repent of your sins,' he was saying, 'for the moment is at hand. Verily, I say unto you, whosoever thinks that his martyrdom will earn him remission of his sins, the same commits a new sin and shall be cast into eternal fire. Every sin you have committed has renewed your Saviour's agony! How dare you believe that the trial which awaits you can be equal to what our Redeemer endured ? Woe unto you, for the lions' teeth will rend your bodies, but will not wipe out your sins, nor the account which you must render to God!'

Vinicius felt a shudder run through him. He who had put all his hope in Christ's mercy now heard that even death in the arena was not enough to win that mercy. Like lightning the idea flashed across his mind that the apostle Peter would have spoken differently to those about to die. But now, reflecting that at any moment the bars might be opened, he began to call aloud for Lygia and Ursus, hoping that if they were not there somebody who knew them would answer.

And so it was, for a man dressed in a bear's skin plucked at his toga and said :

'Master, they were left behind in the prison. I was the last to leave, and I saw her lying ill on her bed.'

'Who are you ? ' asked Vinicius.

'The quarryman in whose hut the apostle Peter baptized you, sir. I was put in prison three days ago, and I am to die to-day.'

Vinicius left the dungeon, and, returning to the amphitheatre, sat down among the Augustans, beside Petronius.

'Is she there ? ' Petronius asked.

'No, she is still in prison.'

'Well, here is a new idea that has struck me ;

but just look in the direction, say, of Nigidia, to make people think we are discussing her coiffure: Tigellinus and Chilon are looking at us. Get Lygia put into a coffin at night, and have her taken out of the prison as though she were dead. The rest you can imagine.'

' I understand,' replied Vinicius.

As a rule, the games opened with wild beast hunts, in which various barbarians from north and south displayed their prowess. But this time it was *andabatæ* who began, gladiators who wore helmets without openings for their eyes, and who had to grope about for their adversaries.

About a dozen of them made their appearance together in the arena, and started to beat the air with their swords, while the whippers-in pushed them towards one another with their long forks. The great folks present were not moved by this essentially contemptible spectacle, but the common people were delighted with the clumsy movements of the gladiators. When they chanced upon each other back to back, roars of laughter broke out, and the people shouted, ' To the right! ' To the left!' ' Straight on!' often intentionally misleading them. But already some of them had come to grips, and were engaged in a bloody struggle. The fiercest of them threw away their shields, and clasping each other tightly by the left hand, fought to the death with their right hands. Those who fell lifted their fingers to beg for mercy, but at the beginning of the shows the people usually clamoured for the death of the wounded, especially the *andabatæ*, who, as their faces were entirely covered, were unrecognisable.

But now came a more important struggle, and one which aroused interest in the people of fashion as well as in the mob. Indeed, the young noblemen often betted enormous sums upon the result, and sometimes lost their last penny in doing so.

At the strident call of the trumpets an ominous silence fell upon the amphitheatre. Thousands of eyes were fixed upon the enormous door, while a man dressed as Charon went up, and, amid universal silence, knocked three times upon it with a hammer, as though to summon to their death the men concealed behind it. The two leaves of the door slowly opened, disclosing a dark passage from which the gladiators swarmed out into the light of the arena.

Thracians, Mirmillones, Samnites, and Gauls advanced in distinct groups of twenty-five, all heavily armed. Then came the *retiarii*, with net in one hand and three-pronged spear in the other. With buoyant, measured step the gladiators marched round the arena, their weapons and rich body-armour flashing in the light, and halted in front of the imperial balcony, haughty, calm, and majestic. They stretched out their right hands, and, with heads and eyes raised towards Cæsar, they chanted in a droning voice:

> ' Ave, Cæsar imperator !
> Morituri te salutant ! '

Then in a twinkling they separated and posted themselves singly all around the arena. They were to fight by companies, but first of all the most renowned among them had the right to engage in single combat, in which their individual strength, skill, and courage were more easily perceived. From among the Gauls stood forth Lanio, a champion well known to frequenters of the amphitheatre and the victor in many a fight. With his great helmet and the coat of mail that encased his mighty body, he appeared in the light which flooded the arena like some great shining beetle. Calendio, an equally well-known *retiarius*, advanced to meet him.

Among the spectators wagers were being made.

' Five hundred sesterces on the Gaul!'

' Five hundred on Calendio!'

' By Hercules, a thousand!'

' Two thousand!'

The Gaul came to the middle of the arena, and then began to retreat, holding out his sword in front of him, his head lowered in order to watch his adversary closely through the openings in his visor. Meantime Calendio, his perfect body naked save for a cloth about his loins, manœuvred nimbly around his ponderous opponent, gracefully flourishing his net, raising and lowering his spear, and singing the customary refrain,—

> ' *Non te peto, piscem peto ;*
> *Quid me fugis, Galle ? '*

> ' A fish, not you, I'm looking for ;
> So wherefore run away, O Gaul ? '

But the Gaul was retreating no longer. He halted, and began imperceptibly to wheel round as he stood, keeping his face turned always towards his adversary. His body and head had now something menacing about them, and the onlookers saw that this mighty bronze-clad mass was about to launch forth in one decisive and overwhelming attack.

The other kept advancing and retiring by sudden leaps, brandishing his three-pronged spear with movements so agile that the eye could scarcely follow them. More than once the teeth of his spear rang against his adversary's shield, but the gigantic Gaul did not even stagger. His whole attention seemed concentrated, not upon the spear, but upon the net that circled above his head like a bird of ill-omen. The spectators followed the wonderful display of the gladiators with bated breath. At last Lanio saw his chance, and hurled himself upon his opponent. The other, with lightning agility, eluded the sword and outstretched arms, and, recovering himself, threw his net.

The Gaul turned round and stopped it with his shield, and then both leapt clear of one another. Shouts of ' *Macte !*' resounded through the amphi-theatre. New wagers were made, and Cæsar himself, who had been talking to the vestal Rubria and paying but scant attention to the contest, now turned his head towards the arena.

Once more they began to fight, and so clever and accurate were they in all their movements that at times it seemed as though this were no longer a matter of life and death, but merely an occasion for the display of their skill. Twice again did Lanio evade the net, and again he started to retreat towards the edge of the ring.

But those who had bet against him wanted to give him no rest, and cried out: ' Go on !' The Gaul obeyed, and attacked. Immediately the arm of the *retiarius* was streaming with blood, and his net sank. Lanio gathered himself together, and sprang forward to deal the finishing stroke. But as he did so Calendio, who had pretended that he could not manage his net any more, bent to one side, eluded the sword-point, slipped his spear between his adversary's knees, and brought him down on the sand.

The other would have risen, but in a twinkling the deadly net was about him, and every movement of hand or foot served only to entangle him the more. The spear kept him pinned to the ground.

He made one supreme effort, raised himself on his arm, stretched himself, and sought to sit up, but in vain. He raised to his head a feeble hand, from which the sword had dropped, and then fell back. Calendio pinned his neck to the earth between the teeth of his fork, and leaning both hands upon the haft, he turned towards the emperor's box.

The whole ring shook with the roars of the people. To those who had laid their money on Calendio he was, for the nonce, a greater than Cæsar; while at the same time all ill-will towards Lanio had disappeared, since at the cost of his own blood he had filled their purses for them.

There was a division of opinion among the spectators, and in every row there were as many in favour of mercy as of death; but Calendio looked only to the box where Cæsar and the vestals sat, and awaited their decision.

Unfortunately for Lanio, he was no favourite of Nero's. At the last games, held before the Fire, the emperor had made a bet against him with Linicius, and had lost a large sum. So he stretched his hand over the balustrade, and turned his thumb down. The vestals immediately followed his example. Then Calendio knelt with one knee upon the Gaul's chest, drew his knife, and unfastening the armour about the neck of his adversary, he plunged the triangular blade up to the hilt in his throat.

' *Peractum est!* ' yelled the crowd.

Lanio quivered like a slaughtered ox, drummed with his feet upon the sand, stiffened, and lay still.

There was no need for Mercury with his hot iron to test if life was extinct.

He was quickly carried out, and fresh couples appeared, after which ensued a raging battle between whole companies. The mob threw themselves into it, eyes, heart, and soul. They howled, shouted, whistled, clapped their hands, laughed, urged on the fighters, and went mad with delight. In the arena the two bodies of gladiators fought with the desperation of wild animals. Breastplates rang, bodies were locked in deadly embrace, mighty limbs cracked in their sockets, swords were plunged into chest or belly, pale lips spat forth blood in torrents. Towards the end some of the novices were so overcome with terror that they extricated themselves from the *mêlée* and ran away, only to be hunted back immediately by the whippers-in with their loaded whips. Dark patches formed upon the sand. Every moment there came fresh bodies, naked or clad in armour, to swell the stacks of corpses.

At last all the vanquished lay dead, save for a few wounded men who kneeled unsteadily in the middle of the arena, with hands stretched out for mercy to the spectators. Prizes of wreaths and olive branches were distributed among the victors. Then came a short interval, which, by the order of the all-powerful emperor, formed the occasion of a feast. Perfumes were burned, and saffron and violet-scented spray rained upon the crowd from vaporisers. Cooling drinks were handed round, roasted meat, sweet cakes, olives, and fruit. The mob ate ravenously, chattered, and shouted in praise of Cæsar, to prompt him to still greater displays of generosity.

The first part of the show was over. People left their seats to stretch their legs in the passages and to talk. The courtiers amused themselves with Chilon, chaffing him about his Hellenic temperament and about his cowardice, which unfitted him to endure such sights as these.

'Well, my Grecian friend, so the sight of torn skin is so very unpleasant to you?' said Vatinius to Chilon as he pulled his beard.

Chilon disclosed his two remaining yellow teeth in a sickly grin.

'My father wasn't a cobbler, so I never learned to patch it,' he replied.

'Good! One to Chilon!' several voices exclaimed together. But the rest continued to tease him.

'It's no fault of his if he has a cheese for a heart,' said Senecio.

'Nor yours, if you have a bladder for a head!' retorted Chilon.

'How will the Christians fare?' asked Festus of Liguria. 'Wouldn't you like to be a dog and be able to bite them?'

'I shouldn't like to be your brother.'

'Go along, you Mæotian leper!'

'And you, you Ligurian mule!'

'Your skin is itching, I see. But don't come and ask me to scratch you.'

'Scratch your own skin! When you scratch out the itch that's the best of you gone!'

So they went on abusing him, while he, amid the laughter of all, repaid them in their own coin. Cæsar clapped his hands, repeated 'Good! good!' and egged on the scoffers. Petronius approached the Greek, and tapping him on the shoulder with his slender rod of carved ivory, said coldly:

'Excellent, O philosopher; but you have made one great mistake. The gods meant you for a pickpocket ; turning fiend was your own idea. That's why you'll not last out to the end.'

The old man looked at him with his red eyes, but this time he had no insulting answer ready. He remained silent for a moment, and then replied with an effort:

' I *will* last out.'

The sound of trumpets announced that the interval was at an end. Scattered over the arena were servants engaged in breaking up the little heaps of sand congealed with blood.

Now came the turn of the Christians.

At a signal from the prefect the same old man dressed as Charon made his appearance in the arena, walked slowly across it, and, amid a dead silence, struck the door three times with his hammer.

Round the amphitheatre ran a murmur:

' The Christians ! The Christians ! '

The iron bars grated. In the dark passages resounded the familiar cry of the whippers-in : ' On to the sand ! ' and in a moment the arena was crowded with a multitude of creatures dressed like satyrs.

All ran with feverish haste to the middle of the arena, and knelt down side by side, with their hands upraised.

The crowd, thinking they were begging for mercy, became enraged at the sight of such cowardice. They began to stamp and whistle, throwing empty dishes and bare bones into the arena, and yelling, ' The beasts ! Let loose the beasts ! '

Then suddenly an unexpected thing happened. From the midst of that shaggy company came the voices of people singing, and for the first time a Roman circus heard the strains of the hymn, ' *Christus regnat !* '

The crowd were dumbfounded. The victims sang on with their eyes uplifted to the awning; their faces were pale, but they looked as though they were inspired. All knew that these men asked for no mercy, and that they saw neither the circus, nor the crowd, nor the senate, nor Cæsar.

A new gate was opened, and out bounded wildly large numbers of dogs—enormous yellow Molossians from the Peloponnese, striped dogs from the Pyrenees, and Irish dogs that looked like wolves, all purposely starved, with lean ribs and bloodshot eyes. Their barking and growling filled the whole amphitheatre. The Christians, having finished their hymn, remained kneeling and motionless, as though turned to stone, moaning out in unison: ' *Pro Christo ! Pro Christo !* '

Scenting men beneath the beasts' skins, but not understanding their immobility, the dogs did not at first venture to attack them. Some of them tried to climb up the front of the boxes, others tore round the ring, barking as though in pursuit of some invisible quarry. The people grew impatient. Thousands of voices rang out, some imitating the howling of wild beasts, others barking like dogs, while others again were urging on the animals in every known language. The amphitheatre trembled with their clamour. The infuriated dogs ran up to the Christians, and then retreated again, gnashing their teeth. But at last one of the Molossian dogs drove his fangs into the shoulder of a woman who was kneeling in front of the others, and bore her to earth with his weight.

Then scores of dogs rushed into the crowd as though through a breach in a wall. The people stopped roaring, the better to observe what was going on. And ever amid the howling and the snarling of the dogs arose the piteous voices of men and women calling, '*Pro Christo! Pro Christo!*' Blood flowed in torrents from dismembered bodies. The dogs tore from each other the bleeding limbs of their victims. The smell of blood and lacerated entrails had drowned the scents of Arabia, and the whole circus reeked with it.

At last only a few people here and there were left kneeling, and soon even these were overwhelmed beneath the writhing howling masses.

Then fresh batches of victims were pushed forward into the arena, wrapped up in the skins of animals. Like those before them, they knelt down at once. But the dogs were quite spent, and would not touch them, Only a few threw themselves on the nearest; the rest lay down, lifted up their mouths, dripping with blood, and began to breathe heavily, their sides heaving.

The people, thoroughly restless but intoxicated with blood and beside themselves with mad fury, shouted aloud in strident tones:

'The lions! The lions! Let out the lions!'

The lions were intended for the next day, but in the amphitheatre the mob imposed its will upon all, including Cæsar himself.

Nero signed to the attendants to open the dungeon, and the crowd was appeased at once. The doors grated upon their hinges, and the lions appeared. At the sight of them the dogs huddled together with smothered yelps on the far side of the ring, while the great tawny beasts, with their noble shaggy heads, came bounding one by one into the arena. Even Cæsar turned a bored look upon them, and put his emerald up to his eye to observe them better. The Augustans hailed them with applause, while the crowd counted them on their

fingers, greedily watching the impression which the
lions would make upon the Christians who knelt
in the middle of the arena, and who had once more
begun their cry, ' Pro Christo ! Pro Christo ! '
which conveyed so little meaning to most of the
spectators, yet rang so hauntingly in the ears of
all.

The lions, although famished, did not hasten to
fall upon their victims. The reddish glare that
flooded the arena blinded them, and made them
blink their dazzled eyes. Some of them stretched
out their tawny limbs in a lazy fashion, while
others opened their mouths and yawned as though
for the purpose of displaying their teeth. But
gradually the smell of blood and of the mangled
bodies that lay heaped upon the arena began to
take effect. They moved about uneasily ; their
manes bristled, and they snorted loudly. Suddenly
one of them leapt upon the body of a woman whose
face had been torn to shreds, and planting his fore-
paws upon her, began to lick the clotted blood with
his rough tongue. Another of them approached a
Christian who held in his arms a child sewn up in a
deer-skin.

The child, shaken with sobs, clung convulsively
to its father, who, anxious to save its life even for a
moment, attempted to unclasp it from his neck, and
pass it to those behind him. But the cries and the
movements irritated the lion. It gave a sharp, hoarse
roar, and with one blow of its paw killed the child ;
then caught the father's head in its mouth and
crushed it.

Instantly the rest sprang upon the huddled group
of Christians. Some of the women could not
restrain their cries of dismay, but these were soon
drowned by the cheers of the crowd, which in turn

were hushed in the anxiety of the people to see all that passed.

Dreadful scenes were enacted. Heads disappeared completely inside gaping jaws ; breasts were ripped open at a single bite, and hearts and lungs torn out ; bones were heard cracking loudly between the lions' jaws. Some of the beasts, grasping their victims by their backs or sides, bounded wildly round the arena as though seeking some quiet corner wherein to devour them. Others fought among themselves, rearing up, closing like wrestlers, and making the circus ring with their thunderous roars. The people rose from their seats ; some left their places and came down to the lower rows in order to obtain a better view, and some of them were crushed to death in doing so. It seemed as though in the end the raving crowd would burst into the arena, and help the lions to tear the Christians to pieces.

At one moment nothing was heard but unearthly cries, at another, nothing but applause : now there were roarings, snarlings, gnashing of teeth, and barking, and now there was nothing but groans !

Cæsar was looking on attentively, with his emerald to his eye. Petronius' face wore an expression of disgust and contempt. Chilon had already fainted and been carried out.

And still the dungeons poured forth fresh victims into the arena.

From the highest tier in the amphitheatre the apostle Peter watched them. Nobody was looking at him, for all eyes were upon the arena. He rose to his feet. And just as once before, in the vineyard of Cornelius, he had blessed in their death, for all eternity, those who were about to be put in prison, so now did he bless with the sign of the cross the

317

victims writhing in their death agony in the jaws of
the wild beasts: he blessed their blood and their
tortures: he blessed the bodies transformed into
shapeless masses and the souls that were taking their
flight far from the blood-stained sand. Some of
them raised their eyes to him ; their faces brightened,
and they smiled when they saw above their heads
the sign of the cross.

But suddenly Cæsar, mad with the lust for blood,
or else desirous of eclipsing all that Rome had ever
seen before, whispered some words to the prefect,
who at once left the scene and hastened to the
passages underground.

Even the crowd gaped in astonishment to see the
gates thrown open again, and animals of every sort
come bounding into the arena. There were tigers
from the Euphrates, panthers from Numidia, bears,
wolves, hyænas, and jackals. The whole arena
swarmed with masses of striped or spotted skins,
yellow, brown, and tawny. In this chaos the eye
could no longer distinguish anything save a dreadful
writhing mass of wild animals' backs. All semblance
of reality was lost. The thing had gone too far.
Above the roaring and yelling and growling there
came from the spectators' seats here and there the
shrill, jerky laugh of women whose nerves were at
last overcome. Some of the people were afraid.
Faces darkened, and many voices were heard crying,
' Enough! enough!'

But it was easier to let loose the beasts than to
drive them from the arena. Cæsar, however, had hit
upon a device for clearing the ring which would at
the same time afford fresh amusement to the people.
From all the passages there emerged numbers
of Numidian negroes, with feathers in their hair and
rings in their ears, and carrying bows in their hands.

The crowd guessed what was coming, and hailed them with shouts of delight. The Numidians spread themselves round the ring, and fitting arrows to their bows, began to discharge them into the wild writhing masses. Here, indeed, was a new spectacle. Their shapely bodies, black as ebony, arched themselves, while their bows, ever on the strain, sent showers of arrows among the beasts. The twanging of the strings and the whistling of the feathered shafts were added to the howling of the animals and the admiring shouts of the onlookers. Wolves, panthers, bears, and those human beings who were still left alive, all went down together. Here and there a lion, feeling the sting of an arrow in his side, would snap at it with a mouth contorted by fury, and attempt to break it off. Others were groaning with pain. The smaller beasts, in an uncontrollable panic, ran blindly about the ring, or else dashed their heads against the bars. Still the arrows whistled on, till soon every living creature had collapsed, quivering in its death-agony.

Then hundreds of slaves ran into the arena with spades, shovels, brooms, wheelbarrows, sacks of sand, and baskets for gathering up and carrying off the mangled remains. The whole ring was a scene of feverish activity. In a trice the bodies had been lifted, the blood and excrement cleaned up, the sand dug up and raked away, and the arena spread with a covering of fresh sand. Then cupids came running in and scattered petals of roses and lilies around. The censers were lit once more, and the awning was taken off, as the sun had now sunk low.

The people looked at each other in astonishment, wondering what new spectacle still awaited them.

A spectacle awaited them that nobody suspected. Cæsar had quitted his box some time before, and now suddenly made his appearance on the flower-strewn arena, wearing a purple robe and a crown of gold. Twelve singers carrying lutes followed him. With majestic tread he advanced to the middle of the ring, a silver lute in his hand, and bowing several times, he raised his eyes to heaven. Thus he stood for a moment, as though awaiting inspiration, and then he struck the strings and began:

> 'Latona's son! O radiant and divine!
> Thou lord of Chios, Tenedos, and Chrysos,
> That hast beneath the shadow of thy wing
> Taken the sacred Ilion:
> Why hast thou left her to the wrath of Atreus' sons,
> And let the blood of Trojans flow, O Smintheus,
> Upon the sacred altars,
> That smoke in honour of thy name eternally?'

The song sank gradually into a plaintive, sorrow-laden elegy. The circus was hushed, and Cæsar went on:

> 'Thy holy lyre, hard-hearted Smintheus,
> Hath drowned all prayers and moans and sighs:
> And still to-day
> The eye is wet with tears; ah, woe is me!
> As flower with drops of dew
> When at the sudden calling of my hymn,
> From out the dismal shroud of ruin
> Arises once again the horrid day of fire—
> Where wert thou, Smintheus, on that day?'

Nero's voice broke and his eyes grew moist. Tears glistened in the eyes of the vestals. Then the people broke the silence with one prolonged hurricane of applause.

Meantime, through the entrance passages, thrown open for ventilation, came the creaking of the tumbrils in which the mangled remains of the Christians, men, women, and children, were to be carried off to the indescribable burying-places known as the 'Stinking Pits.'

CHAPTER 15

THE spectacle was at an end. The crowd left the amphitheatre, and streaming out through the *vomitoria,* made their way towards the city.

Petronius and Vinicius did not break silence on their way home. The litter came to a stop before the house, and they got down. Immediately a dark figure advanced towards them.

'Is the noble Vinicius here ? '

'Yes,' replied the tribune. 'What is it ? '

'I am Nazarius, Myriam's son. I have come from the prison with news of Lygia.'

Vinicius leant upon his arm, and looked into his eyes by the light of the torches, incapable of uttering a word. But Nazarius guessed at the question which died away on his lips.

'She is alive. Ursus sent me to you, sir, to say that in her fever she prays to the Lord, and often mentions your name.'

'Glory be to Christ,' replied Vinicius. 'He can give her back to me if He will.'

He took Nazarius into the library, where Petronius soon joined them.

The latter looked more closely at the boy's handsome face, his blue eyes, and his thick black hair, and asked :

'What country do you come from, my boy ? '

'I am a Galilean, sir.'

'Would you be glad if Lygia were at liberty ? '

'Yes, though I had to die for it.'

Vinicius now spoke.

'Tell the warders to put her in a coffin as if she were dead. Then get some people to help you to remove her by night. Near the burying-place you will meet some men with a litter; hand the coffin over to them. Promise the warders from me as much gold as each can take away in his cloak.'

As he spoke his face lost the expression of stupor that was now habitual to it. The soldier in him awoke, and hope restored to him his former energy.

Nazarius lifted up his hands and exclaimed:

'May Christ give her back her health, for now she will escape.'

'Do you think the warders will do it?' asked Petronius.

'Yes,' said Vinicius. 'They were already willing to let her escape, and they will be the more willing since she is to be taken away as a corpse.'

'There is a man who touches the bodies we take away with a hot iron to test if they are really dead,' said Nazarius; 'but for a few sesterces he will spare the face, and for a piece of gold he will spare the body altogether, and only touch the coffin.'

Petronius reflected.

'Everybody must believe her dead,' he said at last. 'Have you no farm steward up in the mountains on whom you could rely?'

'Yes, I have,' replied Vinicius. 'Up near Corioli there is a faithful fellow who carried me in his arms when I was a child, and who is devoted to me.'

Petronius handed him the tablets.

'Write and tell him to come here to-morrow. I will send off a messenger at once.'

A few moments later a slave set out for Corioli on horseback.

Next day Niger, Vinicius' steward, arrived. For

greater safety he had left behind at an inn in the Suburra, along with the mules and the litter, the four trustworthy men whom he had picked from among the British slaves.

The man was affected at the sight of his young master, and kissing his hands and eyes, he said :

' Are you ill, dear master, or is it sorrow that has drained the blood from your face ? I scarcely recognised you at first.'

Vinicius led him beneath the inner colonnade, and there told him the whole story.

' So she is a Christian ? ' exclaimed Niger, as he looked searchingly at Vinicius.

' And I am one too,' replied the tribune.

Tears glistened in Niger's eyes.

' Thanks be to Thee, O Christ, for lifting the veil from these eyes, which are dearer to me than any-thing else in the world!'

Then Petronius entered along with Nazarius.

' Good news !' he cried when he saw them.

And good news indeed he had. First of all, Glaucus the doctor undertook that Lygia would recover, although she was suffering from the same prison fever that was carrying off scores of people daily, in the Tullianum and elsewhere. As for the warders and the man who tested the dead bodies with his hot iron, they had all been bought over, as well as an assistant called Attys.

' We have bored holes in the coffin,' said Nazarius. ' The only danger is that she might give a groan or speak as we are passing the guards. However, Glaucus will give her a sleeping-draught. The lid of the coffin will not be nailed down. You can easily lift it, and take her into your litter, while we will put a bag of sand into the coffin.'

'Will other bodies be taken out of the prison ? ' said Petronius.

'About twenty people died last night, and there will be more dead before this evening,' replied Nazarius. 'We must go with the rest, but we will loiter and fall behind. At the first street-corner my companion will go lame, and so they will get ahead of us. You wait for us outside the little Temple of Libitina. Pray God the night be dark.'

There the conversation ended, Niger returning to his men at the inn, while Nazarius went off to the prison with a bag of gold under his clothes.

At nightfall there came a heavy rain, which, falling upon the stones, still warm after the long, hot day, condensed into vapour, and filled the streets with mist. The rest of the night was broken by showers at intervals.

Vinicius and Petronius put on Gallic cloaks with hoods. The bad weather had emptied the streets. Now and then a blinding flash of lightning illumined the walls of newly-built houses or houses in course of erection. By one of the flashes they saw at last the rising ground on which stood the little Temple of Libitina, and at the foot a number of mules and horses.

'Niger!' called out Vinicius softly.

'Here I am, sir,' replied a voice through the rain.

'Is everything ready ? '

'Everything is ready, dear master. But take shelter under the embankment or you will be soaked. What a night! I think there's going to be hail.'

And indeed hail did begin to fall, and the air at once became much colder.

They waited, with ears alert to every sound. The hail had ceased, but the rain was now descending in torrents. Occasionally a gust of wind wafted from the direction of the pits the dreadful smell of decomposing bodies lying buried only a short distance below the surface.

Suddenly Niger exclaimed:

'I see a light through the mist; there's another, and another. They are torches.'

He turned to his men:

'Look to your mules; be ready!'

'They are coming,' said Petronius.

The lights were growing more distinct. The flames of the torches could be seen flickering in the gusts of wind. Niger crossed himself, and began to pray.

When the dismal procession came up to the temple it halted.

Petronius, Vinicius, and the steward silently flattened themselves against the embankment in great anxiety. But the men had only stopped to cover their faces and mouths with cloths as a protection against the stench, which at the edge of the pits was intolerable. Then they took up the shafts again and continued on their way. One coffin alone remained opposite the little temple.

Vinicius rushed forward, followed by Petronius, Niger, and the two Britons with the litter.

But Nazarius' voice came sadly out of the night:

'Master, they have taken Ursus and her to the Esquiline Prison. This is another body. They took her away before midnight.'

CHAPTER 16

THE first event on the next day of the games was to be a fight among the Christians themselves. For this purpose they had been equipped as gladiators with the proper weapons, offensive and defensive, of professional fighters. But here a miscalculation had been made, for the Christians threw away nets, tridents, lances, and swords, and fell to embracing each other and exhorting each other to resignation. At a word from Cæsar, real gladiators were let loose upon the kneeling crowd and slaughtered them in an instant.

When the bodies had been cleared away, a series of mythological *tableaux* of Cæsar's contriving were shown. Hercules was seen dying upon Mount Oeta in the midst of real flames. In the next scene, Chilon, who had been compelled by Cæsar to continue his attendance, saw some of his old friends again. It was the story of the death of Dædalus and Icarus. The part of Dædalus had been assigned to Euricius, the old man who not long ago had traced the fish in front of Chilon, while the part of Icarus was played by his son Quartus. Both were raised to an enormous height by a special contrivance, and then hurled into the arena. Quartus fell so close to the imperial box that the ornamentations on the outside and even the purple-covered ledge were bespattered with his blood. Chilon did not see him fall, for he had closed his eyes. He only heard the dull thud of the body, and when, a moment later, he noticed the blood near him, he almost fainted. The scenes succeeded each other rapidly. The crowd were overjoyed at the sight of Christian maidens ravished before their eyes by gladiators clad in wild beasts' skins. Here they saw the priestesses of Cybele and Ceres; there the Danaids, Dirce, and Pasiphae. Finally, they saw little girls of tender years being torn to pieces by wild horses.

Now the arena was again raked over and holes dug in the sand, the outermost of which were only a few steps from the emperor's box. The dungeons were opened, and from each one there poured forth hordes of Christians, entirely naked, and carrying crosses upon their shoulders.

The sand swarmed with people. Old men ran forward, bowed down by the weight of the beams; beside them came men in the prime of life, women striving to cover their nakedness with their flowing hair, youths, and even little children. Most of the victims and their crosses were wreathed with flowers. The attendants lashed the poor wretches with their whips, forcing them to set up their crosses opposite the holes that had been dug and wait beside them. Those who had not been thrown to the dogs and wild beasts on the first day of the games were now to die.

The negro slaves seized the victims and stretched them on the crosses, nailing their hands to the cross-bars. The amphitheatre rang with the sound of hammering.

Among the victims was Crispus. The lions had not had time to rend him, and so he was reserved for the cross. Always ready to die, he rejoiced to think that at last his hour was come. His emaciated body was naked, save for an ivy wreath about his loins. A crown of roses was upon his head. His eyes still shone with their old unquenchable fire, and underneath the flowers was still the same hard, fanatical face. Nor had his heart softened. Just as in the dungeon he had threatened his brethren in their wild beasts' skins with the wrath of Heaven, so now, instead of comforting them, he thundered forth:

'Give thanks to the Saviour, who allows you to die through the same tortures as brought death to Him. Maybe He will forgive some of your sins for that ; yet tremble, for the day of wrath is come!'

But suddenly from the seats nearest to the ring there came a calm and solemn voice, which said:

'Not the day of wrath, but the day of mercy ; the day of deliverance and of joy. I say unto you that Christ will gather you around Him, will comfort you, and set you at His right hand. Have faith, for behold the heavens are opening to receive you.'

At these words all eyes were turned to the seats. Those who were already on the cross raised their pale, tortured faces, and looked at him who spoke.

He came up to the barrier between the seats and the arena, and began to bless them with the sign of the cross.

Crispus stretched out his arm as though to thunder reproaches at him, but recognised him, and let his hand fall. His knees gave way, and he murmured:

'The Apostle Paul!'

To the astonishment of the attendants, all who had not yet been crucified fell upon their knees. Paul of Tarsus turned to Crispus, and said:

'Threaten them not, Crispus, for this day they shall be with you in Paradise. You think they will be condemned. But who will condemn them ? Will it be He who gave His Son to save them ? How should He condemn them who loves them ? Who would accuse God's elect ? Who would say of their blood: " It is accursed " ? '

'I hated evil,' said the old man.

'Above the hatred of evil, Christ has set the love of men. For His religion is love, and not hatred.'

'I have sinned in the very hour of death,' replied Crispus, beating his breast.

An attendant came up to the apostle, and said:

'Who are you who speak to the prisoners?'

'I am a Roman citizen,' replied Paul quietly.

Then turning towards Crispus he said:

'Take comfort, since to-day is the day of mercy, and die in peace, servant of God!'

Two negroes came up to Crispus to lift him on to the cross.

'Pray for me, my brethren!' he exclaimed.

His face was no longer stern, and his hard features wore now an expression of gentle peacefulness. He helped his executioners with their task by himself stretching out his arms on the cross-piece, and then, with eyes upturned to heaven, he began to pray fervently.

The ring now looked like a forest, with a human being crucified on every tree. The arms of the crosses and the martyrs' heads were lit up by the sun, while the arena was covered with shadows that formed a dark chequered pattern, with here and there a patch of yellow sand. The whole pleasure of the spectacle lay in watching the slow torture of the victims. The forest of crosses was so thick that the servants had scarcely room to pass between them. The outermost crosses were chiefly hung with women, but Crispus, as leader, was placed directly opposite to the imperial box, upon an immense cross decked at the foot with hawthorn blossom.

None of the martyrs had yet expired, but some of those who were first hung up had fainted. Not

one of them groaned or begged for mercy. Some
hung with heads bent upon their shoulders or
upon their breasts, as though overcome by drowsi-
ness; others appeared to be meditating, while others
were looking to the sky, their lips moving faintly. In
presence of this appalling forest of crosses, those
outstretched bodies, and this deathly silence, the
joyful shouts of the populace suddenly died away.
Even the stiff and contorted bodies of the naked
women had lost their attraction.

And then Crispus opened his eyes and beheld
Nero. Once again so relentless an expression stole
over his face and his eyes lit up so fiercely that the
Augustans whispered together, and pointed at him,
and at last Cæsar turned his attention upon him,
slowly raising his emerald to his eye. There was
perfect silence. All eyes were fixed on Crispus, who
was striving to tear his right hand free from the
cross.

Then his chest heaved, his ribs stood out, and
he cried:

'Woe unto you, matricide!'

This insult, uttered before all his subjects, made
Cæsar shudder and drop his emerald. Crispus'
voice rang out ever louder and louder through the
amphitheatre:

'Woe unto you, slayer of mother and brother!
Woe unto you, Antichrist! The pit is yawning
below your feet, and the arms of death are stretched
out to embrace you! The grave awaits you! Woe
unto you, you living corpse, for you shall die in
terror, and be damned to all eternity!'

Stretched out in dreadful fashion, like a living
skeleton, he shook his white beard over the imperial
box, scattering the petals of the roses that encircled
his head.

'Woe unto you, murderer! Your hour is at hand!'

He made one supreme effort, and for a moment it seemed as though he would free his captive hand, and shake it at Cæsar. But suddenly his arms relaxed, his whole body became limp, his head sank upon his breast, and he died.

In the forest of crosses the weakest of the martyrs fell one by one into the sleep from which there is no awakening.

CHAPTER 17

VINICIUS, remembering that Nazarius had, despite all obstacles, succeeded in gaining admission to the Tullianum as one of those who carried the corpses to burial, determined to resort to the same device. The overseer of the burial pits consented for an enormous sum of money to take him as one of the servants whom he sent each night to remove the bodies from the prisons. What with the darkness of the night, his slave's dress, the cloth soaked in turpentine about his head, and the wretched lighting of the prisons, he might well hope to escape detection.

When the centurion on duty had seen their passes the great iron door of the Esquiline Prison opened before them, and Vinicius beheld a spacious central vault, from which many others opened off. By the light of the candles he saw that it was full of prisoners. Some were lying along the walls asleep, or possibly dead; others were crowding round a water-trough in the middle, from which they drank; others were sitting on the ground, their elbows resting on their knees and their heads in their hands.

Here and there children were sleeping, huddled close to their mothers. On every side were heard the moans of the sick, sobs, and murmured prayers, the singing of hymns in low tones, and the cursing of the warders.

Vinicius' legs shook beneath him. His hair stood on end and his gorge rose at the idea that Lygia was in this Gehenna. The amphitheatre, the wild beasts' jaws, the crosses—anything rather than these horrible dungeons, reeking with decomposing bodies.

'How many dead to-day ? ' asked the overseer of the pits.

'A good dozen,' replied the chief warder ; 'but before morning there will be more, for some of these along the wall there are at their last gasp already.'

He began to complain about the women who hid their dead children in order to keep them as long as possible. They were only discovered by their smell.

'I would rather be a slave in a prison in the country,' said the man, 'than look after these dogs that rot before they die.'

Meanwhile Vinicius searched in vain for Lygia, and he began to think he would never see her again alive.

Fortunately the overseer came to his assistance.

'You must have the corpses taken away at once,' he said, 'if you don't all want to become corpses yourselves as well as the prisoners.'

'There are only ten of us for all the dungeons,' replied the gaoler, 'and we must sleep sometime.'

'Then I'll leave you four of my men. They will make a round of the dungeons to see if there are any dead.'

'I'll give you a drink tomorrow if you do. But

tell them to report all the bodies, for we received orders today to cut their throats before they are taken away to be buried.'

'All right; and you'll pay for the drink?'

So saying, he pointed out four men, of whom Vinicius was one, and along with the others he began to pile the corpses on the barrows.

Vinicius breathed again, for now he was sure of finding Lygia. First of all, he carefully searched the first dungeon, but found nothing. Equally unsuccessful were his searches in the second and third.

Then he entered a fourth dungeon, smaller than the others, and raised his lantern.

Suddenly he started, for he thought he saw underneath the bars of an air-hole the gigantic figure of Ursus. He instantly blew out the light and drew near to him.

'Is that you, Ursus?'

The giant raised his head.

'Who are you?' said he.

'Don't you recognise me?'

'You have blown out the light, so how can I recognise you?'

But Vinicius caught sight of Lygia lying beside the wall upon a cloak, and without a word he knelt down close beside her.

Then Ursus recognised him, and said:

'Blessed be the Lord! But do not waken her, master.'

Vinicius gazed upon her through his tears. Despite the darkness, he could distinguish her face, pale as marble, and her emaciated shoulders. And the spectacle filled him with a love that was closely allied to the most harrowing grief—a love full of pity and respectful adoration. He fell upon his face, his lips touching the edge of the cloak on which the maiden lay.

Suddenly Lygia opened her eyes and laid her burning hands upon those of her lover as he knelt beside her.

'I see you,' she said. 'Oh, I knew you would come!'

'Yes, darling, I have come. May Christ protect you and save you, my beloved Lygia!'

He could say no more, unwilling to let her see his grief.

'I am ill, Marcus, and here or in the arena I must die. I prayed to see you before I died, and you have come! Christ has heard my prayer!'

Unable to utter another word, he pressed her to his heart.

'I knew you would come,' she went on. 'Today the Saviour has allowed us to say farewell. I am going to Him, Marcus, now; but I love you, and will love you always.'

Vinicius mastered his sorrow with an effort, and said in a voice that he strove to render calm:

'No, my darling, you are not going to die. The apostle bade me have faith, and he promised to pray for you. Christ will take pity upon me. He does not want you to die; He will not suffer it.'

The single lamp that hung above the door had gone out, but the light of the moon was now streaming through the air-hole. In the far corner a child gave a plaintive cry and then was silent. Outside could be heard the voices of the Prætorians off duty, who were playing *scriptæ duodecim* beneath the walls.

After a short silence Lygia replied:

'When the guards came to look for us I was afraid of torture and of death, but now I am not afraid.

334

See what a dreadful place this prison is, and think that I am going to heaven. Think that here there is Cæsar, while up there is the Saviour, who is kind and merciful. You love me, so remember how happy I shall be. And remember, dear Marcus, that you will come and join me there.'

She paused for breath, and then caught Vinicius' hand and put it to her lips.

' Marcus.'

' Yes, my darling.'

' You must not weep for me. Remember that you will come and join me up there. My life has not been a long one, but God has given me your heart. And I can say to Christ that though I am dead, and though you saw me die, and though you were left desolate, yet you did not murmur against His will. He will bring us together again. I love you, and I want to be with you.'

Once again her breath failed her, and she finished in scarce audible tones :

' Promise that, Marcus.'

' By your dear head, I swear it.'

In that dismal light he saw that her face was radiant. She took his hand once more and raised it to her lips, murmuring :

' Your wife ; I am your wife.'

From outside came the voices of the Prætorians quarrelling over their game.

But these two were oblivious of prison, of warders, and of the whole world, and with souls in perfect communion, they were praying to their God.

CHAPTER 18

DARKNESS had not yet completely fallen when the crowd began to wend its way towards the emperor's gardens. On went the people, clad in holiday attire, wreathed with flowers and singing lustily, to witness a new and splendid spectacle. Almost all of them were drunk. The Via Tecta, the Æmilian Bridge, the Via Triumphalis beyond the Tiber, the environs of the Circus Neronis, and even the Vatican Hill rang with shouts of ' Semaxii! Sarmentitii!'

Anxious to have done with the Christians and to check the epidemic that was raging ever more fiercely throughout the city, Cæsar and Tigellinus had cleared out all the dungeons, and had left only a few dozen people for the last day of the games.

When the crowd passed through the gates of the garden they paused, dumbfounded. All the principal walks—all those which ran through the shrubberies, meadows, and trees ; those which led past the lakes, the fish ponds, and the lawns studded with flowers —all were bristling with resinous stakes, to which Christians were bound.

From the rising ground, where the view was not impeded by the trees, could be seen whole rows of bodies decked with flowers, ivy, and myrtle leaves.

Darkness had now fallen, and the first stars appeared in the sky. Slaves with torches took their stand beside the victims, and when the trumpet rang out for the show to begin, they set fire to the foot of the stakes.

Concealed beneath the flowers was straw soaked in pitch, and this sprang at once into a bright flame, which spread till it loosened the ivy wreaths and

336

began to lick the feet of the victims. The crowd
fell silent, while the whole garden resounded with
one mighty groan, proceeding from thousands of
agonised throats. Some of the victims, however,
raised their eyes to the starry heavens, and sang
praises to Christ, while the crowd listened. But the
hardest hearts were filled with horror when from
the tops of the smaller posts came the harrowing
voices of children crying 'Mother! mother!' Even
drunken men shuddered to see the little heads and
the innocent faces drawn with pain or wreathed in
the smoke that was already beginning to suffo-
cate the victims. As the smell of burning flesh
spread through the garden, the slaves threw myrrh
and aloes into the censers which were placed among
the posts.

At the beginning of the spectacle Cæsar appeared
among the people in a magnificent racing chariot
drawn by four white stallions. He was dressed as
a charioteer of the Greens, which was the party
supported by himself and his court. Other cars
followed, crowded with richly dressed courtiers,
senators, priests, and naked, drunken women with
wreaths of roses on their heads and wine-jars in
their hands, uttering wild cries. Musicians in the
guise of fauns and satyrs played on lyres, harps,
flutes, and horns. In other chariots came Roman
matrons and virgins, also drunk and half naked.
Youths walked on both sides of the chariots, some
waving rods decked with ribbons or playing on the
cymbals, while others scattered flowers beneath the
horses' feet.

Amid the smoke and the human torches the
procession passed down the principal walk, shouting
'Evoe!' Cæsar, accompanied by Tigellinus, and by
Chilon, whose terror afforded him much amusement,

drove his horses at a walking pace, gazing at the burning bodies and drinking in the acclamations of the people. His enormous arms seemed, as he held the reins, to be stretched out to bless his people. His face and half-closed eyes wore a smiling expression, and he towered above the rest in his golden crown —a dazzling, god-like vision.

At last, on arriving at the great fountain, where two roads crossed, he descended from his chariot, and beckoning to his followers, he joined the crowd, stopping now and then to make some remarks about the victims or to laugh at Chilon, whose face was a picture of unutterable despair.

They came to a lofty pole hung with myrtle and ivy. The red tongues of flame were still flickering around the knees of the victim, but his face could no longer be seen, as it was obscured by the smoke from the green twigs. But a sudden gust of wind swept aside the smoke and disclosed the head of an old, gray-bearded man. When Chilon saw this he writhed like a wounded snake and uttered a cry that resembled more the hoarse note of a raven than any human sound:

'Glaucus! Glaucus!'

From the top of the blazing post Glaucus the doctor was looking down upon him.

His head bowed upon his breast and his face drawn with pain, he gazed upon the man who had betrayed him, who had robbed him of wife and children, who had drawn him into a den of murderers, and who, after all these crimes had been forgiven him for Christ's sake, had once more sold him to the executioners. His eyes were riveted on the face of the Greek. Everybody saw that something was passing between those two, but laughter died upon their lips, for Chilon's face was a dreadful sight: the tongues of fire might have been devouring his own body. Suddenly he tottered forward, stretched out his arms, and cried in a fearful, harrowing voice:

'Glaucus! Forgive me, for Christ's sake!'

Nobody spoke, but everybody shuddered and raised their eyes to the stake.

The martyr's head moved feebly, and from the top of the pole a voice moaned:

'I forgive!'

Chilon fell upon his face, howling like a wild beast, and began with both hands to throw earth upon his head. The flames suddenly leapt up and enveloped the face and breast of Glaucus, loosened the myrtle wreath upon his head, and devoured the ribbons at the top of the pole, which was now a blazing mass from top to bottom.

But Chilon rose up with a face so transfigured that the Augustans thought it was another man who stood before them. His eyes shone and his face was aglow with ecstasy. The mean, cowardly Greek of a moment ago now looked like a priest, inspired by his God, and about to utter some great truths.

'What has happened to him? He is mad!' people murmured.

He turned towards the crowd, and with his right hand uplifted, he said, or rather shouted in a piercing voice, so that not only the Augustans but the whole throng might hear him:

'Citizens of Rome! As I live, I swear to you that they who perish are innocent! There is the incendiary!'

And he pointed to Nero.

There was silence for a moment. The courtiers were dumbfounded. Chilon stood perfectly still, his hand quivering and his finger pointed towards Cæsar.

Then a turmoil arose. Like waves suddenly stirred up by a squall, the people surged down upon the old man to see him nearer at hand. Some cried out, 'Seize him!' others, 'Woe unto us!' A storm of yells and hisses broke forth, mingled with cries of 'Brazenbeard! Matricide! Incendiary!' The confusion increased, and the Bacchants, with loud cries, ran towards the chariots. Suddenly some of the burnt-out poles came crashing down amid showers of sparks, and Chilon was whirled to the middle of the gardens in the wild eddying of the crowd.

On all sides the stakes, devoured by the flames, were beginning to fall across the paths, filling the walks with smoke and sparks and with the smell of burning wood and flesh. Lights went out all around, and the gardens were wrapped in darkness.

Chilon wandered about not knowing whither to turn. He stumbled against half-roasted bodies and pieces of charred wood that covered him with dangerous showers of sparks. Now and then he sat down and looked stupidly around him. At last he emerged from the shadows, and, urged by an irresistible force, he made his way towards the fountain where Glaucus had given up the ghost.

He felt a hand upon his shoulder.

The old man turned round, and seeing a stranger before him, he exclaimed :

'Well ? Who are you ? '

'An apostle : Paul of Tarsus.'

'I am accursed. What do you want with me ? '

The apostle replied :

'I want to save you.'

Chilon leant against a tree.

'For me there is no salvation now,' he said in a dull voice.

'Then know you not that God forgave the thief who repented ? ' said Paul.

'Then know you not what it is that I have done ? '

'I saw your grief, and I heard you bear witness to the truth.'

'Oh, master!'

'And if a servant of Christ forgave you in the hour of his anguish and death, how should Christ not forgive you ? '

Chilon clutched his head in his hands as though he felt himself going mad.

'Forgiveness ? For me ? Forgiveness ? '

'Our God is a God of mercy,' replied Paul.

'Forgiveness for me!' groaned Chilon.

'Lean upon my arm and come with me,' said the apostle. He walked in the direction of the crossing, guided by the sound of the fountain, which seemed in the stillness of the night to be weeping over the bodies of the martyrs.

'Our God is a God of mercy,' the apostle repeated. 'If you stood at the edge of the sea and threw in pebbles, could you ever fill it up ? Well, I say that Christ's mercy is like the sea, and the sins and faults of men will be swallowed up in it, as stones are swallowed up in the depths of the sea. You suffered before Glaucus as he hung there, and Christ saw your sufferings. Without any thought of the consequences, you exclaimed, " There is the incendiary! " and Christ has not forgotten your words. You have done with meanness and lying, and there is nothing left in your heart save an infinite penitence.'

Chilon fell upon his knees, hid his face in his hands, and remained motionless. Paul lifted his face towards the stars and prayed.

Suddenly at his feet he heard a piteous appeal:

'Christ! Christ! Forgive me!'

Paul went to the fountain, and taking some water in the palms of his hands, returned to the kneeling wretch.

'Chilon, I baptize you in the name of the Father, and of the Son, and of the Holy Ghost! Amen!'

Chilon lifted his head, and stretched out his arms, while the soft light of the moon lit up his white hair and pale, mask-like countenance. The minutes followed each other, and soon from the cages in the gardens of Domitia came the sound of a cock crowing. Still Chilon kneeled, like some sepulchral monument.

But at last he said:

'What must I do before I die, master?'

Paul awoke from his meditations upon the boundless power from whose influence even souls such as the Greek's could not escape. He replied:

'Have faith, and bear witness to the truth.'

They left the gardens together. At the gates the apostle blessed the old man once again, and then they parted at Chilon's own desire, for he suspected that Cæsar and Tigellinus would cause search to be made for him.

Nor was he mistaken. On arriving home he found his house surrounded by Prætorians, who laid hold of him and led him off to the Palatine.

Cæsar had retired, but Tigellinus was waiting for him. He welcomed the unfortunate Greek with a calm but sinister look.

'You have committed the crime of high treason,' he said, 'and you shall not escape punishment. But if, tomorrow, you declare in the middle of the amphitheatre that you were drunk and talking nonsense, and that the Christians are indeed to blame for the fire, your punishment will be limited to scourging and banishment.'

'I cannot, sir,' Chilon said quietly.

Tigellinus walked slowly up to him, and in a quiet yet menacing voice said:

'What? You cannot, you Grecian dog? You were not drunk? You do not seem to understand what is in store for you. Look there!'

And he pointed to a dark corner of the atrium, where, beside a broad wooden bench, stood four Thracian slaves with ropes and pincers in their hands.

Chilon only said:

'I cannot, sir!'

Wrath filled the soul of Tigellinus, but he controlled himself again and said:

'You saw how the Christians died? Do you want to die in the same way?'

The old man lifted up his pallid face, and for a moment his lips moved silently. Then he said:

'I too believe in Christ.'

Tigellinus looked at him in amazement.

'You dog! You must be mad, I think!'

He sprang upon Chilon, seized him by the beard with both hands, threw him to the ground and trampled on him, foaming at the mouth the while, and saying:

'You shall retract! You shall retract!'

'I cannot,' groaned Chilon, beneath his heel.

'Take the fellow and torture him!'

The Thracians seized him, and laying him on the trestle they tied him down with cords and set to work to break his wasted legs with their pincers. But all the while they were tying him he humbly kissed their hands, and then, shutting his eyes, remained motionless, as if he were dead.

But he was still alive, and when Tigellinus bent over him and asked him once more, 'Will you retract ? ' his pale lips moved feebly, and a scarce perceptible murmur escaped them :

' I—cannot—sir ! '

Tigellinus bade them stop the torture. As he paced up and down the atrium a new idea seemed to occur to him, and, turning to the Thracians, he said :

' Tear out his tongue ! '

CHAPTER 19

THE drama of *Aureolus* was usually presented in theatres and amphitheatres so constructed that they could be opened up and disclose two separate stages. But after the spectacle in the Imperial Gardens it was resolved not to employ the ordinary device, as the object was to allow all the spectators to witness the death of the crucified slave, who, in the play, is devoured by a bear. In the theatre the part of the bear was played by an actor sewn up in a skin, but this time the bear was to be a real one. It was a new idea of Tigellinus'.

By nightfall the whole circus was full to overflowing. The Augustans, with Tigellinus at their head, were present in full force, not so much for the sake of the spectacle as in order to testify their loyalty to Cæsar after the incident in the garden, and to discuss Chilon, about whom the whole city was talking.

At last the moment arrived, and the servants brought in a wooden cross low enough to permit of the bear reaching the victim's chest by standing on his hind legs. Then two men led, or rather dragged, Chilon into the ring, for his legs were broken, and he could not walk. He was nailed to the cross so quickly that the Augustans had not time to obtain a good view of him. Only after the cross was fixed up were all eyes turned in his direction. But few of those present recognised in this naked old man the Chilon of the day before.

As a result of the torture inflicted by Tigellinus, his face was quite bloodless. A red streak upon his hoary beard told of the tongue that had been torn out. Through his transparent skin the bones could almost be seen. His face bore traces of suffering, but it was as calm and benign as that of a man asleep. Along with repentance, peace seemed to have settled on this chastened soul.

Nobody laughed, for there was something so peaceful about the old man—he looked so decrepit and helpless, so wretched and pitiable in his abjection—that everybody asked himself why they should torture and crucify one already so near death.

At last the bear came lumbering into the arena, his head low down, swaying from side to side as he looked along the ground. He appeared to be meditating something or on the lookout for something. When he saw the cross and the naked body he went up to them, stood upon his hind legs and sniffed. But he soon fell on all fours again, and sitting down under the cross he began to grunt, as though his savage heart took pity on this poor wreck of a man.

The attendants sought to excite the bear by shouting. The crowd remained silent.

Meanwhile Chilon slowly raised his head and looked at the spectators. His eyes riveted themselves high up on the last rows of the amphitheatre. Then his chest heaved more quickly, and to the astonishment of the crowd his face lit up with a smile. A halo of light encircled his brow, he lifted his eyes to the sky, and from under his drooping eyelids two tears stole slowly down his face.

He was dead.

Suddenly, from near the awning, a deep voice rang out:

'Peace be with the martyrs!'

A deathly silence reigned in the amphitheatre.

CHAPTER 20

DURING Nero's reign evening displays in circus and amphitheatre had became popular. Although the people had had their fill of bloodshed, the news that the end of the games was close at hand, and that the last of the Christians were to die in the ring that evening, filled the benches with a countless throng. The Augustans were there to a man, surmising that Cæsar meant to treat himself to an exhibition of grief on the part of Vinicius. Tigellinus had given no hint as to the kind of torture in store for the young tribune's betrothed, but his very silence aroused universal curiosity.

Cæsar arrived earlier than usual. Besides Tigellinus and Vatinius, he brought with him Cassius, a broad-shouldered centurion of prodigious strength. The guard of Prætorians was reinforced, and was commanded, not by a centurion, but by the tribune Subrius Flavius, whose blind devotion to the person of the emperor was notorious. Plainly, Cæsar's intention was to protect himself against a possible desperate outburst by Vinicius. The interest deepened.

All eyes were kept greedily fixed upon the place where sat the unhappy lover, with pale countenance and drops of perspiration standing on his forehead. His heart beat faintly still with a remnant of hope ; perhaps Lygia was not among those condemned, and perhaps all his fears were vain.

At last, like a man who, falling over a precipice, catches at anything that projects from the face of it, Vinicius caught at the idea that only by faith could he save her now. All was gone, save faith! And had not Peter told him that faith could shake the earth to its foundations ?

Wrapped up in this hope he repressed his fears, and concentrating his whole soul in the three words ' I have faith,' he awaited a miracle.

At last the prefect threw a red handkerchief on to the sand. The door opposite to the imperial box grated on its hinges, and from the dark recesses Ursus stepped forth into the brightly lit arena. The giant blinked his dazzled eyes, and, advancing to the middle of the arena, looked around him to discover his foe. The Augustans and most of the spectators knew that this was the man who had strangled Croton, and a loud murmur rose from tier to tier. Gladiators far beyond the normal size were not uncommon at Rome, but never had Roman eyes beheld so mighty a giant as this.

He stood quite still in the middle of the ring, naked, like some great Colossus hewn out of granite, with a look of grief and suffering upon his ragged face. Seeing the arena empty, he turned his blue, childlike eyes in astonishment upon the audience, upon Cæsar, and then upon the gates of the cells whence he expected death to come.

When he entered the arena his heart had once more beat high with the hope that perhaps he was to die upon the cross. But seeing neither cross nor hole dug for it, he concluded that he was unworthy of such an honour, and that he would have to die in some other way, probably in the jaws of the wild beasts. He was unarmed, and had determined to die with resignation, as became a follower of Christ. And desiring once again to pray to his Redeemer, he knelt down, clasped his hands, and lifted up his eyes towards the stars that shone through the opening in the canopy.

This posture was displeasing to the crowd, who were tired of seeing men die like sheep. If the giant would not fight, the exhibition would be a failure. Here and there arose the sound of hissing, and voices clamoured for the men with the whips. But they gradually died away, for nobody knew who the giant's opponent was to be nor whether when the time came he would refuse to fight.

They were not left long in suspense, for suddenly the trumpets gave forth a deafening blast; the gate opposite the imperial box was thrown open, and amid the shouts of the gladiators, an enormous German bull rushed into the ring with a naked woman bound to his horns.

'Lygia! Lygia!' cried Vinicius.

And clutching the hair upon his forehead with both hands he writhed about like a man who feels the cold steel enter his vitals, and groaned in a hoarse, unearthly voice:

'I have faith! I have faith! A miracle, O Christ!'

He was not even aware that at that moment Petronius threw his toga over his head. He thought that it was death or grief that darkened his eyes. He looked at nothing—saw nothing. A dreadful feeling of emptiness overcame him. He could not fix his thoughts on anything, and from his lips alone came the frenzied words :

'I have faith! I have faith! I have faith!'

Suddenly a hush fell upon the audience. Like one man the Augustans had risen from their seats, for there, upon the arena, an unheard-of thing was happening. At the sight of his mistress tied to the horns of the wild bull, the Lygian, a moment before humble and ready to die, started as though at the touch of a hot iron and rushed across towards the maddened beast.

A short cry of amazement burst from every throat, and then there was a dead silence.

At one bound the Lygian made up on the bull and seized him by the horns.

'Look!' exclaimed Petronius, drawing the toga from Vinicius' head.

Vinicius lifted up his chalk-white face and began to look around the ring with wild staring eyes.

Everybody held his breath. The buzzing of a fly might have been heard in the amphitheatre.

Never had the like been seen since Rome began.

The man had the beast by the horns. His feet were ankle deep in the sand ; his spine was bent like a bow ; his head was hidden between his shoulders and the muscles of his arms stood out so that it seemed as though they must burst through the skin. But he had stopped the bull dead, and man and beast stood there so still that they looked like some sculptured piece representing the labours of Theseus or Hercules. But beneath the stillness lay the fearful tension of two warring forces. The bull's legs were buried in the sand, and his dark, shaggy body was curved into an enormous ball. The question which of the two would be the first to tire and give in was at the moment of greater importance to the

frenzied crowd than their own fate, than the fate of
Rome, and of the whole Roman empire. The
Lygian was a demi-god! Even Cæsar was upon his
feet. He and Tigellinus, knowing the man's
strength, had devised this exhibition, saying ironically
to each other:

'Let him try, this slayer of Croton—let him try
to kill the bull we shall find for him!'

Some of the audience were standing motionless
with arms uplifted; the faces of others were wet
with perspiration, as though they themselves were
fighting with the animal. Not a sound was heard
save the flaring of the lamps and the crackling of
sparks as they dropped from the torches. Words
died away half-uttered on the speakers' lips, and
their hearts thumped loudly within their breasts.
It seemed to all that the struggle had lasted for
ages.

And man and beast stood locked in their dreadful
struggle as though riveted to the earth.

Suddenly a low, moaning bellow arose from the
arena.

From every throat there came a shout, and then
once again there was dead silence. As though in
a dream, the people saw the monstrous head twisted
slowly round in the barbarian's iron grip.

The Lygian's face and neck and arms were
purple, and his back was still further bent. He was
evidently summoning all that remained of his super-
human strength, now wellnigh exhausted.

Even hoarser, more stifled and more agonised
came the bellowing of the bull, mingled with the
man's loud breathing. The animal's head was
wrenched still farther, and suddenly a great dripping
tongue escaped from his jaws.

A moment later the spectators nearest to the

ring heard the dull noise of breaking bones, and the beast collapsed dead in a heap, with his neck broken.

In an instant the giant unwound the cords from the horns and took the maiden in his arms. He was panting for breath; his face was pale, his hair lank with sweat, his arms and shoulders streaming. For a moment he stood motionless as though in a trance, then he raised his eyes and looked at the spectators.

The whole amphitheatre had gone mad.

The walls of the great building trembled with shouts from tens of thousands of throats. The spectators on the upper tiers left their places and thronged down the passages to the ring in order to have a better view of this Hercules.

On every side rose voices clamouring for his release — persistent, passionate voices that soon merged into one great roar. The giant was the hero of the crowd, devoted as they were to the worship of physical strength: he was the first personage in Rome.

Ursus knew that the people were begging for his life and liberty. But that was not what he cared about. He looked around him for a moment, and then advanced towards the imperial box, holding out the young girl in his arms, his eyes raised in supplication as though to say, 'It is mercy for her that I ask! It is she you have to spare! I did it for her!'

At the sight of the fainting girl, who looked like a little child beside the Lygian's immense body, the people, the knights, and the senators were overcome with emotion. Some thought it was a father begging mercy for his child. Pity spread like lightning among them. They had had enough of blood and death and tortures, and voices choked with sobs demanded mercy for both of them.

Suddenly Vinicius started from his seat, and clearing the wall of the arena he ran towards Lygia and covered her naked body with his toga. Then, tearing open his tunic, he pointed to the scars of his Armenian campaign upon his chest, and stretched out his arms towards the people.

Frenzy broke out surpassing all that had ever been seen in the amphitheatre. The crowd began to stamp and to howl; the voices that clamoured for mercy grew threatening; thousands shook their fists at Cæsar, and all eyes blazed with fury.

Nero was in a quandary.

He had no animosity towards Vinicius, and Lygia's death was a matter of no particular moment to him. But his vanity would not allow him to bow to the will of the crowd, and yet his natural cowardice made him hesitate to refuse.

So he began to look around to see if among the Augustans at any rate there was not one thumb turned down to seal the victims' doom. But Petronius' hand was turned upwards and he was looking him full in the face, with a touch of defiance in his look. The senator Scævinus did likewise; so did Nerva; so did Tullius Senecio; so did the famous veteran Ostorius Scapula; so did Austitius, Piso, Vetus, Crispinus, Minucius Thermus, Pontius Telesinus, and even austere Thrasea, the darling of the crowd. Seeing this, Cæsar took his emerald from his eye with a contemptuous and spiteful look, but Tigellinus, anxious at all costs for a victory over Petronius, bent forward and said:

'Do not give in, your Majesty; the Prætorians are with us.'

Nero turned to where at the head of the guard

stood the stern Subrius Flavius, who had always been devoted to him body and soul. An unprecedented spectacle met his eyes, for there stood the old tribune with tears running down his crabbed face and his right hand raised as a sign of mercy.

But now the multitude became enraged. The incessant stamping had raised a cloud of dust in the amphitheatre. Curses mingled with the shouts: 'Brazenbeard! Matricide! Incendiary!' Nero took fright. As actor and as singer he needed the people's support; he would some day need them at his back in his struggle with the senate and the patricians, and since the great fire, he had been striving to win them over by turning his wrath against the Christians and by all the other means in his power. He saw that it would be dangerous to withstand them any longer. Disaffection might spread from the Circus to the city with consequences which it was impossible to foresee.

He cast a hasty glance at Subrius Flavius, at the centurion Scævinus, a relative of the senator's, and at the soldiers; he saw on all sides drawn brows, faces moved with pity, stern looks bent upon himself, and so he gave the sign to spare the prisoners.

The Circus rang with thunderous applause from top to bottom. The people had made sure of the victims' lives. From that moment they were under their protection, and nobody, not even Cæsar himself, would have dared to persecute them further.

CHAPTER 21

FOUR Bithynian slaves carried Lygia tenderly to Petronius' house. Vinicius and Ursus walked along beside the litter in silence, for after the events of that day they had no strength left to talk. Vinicius was still half dazed. He kept telling himself that Lygia was safe and in no danger of prison or of death in the ring, that their troubles were over, and that he was taking her home, never more to part with her. It seemed more like the dawn of a new life than reality. From time to time he would bend over the open litter and gaze by the light of the moon upon her dear face, seemingly wrapped in slumber, saying to himself the while:

' It is she! Christ has saved her!'

They went forward quickly between the newly built houses with their white walls shining in the moonlight. The city was deserted save for here and there an ivy-wreathed crowd of people singing and dancing in front of the colonnades to the sound of flutes, enjoying to the full their holiday, which was to last till the end of the games, and making the most of the glorious night.

And now they were at the house, where the entire household, warned of their coming by one of the slaves, had turned out to meet them. Most of them had already been converted at Antium by Paul of Tarsus. Vinicius' misfortunes were well known to them, and they were overjoyed to see the victims who had been snatched from the cruel Nero's clutches. Their joy was increased when Theocles the doctor declared that Lygia had received no serious injury, and that although weakened by the prison-fever, she would soon recover her strength.

That same night consciousness returned to her. On awakening in a splendid bedroom, lit by Corinthian lamps and scented with verbena, she could not understand where she was nor what had happened to her. She remembered being tied by the men to the bull's horns, and when she saw Vinicius' face looking down at her in the soft light she thought she was no longer upon earth. Feeling no pain, she smiled to Vinicius and sought to question him, but her lips only gave forth a scarce audible murmur in which Vinicius made out nothing save his own name.

He knelt beside her and laid his hand lightly on her forehead.

'Christ has saved you and given you back to me,' he said.

Once again her lips moved and murmured something indistinctly. Her eyelids closed and she fell into a deep sleep, which Theocles expected and pronounced to be a good sign. Vinicius knelt on in prayer beside the bed. A boundless love melted his heart and transported him beyond consciousness. Theocles entered the room several times, and more than once Eunice's golden head appeared round the curtain. At last the cranes that were kept in the garden announced the daybreak with their cries, but Vinicius still knelt at the feet of Christ, seeing and hearing nothing, his heart ablaze as with the flame of some mighty sacrifice.

CHAPTER 22

IT was many a day since the apostle Peter had dared to show himself at Petronius' house, but one evening

Nazarius announced that he was coming. Lygia, who could now walk, went out to meet him with Vinicius, and they both threw themselves at his feet. He welcomed them with an emotion that was all the greater because so few remained of the flock entrusted to his charge by Christ. And when Vinicius said, ' Master, it is thanks to you that the Saviour has restored her to me,' the apostle replied, ' He has restored her to you because of your trust in Him, and in order that all the lips that confess His name may not be for ever dumb.'

A few days later Petronius brought alarming news from the Palatine. One of Cæsar's freedmen had turned out to be a Christian, and in his possession had been found letters from the apostles, Paul of Tarsus and Peter, and from James, Judas, and John. Tigellinus imagined that the apostle was one of the thousands of Christians who had perished, and now it appeared that the two leaders of the new faith were still alive and actually in Rome. And so it was decided to lay hands on them at all costs and wipe out with them the last traces of the accursed sect. With this end in view, whole companies of soldiers had been sent to search the houses across the Tiber.

Vinicius resolved to go at once and warn the Apostle, and that very evening he and Ursus visited Myriam's house, where they found Peter among a handful of his followers, Timothy, the companion of Paul, and Linus being also there.

' Master,' said Vinicius, ' let somebody take you away to-morrow at daybreak to the Alban Mountains. We shall come there for you and take you to Antium, where a ship is lying ready to sail with us to Naples and then to Sicily.'

The others urged the apostle to agree.

'You must hide, master, for you cannot remain in Rome. You must keep the truth alive, that it may not die with us and with you. Hear us, we beseech you as our father!'

Many a time had the Fisher of Men stretched out his hand in solitude to heaven and said: 'Lord what must I do ?'

Since the death of his Master, thirty-four years ago, he had known no rest. With his pilgrim's staff in his hand he had travelled through the world carrying the good tidings. His strength was exhausted with his labours and his travels, and now, when he had at last established his Master's church in the city that was mistress of the world, it had been overwhelmed by one scorching blast of a madman's fury. So once again he must renew the struggle. And what a struggle! On the one side stood Nero, the senate, the people, legions that encircled the whole world with a girdle of iron, countless cities and countries—a force such as human eye had never seen ; and on the other side stood he himself, so bowed down by age and hardship that his trembling hands could scarce hold his staff.

At times he told himself that it was not his task to measure himself against the Roman emperor, and that Christ alone could accomplish that.

His friends crowded ever closer about him, saying in tones of entreaty:

'Hide yourself, rabbi, and save us from the clutches of the Beast.'

At last Linus bowed his tortured head before him:

'Master, the Saviour said to you, "Feed my sheep." But the sheep are no more or will be no more tomorrow. Return to where you may still find them. The Word of God still lives at Ephesus, Jerusalem, and Antioch, as well as in other places.

Why then remain in Rome ? If you die, you make the triumph of the Beast still greater. The Lord has set no term to John's life ; Paul is a Roman citizen, whom they cannot put to death without a trial. But if you, our leader, fall into the clutches of this fiend, then those whose courage is already failing them will say, " Is there truly one greater than Nero ? ' You are the rock on which God's church is built. Allow us to die, but do not allow Antichrist to prevail over the Vicar of God, and do not return till God has blotted out him who has made the blood of innocents to flow in torrents.'

' Behold our tears !' the others cried.

Tears were streaming down Peter's face as he rose, and stretching out his hands above his kneeling flock said :

' May the Lord's name be praised and His will be done !'

CHAPTER 23

On the following morning at daybreak two dark figures might have been seen walking along the Appian Way towards the plains of the Campagna.

One was Nazarius, and the other was Peter, who was leaving behind him Rome and his persecuted followers.

To the east there was a faint tinge of green in the sky, with an ever-spreading border of saffron low down upon the horizon.

The silvery foliage of the trees, the white marble walls of the houses, and the arches of the aqueducts that ran across the plain to Rome, emerged slowly from the darkness. The sky grew gradually brighter, diffused with a golden light. The rising sun tinged with pink the Alban Mountains, which stood up like some wondrous flowers, fashioned out of light. The dawn was mirrored in the drops of dew that shone on every rustling leaf. Gradually the veil of mist lifted, disclosing here and there the expanse of plain, with its houses, cemeteries, villages, and temple pillars gleaming white amid the trees.

The road was deserted. The country folks who took their vegetables each morning to the city had not yet harnessed their carts. The wooden sandals of the two pilgrims resounded faintly upon the stone pavement, with which the road was laid as far as the Alban Mountains.

The sun rose above the brow of the hills, and a strange sight met the eyes of the apostle. The golden orb, instead of rising in the heavens, seemed to have slipped down from the mountains, and to be advancing along the road.

Peter stopped and said:

' Do you see that light coming towards us ? '

' I see nothing,' Nazarius replied.

But Peter shaded his eyes with his hand and said:

' There is a man coming towards us in the rays of the sun.'

Yet no sound of footsteps reached their ears. There was a dead silence all about them. Nazarius only noticed that the distant trees rustled as though shaken by some unseen hand, and he saw the brightness spreading farther and farther over the plain.

He looked in amazement at the apostle.

' Rabbi, what is the matter ? ' he exclaimed in an anxious voice.

Peter's staff had fallen on the road; his eyes

stared fixedly in front of him; his lips were parted, and upon his face was a look of bewildered joy and ecstasy.

He fell upon his knees, with hands outstretched, and from his lips broke the cry,—

'Christ! Christ!'

And he fell with his face to the ground as though he would have kissed some invisible feet. There was a long pause, and then the old man said in a voice shaken with sobs:

'*Quo vadis, Domine?*'

The reply was not audible to Nazarius, but upon the ears of the apostle fell a sweet, sad voice, which said:

'Since you are forsaking my people I am going to Rome to be crucified once again.'

The apostle lay at full length upon the road with his face in the dust, silent and motionless. Nazarius began to think that he had fainted or that perhaps he was dead. But at last he rose, and picking up his staff in his trembling hands, he turned round without a word and faced the seven hills.

Like an echo came the boy's question:

'*Quo vadis, Domine?*'

'To Rome,' said the apostle quietly.

And he returned towards Rome.

Paul, John, Linus, and the other Christians were surprised and uneasy when they saw him. After his departure the Prætorians had surrounded Myriam's house in their search for him. But in reply to all their questions Peter only replied, quietly and happily:

'I have seen the Lord!'

That evening he went to the cemetery at the Ostrianum to teach the Word of God, and to baptize all who desired to be bathed in the water of life. From that time onwards he went there every day, and ever-increasing multitudes followed him. It was as though from every martyr's tear had sprung fresh converts, and as though every groan from the arena had found an echo in thousands of hearts. Cæsar swam in blood ; Rome and the rest of the heathen world were raving in delirium. But those who were sick of crime and madness ; those who were trodden underfoot ; those whose life was one of misfortune and want—all the tortured and oppressed and wronged—these came to hear the wondrous story of a God who let Himself be crucified out of His love for men, and for the redemption of their sins.

And finding a God whom they could love, they found that which till then the world had never been able to give them, the joy that is born of love.

Peter saw that Cæsar and all his legions could never now overcome the living Truth, that neither by tears nor by blood could it be overwhelmed, and that already its hour of victory was at hand. He saw why Christ had bidden him return ; he saw that already the proud, wicked, depraved, but all-powerful city was being won to his side. Already she was assuming her double role as ruler both of souls and of bodies.

CHAPTER 24

THEN came the hour of martyrdom. Cæsar was absent from Rome, and the death sentence had been signed by Helius and Polythetes, two freedmen to whom in his absence he had delegated his powers.

First of all the venerable apostle underwent the

scourging prescribed by law, and on the following day he was to be taken outside the walls to the Vatican Hill and suffer the fate to which he had been condemned.

The soldiers were surprised at the large numbers of people who hung about in front of the prison. The death of a man of the people, and a foreigner to boot, was surely not a matter of such moment. However, they were no mere curious idlers who formed the crowd, but those of the faithful who desired to accompany the great Apostle to the place of his death. At last the doors opened, and Peter appeared with an escort of Prætorians. The sun was already sinking towards Ostia, and the afternoon was clear and calm.

In consideration of his age, Peter was not forced to carry his cross, and in order not to impede his walking his neck had not been confined in the yoke. And he wore no fetters. From all sides he was clearly in view of his followers. When they beheld his white head, the sound of sobbing arose, which, however, soon ceased when they saw his radiant, joyful face. All perceived then that here was no victim going to his death, but a conqueror going forward to his triumph.

And so indeed it was. The fisherman, usually so humble and bent, now walked erect and towered above the soldiers. Never had his bearing seemed so majestic. He walked along like a monarch surrounded by his bodyguard and his subjects.

His face shone with an ever-growing joy, for his view could scarce embrace the legions of his followers. He knew that he had achieved his task. This truth which he had taught all his life was to be as a stream that carried all before it, never more to be stemmed.

As he passed the temples he said: 'Ye shall
be the temples of Christ.' Then, looking at the
multitudes that he beheld before him, he said:
'Your children shall be the servants of Christ!'
And he passed on, rejoicing in his victory, his
services, and his power, and majestic in his tran-
quil joy. The soldiers conducted him across the
Pons Triumphalis in the direction of the Naumachia and the Circus. The Christians dwelling
across the river came to swell the procession, and
the crowd then grew so great that the centurion,
suspecting at last that this was some high priest
surrounded by members of his cult, began to
grow uneasy about the insufficiency of the escort.
But no cry of anger or indignation came from the
crowd.

At last the procession halted between the Circus
and the Vatican Hill. Some of the soldiers began to
dig a hole, while others laid down the cross, with the
hammers and nails, until all should be ready. The
crowd still peaceful and absorbed in the proceedings,
fell upon their knees.

With a golden halo from the setting sun around
his head the apostle turned towards the city. The
Tiber gleamed at his feet; on the other side was
the Campus Martius dominated by the Mausoleum
of Augustus; lower down were the immense baths
built by Nero, while lower still was the Theatre of
Pompey.

The sun was setting fast over Ostia—a great
blood-red globe. The west was aflame with a
brilliant light. The soldiers came up to Peter to
strip him of his clothes.

He raised himself to his full height, a prayer upon
his lips, his right hand raised on high. The executioners paused in awe. The Christians held their

breath while he spoke, and a dead silence fell upon all.

Standing above them with right hand outstretched, Peter made the sign of the cross, and in his dying hour extended his blessing: ' *Urbi et orbi.*'

On that same momentous evening another company of soldiers was conducting the apostle Paul of Tarsus along the Ostian road in the direction of Aquæ Salvianæ. Behind him came a band of Christians, all converts of his own. When he saw some well-known face, he would stop and talk, having the right as a Roman citizen to a certain deference from the guard. Outside the Porta Tergemina he met the daughter of the prefect, Flavius Sabinus, and seeing her young face wet with tears he said to her: ' Go your way in peace, Plautilla, daughter of eternal salvation ; but give me your veil to put over my eyes at the moment when I go to the Lord.' And he went on his way with a face joyful as that of the labourer returning home after his day of toil. His soul, like Peter's, was peaceful and serene as the evening sky. His eyes dwelt thoughtfully upon the plain that stretched in front of him and upon the Alban Mountains, bathed in light. He thought of his travels, his labours and fatigues, the victories he had won, and the churches which he had established on every continent and beyond all the seas. He felt that he deserved his rest. His work was done, and the good seed would never be dispersed by the blasts of persecution. He was departing in the knowledge that truth would prevail in the contest which it was waging against the world, and the thought filled him with profound tranquillity.

The way was long, and evening was coming on.

The hills turned purple, and little by little the shadows about the foot of them grew denser. The flocks were seeking the fold, and bands of slaves were returning with their tools upon their shoulders. Children were playing in front of the houses that lined the road, and they looked with eyes of wonder upon the procession as it passed.

Paul remembered his teaching about charity, and how he had told men that even though they parted with all their goods to feed the poor, and though no mysteries were hidden from their eyes, yet they were as nothing without charity—charity that was long-suffering, gentle, and kindly, not puffed up with pride, embittered never, bearing all things, believing all things, hoping all things, enduring all things—charity that would never end!

The years of his life had been passed in the teaching of charity, and he said in his heart: What power can withstand it or who can overcome it ? Could Cæsar quell it, though he were lord of twice as many legions, twice as many cities, seas, countries, and nations ?

And he went forward in triumph to receive his reward.

At last the escort left the high road, and turned eastwards along a narrow path in the direction of Aquæ Salvianæ. By this time the red sun was just visible above the heather. The centurion halted his men beside the spring. The moment had arrived.

Paul laid Plautilla's veil on his shoulder in order to bind it over his eyes. For the last time he lifted up his eyes, sublimely calm, towards the undying light of evening, and began to pray. His hour had come, and he saw in front of him the broad track of the setting sun that led straight to heaven. He repeated in his heart the words which he had written in the consciousness of a task accomplished, and of the end that was at hand:

'I have fought a good fight, I have kept the faith, I have finished my course, and behold, there is laid up for me the incorruptible crown of righteousness.'

CHAPTER 25

VINICIUS to Petronius:

'Even here, my dear uncle, we learn from time to time what is going on at Rome, and for our fuller information we have your letters. You ask me if we are secure. I give you the simple answer—we are forgotten. That must suffice.

'From the peristyle where I sit writing this I see our quiet bay, with Ursus in a boat, casting his net into the shining waves. My wife is beside me, winding a ball of red wool, and I can hear the slaves singing under the almond trees in the garden. Here is peace, dear uncle, and sweet oblivion of the terrors and sufferings of yesterday.

'We are not strangers to grief and tears, for our faith bids us mourn for the misfortunes of others. But even in these tears lies a consolation that is denied to such as are not Christians. Some day, when our appointed course is run, we shall see again all those dear ones who have perished and those who are still to die for the sake of God's word.

'And so we pass the days and months in peace of mind. Our servants and our slaves believe in Christ, and, in accordance with His commandment, we love each other. Often, when the sun is sinking, or when the waves are turning to silver in the moonlight,

Lygia and I talk of the old times, which seem like a dream to-day. And when I think how narrowly my dear love escaped torture and death, I bless the Lord with all my heart. He alone could have saved her from the arena and given her back to me for ever.

'You have seen, Petronius, how this faith can comfort and strengthen in time of trouble, and what patience and courage it gives men to face death. Come and live with us, and you shall see what a source of happiness it can be in the life of every day. Until now, men never knew a God whom they could love. Neither lawgivers nor philosophers ever taught such a thing. No such thing existed either in Greece or at Rome, and Rome means the whole world. The dry, frigid doctrine of the Stoics, which attracts upright men, tempers the soul like a blade of steel, but only confers upon it greater endurance, and does not improve it.

'You yourself knew Paul of Tarsus, and you often had long talks with him. You can understand better than anybody else that beside his teaching the doctrines of all your philosophers and rhetoricians are so much empty show and noise. Do you remember the question he put to you: " Supposing Cæsar were a Christian, should you not feel more secure, more firmly established in your own possessions, freer from alarms, and surer of the future ? " You used to say to me that our faith was the enemy of life. Well, I can assure you that if I had done nothing but repeat the three words " I am happy " throughout this letter, it would but faintly have expressed my happiness.

'You will say that my happiness lies in Lygia. Yes, and that is because I love her immortal soul and because we love each other in Jesus. When youth and beauty are past, when our bodies lose their freshness and death knocks at our door, our love will survive, because our souls will survive. Before my eyes were opened to the light I was ready, for Lygia's sake, to set fire to my own house, and yet today I can assure you that I did not love her then. No, I did not love her, for it is Christ who has taught me what love means.

' He is an everlasting fountain of peace and happiness. Compare with the Christian life your pleasures and their bitter consequences ; your drunken revellings on the eve of—you know not what, and your orgies that more resemble a funeral feast. But to make the contrast clearer, come and see us here in the midst of our thyme-scented hills, our shady groves of olive trees, and our ivy-covered shores. Here are two hearts that love you well. One who is so noble and so good as you ought to be happy. A mind like yours will see the truth, and you will come to love it ; for although, like Cæsar or Tigellinus, a man may be an enemy of the truth, yet it cannot be treated with indifference. Lygia and I, dear Petronius, are glad to think that we may see you soon. Keep yourself well and happy, and come as soon as you can.'

Petronius received this letter at Cumæ, whither he had gone with Cæsar. Every day saw the emperor lower himself still more by some further exhibition of his skill as actor, mountebank, or charioteer ; every day he sank deeper in the morass of abject, loathsome debauchery. The refinement of the Arbiter was now only burdensome to him. When Petronius was silent, Nero read disapproval in his silence ; when he did approve, Nero thought he detected irony in what he said. The lofty patrician both aroused his jealousy and offended his vanity.

Besides, the master and his all-powerful minister had cast eyes of longing upon the wealth and the magnificent art collection of Petronius. They had tolerated him till now because of the projected voyage to Achæa, where his taste and experience in matters Hellenic might prove useful. But Tigellinus had been at great pains to convince Cæsar that Carinas surpassed Petronius in taste and experience, and, moreover, that he would be able to organise games, receptions, and triumphs when they arrived in Greece. From that day Petronius was doomed.

When he was invited to Cumæ with the rest, he went, although he suspected a trap. Perhaps he meant to avoid all show of open resistance, or perhaps it was that he wanted once again to appear before Cæsar and the Augustans with his gay, untroubled countenance, and win a last victory over Tigellinus.

He had scarcely left Rome when Tigellinus accused him of complicity in the abortive conspiracy which Scævinus the senator had led. Those of his household who had remained in Rome were put in prison, and his house was guarded.

Far from being dismayed, Petronius showed not the slightest concern, and he smiled as he welcomed the Augustans to his splendid house at Cumæ, saying :

' Brazenbeard does not like straight questions, so just watch his face when I ask him if it was by his orders that my slaves were put in prison.'

He invited them all to a banquet before he set out on his voyage, and it was while preparations were being made for it that he received the letter from Vinicius.

For a moment it left him pensive. Then his face brightened again, and that same evening he wrote in reply :

' I rejoice that you are so happy, my dear Vinicius, and I wonder at your generosity, for I had no idea that two lovers could remember anybody at all, especially a friend who was far away. Not only do you remember me ; you actually want to bring me to Sicily, and share with me your daily bread and also your Christ, who has, as you say, loaded you with happiness in such generous measure

' If it be really so, then of course pay Him honour. But at the same time I will not hide from you my opinion that Ursus had a certain share in saving Lygia, and that even the people of Rome had some cognizance of the matter. But if you assure me that you consider it Christ's doing, then I will say no more. Do not be sparing in your sacrifices to Him. Prometheus also, you know, sacrificed himself for mankind ; but Prometheus is apparently only an invention of the poets, while certain credible persons have stated that they saw Christ with their own eyes. Like you, I consider Him the best of all the gods. I remember Paul's question well, and I agree that if Ahenobarbus lived in accordance with Christ's teaching, I might perhaps have time to come and see you in Sicily. Then, beside the fountains and in the shade of the trees, we should have long discussions about deities and about truth in all its forms after the fashion of the Greek philosophers. But as it is, my answer must be brief.

' In my opinion there are only two philosophers. One is Pyrrho, the other Anacreon. I'll make you a bargain of the rest, and throw in all the Greek and Roman Stoics as well. Truth dwells in regions so inaccessible that the very gods cannot perceive it from the summit of Olympus. Your Olympus seems higher still, and you stand at the top and cry out:

"Climb up, and you will see things that you never dreamt of!" Very possibly; and yet I reply: "I have not legs for it now!" When you have read to the end, I think you will find me justified.

'Well, then, most fortunate spouse of the Princess Aurora, your religion is not for me. It would mean that I must love my Bithynians and my Egyptian bath-men. I should have to love Tigellinus and Brazenbeard. By the white knees of the Graces, I swear to you that even though I tried I should be incapable of it. There are at least a hundred thousand people in Rome with crooked backs, swollen knees, thin legs, staring eyes, or overgrown heads. Do you ask me to love them all alike? And where am I to find this love which does not exist in my heart? If your God claims that I should love them all equally, why has he not in his omnipotence endowed them with a more prepossessing exterior and created them in the likeness of the Niobides that you have seen at the palace? One who loves beauty is thereby rendered incapable of loving ugliness. It is not a question of believing in the gods: we can love them as Pheidias, Praxiteles, Scopas, Miron, and Lysias did, without believing in them.

'And then, even though I had any desire to go along the way which you point out, I could not do it. But in any case I don't want to do it, so for two reasons it can't be done. You believe that one day, in some Elysian field or another beyond the Styx, you will see your Christ. Very well: ask Him whether he would have taken me with my gems, my Myrrhine vase, my fine books, and my darling with the golden hair. The very idea makes me want to laugh. Even your Paul of Tarsus told me how for Christ's sake one must give up garlands of roses, banquets, and all worldly pleasures. He promised me another kind of happiness in exchange, but I told him that I was too old for such happiness, that my eyes would always be rejoiced by the sight of roses, and that the scent of violets would always be infinitely more agreeable to me than that of my dirty " neighbour " from the Suburra.

'These are my reasons. Your happiness is not made for me. But the decisive reason I have kept for the end: death calls me! Life for you has scarce reached its dawn ; for me the sun has set, and the twilight is upon me. In other words, dear Vinicius, I must die.

'It is no use dwelling on the matter. It had to come, as you who know Ahenobarbus will easily understand. Tigellinus has beaten me, or I should say rather that my victories over him are drawing to a close. I have lived as I wanted to live, and I will die as I please.

'Do not take it too much to heart. No god has promised me immortality, and this is no unexpected thing that is happening. You are wrong, Vinicius, in stating that your God alone can teach men to die calmly. No, our world knew before yours that when the last cup was drained it was time to vanish among the shadows, and our world still knows how to do it with countenance unmoved. Plato states that virtue is a kind of music, and that the philosopher's life is harmony. So I shall have lived and I shall die virtuous.

'I should like to bid farewell to your angelic wife in the words with which I once greeted her in Aulus' house: "I have seen countless people in my life, but a woman such as you I never saw."

'And in conclusion let me say that if, contrary to Pyrrho's view, some part of our soul lives on after death, my soul, as it takes its way to the shores of the ocean, will alight near your house in the shape of a butterfly, or perhaps, if the Egyptians are to be believed, of a hawk.

'To come in any other way—impossible!

'But for you, may Sicily be transformed into the garden of the Hesperides; may the goddesses of fields, woods, and fountains strew flowers beneath your feet, and in every acanthus on your colonnade may doves, white as lilies, build their nests.'

CHAPTER 26

Two days later, young Nerva, who was much attached to Petronius, sent a freedman to him with the latest news of the Court.

His fate had been decided. The following evening a centurion was to bring him the order not to leave Cumæ, but to wait there for the orders that would be sent him later on. Some days after that, another message would announce the death sentence.

Petronius listened, calm and unmoved. Then he said:

'You will take a valuable vase to your master, which will be given to you when you depart. Tell him I thank him most heartily, for this will enable me to anticipate the sentence.'

And he burst out laughing, like a man who has hit upon a splendid idea and is enjoying the thought of carrying it out.

That same evening his slaves were sent out through the city with invitations to all the Augustans who were in Cumæ and all their ladies to be present at a banquet in the Arbiter's splendid house.

Petronius spent the afternoon writing in his library. Then he bathed, and, with the aid of his attendants, arrayed himself in his toga.

In all his splendour he passed into the triclinium, to view the preparations for the feast, and thence into the gardens, where youths and young girls from the islands were weaving wreaths of roses for the evening. There was not the slightest look of anxiety on his face. The slaves understood that the banquet was to be one of extraordinary magnificence, for he ordered unusual rewards to be given to those with whom he was pleased and but a small number of stripes to those who had incurred his displeasure. The lute-players and singers were to be paid beforehand, and very generously. Seating himself beneath a beech tree, through whose leaves the sun shone and lit up broad patches on the ground, Petronius sent to invite Eunice to come.

She appeared in a white robe, with a spray of myrtle in her hair, fair as one of the Graces. He made her sit down beside him, and passing his hand lightly over her temples, he gazed upon her for a long time with eyes of admiration and delight.

'Eunice,' he said, 'do you know that for many a day you have not been a slave?'

She lifted her calm blue eyes to his and gently shook her head.

'I am your slave for ever, master.'

'But perhaps you are not aware that these slaves weaving wreaths over there, this house and all it contains, and all my fields and flocks, belong to you from this day.'

Eunice drew back from him, and with a voice trembling with anxiety she said:

'Why, oh, why do you say that to me?'

Then she came closer to him again and began

to look at him, while her eyelids trembled with apprehension.

He said but one word:

'Yes!'

There was silence, save for the rustling of the leaves in the light wind.

Petronius might have had before him a marble statue.

'Eunice,' he said, 'I am anxious to die calmly.'

With a heartrending smile she replied:

'I understand, master.'

In the evening the guests arrived in crowds. Compared with the banquets which Petronius gave, those of Nero were tedious and extravagant. But the idea that this was to be the last 'symposium' had occurred to nobody.

The scent of violets filled the hall, and globes of Alexandrian glass shed their many-coloured rays around. Beside the couches stood little girls whose duty was to anoint the feet of the guests with perfumes. Round the wall were the lute-players and singers, awaiting the signal from their leader.

Petronius was talking. His conversation turned upon the latest news, the latest divorces, love affairs, intrigues, the races, a gladiator who had lately become famous by his exploits, and the latest books brought out by Atractus and the Sosii. He spilled wine upon the floor, and declared that the libation was intended only for the Queen of Cyprus, the oldest and greatest of all the gods, who alone was enduring, eternal, and sovereign.

He gave the sign, and the lutes sighed forth their melody, while fresh voices arose in harmony with them. Then dancing-girls from Cos, Eunice's country, spun around with their rosy bodies scarce hidden beneath the filmiest of gauzes.

After that an Egyptian seer took up a crystal vase containing brightly-coloured dorados and told the guests their fortunes.

When the display was at an end, Petronius lifted himself on his Syrian cushion and carelessly remarked:

'Forgive me for asking favours of you during the banquet, but I should like each of you to accept as a present the cup which he has used for his libations to the gods and in my honour.'

He raised his Myrrhine cup—a priceless cup that glistened with all the colours of the rainbow—and said to his guests:

'This is the cup that held my libation to the Queen of Cyprus. May no lips ever touch it again, and may no hand ever lift it in honour of another god!'

And he dashed the cup to pieces upon the saffron-strewn tiles. Then, seeing their amazement, he went on:

'My dear friends, do not be downcast. Old age and feebleness are the gloomy comrades of our declining years. I am giving you a good example and good advice: you see that a man need not await them, but may depart of his own free will before their coming.'

'What do you intend to do?'

'I intend to be happy, to drink, to listen to the music, to gaze upon the heavenly form that is beside me, and then to fall asleep with my head wreathed in roses. I have already taken leave of Cæsar. Listen to the farewell letter I have written.'

From under the purple cushion he took a letter and read:

'I know, divine Cæsar, that you are impatiently awaiting me, and that your faithful heart is

languishing for me day and night. I know that you
are dying to shower your favours upon me, to make
me prefect of your guard, and to appoint Tigellinus
custodian of the mules on the estates you became
master of after the poisoning of Domitia — a
position for which the gods seem to have created
him.

'But, unfortunately, I must excuse myself. I
swear to you by Hades, and more particularly by the
shades of your mother, your wife, your brother, and
Seneca, that I cannot come to you. Life, my dear
friend, is a treasure, from which I flatter myself
I have contrived to extract the most precious gems.
But life contains also some things that I declare
I can no longer endure.

'Do not imagine, I pray you, that I was disgusted
by the murder of your mother, your wife, and your
brother, or that I was indignant at the burning of
Rome, or shocked at your method of despatching all
the honest men in your empire to Erebos.

'No, beloved grandson of Chronos, death is the
common inheritance of all sublunary beings, and
nobody could expect you in any case to act otherwise.

'But to have your singing jar upon my ears for
long years still, to see your very Domitian legs, like
vine-props, jumping about in the Pyrrhic dance, to
listen to your declamations, and to hear you recite
your own poetry, you poor suburban scribbler,
really such a prospect was too much for me, and
I felt irresistibly the need to return to my fathers.
Rome stops her ears, and all the world laughs at
you. And I will not blush for you any longer.
I will not—I cannot! The howling of Cerberus,
despite its resemblance to your singing, would be
less painful to me ; for I was never a friend of the

said Cerberus, and do not need to be ashamed of his voice.

'All good wishes, but leave singing alone. Kill on, but give poetry a rest. Poison, but do not dance. Fire more cities, but give up the lute. Such is the last wish and the very friendly advice of the ARBITER OF ELEGANCE.'

The guests were dumbfounded. They knew that the ruin of the Empire would hurt Nero less. The writer of the letter was bound to die, and they turned pale with dismay at having heard it.

But Petronius gave an honest, merry laugh as though at some innocent joke, and looking round the company he said:

'Banish your fears. Nobody need boast about hearing the letter read. As for me, I can boast about it when I meet Charon the ferryman.'

With that he beckoned to the doctor, and stretched out his arm. Instantly the skilful Greek put a gold bracelet round it and opened an artery in the wrist. The blood spurted out on to the cushion, and upon Eunice, who was supporting Petronius' head. She bent over him:

'Master,' she said, 'Did you think I meant to desert you ? Though the gods should offer me immortality and Cæsar give me his Empire, still I would go with you.'

Petronius smiled, and raising himself he kissed her on the lips:

'Come with me.'

And he added:

'Yours has been a real love, my darling.'

She stretched out her pink arm to the doctor. Next moment her blood mingled indistinguishably in one stream with her lover's.

Petronius made a sign to the musicians, and once

again the lutes and the voices resounded, first of all to the music of the 'Harmodios.' Then came the hymn of Anacreon in which the poet bewails the discovery at his door of the chilled and weeping son of Aphrodite. He had warmed him and dried his wings, and then the ingrate had pierced his heart with an arrow. From that day his mind had known no peace.

They leant upon each other and listened, smiling and growing ever paler in their beauty.

When the hymn was over, Petronius ordered fresh wine and courses. Then he began to talk with his neighbours about a thousand simple, charming trifles that make up conversation on those occasions. At last he summoned the Greek and bade him tie up the artery, as he felt drowsy and desired once more to give himself up to Hypnos ere Thanatos put him to sleep for ever. He fell asleep.

When he awoke, Eunice's head was lying on his breast like a white flower. He laid it upon the cushion to gaze upon it once more, and then his veins were opened again.

The singers began another hymn of Anacreon's, while the lutes accompanied them softly in order not to drown the words. Petronius was growing paler and paler, and when the last chords had died away, he turned to the guests:

' Admit that with us dies——'

He could not finish. With one last effort he threw his arm about Eunice, and his head fell.

And the guests, looking upon these two pale figures like two wonderful statues, felt that the last appanage of the Roman world had passed away—its beauty and its poetry.

EPILOGUE

AT first, the revolt of Vindex and the legions in Gaul did not seem to be a very serious matter. Cæsar himself, to whom the revolt served as a pretext for fresh depredations, troubled himself but little about Vindex, and even expressed satisfaction at his doings.

But when he learned that Vindex had called him a pitiful artist, he set out with all haste for Rome.

His entry into the city was an unprecedented spectacle. He himself used the chariot in which Augustus had driven in his triumph. An arch of the Amphitheatre was pulled down to allow of the passage of the procession. The Senate, the knights, and a countless multitude went out to meet him. The walls rang with shouts of 'Hail, Augustus! Hail, Hercules! Hail, divine Majesty! Hail, Olympian and Immortal!' Behind him were borne the wreaths that he had won, with the names of the cities where he had enjoyed his triumphs, and tablets on which were inscribed the names of the great artists whom he had vanquished. The idea that a mortal should dare to raise his hand against a demi-god like himself appeared to him absurd and nonsensical. He believed himself to be really an Olympian and therefore inviolable.

But meantime, in the West, the cloud was growing ever denser and blacker. The measure was full: the farce was drawing to a close. When he learned that Galba and the troops in Spain had joined in the revolt, Nero was smitten with an access of blind fury. He smashed cups and overturned the banqueting table, and issued orders that neither Helius nor even Tigellinus dared to carry out. A plan of massacring all the Gauls in Rome, of setting fire to the city again, of letting loose the wild beasts, and of transferring the capital to Alexandria, commended itself to him as a work of stupendous grandeur, yet easy of execution. But the days of his omnipotence were over, and even his companions in ill-doing looked upon him now as a madman.

The death of Vindex and dissension among the armies of rebellion seemed once again to turn the scales in Cæsar's favour. New feasts and triumphs had been announced, and new sentences already proclaimed, when one night a messenger from the Prætorian headquarters rode in upon a foaming horse with the news that the soldiers had raised the standard of revolt in the city itself and proclaimed Galba emperor.

Cæsar, who was asleep, woke up with a start and called out to the sentries on duty at his door. The palace was deserted. In out-of-the-way corners slaves were hastily laying hands on all they could find. They took to their heels at sight of Nero, who wandered all over the palace, filling the night with his cries of terror and despair.

At last his freedmen, Phaon, Spirus, and Epaphroditus, came to his assistance. They urged him to fly instantly, as there was not a moment to be lost, but still he deluded himself. What if he were to dress in mourning and harangue the Senate? Could the fathers resist his eloquence and his tears? If he put forth all his art, all his charm, all his actor's wiles, was he not bound to persuade them? Would they not at least make him Exarch of Egypt?

Accustomed as they were to flatter him, they did not dare contradict him outright. But they warned

him that he would be torn to pieces by the crowd
ere he reached the Forum, and then they threatened
to abandon him if he did not at once mount his
horse.

Phaon offered him shelter in his house, which lay
outside the Porta Nomentana.

They wrapped their cloaks round their heads and
galloped off towards the city walls. Morning was
approaching. The unwonted bustle in the streets
told of the disturbed nature of the times. Soldiers
were scattered, singly or in bands, throughout the
city. As they passed the camp they heard thunderous
acclamations in honour of Galba. Nero saw then
that his hour had come. He was seized with terror
and remorse. He professed to see a black cloud in
front of him, and the faces of his mother, his wife,
and his brother looking at him out of it. But
although his teeth were rattling in his head, his
actor's soul could find a certain charm in the very
horror of the moment. To be lord omnipotent of
all the world, and to lose all, seemed to him the quin-
tessence of tragedy. And, true to himself, he played
the leading part to the end. He was seized with a
fever of quotations, and with a passionate desire that
his hearers should remember them for the sake of
posterity. Now and again he would declaim:

' My mother, my wife, and my father are calling
me!'

Even now, faint, childish hopes glimmered within
him. He knew that death had come, and yet he
could not believe it.

They found the Porta Nomentana open. They
passed the Ostrianum where the Apostle had taught
and baptized, and at daybreak they reached Phaon's
house.

Once there, the freedmen no longer disguised from

him that it was time to die. He caused a grave to be dug, and lay down upon the ground that they might measure him exactly.

But the sight of the shovelfuls of earth frightened him. His great swollen face turned pale, and drops of sweat stood out like dew upon his forehead. He turned irresolute and declared in a jerky voice, which he did his best to render tragical, that it was not yet time. Then once again he began his quotations. Finally he asked that his body should be burned. 'What an artist is perishing!' he repeated in a stupid fashion.

Suddenly a messenger of Phaon's arrived with the news that the Senate had already pronounced its judgment, and that the parricide would be punished in the customary way.

'What is the customary way?' asked Nero, with pale lips.

'They put a yoke on your neck, scourge you to death, and throw your body into the Tiber!' said Epaphroditus in a surly tone.

Cæsar threw open his cloak.

'Then it is time!' he said, raising his eyes to heaven.

And once more:

'What an artist is perishing!'

At that moment the galloping of a horse was heard. It was, no doubt, the centurion coming with his men to look for Ahenobarbus.

'Go on!' shouted the freedmen.

Nero put the knife to his throat. But his hand was timid in its efforts, and they saw that he would never have the courage to drive the blade home. Suddenly Epaphroditus gave his hand a push, and the knife was buried up to the hilt. His great terrified eyes protruded horribly.

' I bring you your life!' cried the centurion.

' Too late,' cried Nero hoarsely.

Then he added:

' Ah! that was loyalty indeed!'

In a trice Death had thrown her mantle about his head. The blood spouted in a dark stream from his thick neck over the flowers in the garden. His feet drummed upon the ground, and he expired.

Next day the faithful Acte covered his remains with costly stuffs and burned them on a scented pyre.

And so passed Nero, as pass storm and tempest and fire and war and pestilence. From that time onwards the Basilica of Peter has dominated the city and the world from the heights of the Vatican.

Not far from the old Porta Capena there stands to-day a tiny chapel, and on its walls is the inscription, half worn away: QUO VADIS, DOMINE ?

Printed in Great Britain by
Thomas Nelson and Sons Ltd, Edinburgh